A FAMILY FIGHT...
TO THE DEATH

READERS LOVE
DANCE OF DEATH!

"DANCE OF DEATH is sheer brilliance from start to finish."
> —GAIL FOSTER (Novato, CA)

"The one word that sums up this book for me is 'compulsive.' I could not put it down, and every page egged me on to the next. It was much more fast-paced than your previous books, but not lacking in any of the beautiful descriptive prose regarding history, society, and landscapes. My only regret is now I have to wait for the next chapter to come out."
> —ROBERT SAUNDERS (Vancouver, B.C., Canada)

"You know a book is in a class of its own when you are happy to miss your subway stop because it means you can keep on reading. DANCE OF DEATH brings together every captivating, rich, eccentric character that Preston and Child have ever created. It's mind candy for your imagination— the only downside being the excruciating wait for these incredible authors' next masterpiece."
> —LINDSAY GENSHAFT (New York, NY)

"I just wanted to say (and I am sure that you have heard this thousands of times) that your books are, by far, the best books that I have ever read . . . Your books just keep getting better and better with each publication."
> —NICHOLAS VANARIA (Romeoville, IL)

"As usual, your latest masterpiece was nearly impossible to put down."
> —PAT & ALICIA COOK (Brier, WA)

more . . .

"I would like to say *excellent* work with DANCE WITH DEATH. I anxiously look forward to your next collaborative effort. I get so absorbed in them. The imagery is so rich and detailed that one can almost see it playing out before them. Keep up the great work."

—JASON PATRICK (Fort Rucker, AL)

"In regards to your latest release of fiction, as the late Jim Backus might have said, 'Ohhh, Magoo, you've done it again!'"

—RILEY COUGER (Mineral Wells, TX)

"I loved this book. Pendergast is a hero for the ages, utterly complex and fiercely fascinating. One would believe that his character alone could carry the novel; however, he is ever in the company of fully realized friends and foes, none more brilliant, insane, and malevolent than frater Diogenes. I have read all ten Preston/Child books and can only wonder . . . how much better can it get?"

—PAMELA BROUSE (Narvon, PA)

"Not only have you managed to deliver another slick thriller complete with the usual engaging cast of characters, touches of humor, and dashes of scientific/historical/literary interest, but you've managed to weave the strands of your other novels together without disrupting the flow of the plot. I absolutely loved it, and await the next installment anxiously."

—JAMES MARCUS
(Larne, Northern Ireland)

BY DOUGLAS PRESTON AND LINCOLN CHILD

Brimstone
Still Life with Crows
The Cabinet of Curiosities
The Ice Limit
Thunderhead
Riptide
Reliquary
Mount Dragon
Relic

BY DOUGLAS PRESTON

The Codex
The Royal Road
Talking to the Ground
Jennie
Cities of Gold
Dinosaurs in the Attic

BY LINCOLN CHILD

Death Match
Utopia
Tales of the Dark 1–3
Dark Banquet
Dark Company

DOUGLAS   LINCOLN
PRESTON & CHILD

DANCE of
DEATH

WARNER BOOKS

NEW YORK   BOSTON

Copyright © 2005 by Lincoln Child and Splendide Mendax, Inc.
Excerpt from *The Book of the Dead* copyright © 2006 by Lincoln Child and Splendide Mendax, Inc.
All rights reserved. No part of this book may be reproduced in any form or by any electronic or mechanical means, including information storage and retrieval systems, without permission in writing from the publisher, except by a reviewer who may quote brief passages in a review.

Original poetry on page 505 is from "Piano" by D. H. Lawrence © 1918.

Warner Books

Time Warner Book Group
1271 Avenue of the Americas, New York, NY 10020
Visit our Web site at www.twbookmark.com

Printed in the United States of America

Originally published in hardcover by Warner Books

First Paperback Edition: January 2006

10 9 8 7 6 5 4 3 2 1

Acknowledgments

At Warner Books, we would like to thank the following: Jamie Raab, Larry Kirshbaum, Maureen Egen, Devi Pillai, Christine Barba and the Sales Team, Karen Torres and Marketing, Martha Otis and the Advertising and Promotions Department, Jennifer Romanello, Dan Rosen, Maja Thomas, Flag Tonuzi, Bob Castillo, Penina Sacks, Jim Spivey, Miriam Parker, Beth de Guzman, and Les Pockell.

A special thanks to our editor, Jaime Levine, for being a tireless champion of the Preston-Child novels. We owe much of our success to her fine editing, enthusiasm, and advocacy.

Thanks also to our agents, Eric Simonoff at Janklow & Nesbit, and Matthew Snyder of Creative Artists Agency. Garlands of laurel leaves to Special Agent Douglas Margini, Jon Couch, John Rogan, and Jill Nowak, for their diverse and sundry ministrations.

And, as always, we want to thank our wives and children for their love and support.

DANCE of DEATH

One

DEWAYNE MICHAELS SAT in the second row of the lecture hall, staring at the professor with what he hoped passed for interest. His eyelids were so heavy they felt as if lead sinkers had been sewn to them. His head pounded in rhythm with his heart and his tongue tasted like something had curled up and died on it. He'd arrived late, only to find the huge hall packed and just one seat available: second row center, smack-dab in front of the lectern.

Just great.

Dewayne was majoring in electrical engineering. He'd elected this class for the same reason engineering students had done so for three decades—it was a gimme. "English Literature—A Humanist Perspective" had always been a course you could breeze through and barely crack a book. The usual professor, a fossilized old turd named Mayhew, droned on like a hypnotist, hardly ever looking up from his forty-year-old lecture notes, his voice perfectly pitched for sleeping. The old fart never even changed his exams, and copies were all over Dewayne's dorm. Just his luck, then, that—for this one semester—a certain *renowned* Dr. Torrance Hamilton was teaching the course. It was as if Eric Clapton had agreed to play the junior prom, the way they fawned over Hamilton.

Dewayne shifted disconsolately. His butt had already fallen asleep in the cold plastic seat. He glanced to his left, to his right. All around, students—upperclassmen, mostly—were typing notes, running microcassette recorders, hanging on the professor's every word. It was the first time ever the course had been filled to capacity. Not an engineering student in sight.

What a crock.

Dewayne reminded himself he still had a week to drop the course. But he needed this credit and it was still possible Professor Hamilton was an easy grader. Hell, all these students wouldn't have shown up on a Saturday morning if they thought they were going to get reamed out . . . would they?

In the meantime, front and center, Dewayne figured he'd better make an effort to look awake.

Hamilton walked back and forth on the podium, his deep voice ringing. He was like a gray lion, his hair swept back in a mane, dressed in a snazzy charcoal suit instead of the usual threadbare set of tweeds. He had an unusual accent, not local to New Orleans, certainly not Yankee. Didn't exactly sound English, either. A teaching assistant sat in a chair behind the professor, assiduously taking notes.

"And so," Dr. Hamilton was saying, "today we're looking at Eliot's *The Waste Land*—the poem that packaged the twentieth century in all its alienation and emptiness. One of the greatest poems ever written."

The Waste Land. Dewayne remembered now. What a title. He hadn't bothered to read it, of course. Why should he? It was a poem, not a damn novel: he could read it right now, in class.

He picked up the book of T. S. Eliot's poems—he'd borrowed it from a friend, no use wasting good money on something he'd never look at again—and opened it. There, next to the title page, was a photo of the man himself: a real weenie, tiny little granny glasses, lips pursed like he had two feet of broomstick shoved up his ass. Dewayne snorted and began turning pages. Waste Land, Waste Land . . . here it was.

Oh, *shit*. This was no limerick. The son of a bitch went on for page after page.

"The first lines are by now so well known that it's hard for us to imagine the sensation—the *shock*—that people felt upon first reading it in *The Dial* in 1922. This was not what people considered poetry. It was, rather, a kind of anti-poem. The persona of the poet was obliterated. To whom belong these grim and disturbing thoughts? There is, of course, the famously bitter allusion to Chaucer in the opening line. But there is much more going on here. Reflect on the opening images: 'lilacs out of the dead land,' 'dull roots,' 'forgetful snow.' No other poet in the history of the world, my friends, ever wrote about spring in quite this way before."

Dewayne flipped to the end of the poem, found it contained over four hundred lines. *Oh, no. No . . .*

"It's intriguing that Eliot chose lilacs in the second line, rather than poppies, which would have been a more traditional choice at the time. Poppies were then growing in an abundance Europe hadn't seen for centuries, due to the numberless putrefying corpses from the Great War. But more important, the poppy—with its connotations of narcotic sleep—seems the better fit to Eliot's imagery.

So why did Eliot choose lilacs? Let's take a look at Eliot's use of allusion, here most likely involving Whitman's 'When Lilacs Last in the Dooryard Bloom'd.' "

Oh, my God, it was like a nightmare: here he was in the front of the class and not understanding a word the professor was saying. Who'd have thought you could write four hundred lines of poetry on a freaking *waste* land? Speaking of wasted, his head felt like it was packed full of ball bearings. Served him right for hanging out until four last night, doing shots of citron Grey Goose.

He realized the class around him had gone still, and that the voice from behind the lectern had fallen silent. Glancing up at Dr. Hamilton, he noticed the professor was standing motionless, a strange expression on his face. Elegant or not, the old fellow looked as if he'd just dropped a steaming loaf in his drawers. His face had gone strangely slack. As Dewayne watched, Hamilton slowly withdrew a handkerchief, carefully patted his forehead, then folded the handkerchief neatly and returned it to his pocket. He cleared his throat.

"Pardon me," he said as he reached for a glass of water on the lectern, took a small sip. "As I was saying, let's look at the meter Eliot employs in this first section of the poem. His free verse is aggressively enjambed: the only stopped lines are those that finish his sentences. Note also the heavy stressing of verbs: *breed*ing, *mix*ing, *stir*ring. It's like the ominous, isolated beat of a drum; it's ugly; it shatters the meaning of the phrase; it creates a sense of disquietude. It announces to us that something's going to happen in this poem, and that it won't be pretty."

The curiosity that had stirred in Dewayne during the unexpected pause faded away. The oddly stricken look had left the professor's face as quickly as it came, and his features—though still pale—had lost their ashen quality.

Dewayne returned his attention to the book. He could quickly scan the poem, figure out what the damn thing meant. He glanced at the title, then moved his eye down to the epigram, or epigraph, or whatever you called it.

He stopped. What the hell was this? *Nam Sibyllam quidem* . . . Whatever it was, it wasn't English. And there, buried in the middle of it, some weird-ass squiggles that weren't even part of the normal alphabet. He glanced at the explanatory notes at the bottom of the page and found the first bit was Latin, the second Greek. Next came the dedication: For Ezra Pound, *il miglior fabbro*. The notes said that last bit was Italian.

Latin, Greek, Italian. And the frigging poem hadn't even started yet. What next, hieroglyphics?

It was a nightmare.

He scanned the first page, then the second. Gibberish, plain and simple. "I will show you fear in a handful of dust." What was that supposed to mean? His eye fell on the next line. *Frisch weht der Wind* . . .

Abruptly, Dewayne closed the book, feeling sick. That did it. Only thirty lines into the poem and already five damn languages. First thing tomorrow morning, he'd go down to the registrar and drop this turkey.

He sat back, head pounding. Now that the decision was made, he wondered how he was going to make it through the next forty minutes without climbing the walls. If only there'd been a seat up in the back, where he could slip out unseen . . .

Up at the podium, the professor was droning on. "All that being said, then, let's move on to an examination of—"

Suddenly, Hamilton stopped once again.

"Excuse me." His face went slack again. He looked—what? Confused? Flustered? No: he looked *scared.*

Dewayne sat up, suddenly interested.

The professor's hand fluttered up to his handkerchief, fumbled it out, then dropped it as he tried to bring it to his forehead. He looked around vaguely, hand still fluttering about, as if to ward off a fly. The hand sought out his face, began touching it lightly, like a blind person. The trembling fingers palpated his lips, eyes, nose, hair, then swatted the air again.

The lecture hall had gone still. The teaching assistant in the seat behind the professor put down his pen, a concerned look on his face. *What's going on?* Dewayne wondered. *Heart attack?*

The professor took a small, lurching step forward, bumping into the podium. And now his other hand flew to his face, feeling it all over, only harder now, pushing, stretching the skin, pulling down the lower lip, giving himself a few light slaps.

The professor suddenly stopped and scanned the room. "Is there something wrong with my face?"

Dead silence.

Slowly, very slowly, Dr. Hamilton relaxed. He took a shaky breath, then another, and gradually his features relaxed. He cleared his throat.

"As I was saying—"

Dewayne saw the fingers of one hand come back to life again, twitching, trembling. The hand returned to his face, the fingers plucking, plucking the skin.

This was too weird.

"I—" the professor began, but the hand interfered with his speech. His mouth opened and closed, emitting nothing more than a wheeze. Another shuffled step, like a robot, bumping into the podium.

"What are these things?" he asked, his voice cracking.

God, now he was *pulling* at his skin, eyelids stretched grotesquely, both hands scrabbling—then a long, uneven scratch from a fingernail, and a line of blood appeared on one cheek.

A ripple coursed through the classroom, like an uneasy sigh.

"Is there something wrong, Professor?" the T.A. said.

"I . . . asked . . . a question." The professor growled it out, almost against his will, his voice muffled and distorted by the hands pulling at his face.

Another lurching step, and then he let out a sudden scream: "My face! Why will no one tell me what's wrong *with my face!*"

More deathly silence.

The fingers were digging in, the fist now pounding at the nose, which cracked faintly.

"Get them off me! They're *eating into my face!*"

Oh, *shit:* blood was now gushing from the nostrils, splashing down on the white shirt and charcoal suit. The fingers were like claws on the face, ripping, tearing; and now one finger hooked up and—Dewayne saw with utter horror—worked itself into one eye socket.

"Out! Get them out!"

There was a sharp, rotating motion that reminded Dewayne of the scooping of ice cream, and suddenly the globe of the eye bulged out, grotesquely large, jittering, staring directly at Dewayne from an impossible angle.

Screams echoed across the lecture hall. Students in the front row recoiled. The T.A. jumped from his seat and ran up to Hamilton, who violently shrugged him off.

Dewayne found himself rooted to his seat, his mind a blank, his limbs paralyzed.

Professor Hamilton now took a mechanical step, and another, ripping at his face, tearing out clumps of hair, staggering as if he might fall directly on top of Dewayne.

"A doctor!" the T.A. screamed. "Get a doctor!"

The spell was broken. There was a sudden commotion, everyone rising at once, the sound of falling books, a loud hubbub of panicked voices.

"My face!" the professor shrieked over the din. "*Where is it?*"

Chaos took over, students running for the door, some crying. Others rushed forward, toward the stricken professor, jumping onto the podium, trying to stop his murderous self-assault. The professor lashed out at them blindly, making a high-pitched, keening sound, his face a mask of red. Someone forcing his way down the row trod hard on Dewayne's foot. Drops of flying blood had spattered Dewayne's face: he could feel their warmth on his skin. Yet still he did not move. He found himself unable to take his eyes off the professor, unable to escape this nightmare.

The students had wrestled the professor to the surface of the podium and were now sliding about in his blood, trying to hold down his thrashing arms and bucking body. As Dewayne watched, the professor threw them off with demonic strength, grabbed the cup of water, smashed it against the podium, and—screaming—began to work the shards into his own neck, twisting and scooping, as if trying to dig something out.

And then, quite suddenly, Dewayne found he could move. He scrambled to his feet, skidded, ran along the row of seats to the aisle, and began sprinting up the stairs toward the back exit of the lecture hall. All he could think about was getting away from the unexplainable horror of what he'd just witnessed. As he shot out the door and dashed full speed down the corridor beyond, one phrase kept echoing in his mind, over and over and over:

I will show you fear in a handful of dust.

Two

VINNIE? VIN? Sure you don't want any help in there?"

"No!" Lieutenant Vincent D'Agosta tried to keep his voice cool and even. "No. It's all right. Just a couple more minutes."

He glanced up at the clock: almost nine. *A couple more minutes. Yeah, right.* He'd be lucky if he had dinner on the table by ten.

Laura Hayward's kitchen—he still thought of it as hers; he'd only moved in six weeks before—was usually an oasis of order, as calm and immaculate as Hayward herself. Now the place looked like a war zone. The sink was overflowing with soiled pots. Half a dozen empty cans lay in and around the wastebasket, dribbling out remnants of tomato sauce and olive oil. Almost as many cookbooks lay open on the counter, their pages obscured by bread crusts and blizzards of flour. The lone window looking down on the snowy intersection of 77th and First was speckled with grease from frying sausages. Although the vent fan was going full blast, the odor of burned meat lingered stubbornly in the air.

For weeks now, whenever their schedules allowed

time with each other, Laura had thrown together—almost effortlessly, it seemed—meal after delicious meal. D'Agosta had been astonished. For his soon-to-be-ex-wife, now up in Canada, cooking had always been an ordeal accompanied by histrionic sighs, clanging of pans, and—more often than not—disagreeable results. It was like night and day with Laura.

But along with his astonishment, D'Agosta also felt a bit threatened. As a detective captain in the NYPD, not only did Laura Hayward outrank him, but she outcooked him as well. Everybody knew men made the best chefs, especially Italians. They blew the French out of the water. And so he'd kept promising to cook her a real Italian dinner, just like his grandmother used to make. Each time he repeated the promise, the meal seemed to grow in complexity and spectacle. And at last, tonight was the night he would cook his grandmother's lasagna *napoletana*.

Except that once he got in the kitchen, he realized he didn't remember exactly how his grandmother cooked lasagna *napoletana*. Oh, he'd watched dozens of times. He'd often helped out. But what precisely went into that *ragù* she spooned over the layers of pasta? And what was it she'd added to those tiny meatballs that—along with the sausage and various cheeses—made up the filling? He had turned in his desperation to Laura's cookbooks, but each one had offered conflicting suggestions. And so now here he was, hours later, everything at varying stages of completion, frustration mounting by the second.

He heard Laura say something from her banishment in the living room. He took a deep breath.

"What was that, babe?"

"I said I'll be home late tomorrow. Rocker's having a state-of-the-force meeting with all the captains on January 22. That leaves me only Monday evening to get status reports and personnel records up to date."

"Rocker and his paperwork. How *is* your pal the commissioner, by the way?"

"He's not my pal."

D'Agosta turned back to the *ragù,* boiling away on the stove. He remained convinced that he'd gotten his old job on the force back, his seniority restored, only because Laura had put a word in Rocker's ear. He didn't like it, but there it was.

A huge bubble of *ragù* rose from the pot, burst like a volcanic eruption, and spewed sauce over his hand. "Ouch!" he cried, dousing the hand in dishwater while turning down the flame.

"What's up?"

"Nothing. Everything's just fine." He stirred the sauce with a wooden spoon, realized the bottom had burned, moved it hastily onto a back burner. He raised the spoon to his lips a little gingerly. Not bad, not bad at all. Decent texture, nice mouth feel, only a slight burned taste. Not like his grandmother's, though.

"What else goes in the *ragù,* Nonna?" he murmured.

If there was any response from the choir invisible, D'Agosta couldn't hear it.

Suddenly, there was a loud hissing from the stove. The giant pot of salted water was bubbling over. Swallowing a curse, D'Agosta turned down the heat on that as well, tore open a box of pasta, dumped in a pound of lasagna.

The sound of music filtered in from the living room: Laura had put on a Steely Dan CD. "I swear I'm going to speak to the landlord about that doorman," she said through the door.

"Which doorman?"

"That new one who came on a few weeks ago. He's the surliest guy I've ever met. What kind of a doorman doesn't even open the door for you? And this morning he wouldn't call me a cab. Just shook his head and walked away. I don't think he speaks English. At least, he pretends he doesn't."

What do you expect for twenty-five hundred a month? D'Agosta thought to himself. But it was her apartment, so he kept his mouth shut. And it was her money that paid the rent—at least for now. He was determined to change that as soon as possible.

When he'd moved in, he hadn't brought any expectations with him. He'd just gone through one of the worst times in his life, and he refused to let himself think more than a day ahead. Also, he was still in the early stages of what promised to be an unpleasant divorce: a new romantic entanglement probably wasn't the smartest thing for him right now. But this had turned out far better than he could ever have hoped. Laura Hayward was more than a girlfriend or lover—she'd become a soulmate. He'd thought that their both being on the job, her ranking him, would be a problem. It was just the opposite: it gave them common ground, a chance to help each other, to talk about their cases without worrying about confidentiality or second-guessers.

"Any new leads on the Dangler?" he heard Laura ask from the living room.

The Dangler was the NYPD's pet name for a perp who'd recently been stealing money from ATMs with a hacked bank card, then exposing his johnson to the security camera. Most of the incidents had been in D'Agosta's precinct.

"Got a possible eyewitness to yesterday's job."

"Eyewitness to what?" Laura asked suggestively.

"To the *face,* of course." D'Agosta gave the pasta a stir, regulated the boil. He glanced at the oven, made sure it was up to temperature. Then he turned back to the messy counter, mentally going over everything. Sausage: check. Meatballs: check. Ricotta, Parmesan, and mozzarella *fiordilatte:* all check. *Looks like I might pull this one out of a hat, after all . . .*

Hell. He still had to grate the Parmesan.

He threw open a drawer, began rummaging frantically. As he did so, he thought he heard the doorbell ring.

Maybe it was his imagination: Laura didn't get all that many callers, and he sure as hell didn't get any. Especially this time of night. It was probably a delivery from the Vietnamese restaurant downstairs, knocking at the wrong door.

His hand closed over the box grater. He yanked it out, set it on the counter, grabbed the brick of Parmesan. He chose the face with the finest grate, raised the Parmesan to the steel.

"Vinnie?" Laura said. "You'd better come out here."

D'Agosta hesitated only a moment. Something in her tone made him drop everything on the counter and walk out of the kitchen.

She was standing in the front doorway of the apartment, speaking to a stranger. The man's face was in shadow, and he was dressed in an expensive trench coat. Something about him seemed familiar.

Then the man took a step forward, into the light. D'Agosta caught his breath.

"You!" he said.

The man bowed. "And you are Vincent D'Agosta."

Laura glanced back at him. *Who's he?* her expression read.

Slowly, D'Agosta released the breath. "Laura," he said, "I'd like you to meet Proctor. Agent Pendergast's chauffeur."

Her eyes widened in surprise.

Proctor bowed. "Delighted to make your acquaintance, ma'am."

She simply nodded in reply.

Proctor turned back to D'Agosta. "Now, sir, if you'd kindly come with me?"

"Where?" But already D'Agosta knew the answer.

"Eight ninety-one Riverside Drive."

D'Agosta licked his lips. "Why?"

"Because someone is waiting for you there. Someone who has requested your presence."

"Now?"

Proctor simply bowed again in reply.

Three

D'AGOSTA SAT in the backseat of the vintage '59 Rolls-Royce Silver Wraith, looking out the window but not really seeing anything. Proctor had taken him west through the park, and the big car was now rocketing up Broadway.

D'Agosta shifted in the white leather interior, barely able to contain his curiosity and impatience. He was tempted to pepper Proctor with questions, but he felt sure the chauffeur would not respond.

Eight ninety-one Riverside Drive. The home—one of the homes—of Special Agent Aloysius Pendergast, D'Agosta's friend and partner in several unusual cases. The mysterious FBI agent whom D'Agosta knew, and yet did not know, who seemed to have as many lives as a cat . . .

Until that day not two months ago, when he'd seen Pendergast for the last time.

It had been on the steep flank of a hill south of Florence, Italy. The special agent had been below him, surrounded by a ravening pack of boar-hunting dogs, backed up by a dozen armed men. Pendergast had sacrificed himself so D'Agosta could get away.

And D'Agosta had let him do it.

D'Agosta stirred restlessly at the memory. *Someone who has requested your presence,* Proctor had said. Was it possible that, despite everything, Pendergast *had* somehow managed to escape? It wouldn't be the first time. He suppressed a surge of hope . . .

But no, it was not possible. He knew in his heart that Pendergast was dead.

Now the Rolls was cruising up Riverside Drive. D'Agosta shifted again, glancing out at the passing street signs: 125th Street, 130th. Very quickly, the well-tended neighborhood surrounding Columbia University gave way to dilapidated brownstones and decaying hulks. The usual loiterers had been chased indoors by the January chill, and in the dim light of evening the street looked deserted.

Up ahead now, just past 137th Street, D'Agosta could make out the boarded-up facade and widow's walk of Pendergast's mansion. The dark lines of the vast structure sent a chill through him.

The Rolls pulled past the gates of the spiked iron fence and stopped beneath the porte-cochère. Without waiting for Proctor, D'Agosta let himself out and stared up at the familiar lines of the rambling mansion, windows covered with tin, looking for all the world like the other abandoned mansions along the drive. Inside, it was home to wonders and secrets almost beyond belief. He felt his heart begin to race. Maybe Pendergast was inside, after all, in his usual black suit, sitting in the library before a blazing fire, the dancing flames casting strange shadows over his pale face. "My dear Vincent," he would say, "thank you for coming. May I interest you in a glass of Armagnac?"

D'Agosta waited as Proctor unlocked, then opened, the heavy door. Pale yellow light streamed out onto the worn brickwork. He stepped forward while Proctor carefully relocked the door behind him. He felt his heart beat still faster. Just being back inside the mansion sent a strange mix of emotions coursing through him: excitement, anxiety, regret.

Proctor turned toward him. "This way, sir, if you please."

The chauffeur led the way down the length of the gallery and into the blue-domed reception hall. Here, dozens of rippled-glass cabinets displayed an array of fabulous specimens: meteorites, gems, fossils, butterflies. D'Agosta's eyes stole across the parquet floor to the far side, where the double doors of the library lay open. If Pendergast was waiting for him, that's where he'd be: sitting in a wing chair, a half-smile playing across his lips, enjoying the effect of this little drama on his friend.

Proctor ushered D'Agosta toward the library. Heart pounding, he stepped through the doors and into the sumptuous room.

The smell of the place was as he remembered it: leather, buckram, a faint hint of woodsmoke. But today there was no fire crackling merrily on the hearth. The room was cold. The inlaid bookshelves, full of leather-bound volumes tooled in gold, were dim and indistinct. Only a single lamp glowed—a Tiffany piece standing on a side table—casting a small pool of light in a vast lake of darkness.

After a moment, D'Agosta made out a form standing beside the table, just outside the circle of light. As he watched, the form advanced toward him across the carpeting. He recognized immediately the young girl as Constance Greene, Pendergast's ward and assistant. She was perhaps twenty, wearing a long, old-fashioned velvet dress that snugged her slender waist and fell in lines almost to the floor. Despite her obvious youth, her bearing had the poise of a much older woman. And her eyes, too—D'Agosta remembered her strange eyes, full of experience and learning, her speech old-fashioned, even quaint. And then there was that something else, something just the other side of normal, that seemed to cling to her like the antique air that exhaled from her dresses.

Those eyes seemed different today. They looked haunted, dark, heavy with loss . . . and fear?

Constance held out her right hand. "Lieutenant D'Agosta," she said in a measured tone.

D'Agosta took the hand, uncertain as always whether to shake it or kiss it. He did neither, and after a moment the hand was withdrawn.

Normally, Constance was polite to a fault. But today she simply stood before D'Agosta, without offering him a chair or inquiring after his health. She seemed uncertain. And D'Agosta could guess why. The hope that had been stirring within him began to fade.

"Have you heard anything?" she asked, her voice almost too low to make out. "Anything at all?"

D'Agosta shook his head, the flame of hope dashed out.

Constance held his glance a moment longer. Then she nodded her understanding, her gaze dropping to the floor, her hands fluttering at her sides like confused white moths.

They stood there together in silence for a minute, perhaps two.

Constance raised her eyes again. "It's foolish for me to continue to hope. More than six weeks have passed without a word."

"I know."

"He is dead," she said, voice even lower.

D'Agosta said nothing.

She roused herself. "That means it is time for me to give you *this*." She went to the mantelpiece, took down a small sandalwood box inlaid with mother-of-pearl. A tiny key already in her hand, she unlocked it and, without opening it, held it out toward D'Agosta.

"I have delayed this moment too long already. I felt that there was still a chance he might appear."

D'Agosta stared at the box. It looked familiar, but for a moment he could not place where he'd seen it before. Then it came to him: it had been in this house, this very room, the previous October. He'd entered the library and disturbed Pendergast in the act of writing a note. The agent had slipped it into this same box. That had been the night before they left on their fateful trip to Italy—the night Pendergast told him about his brother, Diogenes.

"Take it, Lieutenant," Constance said, her voice breaking. "Please don't draw this out."

"Sorry." D'Agosta gently took the box, opened it. Inside lay a single sheet of heavy cream-colored paper, folded once.

Suddenly, the very last thing D'Agosta wanted to do was to take out that piece of paper. With deep misgivings, he reached for it, opened it, and began to read.

My dear Vincent,

If you are reading this letter, it means that I am dead. It also means I died before I could accomplish a task that, rightfully, belongs to me and no other. That task is preventing my brother, Diogenes, from committing what he once boasted would be the "perfect" crime.

I wish I could tell you more about this crime, but all I know of it is that he has been planning it for many years and that he intends it to be his apotheosis. Whatever this "perfect" crime is, it will be infamous. It will make the world a darker place. Diogenes is a man with exceptional standards. He would not settle for less.

I'm afraid, Vincent, that the task of stopping Diogenes must now fall to you. I cannot tell you how much I regret this. It is something I would not wish on my worst enemy, and especially not on somebody I've come to regard as a trusted friend. But it is something I believe you are best equipped to handle. Diogenes's threat is too amorphous for me to take to the FBI or other law enforcement agency, since he contrived his own false death some years ago. A single, dedicated individual has the best chance of preventing my brother from carrying out this crime. That individual is you.

Diogenes has sent me a letter consisting of only one thing: a date, January 28. In all likelihood, the crime will be committed on that date. I would not, however, make any assumptions—the date could mean nothing at all. Diogenes is, if anything, unpredictable.

You will need to take a leave of absence from the Southampton P.D. or wherever you are currently employed. This cannot be avoided. Get all the information you can from Detective Captain Laura Hayward, but for her own sake minimize her involvement. Diogenes is an expert on forensics and police procedure, and any information left at the scene of the crime—assuming, God forbid, you are not in time to stop said crime—will no doubt be cleverly contrived to mislead the police. Hayward, as fine an officer as she is, is no match for my brother.

I've left a separate note for Constance, who will

at this point know all the particulars of this matter. She will make my house, my finances, and all my resources available to you. She will immediately put at your disposal a bank account containing $500,000 in your name, to use as you see fit. I recommend that you use her invaluable research skills, though I ask that you keep her out of your direct investigation for obvious reasons. She must never leave the mansion—ever. And you must watch her very, very carefully. She is still fragile, both mentally and physically.

As a first step, you should pay a visit to my Great-Aunt Cornelia, who is confined to a hospital on Little Governors Island. She knew Diogenes as a boy, and she will provide you with the personal and family information you will undoubtedly need. Treat this information—and her—with great care.

One final word. Diogenes is consummately dangerous. He is my intellectual equal, but he was somehow formed without the slightest shred of moral conscience. In addition, a severe childhood illness left him damaged. He is motivated by an undying hatred of myself and an utter contempt for humanity. Do not gain his attention any earlier than you have to. Be vigilant at all times.

Goodbye, my friend—and good luck.

Aloysius Pendergast

D'Agosta looked up. "January 28? My God, that's just *one week away.*"
Constance only bowed her head.

Four

IT WAS THE SMELL of the place, she thought, that really brought home the fact she was back in the museum: that mixture of mothballs, dust, old varnish, and a whiff of decay. She walked down the great fifth-floor corridor, past the oaken office doors, each sporting the name of a curator in black-edged gold leaf. She was surprised at how few new names there were. A lot of things had changed in six years, but here, in the museum, time seemed to run at a different pace.

She had been worried—more worried than she cared to admit—about how it would feel to be back in the museum several years after the most frightening experience of her life. In fact, that worry had delayed her decision to return. But she had to admit, after a slightly rough first couple of days, that little of the old terror still clung to the place. Her nightmares, the lingering sense of vulnerability, had faded with the years. The old events, the bad events, were now ancient history. And the museum was still a wonderful old pile, a Gothic castle of Brobdingnagian proportions, full of wonderful, eccentric people—and bursting with strange and fascinating specimens. The most extensive collection of trilobites in the world. Lucifer's Heart, the most precious diamond ever found. "Snaggletooth," the largest and best-preserved T. rex fossil known.

Nevertheless, she had been careful not to stray into the museum's sub-basement. And it was not laziness that made her limit the number of nights she worked much past closing.

She remembered the time when she had walked down this august corridor for the first time as a graduate student of no account. Graduate students were so low on the museum's totem pole they were not even despised—they were simply invisible. Not that she'd been resentful: it was a rite of passage everyone had to go through. Back then she was a nobody—a "you," or, at best, a "Miss."

How things had changed. Now she was "Doctor," sometimes even "Professor," and her name appeared in print with a string of titles after it: Pierpont Research Fellow (the "fellow" part always made her smile); adjunct professor of ethnopharmacology; and her most recent title, only three weeks old: editor in chief of *Museology*. While she'd always told herself that titles meant nothing, she was surprised to discover that, once she'd acquired them, they were most gratifying. *Professor* . . . that had a nice round sound to it, especially on the lips of those crusty old curators who, six years ago, wouldn't even give her the time of day. Now they went out of their way to ask her opinion or press their monographs on her. Just that morning, no less a personage than the head of anthropology and her titular boss, Hugo Menzies, had asked solicitously after the subject of her panel discussion for the forthcoming Society of American Anthropologists meeting.

Yes: a refreshing change, indeed.

The office of the director lay at the end of the hall, in one of the coveted tower offices. She paused before the great oaken door, darkened with the patina of a century. She raised her hand, then lowered it, suddenly feeling nervous. She took a deep breath. She felt happy to be back in the museum, and she wondered yet again if the sudden controversy she was about to launch herself into wasn't a serious mistake. She reminded herself that this controversy had been forced on her and that as editor of *Museology* she had to take a stand. If she ducked this one, she would immediately lose her credibility as an arbiter of ethics and free expression. Worse, she wouldn't be able to live with herself.

Her hand fell firmly upon the oaken door, once, twice, three times, each knock firmer than the last.

A moment of silence. Then the door was opened by Mrs. Surd, the dry and efficient secretary to the museum's director. The sharp blue eyes gave her a rapid once-over as she stepped aside.

"Dr. Green? Dr. Collopy is expecting you. You may go straight in."

Margo approached the inner door, if anything darker and more massive than the other, grasped the ice-cold brass knob, turned it, and pushed it open on well-oiled hinges.

There, behind the great nineteenth-century desk, under a vast painting by De Clefisse of Victoria Falls, sat Frederick Watson Collopy, director of the New York Museum of Natural History. He rose graciously, a smile creasing his handsome face. He was dressed in a somber gray suit of old-fashioned cut, the starched white shirtfront enlivened only by a bright red silk bow tie.

"Ah, Margo. How good of you to come. Please take a seat."

How good of you to come. The note she had received had more the flavor of a summons than an invitation.

Collopy came around his desk and indicated a plush leather armchair which formed part of a group arrayed before a pink marble fireplace. Margo sat down and Collopy followed, taking a seat opposite her.

"Care for anything? Coffee, tea, mineral water?"

"Nothing, thank you, Dr. Collopy."

He leaned back, threw one leg casually over the other.

"We're so pleased to have you back at the museum, Margo," he said in his old New York society drawl. "I was delighted when you agreed to accept the editorship of *Museology*. We felt so lucky to lure you away from GeneDyne. Those research papers you published really impressed us, and your background here in ethnopharmacology made you the perfect candidate."

"Thank you, Dr. Collopy."

"And how do you find it? Everything to your satisfaction?" His voice was genteel, even kind.

"Everything is well, thank you."

"I am glad to hear it. *Museology* is the oldest journal in its field, publishing continuously since 1892, and still the most respected. It is a great responsibility and challenge you've taken on, Margo."

"I hope to carry on the tradition."

"And so do we." He stroked his closely trimmed iron-gray beard meditatively. "One of the things we are proud of is the strongly independent editorial voice of *Museology.*"

"Yes," said Margo. She knew where this was going, and she was ready.

"The museum has never interfered with the editorial opinions expressed in *Museology,* and we never will. We consider the editorial independence of the journal to be well-nigh sacred."

"I'm glad to hear that."

"On the other hand, we would not like to see *Museology* devolve into a . . . what should one call it? An *op-ed* organ." The way he said it made it sound like another kind of organ entirely. "With independence comes responsibility. After all, *Museology* bears the name of the New York Museum of Natural History."

The voice remained soft-spoken, and yet it had taken on an edge. Margo waited. She would remain cool and professional. In fact, she had already prepared her response—even written it out and memorized it so she could express herself more eloquently—but it was important to let Collopy have his say.

"That is why the previous editors of *Museology* have always been exceedingly careful about how they exercised their editorial freedom." He let the words hang in the air.

"I assume you're referring to the editorial I am about to publish on the repatriation request of the Tano Indians."

"Exactly. The letter from the tribe, asking for the return of the Great Kiva masks, arrived only last week. The board of trustees has not yet discussed it. The museum hasn't even had time to consult its lawyers. Isn't it a bit premature to be editorializing on something that hasn't even begun to be evaluated? Especially when you're so new to the position?"

"It seems to me a straightforward issue," she said quietly.

At this, Collopy leaned back in his chair, a patronizing smile on his face. "It is anything *but* straightforward, Margo. Those masks have been in the museum's collections for one hundred and thirty-five years. And they're to be the centerpiece of the Sacred Images show, the biggest exhibition in the museum since Superstition, six years ago."

Another heavy silence.

"Naturally," Collopy went on, "I'm not going to ask you to alter your editorial stand. I will merely point out that there may be a few facts you are unaware of." He pressed an almost invisible button on his desk and said into an equally invisible speaker: "The file, Mrs. Surd?"

A moment later, the secretary appeared with an ancient file in her hand. He thanked her, glanced at it, then handed it to Margo.

Margo took the file. It was very old and brittle and gave off a fearful smell of dust and dry rot. She opened it carefully. Inside were some handwritten papers in spidery mid-nineteenth-century script, a contract, some drawings.

"That is the original accession file of the Great Kiva masks you seem so anxious to return to the Tano Indians. Have you seen it?"

"No, but—"

"Perhaps you should have before you drafted your editorial. That first document is a bill of sale, itemizing two hundred dollars for the masks: a lot of money back in 1870. The museum didn't pay for those Great Kiva masks in trinkets and beads. The second document is the contract. That *X* is the signature of the chief of the Great Kiva Society—the man who sold the masks to Kendall Swope, the museum's anthropologist. The third docu-

ment, there, is the letter of thanks the museum wrote to
the chief, in care of the Indian agent, which was read to
him by the agent, promising the chief that the masks
would be well taken care of."

Margo stared at the ancient papers. It continually
amazed her how tenacious the museum was with everything, especially documents.

"The point is, Margo, the museum bought those masks
in good faith. We paid an excellent price for them. We've
now owned them for almost one and a half centuries.
We've taken beautiful care of them. On top of that,
they're among the most important objects in our entire
Native American collection. Many thousands of people
view them—are *educated* by them, make career choices
in anthropology or archaeology because of them—every
week. Not once in a hundred and thirty-five years did any
member of the Tano tribe complain or accuse the museum of acquiring them illegally. Now, doesn't it seem
just a tad unfair for them to suddenly be demanding them
back? And right before a blockbuster exhibition in which
they are the featured attraction?"

Silence fell in the grand tower office, with its tall windows overlooking Museum Drive, its dark-paneled walls
graced with Audubon paintings.

"It does seem a bit unfair," Margo said evenly.

A broad smile creased Collopy's face. "I knew you
would understand."

"But it won't change my editorial position."

A gradual freezing of the air. "Excuse me?"

It was time for her speech. "Nothing in that accession
file changes the facts. It's quite simple. The chief of the
Great Kiva Society didn't own the masks to begin with.
They weren't his. They belonged to the entire tribe. It

would be like a priest selling off church relics. By law, you can't sell something you don't own. That bill of sale and contract in that folder are not legally valid. What's more, when he bought the masks, Kendall Swope knew that, and that is clear from the book he wrote, *Tano Ceremonials*. He knew the chief didn't have the right to sell them. He knew the masks were a sacred part of the Great Kiva ceremony and must never leave the kiva. He even admits the chief was a crook. It's all right there in *Tano Ceremonials*."

"Margo—"

"Please let me finish, Dr. Collopy. There's an even more important principle at stake here. Those masks are *sacred* to the Tano Indians. Everyone recognizes that. They can't be replaced or remade. The Tanos believe each mask has a spirit and is alive. These aren't conveniently made-up beliefs; they're sincere and deeply held religious convictions."

"But after one hundred and thirty-five years? Come, now. Why hadn't we heard a peep from those people all this time?"

"The Tano had no idea where the masks had gone until they read about the upcoming exhibition."

"I simply cannot believe they were mourning the loss of those masks for all this time. They were long forgotten. This is all too convenient, Margo. Those masks are worth five, maybe ten million dollars. It's about money, not about religion."

"No, it isn't. I've spoken to them."

"You've *spoken* to them?"

"Of course. I called and spoke to the governor of Tano Pueblo."

For a moment, Collopy's mask of implacability fell away. "The legal implications of this are staggering."

"I was simply fulfilling my responsibility as editor of *Museology* to learn the facts. The Tanos *do* remember, they remembered all along—those masks, as your own carbon dating proved, were almost seven hundred years old when they were collected. Believe me, the Tanos remember their loss."

"They won't be properly curated—the Tanos don't have the proper facilities to take care of them!"

"They should never have left the kiva to begin with. They aren't 'museum specimens'—they're a living part of Tano religion. Do you think the bones of St. Peter under the Vatican are being 'properly curated'? The masks belong in that kiva, whether it's climate-controlled or not."

"If we give these masks back, it would set a terrible precedent. We'll be inundated with demands from every tribe in America."

"Perhaps. But that's not a valid argument. Giving back those masks is the *right* thing to do. You know it, and I'm going to publish an editorial saying so!"

She stopped, swallowed, realizing she had violated all her resolutions by raising her voice.

"And that is my final, and *independent,* editorial judgment," she added more quietly.

Five

THERE WERE NO secretaries, receptionists, or low-echelon flunkies seated outside the entrance to Glen Singleton's office. The room itself was no larger than any of the other few dozen offices scattered around the cramped and dusty confines of the precinct house. There was no sign on the door announcing the exalted status of its tenant. Unless you were a cop yourself, there would be no way of knowing this was the office of the head honcho.

But that, D'Agosta reflected as he approached, was the captain's style. Captain Singleton was that rarest of police brass, a guy who'd worked his way up honorably through the ranks, built a reputation not from kissing ass, but by solving tough cases with solid police work. He lived and breathed for one reason: to get criminals off the streets. He was perhaps the hardest-working cop D'Agosta had ever known, save Laura Hayward. D'Agosta had worked for more than his fair share of incompetent desk jockeys, and that made him respect Singleton's professionalism all the more. He sensed that Singleton respected him, too, and to D'Agosta that meant a great deal.

All this made what he was about to do even harder.

Singleton's door was wide open, as usual. It wasn't his style to limit access—any cop who wanted to see him could do so at any time. D'Agosta knocked, half leaning into the doorway. Singleton was there, standing behind the desk, talking into the phone. Even at his desk, the man never seemed to sit down. He was in his late forties, tall and lean, with a swimmer's physique—he swam laps every morning at six, without fail. He had a long face and an aquiline profile. Every other week he had his salt-and-pepper hair cut by the ridiculously expensive barber in the basement of the Carlyle, and he always looked as well groomed as a presidential candidate.

Singleton flashed a smile at D'Agosta and gestured for him to come in.

D'Agosta stepped inside. Singleton pointed to a seat, but D'Agosta shook his head: something about the captain's restless energy made him feel more comfortable on his feet.

Singleton was clearly talking to somebody in NYPD public relations. His voice was polite, but D'Agosta knew that, inside, Singleton was doing a slow boil: his interest lay in police work, not P.R. He hated the very concept, telling D'Agosta, "Either you catch the perp or you don't. So what's there to spin?"

D'Agosta glanced around. The office was decorated so minimally it was almost anonymous. No photos of family; no obligatory picture of the captain shaking hands with the mayor or commissioner. Singleton was one of the most decorated cops on active duty, but there were no commendations for bravery, no plaques or citations framed on the walls. Instead, there was just some paperwork sitting on a corner of his desk, fifteen or twenty manila folders on a nearby shelf. On a second shelf, D'Agosta could see handbooks on forensic technique and crime scene investigation, half a dozen well-thumbed books on jurisprudence.

Singleton hung up the phone with a sigh of relief. "Hell," he said. "I feel like I spend more time juggling community action groups than I do catching bad guys. It's enough to make me wish I was on foot patrol again." He turned toward D'Agosta with another short smile. "Vinnie, how's it going?"

"Okay," D'Agosta replied, not feeling okay at all. Singleton's friendliness and approachability made this little visit all the more difficult.

The captain hadn't requested D'Agosta: he'd been assigned to the division by the commissioner's office. This would have guaranteed D'Agosta a suspicious, hostile reception from other brass he'd known—Jack Waxie, for instance. Waxie would have felt threatened, kept D'Agosta at arm's length, made sure he got the low-profile cases. But Singleton was just the opposite. He'd welcomed D'Agosta, personally brought him up to speed on the details and procedures unique to his office, even put him in charge of the Dangler investigation—and, at the moment, cases didn't get any higher-profile than that.

The Dangler hadn't killed anybody. He hadn't even used a gun. But he'd done something almost as bad: he'd subjected the NYPD to public ridicule. A thief who emptied ATMs of cash, then whipped out his dong for the benefit of their security cameras, was perfect fodder for the daily tabloids. So far, the Dangler had paid visits to eleven ATMs. Each new robbery meant more front-page headlines, smirking, full of innuendo. Each time, the NYPD had its face rubbed in it afresh. *Dangler's streak grows longer,* the *Post* had trumpeted after the last robbery, three days before. *Police find themselves short.*

"How's our witness?" Singleton asked. "She panning out?" He stood behind his desk, looking at D'Agosta. The captain had piercing blue eyes, and when they looked at you, it was like you were the center of the universe: for that brief moment, at least, you had his complete and undivided attention. It was unnerving.

"Her story checks out against the security cam."

"Good, good. Hell, you'd think in this digital age the banks would be able to manage better coverage with their security cams. The guy seems to know their sweep, their range—you think he worked in security once?"

"We're looking into that."

"Eleven hits and all we still know for sure is he's Caucasian."

And circumcised, D'Agosta thought mirthlessly. "I had our detectives call all the branch managers on the hot list. They're installing additional hidden cameras."

"The perp might be working for the security firm that provides the cameras."

"Looking into that, too."

"One step ahead of me. That's what I like to hear." Singleton moved toward the pile of paperwork, began riffling through it. "This guy's pretty territorial. All his jobs have been within a twenty-square-block area. So the next step is to stake out the choicest machines he hasn't hit yet. Unless we can narrow down the list of potentials, we'll be spread too thin. Thank God we aren't working any active homicides at the moment. Vinnie, I'll leave it to you to interface with the task force, draw up a list of most likely ATMs based on the earlier hits, and allocate manpower for the stakeouts. Who knows? We might just get lucky."

Here it comes, D'Agosta thought. He licked his lips. "Actually, that's what I came in to talk to you about."

Singleton stopped, fixed him once again with his intense gaze. Wrapped up in his work the way he was, it hadn't occurred to the captain that D'Agosta might have come in about anything else. "What's on your mind?"

"I don't really know how to say this, but . . . sir, I wish to request a leave of absence."

Singleton's eyebrows shot up in surprise. "A leave of absence?"

"Yes, sir." D'Agosta knew how it sounded. But no matter how he'd rehearsed in his mind, it never seemed to come out right.

Singleton held his gaze a moment longer. He didn't say anything; he didn't need to. *A leave of absence. You've been here six weeks, and you want a leave of absence?*

"Anything I should know, Vinnie?" he asked in a low voice.

"It's a family matter," D'Agosta replied after a brief pause. He hated himself for stammering under Singleton's gaze, and hated himself even more for lying. But just what the hell was he supposed to say? *Sorry, Cap, but I'm taking unlimited time off to go chase a man who's officially dead, whose whereabouts are unknown, for a crime that hasn't yet been committed?* There was no question in his mind, no question at all, this was something he had to do. It was so important to Pendergast that he'd left instructions from beyond the grave. That was more than enough. But that didn't make this any easier or feel any more right.

Singleton held him in a look that was both concerned and speculative.

"Vinnie, you know I can't do that."

With a sinking sensation, D'Agosta realized it was going to be even harder than he anticipated. Even if he had to quit, he would—but that would be the end of his career. A cop could quit once, but not twice.

"It's my mother," he said. "She's got cancer. They think it's terminal."

Singleton stood quite still for a moment, taking this in. Then he rocked slightly on his heels. "I'm very, very sorry to hear that."

There was another silence. D'Agosta wished somebody would knock on the door, or the phone would ring, or a meteor would strike the precinct house—anything to deflect Singleton's attention.

"We just found out," he went on. "It was a shock, a real shock." He paused, sick at heart. He'd just blurted out the first excuse he could think of, but already it seemed an appalling choice. His own mother, *cancer* . . . shit, he'd have to go to confession after this, big-time. And call his mom in Vero Beach, send her two dozen roses.

Singleton was nodding slowly. "How much time do you need?"

"The doctors don't know. A week, maybe two."

Singleton nodded again, even more slowly. D'Agosta felt himself flushing all over. He wondered what the captain was thinking.

"She doesn't have much time left," he went on. "You know how it is. I haven't exactly been a model son. I just feel I need to be with her, right now, through this . . . Just like any son would," he concluded lamely. "You could rack it up against future vacation and sick leave."

Singleton listened closely, but this time he didn't nod. "Of course," he said.

He gazed at D'Agosta a long time. His look seemed to say: *A lot of people have sick parents, personal tragedies. But they're professionals. What's so different about you?* Breaking eye contact at last, he turned away, picking up the sheaf of papers that lay on his desk.

"I'll have Mercer and Sabriskie coordinate the stake-outs," he said crisply over his shoulder. "Take whatever time you need, Lieutenant."

Six

A DENSE FOG lay over the stagnant marshlands of Little Governors Island. From out of the murk came the mournful blast of a tugboat drifting down the East River. Manhattan was less than a mile across the icy black waters, but no lights from the cityscape pierced the veil of mist.

D'Agosta sat in the front passenger seat, holding grimly to the door handle as Laura Hayward's unmarked pool car bounced and swayed over the rough one-lane road. The headlights stabbed into the gloom, twin shafts of yellow that caromed wildly up and down, briefly illuminating the rutted drive and the skeletal chestnut trees that lined it.

"I think you missed one pothole back there," he said.

"Never mind about that. Let me get this straight. You told Singleton your mom has cancer?"

D'Agosta sighed. "It was the first thing that came into my head."

"Jeez, Vinnie. Singleton's own mother died of cancer. And guess what? He never missed a day of work. Had the funeral on a Sunday. *Everybody* knows that story."

"I didn't." D'Agosta winced, thinking back over what

he'd said to his captain that morning. *You know how it is. I just feel I need to be with her, right now, through this. Just like any son would.* Nice going, Vinnie.

"And I still can't believe you're taking a leave of absence to hunt for this brother of Pendergast's, based on a letter and a hunch. Don't get me wrong: nobody respected Pendergast more than me, he was the most brilliant law enforcement officer I ever met. But he had a fatal weakness, Vinnie, and you know what it was. He didn't respect the rules. He thought he was above the rest of us schmucks who are bound by the regulations. And I hate to see you picking up that attitude."

"I'm not picking up that attitude."

"This search for Pendergast's brother is so far beyond the rule book it isn't even funny. I mean what, exactly, are you planning to do if you find this Diogenes?"

D'Agosta didn't answer. He hadn't gotten that far yet.

The car shuddered as the front left tire sank into a rut. "Are you sure this is the right way?" she asked. "I can't believe there's a hospital out here."

"It's the right way."

Ahead, vague shapes were gradually becoming visible through the fog. As the car approached, the shapes resolved themselves into the pointed bars of a wrought-iron gate, set in a ten-foot-high wall of moss-covered bricks. The sedan pulled up before the closed gate, an ancient guardhouse beside it. A plaque on the gate read *Mount Mercy Hospital for the Criminally Insane.*

A guard appeared, flashlight in hand. D'Agosta leaned across Hayward, displaying his badge. "Lieutenant D'Agosta. I have an appointment to see Dr. Ostrom."

The man retreated into the guardhouse, checked a printed list. A moment later, the gate creaked slowly open. Hayward drove past and up a cobbled drive to a rambling structure, its battlements and towers half obscured by drifting mist. Along its upper edge, D'Agosta could see rows of crenellated stone, like broken teeth against the blackness.

"My God," Hayward said, peering through the windshield. "Pendergast's great-aunt is in *there*?"

D'Agosta nodded. "Apparently, this place used to be an expensive sanatorium for tubercular millionaires. Now it's a loony bin for murderers found not guilty by reason of insanity."

"What did she do, exactly?"

"Constance tells me she poisoned her whole family."

Hayward glanced at him. "Her whole family?"

"Mother, father, husband, brother, and two children. She thought they'd been possessed by devils. Or maybe the souls of Yankee soldiers shot dead by her father. Nobody seems to be quite sure. Whatever the case, be sure to keep your distance. She's apparently skilled at acquiring razor blades and concealing them on her person. Put two orderlies in the emergency room in the last twelve months."

"No kidding."

Inside, Mount Mercy Hospital smelled of rubbing alcohol and damp stone. Beneath the drab institutional paint, D'Agosta could still glimpse the remains of an elegant building, with hand-carved wood ceilings and paneled walls, the hallway floors of well-worn marble.

Dr. Ostrom was waiting for them in a "quiet room" on the second floor. He was a tall man in a spotless medical coat who, even without speaking, managed to convey the air of having several more important things to do. Glancing around the sparsely appointed space, D'Agosta noticed that everything—table, plastic chairs, light fixture—was either bolted to the floor or hidden behind steel mesh.

D'Agosta introduced himself and Hayward to Ostrom, who nodded politely in return but did not offer to shake hands. "You're here to see Cornelia Pendergast," he said.

"At her grandnephew's request."

"And you're familiar with the, ah, special requirements necessary for such a visit?"

"Yes."

"Keep well back at all times. Make no sudden movements. Do not, at any time, touch her or allow her to touch you. You'll only be able to spend a few minutes with her; any longer and she's likely to become excited. And it's of paramount importance she not become excited. When I see any such indications, I'll be forced to conclude the interview immediately."

"I understand."

"She doesn't like receiving strangers and may not see you, and there's nothing I can do to force the issue. Even if you had a warrant . . ."

"Tell her I'm Ambergris Pendergast. Her brother." This was the name Constance Greene had suggested.

Dr. Ostrom frowned. "I don't approve of deception, Lieutenant."

"Then don't call it deception. Call it a white lie. It's important, Doctor. Lives may be at stake."

Dr. Ostrom seemed to consider this. Then he nodded brusquely, turned, and left the room through a heavy steel door set in the back wall.

All was silent for several minutes. Then—at what seemed a great distance—the voice of an elderly lady could be heard raised in querulous complaint. D'Agosta and Hayward exchanged glances.

The raillery grew louder. Then the steel door opened again and Cornelia Pendergast was wheeled into view.

She was sitting in a wheelchair whose every surface was encased in thick black rubber. A small needlepoint pillow sat in her lap, on which rested her two withered hands. Ostrom himself pushed the wheelchair, and behind him came two orderlies wearing padded protective garments. She was wearing a long, old-fashioned dress of black taffeta. She looked tiny, with sticklike arms and a narrow frame, her face obscured by a mourning veil. It seemed impossible to D'Agosta that this frail-looking creature had recently slashed two orderlies. As she came into view and the wheelchair stopped, the string of invectives ceased.

"Raise my veil," she commanded. Her southern accent was cultivated, almost British, in its modulations.

One of the orderlies approached and—standing at arm's length—lifted the veil with a gloved hand. Unconsciously, D'Agosta leaned forward, staring curiously.

Cornelia Pendergast stared back. She had a sharp, cat-like face and pale blue eyes. Despite her advancing years, her liver-spotted skin had a strangely youthful glow. As he looked at her, D'Agosta's heart accelerated. He could see—in her intent gaze, in the lines of her cheekbones and jaw—faint outlines of his vanished friend. The resemblance would have been stronger but for the gleam of madness in her eyes.

For a moment, the room fell utterly silent. As Great-Aunt Cornelia held his gaze, D'Agosta became afraid she would erupt with anger at his lie.

But then she smiled. "Dear brother. So good of you to

come all this way to visit me. You've kept away so *very* long, you bad creature. Not that I blame you, of course— it's almost more than I can bear, living in the North with all these barbarous *Yankees*." She gave a little laugh.

Okay, D'Agosta thought to himself. Constance had told him Great-Aunt Cornelia lived in a fantasy world and would believe herself to be in one of two places: Ravenscry, her husband's estate north of New York City, or in the old Pendergast family mansion in New Orleans. Obviously, today she was in the former.

"Nice to see you, Cornelia," D'Agosta replied guardedly.

"And who is this lovely young lady at your side?"

"This is Laura, my . . . my wife."

Hayward shot him a glance.

"How delightful! I always wondered when you'd take a bride. High time the Pendergast line was invigorated by new blood. May I offer you some refreshment? Tea, perhaps? Or better still, your favorite, a mint julep?"

She glanced at the orderlies, who had taken up positions as far away from the woman as possible. They remained motionless.

"We're fine, thank you," D'Agosta said.

"I suppose it's just as well. We have such *dreadful* help these days." She flapped a hand toward the two orderlies behind her, who fairly jumped. Then she leaned forward, as if to impart a confidence across the room. "I envy you. Life is so much more gracious in the South. People up here take no pride in being members of the servile class."

As D'Agosta nodded in sympathy, a strange, dream-like unreality began to settle over him. Here was this elegant old woman chatting amiably to a brother she'd poisoned almost forty years before. He wondered just how he was going to go about this. Ostrom had said to keep the meeting short. He'd better get to the point.

"How, ah, how is the family?" he asked.

"I'll never forgive my husband for bringing us up to this drafty pile. Not only is the climate dreary, but the lack of culture is shocking. My dear children are my comfort."

The fond smile that accompanied this observation chilled D'Agosta. He wondered if she'd watched them die.

"Of course, there are no neighbors fit for company. As a result, my days are my own. I try to walk for the sake of my health, but the air is so raw I'm frequently driven inside. I've gone as pale as a ghost. See for yourself." And from the pillow, she lifted up a thin, palsied hand for his inspection.

Automatically, D'Agosta stepped forward. Ostrom frowned and nodded for him to stay back.

"How about the rest of the family?" D'Agosta asked. "I haven't heard from—from our nephews in a long time."

"Aloysius comes to visit me here every now and then. When he needs advice." She smiled again, and her eyes flashed. "He's such a good boy. Attentive to his elders. Not like the other one."

"Diogenes," D'Agosta said.

Great-Aunt Cornelia nodded. "Diogenes." She gave a shudder. "From the day he was born, he was different. And then there was his illness . . . and those peculiar eyes of his." She paused. "*You* know what they said about him."

"Tell me."

"Dear me, Ambergris, have you forgotten?"

For an uncomfortable moment, D'Agosta thought a look of skepticism passed over the old woman's face. But it soon vanished as her expression turned inward. "The Pendergast bloodline has been tainted for centuries. There but for the grace of God go you and I, Ambergris."

A suitably pious pause followed this statement. "Young Diogenes was *touched* even from the beginning. A bad seed indeed. After his sudden illness, the darker side of our lineage reached full flower in him."

D'Agosta remained silent, not daring to say more. After a moment, Great-Aunt Cornelia stirred and began again.

"He was a misanthrope from the beginning. Both boys were loners, of course—they were Pendergasts—but with Diogenes it was different. Young Aloysius had one close friend his age, I recall—he became quite a famous painter. And, dear me, Aloysius *would* spend a lot of time in the bayou among the Cajuns and others of that sort, to which I naturally objected. But Diogenes had no friends at all. Not a one. You remember how none of the other children would go near him. They were all scared to death of him. The illness made it so much worse."

"Illness?"

"Very sudden—scarlet fever, they said. That's when his eye changed color, went milky. He's blind in that eye, you know." She shuddered.

"Now, Aloysius, he was just the opposite. The poor boy was bullied. You know how we Pendergasts are frequent objects of scorn among the common folk. Aloysius was ten, I believe, when he began visiting that queer old Tibetan man down on Bourbon Street—he always had the most uncommon acquaintances. The man taught him all that Tibetan nonsense, you know, with the unpronounceable name, *chang* or *choong* something or other. He also taught Aloysius that peculiar way of fighting which guaranteed he was never bothered by bullies again."

"But the bullies never picked on Diogenes."

"Children have a sixth sense about that kind of thing. And to think Diogenes was younger and smaller than Aloysius."

"How did the two brothers get along?" D'Agosta asked.

"Ambergris, you're not getting forgetful in your old age, are you, dear? You know Diogenes *hated* his older brother. Diogenes never cared for anyone but his mother, of course, but he seemed to put Aloysius in a special category altogether. After the illness particularly."

She paused, and for a moment her mad eyes seemed to dim, as if she was peering far into the past. "Surely, you remember Aloysius's pet mouse."

"Oh, sure. Of course."

"Incitatus he called it, after the emperor Caligula's favorite horse. He was reading Suetonius at the time, and he used to walk around with the tiny beast on his shoulder, chanting: 'All hail Caesar's beautiful mouse, Incitatus!' I have a perfect horror of mice, you know, but the little white thing was so friendly and calm I found myself able to bear it. Aloysius was so patient with the creature, he loved it so. Oh, the tricks he taught it! Incitatus could walk upright on his hind legs. He must have responded to a dozen different commands. He could fetch a Ping-Pong ball for you and balance it on his nose like a seal. I remember you laughing so, dear, I feared your sides would split."

"I remember."

Great-Aunt Cornelia paused. Even the impassive guards seemed to be listening.

"And then one morning young Aloysius woke to find a wooden cross planted at the foot of his bed. A little cross, no more than six inches high, beautifully and lovingly made. Incitatus had been crucified upon it."

D'Agosta heard Laura Hayward inhale sharply.

"Nobody had to ask. Everyone knew who'd done it. It changed Aloysius. He never had another pet after Incitatus. As for Diogenes, that was just the beginning of his, ah, *experiments* on animals. Cats, dogs, even poultry and livestock began to disappear. I recall one particularly unpleasant incident with a neighbor's goat . . ."

At this, Great-Aunt Cornelia stopped speaking and began to laugh, quite softly, under her breath. It went on for a long time. Dr. Ostrom, growing alarmed, frowned at D'Agosta and pointed to his watch.

"When did you last see Diogenes?" D'Agosta asked quickly.

"Two days after the fire," the old woman replied.

"The fire," D'Agosta repeated, trying not to make it sound like a question.

"Of *course,* the fire," Great-Aunt Cornelia said, her voice suddenly agitated. "When else? The dreadful, dreadful fire that destroyed the family and convinced my husband to bring me and the children up to this drafty mansion. Away from New Orleans, away from all *that.*"

"I think we're done here," Dr. Ostrom said. He nodded to the guards.

"Tell me about the fire," D'Agosta pressed.

The old woman's face, which had gone almost fierce, now took on a look of great sorrow. Her lower lip trembled, and her hands twitched beneath the restraints. Despite himself, D'Agosta couldn't help but marvel at the suddenness with which these changes overtook her.

"Now, listen," Dr. Ostrom began.

D'Agosta held up his hand. "One minute more. Please." When he looked back at Great-Aunt Cornelia, he found she was staring directly at him.

"That superstitious, hateful, ignorant mob. They burned our ancestral home, may the curse of Lucifer be on them and their children for all eternity. By that time, Aloysius was twenty and away at Oxford. But Diogenes was home that night. He saw his own mother and father burned alive. The look on his face when the authorities pulled him from the basement, where he'd gone to hide . . ." She shuddered. "Two days later, Aloysius returned. We were staying with relatives by then, in Baton Rouge. I recall Diogenes taking his older brother into another room and closing the door. They were only inside for five minutes. When Aloysius came out, his face was dead white. And Diogenes immediately walked out the front door and disappeared. He didn't take anything, not even a change of clothing. I never saw him again. The few times we heard from him, it was either by letter or through family bankers or solicitors, and then nothing. Until, of course, the news of his death."

There was a moment of tense silence. The sorrow had left the old woman's face, leaving it calm, composed.

"I do believe it's time for that mint julep, Ambergris." She turned sharply. "John! Three mint juleps, well chilled, *if* you please. Use the icehouse ice, it's so much sweeter."

Ostrom spoke sharply. "I'm sorry, your guests have to go."

"A pity."

An orderly arrived with a plastic cup of water. He handed it gingerly to the old woman, who took it in her withered hand. "That's enough, John. You are dismissed."

She turned to D'Agosta. "Dear Ambergris, you're leaving an old woman to drink alone, shame on you."

"It was nice seeing you," D'Agosta said.

"I do hope you and your lovely bride will come again. It's always a pleasure to see you . . . *brother*." Then she abruptly bared her teeth in what seemed half-smile, half-snarl; raised a spotted hand; and drew the black veil down over her face once again.

Seven

SOMEWHERE, a clock chimed midnight, its deep, bell-like tones muted by the plush drapes and hanging tapestries of the library in the old mansion at 891 Riverside Drive.

D'Agosta sat back from the table and stretched in the leather armchair, fingertips working the kinks out of the small of his back. This time the library felt a lot more cheery: a fire was crackling atop wrought-iron firedogs, and light from half a dozen lamps threw a mellow glow into the remotest corners. Constance was sitting beside the fire, sipping tisane from a china cup and reading Spenser's *Faerie Queene.* Proctor, who had not forgotten D'Agosta's own taste in beverages, had drifted in a few times, replacing warm, half-finished glasses of Budweiser with chilled ones.

Constance had produced all the materials Pendergast saved concerning his brother, and D'Agosta had spent the evening poring over them. Here, in this familiar room, with its walls of books and its scent of leather and woodsmoke, D'Agosta could almost imagine Pendergast at his side, helping him take up the long-cold trail, pale eyes glittering with curiosity at the onset of the chase.

Except there was precious little here to chase. D'Agosta glanced over the documents, clippings, letters, photographs, and old reports that littered the table. Pendergast had clearly taken his brother's threat seriously: the collection was beautifully organized and annotated. It was almost as if Pendergast knew that, when the time ultimately came, he might not be around to face the challenge; that the task might be left to others. He'd saved every scrap of information, it seemed, that he had been able to obtain.

Over the last several hours, D'Agosta had read everything on the table two and, in some cases, three times. After Diogenes had severed his connection with the Pendergast clan following the death of his mother and father, he had gone largely into hiding. For almost a year, there was no word at all. Then a letter arrived from a family lawyer, asking that a sum of $100,000 be wired to a Zurich bank for Diogenes's benefit. This was followed a year later by another, similar letter, demanding that $250,000 be wired to a bank in Heidelberg. The family rejected this second request, and it prompted a response from Diogenes. That letter now sat on the table, sealed between two panels of clear Lucite. D'Agosta glanced once again at the spidery, meticulous script, so curiously inappropriate for a boy of seventeen. There was no date or location, and it was addressed to Pendergast:

Ave, frater—

I find it disagreeable to write you on this subject, or any other for that matter. But you force my hand. For I have no doubt you are the one behind the denial of my request for funds.

I need not remind you I will come into my inheritance in a few years. Until that time I shall now and then require certain trifling sums such as I requested last month. You will find it in your best interests, and in the best interests of others you may or may not know, to honor such requests. I should have thought our final discussion in Baton Rouge would have made that clear. I am very much preoccupied at present with various lines of research and study and have no time to earn money in the conventional manner. If forced to do so, I *will* obtain the funds I need—in a manner amusing to myself. If you do not wish to see my attentions diverted in this way, you will honor my request with all haste.

The next time I write you, it shall be on a matter of my own choosing, not yours. I will not bring this up again. Good-bye, brother. And *bonne chance*.

D'Agosta put the letter aside. Records showed that the money was promptly sent. The following year, a similar sum was wired to a bank in Threadneedle Street, London. A year later, another sum was sent to a bank in Kent. Diogenes surfaced briefly on his twenty-first birthday to claim his inheritance—eighty-seven million dollars. Two months later, he was reported to have been killed in an automobile accident in Canterbury High Street. Burned beyond recognition. The inheritance was never found.

D'Agosta turned the bogus death certificate over in his hands.

I am very much preoccupied at present with various lines of research and study. But what, exactly? Diogenes certainly didn't say, and his brother was silent on the matter. Or almost silent. D'Agosta let his eye fall on a pile of news clippings. They had been taken from a variety of foreign magazines and newspapers. Each had been labeled with an attribution and a date, and those in foreign languages had translations attached—once again, Pendergast thinking ahead.

Most of these clippings dealt with unsolved crimes. There was an entire family in Lisbon, killed by botulism, yet without any trace of food found in their stomachs. A chemist at the University of Paris, Sorbonne, was discovered with radial arteries of both wrists severed and the body carefully exsanguinated. Yet there was no blood at the murder scene. Files on several of the chemist's experiments were found to be missing. Additional clippings described still other deaths, more grisly, in which the corpses seemed to have been victims of various tortures or experimentation—the bodies were too badly damaged to be certain. And yet other clippings were mere obituaries. There seemed to be no logic or pattern to the deaths, and Pendergast did not leave any commentary on what it was that he had found interesting.

D'Agosta picked up the pile, riffled through it. There was a variety of thefts, too. A pharmaceutical manufacturing company, reporting the robbery of a freezer full of experimental drugs. A collection of diamonds mysteriously vanished from a vault in Israel. A rare, fist-sized piece of amber containing a leaf from a long-extinct plant, lifted from a wealthy couple's apartment in Paris. A unique, polished T. rex coprolite, dating precisely from the K-T boundary.

He replaced the clippings on the table with a sigh.

Next his eye fell on a small sheaf of papers from Sandringham, a private school in the south of England that

Diogenes attended—unknown to his family—to finish out his last year of upper school. He had managed to get himself accepted on the strength of several forged documents and a phony set of parents hired for the occasion. Despite a first-semester report card putting him in the first of every form, he was expelled a few months later. Judging from the paperwork, the school gave no reason for the expulsion and responded to Pendergast's queries with evasion, even agitation. Other papers showed that Pendergast had contacted a certain Brian Cooper on several occasions—Cooper had briefly been the roommate of Diogenes at Sandringham—but it seemed the boy refused to respond. A final letter from the youth's parents said Brian had been placed in an institution, where he was being treated for acute catatonia.

Following the expulsion, Diogenes slipped completely out of view for more than two years. And then he had surfaced to claim his inheritance. Four months later, he staged his own death in Canterbury.

After that, silence.

No—that wasn't quite true. There was one final communication. D'Agosta turned toward a folded sheet of heavy linen paper, sitting alone at one corner of the table. He reached for it, opened it thoughtfully. At the top was an embossed coat of arms, a lidless eye over two moons, a lion crouched beneath. And at the very center of the sheet was a date, written in violet ink with what D'Agosta now recognized as Diogenes's handwriting: *January 28*.

Inexorably, D'Agosta's mind returned once again to the October day when he'd first held the letter—here, in this room, on the eve of their departure to Italy. Pendergast had shown it to him and spoken briefly of Diogenes's plan to commit the perfect crime.

But D'Agosta had returned from Italy alone. And now it was up to him—and nobody else—to follow through for his dead partner, to stop the crime that presumably would occur on January 28.

Less than a week away.

He felt a rising panic; there was so little time left. The roommate at Sandringham: now, there was a lead. He'd call the parents tomorrow, see if the boy was talking. Even if he struck out there, undoubtedly there were other boys at the school who had known Diogenes.

D'Agosta folded the paper carefully and returned it to the table. Beside it lay a single black-and-white photograph, scuffed and creased with age. He picked it up, held it to the light. A man, a woman, and two young boys, standing before an elaborate wrought-iron railing. An imposing mansion could be seen in the middle distance. It was a warm day: the boys were in shorts, and the woman wore a summer dress. The man stared at the camera with a patrician face. The woman was beautiful, with light hair and a mysterious smile. The boys were perhaps eight and five. The elder stood straight, arms behind his back, looking gravely into the lens. His light blond hair was carefully parted, his clothes pressed. Something about the shape of the cheekbones, the aquiline features, told D'Agosta this was Agent Pendergast.

Beside him was a younger boy with ginger hair, hands pressed together, fingers pointed skyward, as if in prayer. Unlike his older sibling, Diogenes seemed faintly disheveled. But there was nothing in his dress or his grooming to account for this. Maybe it was something in the relaxed, almost languid draping of his limbs, so out of context with the chastely positioned hands. Maybe it was the parted lips, too full and sensual for a person so young. Both eyes looked the same—this must have been before the illness.

Still, D'Agosta was drawn to the eyes. They weren't looking at the camera, but at some point past it if they were looking at anything at all. They seemed dull, almost dead, out of place in that childish little face. D'Agosta felt an uncomfortable sensation in the pit of his stomach.

There was a rustle beside him and D'Agosta jumped. Constance Greene had suddenly materialized at his side. She seemed to have Pendergast's ability to approach with almost total silence.

"I'm sorry," Constance said. "I didn't mean to startle you."

"No problem. Looking at all this stuff is enough to creep anyone out."

"Excuse me. Creep out?"

"It's just an expression."

"Have you found anything interesting? Anything at all?"

D'Agosta shook his head. "Nothing we didn't talk about earlier." He paused. "The only thing is, I didn't see anything in here about Diogenes's illness. Scarlet fever, according to Aunt Cornelia. She said it changed him."

"I wish there was more information I could give you. I've searched the collections and the family papers, just in case there was something Aloysius overlooked. But he was very thorough. There's nothing else."

Nothing else. Diogenes's whereabouts, his appearance, his activities, even the crime he planned to commit: everything was a blank.

There was only a date—January 28. Next Monday.

"Maybe Pendergast was wrong," D'Agosta said, trying to sound hopeful. "About the date, I mean. Maybe it's not for another year. Or maybe it's something else entirely." He gestured at the documents strewn across the table. "All this seems so far away and long ago. It's hard to believe something big's about to happen."

The only response from Constance was a faint, and fleeting, smile.

Eight

ORACE SAWTELLE passed the oversize vellum menu back to the waiter with relief. He wished that once—just once—a client would come to *him*. He hated the sprawling concrete jungles they all worked in: Chicago, Detroit, and now New York. Once you got to know it, Keokuk wasn't so bad. He knew all the best watering holes and titty bars. Some of his clients might even develop a deep admiration for certain Iowan charms.

Across the table, his client was ordering something that sounded like cough-up of veal. Horace Sawtelle wondered if the man really knew what the hell he was asking for. He himself had scanned the menu, first one side and then the other, with deep misgivings. Handwritten French script, and unpronounceable at that. He'd settled on something called steak tartare. Hell, how bad could it be? Even the French couldn't ruin steak. And he liked tartar sauce on fish sticks.

"You don't mind if I glance through them once more before signing?" the client asked, holding up the sheaf of contracts.

Sawtelle nodded. "You go right ahead." Never mind

that they'd spent the last two hours going over them with a damn magnifying glass. You'd think the guy was buying a million dollars' worth of Palm Beach real estate instead of fifty grand in machine parts.

The client buried his nose in the paperwork and Sawtelle looked around, idly crunching on a breadstick. They were sitting in what looked to him like a glassed-in sidewalk café, protruding out into the sidewalk from the main restaurant. Every table was full: these pasty-faced New Yorkers needed all the sunlight they could get. Three women sat at the next table, black-haired and gaunt, picking at huge fruit salads. On the far side, a fat businessman was digging into a plate of something yellow and slippery.

A truck passed in a shriek of grinding gears, seemingly inches away from the glass wall, and Sawtelle's hand closed reflexively, breaking the breadstick. He wiped his hand on the tablecloth in disgust. Why the hell had the client insisted on eating out here, in the January chill? He glanced up through the glass ceiling at the pink awning, *La Vielle Ville* stitched on it in white. Above towered one of the huge cliff dwellings that passed for apartments in New York City. Sawtelle eyed the rows of identical windows rising toward the sooty sky. Like a damn high-rise prison. Probably held a thousand people. How could they stand it?

There was a flurry of activity near the entrance to the kitchen and Sawtelle glanced over disinterestedly. Maybe it was his lunch. Prepared tableside, the menu had said. And just how the hell were they going to do that: wheel a Weber grill over and fire up the charcoal? But sure enough, here they came, a whole damn procession of men in white smocks, pushing what looked like a small gurney in front of them.

The chef parked the rolling table at Sawtelle's elbow with a proud flourish. He barked a few orders in rapid-fire French and several underlings began to scurry around, one chopping onions, another frenziedly beating a raw egg. Sawtelle scanned the rolling table. There were little white toast points, a pile of round green things he guessed were capers, spices and dishes of unknown liquids, and a cupful of minced garlic. In the center, a fist-sized wad of raw hamburger. No steak or tartar sauce to be had for love or money.

With great ceremony, the chef dropped the hamburger into a stainless bowl, poured in the raw egg, the garlic, and onions, then began mashing everything together. In a few moments, he removed the sticky mass and dropped it back onto the rolling table, working it slowly between his fingers. Sawtelle glanced away, making a mental note to ask that the hamburger be cooked extra-well-done. *You never know what kinds of diseases these New Yorkers carry around.* And where was the damn grill, anyway?

At that moment, a waiter appeared at the client's side and slipped a plate onto the table. Sawtelle looked over in surprise just as another waiter darted in and slid something in between his own knife and fork. Looking down, Sawtelle saw with incredulity that the glistening patty of raw beef—now tamped down into a neat little mound— sat in front of him, surrounded by wedges of toast, chopped eggs, and capers.

Sawtelle looked up again quickly, uncomprehending. Across the table, the client was nodding approvingly.

The chef beamed at them briefly from the far side of

the table, then stepped back as his flunkies began wheeling the apparatus away.

"Excuse me," Sawtelle said in a low voice. "You haven't cooked it."

The chef stopped. "*Pourquoi?*"

Sawtelle jerked a finger in the direction of his plate. "I said, you haven't *cooked* it. You know, heat. Fire. Flambé."

The chef shook his head vigorously. "No, *monsieur.* Is no cook."

"You don't cook steak tartare," the client said, pausing as he was about to sign the contracts. "It's served raw. You didn't know?" A superior smile came briefly to his lips, then vanished.

Sawtelle sat back, rolling his eyes heavenward, struggling to keep his temper. *Only in New York. Twenty-five bucks for a mound of raw hamburger.*

Suddenly, he stiffened. "Sweet Caesar, what the hell is that?"

Far above him, a man dangled in the sky: limbs flung wide and flailing silently in the chill air. For a moment, it seemed to Sawtelle that the man was just hovering there, as if by magic. But then he made out the thin taut line of rope that arrowed upward from the man's neck. It disappeared into a window above, black and broken. Sawtelle stared openmouthed, thunderstruck by the sight.

Others in the restaurant had followed his gaze. There were sharp intakes of breath, a sudden gasp.

The figure jerked and shuddered, its back arching in agony until the victim seemed almost bent double. Sawtelle watched, transfixed with horror.

Then, suddenly, the rope parted. The man, flapping his arms and churning his legs, dropped directly toward him.

Just as suddenly, Sawtelle found he could move again. With an inarticulate cry, he threw himself backward in his chair. A split second later, there came an explosion of glass, and a shape hurtled past in a shower of glass and landed with a deafening crash on the women and their fruit salads, which disintegrated into a strange pastel eruption of reds and yellows and greens. From his position on his back on the floor, Sawtelle felt something warm and wet slap him hard across the side of the face, followed almost immediately by a shower of broken glass, dishes, cups, forks, spoons, and flowers, all raining down from the impact.

A strange silence. And then the cries began, the screams of pain, horror, and fear, but they seemed strangely soft and far away. Then he realized that his right ear was full of an unknown substance.

As he lay on his back, the full impact of what had just happened finally registered. Disbelief and horror washed over him once again. For a minute, maybe two, he found himself unable to move. The cries and shrieks grew steadily louder.

At last, with a heroic effort, he forced his unwilling limbs to respond. He rose to his knees, then staggered to his feet. Other people were now climbing to their feet, the room filling with the muffled shrieks and moans of the damned. Glass lay everywhere. The table at his right had turned into a crumpled mound of food, gore, flowers, tablecloth, napkins, and splintered wood. His own table was covered with glass. The twenty-five-dollar mound of raw hamburger was the only thing that had been spared, and it sat in solitary splendor, fresh and gleaming, all by itself.

His eyes moved to his client, who was still sitting, motionless, his suit splattered with something indescribable.

Abruptly, involuntarily, Sawtelle's limbs went into action. He swiveled about, found the door, took a step, lost his balance, recovered, took another.

The client's voice followed him. "Are—are you going?"

The question was so inane, so inappropriate, that Sawtelle broke into a choking, hoarse laugh. "Going?" he repeated, clearing his ear with a tug. "Yeah. I'm *going*." He lurched toward the door, coughing with laughter, his feet crunching across glass and ruin, anything to get away from this terrible place. He hit the sidewalk and turned south, his walk breaking into a run, scattering pedestrians in his wake.

From now on, people would just have to come to Keokuk.

Nine

ILLIAM SMITHBACK JR. got out of the cab, tossed a crumpled twenty through the front passenger window, and looked up Broadway toward Lincoln Center. A few blocks uptown he could make out a vast throng of people. They'd spilled out into Columbus and across 65th Street, creating one mother of a traffic jam. He could hear people leaning on their horns, the shriek of sirens, the occasional earth-shuddering *blaaaat* of a truck's air horn.

Smithback threaded his way through the sea of motionless vehicles, then turned north and began jogging up Broadway, his breath misting in the cold January air. It seemed he ran just about everywhere these days. Gone was the dignified, measured step of the ace *New York Times* reporter. Now he rushed to get his copy in on time, dashed to each new assignment, and sometimes filed two stories a day. His wife of two months, Nora Kelly, was not happy. She'd had expectations of unhurried dinners, sharing with each other the events of the day, before retiring to a night of lingering pleasure. But Smithback found he had little time for either eating or lingering. Yes, he was on the run these days: and for good reason. Bryce

Harriman was running, too, and he was hard on Smith-back's heels.

It had been one of the worst shocks of Smithback's life to return from his honeymoon and find Bryce Harriman lounging in his office doorway, grinning smugly, wearing the usual insufferably preppie clothes, welcoming him back to "our paper."

Our paper. Oh, God.

Everything had been going his way. He was a rising star at the *Times,* had nailed half a dozen great scoops in as many months. Fenton Davies, his editor, had started turning automatically to Smithback when it came time to hand out the big assignments. He'd finally convinced his girlfriend Nora to stop chasing old bones and digging up pots long enough to get hitched. And their honeymoon at Angkor Wat had been a dream—especially the week they'd spent at the lost temple of Banteay Chhmar, hack-ing through the jungle, braving snakes, malaria, and stinging ants while exploring the vast ruins. He remem-bered thinking, on the plane ride home, that life couldn't possibly get any better.

And he'd been right.

Despite Harriman's smarmy collegiality, it was clear from day one that he was gunning for Smithback. It wasn't the first time they'd crossed swords, but never be-fore at the same paper. How had he managed to get re-hired by the *Times* while Smithback was halfway around the world? The way Harriman sucked up to Davies, bringing the editor lattes every morning, hanging on his every word like he was the Oracle of Delphi, made Smithback's gorge rise. But it seemed to be working: just last week, Harriman had bagged the Dangler story, which by rights belonged to Smithback.

Smithback quickened his jog. Sixty-fifth and Broadway—the spot where some guy had reportedly fallen right into the midst of dozens of people eating lunch—was just ahead now. He could see the cluster of television cameras, reporters checking their cassette recorders, soundmen setting up boom microphones. This was his chance to outshine Harriman, seize the momentum.

No briefing under way yet, thank God.

He shook his head, muttering under his breath as he elbowed his way through the crowd.

Up ahead, he could see the glassed-in café of La Vielle Ville. Inside, police were still working the scene: the periodic flash of the police photographer lit up the glass restaurant. Crime scene tape was draped everywhere like yellow bunting. His eye rose to the glass roof of the café and the huge, jagged hole where the victim had fallen through, and still farther, up the broad facade of Lincoln Towers, until it reached the broken window from which the victim had precipitated. He could see cops there, too, and the bright bursts of a flash unit.

He pushed forward, looking around for witnesses. "I'm a reporter," he said loudly. "Bill Smithback, *New York Times*. Anybody see what happened?"

Several faces turned to regard him silently. Smithback took them in: a West Side matron carrying a microscopic Pomeranian; a bicycle messenger; a man balancing a large box filled with Chinese takeout on one shoulder; half a dozen others.

"I'm looking for a witness. Anybody see anything?"

Silence. *Most of them probably don't even speak English,* he thought.

"Anybody *know* anything?"

At this, a man wearing earmuffs and a heavy coat nodded vigorously. "A man," he said in a thick Indian accent. "He fall."

This was useless. Smithback pushed himself deeper into the crowd. Up ahead, he spotted a policeman, shooing people onto the sidewalk, trying to clear the cross street.

"Hey, Officer!" Smithback called out, using his elbows to dig through the gawking herd. "I'm from the *Times*. What happened here?"

The officer stopped barking orders long enough to glance his way. Then he went back to his work.

"Any ID on the victim?"

But the cop ignored him completely.

Smithback watched his retreating back. Typical. A lesser reporter might be content to wait for the official briefing, but not him. He'd get the inside scoop, and he wouldn't even break a sweat trying.

As he looked around again, his eye stopped at the main entrance to the apartment tower. The building was huge, probably sported a thousand apartments at least. There'd be people inside who knew the victim, could provide some color, maybe even speculate on what happened. He craned his neck, counting floors, until he again reached the open window. Twenty-fourth floor.

He began pushing his way through the crowd again, avoiding the megaphone-wielding cops, tacking as directly as he could toward the building's entrance. It was guarded by three large policemen who looked like they meant business. How on earth was he going to get in? Claim to be a tenant? That wasn't likely to work.

As he paused to survey the milling throng of press outside, his equanimity quickly returned. They were all waiting, like restless sheep, for some police brass to come out and begin the briefing. Smithback looked on pityingly. He didn't want the same story everybody else got: spoon-fed by the authorities, telling only what they wanted to tell with the requisite spin attached. He wanted the *real* story: the story that lay on the twenty-fourth floor of Lincoln Towers.

He turned away from the crowd and headed in the opposite direction. All big apartment buildings like this had a service entrance.

He followed the facade of the building up Broadway until he finally reached its end, where a narrow alley separated it from the next building. Thrusting his hands back into his pockets, he turned down the alley, whistling jauntily.

A moment later, his whistling stopped. Up ahead lay a large metal door marked *Service Entrance—Deliveries*. Standing beside the door was another cop. He was staring at Smithback and speaking into a small radio clipped to his collar.

Damn. Well, he couldn't just stop dead in his tracks and turn around—that would look suspicious. He'd just walk right past the cop like he was taking a shortcut behind the building.

"Morning, Officer," he said as he came abreast of the policeman.

"Afternoon, Mr. Smithback," the cop replied.

Smithback felt his jaw tighten.

Whoever was in charge of this homicide investigation was a pro, did things by the book. But Smithback was not some third-rate line stringer. If there was another way in, he'd find it. He followed the alley around the back of the building until it turned a right angle, heading once again toward 65th.

Yes. There, not thirty yards in front of him, was the staff entrance to La Vielle Ville. Deserted, with no cop loitering around outside. If he couldn't get to the twenty-fourth floor, at least he could check out the place where the man had landed.

He moved forward quickly, excitement adding spring to his step. Once he'd checked out the restaurant, there might even be a way to get into the high-rise. There had to be connecting passages, perhaps through the basement.

Smithback reached the battered metal door, pulled it ajar, began to step in.

Then he froze. There, beside a brace of massive stoves, several policemen were taking statements from cooks and waiters.

Everybody slowly turned to look at him.

He put a tentative foot in, like he was going somewhere.

"No press," barked one of the cops.

"Sorry," he said, flashing what he feared was a ghastly smile. "Wrong way."

And, very gently, he closed the door and stepped back, walking back around to the front of the building, where he was once more repelled by the sight of the vast herd of reporters, all waiting like sheep to the slaughter.

No way, not him, not Bill Smithback of the *Times.* His eye cast around for some angle of attack, some idea that hadn't occurred to the others—and then he saw it: a pizza delivery man on a motorbike, hopelessly trying to work his way through the crowd. He was a skinny man with no chin wearing a silly hat that said *Romeo's Pizzeria,* and his face was splotched and red with frustration.

Smithback approached him, nodded toward the carrier mounted on the back. "Got a pizza in there?"

"Two," the man said. "Look at this shit. They're gonna be stone-cold, and there goes my tip. On top of that, if I don't get it there in twenty minutes, they don't have to pay—"

Smithback cut him off. "Fifty bucks for your two pizzas and the hat."

The man looked at him blankly, like a complete idiot.

Smithback pulled out a fifty. "Here. Take it."

"But what about—"

"Tell them you got robbed."

The man couldn't help but take the money. Smithback swiped the hat off the man's head, stuck it on his own, opened the rear carrier on the motorbike, and hauled out the pizza boxes. He moved through the crowd toward the door, carrying the pizzas in one hand and jerking off his tie with the other, stuffing it in his pocket.

"Pizza delivery, coming through!" He elbowed his way to the front, came up against the blue barricades draped in crime scene tape.

"Pizza delivery, SOC team, twenty-fourth floor."

It worked like a dream. The fat cop manning the barricade shoved it aside and Smithback hiked through.

Now for the triumvirate at the door.

He strode confidently forward as the three cops turned to face him.

"Pizza delivery, twenty-fourth floor."

They moved to block his way.

"I'll take the pizzas up," one said.

"Sorry. Against company rules. I got to deliver directly to the customer."

"Nobody's allowed in."

"Yeah, but this is for the SOC team. And if you take it up, how am I going to collect my money?"

The cops exchanged an uncertain glance. One shrugged. Smithback felt a glow. It was going to work. He was as good as in.

"They're getting cold, come on." Smithback pressed forward.

"How much?"

"Like I said, I have to deliver *directly to the customer.* May I?" He made one more tentative step, almost bumped into the large gut of the lead cop.

"No one's allowed up."

"Yes, but it's just for a—"

"Give me the pizzas."

"Like I said—"

The cop reached out. "I *said,* give me the damn *pizzas.*"

And just like that, Smithback realized he was defeated. He docilely held them out and the cop took them.

"How much?" the cop asked.

"Ten bucks."

The cop gave him ten, no tip. "Who's it for?"

"The SOC team."

"Your customer got a name? There're a dozen SOC up there."

"Ah, I think it was Miller."

The cop grunted, disappeared in the dim lobby carrying the pizzas, while the other two closed rank, blocking the door. The one who had shrugged turned back. "Sorry, pal, but could you bring me a fifteen-inch pie, pepperoni, garlic, and onions with extra cheese?"

"Up yours," Smithback said, turning and walking back to the barriers. As he squeezed through the press of reporters, he heard some snickers and someone called out, "Nice try, Bill." And another shrilled out in an effeminate voice, "Why, Billy darling, that hat looks *dreamy* on you."

Smithback pulled the hat off in disgust and tossed it. For once, his reportorial genius had failed. He was already getting a bad feeling about this assignment. It had barely started and already it was smelling rotten. Despite the January frost in the air, he could almost feel Harriman's hot breath on the back of his neck.

He turned and—with heavy heart—took his place in the crowd to wait for the official briefing.

Ten

*L*IEUTENANT VINCENT D'AGOSTA pushed open the door of McFeeley's Ale House, feeling bone-tired. McFeeley's was about as cozy an Irish bar as you could still find in New York, and D'Agosta needed a little comfort right about now. The place was dark, long, and narrow, with a thickly varnished wooden bar on one side, booths along the other. Ancient sporting prints hung from the walls, indistinguishable underneath a heavy mantle of dust. Behind the bar, bottles stood six rows deep in front of the mirrored wall. An old jukebox sat near the door, the kind where the Irish selections were printed in green ink. On tap were Guinness, Harp, and Bass. The place smelled of greasy cooking and spilled beer. Just about the only nostalgic touch missing, in fact, was tobacco smoke, and D'Agosta didn't miss that at all: he'd given up cigars years before, when he quit the force and moved to Canada to write.

McFeeley's was half empty, the way D'Agosta liked it. He chose a stool, pulled it up to the bar.

Patrick, the bartender, caught sight of him and came over. "Hey, Lieutenant," he said, sliding a coaster in front of him. "How's it going?"

"It's going."

"The usual?"

"No, Paddy, a black and tan, please. And a cheese-burger, rare."

A pint appeared a moment later and D'Agosta sank his upper lip meditatively into the mocha-colored foam. He almost never allowed himself this kind of indulgence anymore—he had lost twenty pounds in the last few months and didn't intend to gain them back—but tonight he'd make an exception. Laura Hayward wouldn't be home until late: she was working the bizarre hanging that had taken place on the Upper West Side at lunchtime.

He'd spent a fruitless morning chasing leads. There was nothing in the public records office on Ravenscry, Great-Aunt Cornelia's estate in Dutchess County. He'd made inquiries with the NOPD about the long-burned Pendergast residence in New Orleans, with similar results. In both cases, there was nothing about Diogenes Pendergast.

From headquarters, he'd journeyed back to 891 Riverside to reexamine Pendergast's scanty collection of evidence. He'd called the London bank to which, according to Pendergast's records, Diogenes had requested money be deposited years before. The account had been closed for twenty years, no forwarding information available. Inquiries at the banks in Heidelberg and Zurich brought the same answer. He spoke with the family in England whose son had briefly been Diogenes's roommate at Sandringham, only to learn the youth had killed himself one day after being removed from protective restraints.

Next, he called the firm of lawyers that had acted as intermediaries in the correspondence between Diogenes and his family. This time the red tape was almost inter-

minable: he was transferred from one legal secretary to
another, each requiring a repetition of his request. At long
last, an attorney who would not identify himself came on
the line and informed D'Agosta that Diogenes Pendergast
was no longer a client; that attorney-client privilege for-
bade giving out further information; and that, besides, all
relevant files had long been destroyed at said person's
request.

Five hours and at least thirty phone calls later,
D'Agosta had learned precisely zip.

Next, he turned to the newspaper clippings Pendergast
had collected of various odd crimes. He'd considered
calling the case officers involved but decided against it.
Pendergast had no doubt done this already; if there had
been any information worth sharing, he would have put it
in the files. Anyway, D'Agosta still had no clue what
Pendergast thought important about these clippings, scattered as they were across the globe, the crimes they
reported bizarre yet seemingly unconnected.

It was now past two o'clock. D'Agosta knew his boss,
Captain Singleton, would be out: he invariably spent his
afternoons in the field, following up personally on the
important cases. So D'Agosta left 891 Riverside and
made his way down to the precinct house, where he slunk
to his desk, turned on his computer terminal, and punched
in his password. For the rest of the afternoon, he had
moused his way through every law enforcement and gov-
ernmental database he could access: NYPD, state, federal, WICAPS, Interpol, even the Social Security
Administration. Nothing. Despite all the crushing, endless documentation generated by the interlocking tangle
of government bureaucracies, Diogenes walked through

it all like a wraith, leaving no impression behind him. It was almost as if the guy were really dead, after all.

That was when he gave up and went to McFeeley's.

His cheeseburger arrived and he began to eat, barely tasting it. His investigation wasn't even forty-eight hours old, and already he'd just about run out of leads. Pendergast's vast resources seemed of little use against a ghost.

He took a few more halfhearted bites from his burger, finished his drink, dropped some bills on the bar, nodded to Patrick, and left. *Get all the information you can from Detective Captain Laura Hayward, but for her own sake minimize her involvement.* D'Agosta had, in fact, told her little of his investigations since their visit to Great-Aunt Cornelia. In a perverse way, it seemed best.

Why?

He thrust his hands into his pockets, bent into the chill January wind. Was it because of the levelheaded things he was certain she'd say? *Vinnie, this is crazy. A letter containing nothing but a date. Some half-baked threats made twenty, thirty years ago. I can't believe you're wasting your time.*

And maybe—just maybe—he was afraid she'd convince him it was crazy, too.

Strolling along, he approached the intersection of 77th and First Avenue. The ugly white brick apartment building he shared with Laura Hayward rose at the corner. Shivering, he glanced at his watch. Eight o'clock. Laura wouldn't be home yet. He'd set the table for her, put what was left of the lasagna *napoletana* in the microwave. He was curious to hear more about this new murder case she was working. Anything to keep his mind from running in circles.

The doorman made a belated, insolent attempt to open

the door for him. D'Agosta walked past into the narrow lobby, sounding his pocket for the key. Ahead, one of the elevators stood open invitingly. D'Agosta stepped in, pressing the button for the fifteenth floor.

Just as the elevator doors were closing, a gloved hand shot in, forcing them open. It was the obnoxious doorman. He stepped in, then turned to face forward, crossing his arms before him and ignoring D'Agosta. The unpleasant smell of body odor filled the small space.

D'Agosta glanced at him with irritation. He was a swarthy-looking fellow with a fleshy face, brown eyes, overweight. Strange: he hadn't pressed a floor button of his own. D'Agosta looked away, losing interest, directing his gaze to the floor indicator as the elevator rose. Five, six, seven . . .

The doorman leaned forward, pressed the stop button. The elevator came to an abrupt halt.

D'Agosta glanced over. "What's your problem?"

The doorman didn't bother looking at him. Instead, he pulled an override key from his pocket, inserted it into the control panel, turned it, and withdrew it. With a jerk, the elevator began descending again.

Laura's right, D'Agosta thought. *This jerk's got a serious attitude problem.* "Look, I don't know where the hell you think you're going, but you can wait until I've reached my floor." D'Agosta pressed the button marked *15* again.

The elevator didn't respond. It was still descending, past the lobby now and heading for the basement.

In a heartbeat, D'Agosta's irritation turned to alarm. His cop radar went off full blast. The cautionary words of Pendergast's note suddenly flashed through his mind: *Diogenes is consummately dangerous. Do not gain his at-*

tention any earlier than you have to. Almost without thinking, he reached into his coat and yanked out his service piece.

But even as he did so, the doorman spun toward him and, with an amazing, lightninglike move, thrust him up against the elevator wall, pinning his arms behind his back in a viselike grip. D'Agosta struggled, only to find he had been expertly restrained. He drew breath to yell for help, but—almost as if by telepathy—a gloved hand clamped down hard over his mouth.

D'Agosta struggled briefly again, hardly believing how swiftly and totally he had been disarmed and immobilized.

And then the doorman did a strange thing. He leaned forward, brought his lips directly to D'Agosta's ear. When he spoke, it was in the faintest of whispers.

"My sincerest apologies, Vincent . . ."

Eleven

DETECTIVE CAPTAIN LAURA HAYWARD walked across the living room and glanced out the window, careful not to brush against the table that had been placed beneath it. Through the shattered hole, she could see that, far below, Broadway was finally quiet. She'd given her men strict orders to seal off the scene, and they'd done a good job: the injured had been quickly removed by ambulance, the gawkers and rubber-neckers had eventually grown tired and cold and had drifted away. The press had been more tenacious, but they, too, had eventually settled for the terse statement she'd given late in the afternoon. It had proved a compli-cated, messy crime scene, involving the apartment and the restaurant below, but she'd coordinated all the inves-tigative teams personally and now—at last—the on-site forensic work was wrapping up. The fingerprint examin-ers, photo technicians, and crime scene analysts had al-ready left. Only the evidence custodian remained, and she would be gone within the hour.

Laura Hayward derived immense satisfaction from a well-worked homicide. Violent death was a disorderly af-fair. But as a scene was analyzed—as wave after wave of forensic investigators, medical examiners, technicians, and criminalists went about their jobs in the scripted fashion—the chaos and horror were compartmentalized, ordered, and labeled. It was as if the investigation itself restored some of the natural order that the act of murder had overturned.

And yet, as she looked over this scene, Hayward felt no satisfaction. She felt instead an inexplicable sense of unease.

She shivered, blew on her hands, buttoned the top button of her coat. What with the broken window, and her instructions to touch nothing (not even the heat), the room was only a few degrees warmer than outside. For a moment, she found herself wishing D'Agosta were there. No matter: she'd tell him about the case when she got home. He'd be interested, she knew, and he often surprised her with practical, creative suggestions. Maybe it would get his mind off his unhealthy obsession with Pendergast's brother. Just when he'd gotten over Pendergast's death, just when his sense of guilt had seemed to ease, he'd been summoned by that damned chauffeur . . .

"Ma'am?" a sergeant said, popping his head into the living room. "Captain Singleton is here."

"Show him in, please." Singleton was the local precinct captain, and Hayward expected he would show up personally. He was one of those old-fashioned captains who felt their place was with their men, working cases, on the street or at the scene of a crime. Hayward had worked with Singleton before and found him one of the best captains in the city when it came to working with Homicide—cooperative, deferring when it came to forensics, but involving himself usefully in every step of the investigation.

And now in the doorway the man himself appeared, natty in a long camel's-hair coat, his carefully trimmed hair impeccable as always. He paused, eyes moving about restlessly, taking in the scene. Then he smiled, stepped forward, and offered his hand. "Laura."

"Glen. Nice to see you." The handshake was brief and businesslike. She wondered if Singleton knew about her and D'Agosta, decided immediately that he didn't: they had both been careful to keep their relationship out of the NYPD rumor mill.

Singleton waved his hand around the room. "Beautiful work, as usual. Hope you don't mind my sticking my nose in."

"Not at all. We're just about squared away."

"How's it going?"

"Just fine." She hesitated. No reason not to tell Singleton: unlike most police brass, he got no joy out of backstabbing potential rivals for advancement—nor was he threatened by being upstaged by Homicide. Besides, he was a captain, too—she could rely on his discretion.

"Actually, I'm not so sure," she said in a quieter tone.

Singleton glanced over at the evidence custodian, who was standing in a far corner of the room jotting some notations on a clipboard. "Want to tell me about it?"

"The lock on the front door was expertly picked. It's a small apartment, just two bedrooms, one converted into an artist's studio. The perpetrator entered the apartment undetected and apparently hid here—" She pointed to a dark corner near the doorway. "He jumped the victim as he entered the living room, probably hit him over the head. Unfortunately, the body was so badly damaged by the fall that it might be difficult to determine the weapon the attacker used." She pointed to the adjoining wall, where a spray of blood defaced a painting of Central Park's boat pond. "Take a look at that impact splatter."

Singleton examined. "Fairly small, medium-velocity drops. A blunt instrument of some kind?"

"That's our take. The cast-off patterns, here and here, back up the assumption. And the height of the spray relative to the wall is what indicates a blow to the head. Judging by the pattern of travel—note the crown droplets moving across the rug—the victim staggered a few feet, then collapsed where that ponding stain has been marked. The amount of blood is also suggestive of a head wound—you know how much they bleed."

"I take it no weapon was recovered?"

"None. Whatever was used, the perp took it with him."

Singleton nodded slowly. "Go on."

"It appears that the attacker then dragged the stunned victim to the sofa, where—and this is strange—he tended the wound he'd just inflicted."

"Tended?"

"Dabbed at it with gauze pads from the medicine cabinet in the bathroom. Several empty packages were found next to the sofa, some bloody pads tossed in the trash."

"Any prints?"

"The guys from Latents lifted about fifty from all over the apartment. Even took a few from the blood of the victim, Duchamp, with an amido black methanol solution. All the prints matched Duchamp, his help, or known acquaintances. There were no others: not on the medicine cabinet, not on the doorknob, not on the packets of gauze."

"The murderer wore gloves."

"Surgical rubber, based on trace residues. The lab will be able to confirm by morning." Hayward gestured at the sofa. "Next the victim was bound, arms tied behind his back in a series of elaborate knots. The same heavy cordage was used to fashion the hangman's noose. I had forensics remove the ropes from the body and bag them. The knots are like nothing I've ever seen before." She nodded to a series of oversize plastic bags which lay, tagged and sealed, atop a blue evidence locker.

"Strange-looking ropes, too."

"It's about the only evidence the perp left behind. That, and a few fibers from his clothing." *It's the only bit of good news in the whole case,* Hayward thought to herself. Rope had almost as many characteristics as fingerprints: type of twist, turns per inch, number of plies, filament attributes. That, along with the particular type and style of knot, could speak volumes.

"By the time Duchamp came to again, he was probably already bound. The murderer shoved that long desk into position there beneath the window. Then—somehow—he forced Duchamp to climb onto the desk and, in effect, walk the plank. Or, I should say, *run* the plank. The man basically leaped out through the window, hanging himself."

Singleton frowned. "You sure about that?"

"Take a look at the desk." Hayward showed him a series of bloody footprints across the desktop, each flagged and labeled.

"Duchamp walked through his own blood on the way to the desk. See how, in the first set of prints, he's standing at rest? As the others lead toward the window, the distance between them grows larger. And look how, in this last print before the window, only the ball of the shoe hit the desk. These are *acceleration* marks."

Singleton stared at the desk for at least a minute. Then

he glanced over at Hayward. "They couldn't have been faked? The murderer couldn't, say, have taken off Duchamp's shoes, made the marks, then replaced them on his feet?"

"I wondered about that, too. But the forensics boys said that would have been impossible. You can't fake prints like that. Besides, the pattern of breakage of the window frame is consistent with somebody leaping through it, rather than somebody being manhandled, or pushed, out of it."

"Holy crap." Singleton stepped forward. The shattered window was like a jagged eye staring out into the Manhattan night. "Imagine Duchamp standing there, arms tied behind his back, a hangman's noose hanging from his neck. What could somebody say that would induce him to take a running leap out his own window?"

He turned back again. "Unless it was voluntary. Assisted suicide. After all, there was no sign of struggle— was there?"

"None. But then, what are we to make of the perp picking the lock? Wearing gloves? Assaulting Duchamp before tying him up? The footprints on the desk show none of the false starts, the hesitation, you usually see in suicide attempts. Besides, we've done preliminary interviews of Duchamp's neighbors, some friends, a few clients. Everybody said he was the sweetest, gentlest man they'd ever met. Always a kind word for everyone, always smiling. His doctor backed that up as well. No psychological troubles. Unmarried, but no signs of any recent breakup. Financially stable. Made plenty of money from his paintings." Hayward shrugged. "No stressors of any kind that we know about."

"Any of the neighbors see anything?"

"Nobody. We've impounded the videotapes from building security. They're being gone over now."

Singleton pursed his lips, nodding. Then, putting his hands behind his back, he strolled slowly around the room, looking carefully at the traces of fingerprint powder, the labeled pins, and the evidence markers. At last, he stopped beside the locker. Hayward came over and together they stared at the heavy length of rope within the sealed bag. It was a very unusual material, glossy rather than rough, and the color was equally strange: dark purple verging on black, the color of eggplant. The hangman's noose was wrapped in the requisite thirteen loops, but they were the strangest loops Hayward had ever seen: thick and complex, like a mass of knotted intestine. In another, smaller bag lay the cord used to bind Duchamp's wrists. Hayward had instructed the workers to cut the cord, not the knot, which was almost as exotic and serpentine as the hangman's noose.

"Look at those," Singleton said, whistling. "Big, fat idiot knots."

"I'm not sure about that," Hayward replied. "I'll have the ligature specialist run them through the FBI's knot database." She hesitated. "Here's something unusual. The rope he was hung from was cut partway through with a sharp knife, maybe a razor, at the center of its length."

"You mean—" Singleton stopped.

"Right. The rope was *supposed* to break the way it did."

They stared a moment longer at the strange coils of rope, shimmering faintly in the incandescent light.

From behind, the evidence custodian cleared her throat. "Excuse me, Captain," she said. "Can I remove that now?"

"Sure." Hayward stepped back as the woman carefully placed the bags into the evidence locker, sealed it, then began wheeling the locker toward the front door.

Singleton watched her go. "Anything taken? Valuables, money, paintings?"

"Not a thing. Duchamp had close to three hundred dollars in his wallet and some really valuable old jewelry on his dresser. Not to mention a studio full of expensive paintings. Nothing was touched."

Singleton's eyes were on her. "And this feeling of uneasiness you spoke about?"

She turned to face him. "I can't really put a finger on it. On the one hand, the whole scene feels a little too clear and cold—almost like it's a setup. This was certainly a carefully, almost masterfully executed crime. And yet nothing makes any sense. Why knock the guy over the head, then doctor the wound? Why tie him up, put a noose around his neck, force him to jump out a window, but then deliberately weaken the rope so he falls to his death after a brief struggle? What could Duchamp possibly have been told that would make him leap to his own death like that? And above all: why go to all this trouble to kill a harmless watercolor artist who never hurt a fly? I get the sense that there's a deep and subtle motive for this crime, and so far we haven't even begun to guess at it. I've already got Psych working on a profile. I can only hope we'll learn what makes him tick. Because unless we find the motive, how the hell are we supposed to find the killer?"

Twelve

FOR A MOMENT, D'Agosta went rigid in shock and disbelief. The voice was familiar and yet strange. Instinctively, he tried to speak again, but the gloved hand clamped down still harder over his mouth.

"Shhhh."

The elevator doors rolled open with a faint chime. Still holding D'Agosta in a tight restraint, the man peered cautiously out into the dark basement corridor, looking carefully in both directions. Then he gave D'Agosta a gentle shove out into the dingy hall, steering him through a series of narrow, high-ceilinged passages of yellow cinder block. At last, he brought D'Agosta up short before a scuffed metal door, unlabeled and painted the same color as the walls. They were near the building's power plant: the low rumble of furnaces was clearly audible. The man glanced around once again, then stopped to examine a small cobweb that stretched across one edge of the door frame. Only then did he withdraw a key from his pocket, unlock the door, and usher D'Agosta quickly inside, closing the door and carefully locking it.

"Glad to see you looking so well, Vincent."

D'Agosta could not summon a word.

"My sincerest apologies for the brusque behavior," the man said, crossing the room with swift steps and checking the lone basement window. "We may speak freely here."

D'Agosta remained astounded by the disconnect between the man's voice—those unmistakable, mellifluous southern tones with the lazy consistency of molasses—and the man himself: a total stranger in a spotty doorman's uniform, stocky, dark-complected, with brown hair and eyes and a round face. Even his bearing, his manner of walking, was unfamiliar.

"Pendergast?" D'Agosta asked, finally finding his voice.

The man bowed. "The very same, Vincent."

"Pendergast!" And before he realized what he was doing, D'Agosta had crushed the FBI agent in a bear hug.

Pendergast went rigid for a few seconds. Then, gently but firmly, he disengaged himself from the embrace and took a step back. "Vincent, I can't tell you how delighted I am to see you again. I have missed you."

D'Agosta seized his hand and shook it, embarrassment mingling with the surprise, relief, and joy. "I thought you were dead. How—?"

"I must apologize for the deception. I'd intended to remain 'dead' even longer. But circumstances have forced my hand." He turned his back. "Now, if you don't mind . . ." He slipped out of the doorman's coat, which D'Agosta could now see was cleverly padded around the shoulders and midriff, and hung it on the back of the door.

"What happened to you?" D'Agosta asked. "How did you escape? I turned Fosco's castle upside down looking for you. Where the hell have you been?" As the initial shock began to recede, he felt himself filling with a thousand questions.

Pendergast smiled faintly under this barrage. "You shall know all, I promise. But first, make yourself comfortable—I'll only be a moment." And with that, he turned and vanished into a back room.

For the first time, D'Agosta examined his surroundings. He was in the living room of a small, dingy apartment. A threadbare sofa was shoved against one wall, flanked by two wing chairs, their arms spotted with stains. A cheap coffee table held a stack of *Popular Mechanics* magazines. A battered rolltop desk sat against one wall, its writing surface bare save for a sleek Apple PowerBook: the only thing out of place in the monochromatic room. Some faded Hummel pictures of big-eyed children hung on the nondescript walls. A bookshelf was stuffed with paperbacks, mostly popular novels and cheesy best sellers. D'Agosta was amused to find a personal favorite, *Ice Limit III: Return to Cape Horn,* among the well-thumbed reads. Beyond the living room, an open door led to a kitchen, small but tidy. The place was about as far removed from Pendergast's digs at the Dakota or his Riverside Drive mansion as you could get.

There was a faint rustle and D'Agosta jumped to find Pendergast—the real Pendergast—standing in the doorway: tall, slender, his silver eyes glittering. His hair was still brown, his skin swarthy, but his face had morphed back into the fine, aquiline features D'Agosta knew so well.

Pendergast smiled again, as if reading D'Agosta's mind. "Cheek pads," he said. "Remarkable how effectively they can change one's appearance. I've removed them for the present, however, since I find them rather uncomfortable. Along with the brown contact lenses."

"I'm floored. I knew you were a master of disguises,

but this beats all . . . I mean, even the room . . ." D'Agosta jerked a thumb in the direction of the bookcase.

Pendergast looked pained. "Even here, alas, nothing can appear out of place. I must keep up the image of doorman."

"And a surly one at that."

"I find that exhibiting unpleasant personality traits helps one evade deeper scrutiny. Once people typecast me as a peevish doorman with a chip on his shoulder, they look no farther. May I offer you a beverage?"

"Bud?"

Pendergast shuddered involuntarily. "My dissembling has its limits. Perhaps a Pernod or Campari?"

"No, thanks." D'Agosta grinned.

"I take it you received my letter."

"That's right. And I've been on the case ever since."

"Progress?"

"Precious little. I paid a visit to your great-aunt. But that can wait a bit. Right now, my friend, you have some serious explaining to do."

"Naturally." Pendergast motioned him to a seat and took a chair opposite. "I recall we parted in haste on a mountainside in Tuscany."

"You could say that. I'll never forget the last time I saw you, surrounded by a pack of boar-hunting dogs, every one eager to take a chunk out of you."

Pendergast nodded slowly, and his eyes seemed to go far away. "I was captured, bound, sedated, and carried back to the castle. Our corpulent friend had me transported deep into the tunnels beneath. There he chained me in a tomb whose former occupant had been unceremoniously swept out. He proceeded—in the most genteel way, of course—to wall me in."

"Good God." D'Agosta shuddered. "I brought the Italian police in to search for you the next morning, but it was no use. Fosco had removed all traces of our stay. The Italians thought I was a lunatic."

"I learned later of the count's curious death. Was that you?"

"Sure was."

Pendergast nodded approvingly. "What happened to the violin?"

"I couldn't leave it lying around the castle, so I took it and . . ." He paused, feeling uncertain how Pendergast would feel about what he had done.

Pendergast raised his eyebrows in query.

"I brought it to Viola Maskelene. I told her you were dead."

"I see. How did she react?"

"She was very shocked, very upset. Although she tried to cover that up. I think . . ." D'Agosta hesitated. "I think she cares for you."

Pendergast was silent, his face a mask.

D'Agosta and Pendergast had first met Viola Maskelene the prior November, while working on a case in Italy. It had been obvious to D'Agosta that, from the moment the two saw each other, something ineffable had passed between Pendergast and the young Englishwoman. He could only guess what Pendergast was now thinking.

Pendergast suddenly roused himself. "You did the correct thing, and now we can consider the case of the Stormcloud violin definitively closed."

"But look," D'Agosta said, "how did you escape the castle? How long were you walled up down there?"

"I was chained in the tomb for almost forty-eight hours."

"In the dark?"

Pendergast nodded. "Slowly suffocating, I might add. I found a certain specialized form of meditation to be most useful."

"And then?"

"I was rescued."

"By who?"

"My brother."

D'Agosta, still reeling from Pendergast's near-miraculous reappearance, felt himself go numb with shock. "Your *brother*? Diogenes?"

"Yes."

"But I thought he hated you."

"Yes. And because he hates me, he needs me."

"For what?"

"For at least the past six months, Diogenes had made it his business to monitor my movements, as part of his preparation for the crime. I regret to say I was completely unaware of it. I had always believed myself the biggest impediment to his success and that someday he would attempt to kill me. But I was wrong—foolishly wrong. The *opposite* was true. When Diogenes learned of my peril, he launched a daring rescue. He entered the castle, disguised as a local—he is more the master of disguise than I am—and freed me from the tomb."

D'Agosta was seized by a sudden thought. "Wait. His eyes are two different colors, right?"

Pendergast nodded again. "One is hazel, the other a milky blue."

"*I saw him.* On the hillside there, above Fosco's castle. Just after we were separated. He was standing in the shadow of a rock ledge, watching the proceedings, as calm as if it was the first race at Aqueduct."

"That was him. After freeing me from my imprisonment, he transported me to a private clinic outside Pisa, where I recuperated from dehydration, exposure, and the wounds inflicted by Fosco's dogs."

"I still don't get it. If he hated you—if he planned to commit this so-called perfect crime—why not just leave you walled up?"

Pendergast smiled again, but this time the smile held no mirth. "You must always remember, Vincent, that we are dealing with a uniquely deviant criminal mind. How little I understood his real plans."

At this, Pendergast abruptly rose and went to the kitchen. A moment later, D'Agosta heard the clink of ice in a glass. When the agent returned, he held a bottle of Lillet in one hand and a tumbler in the other.

"Are you sure I can't interest you in a drink?"

"No. Now tell me, for God's sake, what you mean."

Pendergast splashed a few fingers of Lillet into the glass. "If I had died, I would have ruined everything for Diogenes. You see, Vincent, *I* am the primary object of his crime."

"*You?* You're going to be the victim? Then why—?"

"I am not *going* to be the victim. I *already am* the victim."

"What?"

"The crime has commenced. It is being successfully executed as we speak."

"You're not serious."

"I have never been more serious in my life." Pendergast took a long gulp of Lillet, refilled the glass. "Diogenes disappeared during my recovery at the private clinic in Pisa. As soon as I recovered, I returned to New York, incognito. I knew his plans were almost mature, and New York seemed the best place to mount the effort to stop him. I had little doubt the crime would take place here. This city offers the greatest anonymity, the best opportunities to hide, adopt an alter ego, develop his plan of attack. And so now—aware that my brother had been keeping tabs on my movements—I remained 'dead' as a way to move about unseen. It meant keeping all of you in the dark. Even Constance." At this, a stab of pain crossed Pendergast's face. "I regret that more than I can say. Still, it seemed the most prudent way to proceed."

"And so you became a doorman."

"The position allowed me to keep an eye on you and, through you, others important to me. I have a better chance of hunting Diogenes from the shadows. And I would not have revealed myself had certain events not forced my hand prematurely."

"What events?"

"The hanging of Charles Duchamp."

"That bizarre murder over by Lincoln Center?"

"Correct. That, and another murder in New Orleans three days ago. Torrance Hamilton, professor emeritus. Poisoned in front of a crowded lecture hall."

"What's the connection?"

"Hamilton was one of my tutors in high school, the man who taught me French, Italian, and Mandarin. We were very close. Duchamp was my dearest—in fact, my *only*—childhood friend. He's the only person from my youth I've remained in touch with. Both murdered by Diogenes."

"It couldn't be a coincidence?"

"Impossible. Hamilton was poisoned by a rare nerve

toxin, placed in his water glass. It's a synthetic toxin, very similar to that produced by a certain spider native to Goa. An ancestor of my father's died of a bite from that same spider when he was a minor functionary in India during the Raj." Pendergast took another sip. "Duchamp was hung from a noose, which then parted, plunging him twenty stories to his death. My Great-Great-Uncle Maurice died in precisely the same manner. He was hanged in New Orleans in 1871 for murdering his wife and her lover. Because the gibbet had been badly damaged in recent riots, they hung him instead from one of the upper courthouse windows on Decatur Street. But Maurice's violent struggles, combined with a defective rope, caused it to part, sending him plummeting to his death."

D'Agosta stared at his friend in horror.

"These deaths, and the manner in which they were staged, were Diogenes's way of attracting my attention. Perhaps now, Vincent, you can understand why Diogenes needs me *alive*."

"You can't mean that he's—"

"Precisely. I had always assumed his crime would be against humanity. But now I know *I* am his target. My brother's so-called perfect crime is to murder *everyone close to me*. That's the real reason he rescued me from Fosco's castle. He doesn't want me dead, he wants me alive—alive so he can destroy me in a far more exquisite way, leaving me filled with misery and self-reproach, torturing myself with the knowledge that I was unable to save those few people on earth . . ." Pendergast paused, took a steadying breath. "Those few people on earth I truly care about."

D'Agosta swallowed. "I can't believe this monster's related to you."

"Now that I know the true nature of his crime, I've been forced to abandon my initial plan and develop a new one. It's not an ideal plan, but it is the best possible under the circumstances."

"Tell me."

"We *must* prevent Diogenes from killing again. That means locating him. And here's where I'll need your help, Vincent. You must use your access as a law enforcement officer to glean as much as you can from the crime scene evidence."

He handed a cell phone to D'Agosta. "Here's a phone I'll use to keep in contact with you. Because time is of the essence, we'll need to start locally, with Charles Duchamp. Dig up whatever evidence you can find and bring it to me. No crumb is too small. Find out everything you can from Laura Hayward—but for God's sake don't tell her what you're up to. Not even Diogenes can leave a totally clean crime scene."

"Good as done." D'Agosta paused. "So what's with the date on the letter? January 28?"

"I no longer have any doubt that is the day he plans to complete his crime. But it is vital you keep in mind that the crime *has already begun*. Today is the twenty-second. My brother has been planning this infamy for years, maybe decades. All his preparations are in place. I shudder to think who he might kill in the next six days." And at this, Pendergast sat forward and stared at D'Agosta, his eyes glittering in the dim room. "Unless Diogenes can be stopped, everyone close to me—and that would certainly include you, Vincent—may die."

Thirteen

SMITHBACK TOOK his usual place in the darkest corner of the Bones, the dingy restaurant behind the museum favored as an after-hours hangout by museum employees who—it seemed—never tired of the sight of bones. The official name of the place was the Blarney Stone Tavern; it had acquired its nickname from the owner's penchant for hammering bones of all shapes, sizes, and sources onto the walls and ceiling.

Smithback looked at his watch. Miracle of miracles, he was ten minutes early. Maybe Nora would be early, too, and they could have a few extra minutes to talk. He felt like he hadn't seen his new wife in ages. She had promised to meet him here for a burger and beer before she returned to the museum to work late on the big upcoming show. And he himself had a story of sorts to write up and file before the 2 A.M. deadline.

He shook his head. What a life: two months married and he hadn't been laid in a week. But it wasn't so much making love he missed as Nora's companionship. Talk. Friendship. The truth was, Nora was Smithback's best friend, and right now he needed his best friend. The Duchamp murder story was going badly: he'd gotten nothing more than the same crap as the other papers. The cops were keeping a tight lid on information, and his usual sources could offer nothing. Here he was, Smithback of the *Times,* and his latest stories were nothing more than the reheated leftovers of a few briefings. Meanwhile, he could almost smell Bryce Harriman's ambition to muscle in on the story, take it away from him, leave him with the damn Dangler assignment he'd managed to slough off so adroitly when the Duchamp case first broke.

"Whence the dark look?"

Smithback looked up, and there was Nora. Nora, her bronze-colored hair spilling over her shoulders, her freckled nose wrinkled by a smile, her green eyes sparkling with life.

"This seat taken?" she asked.

"Are you kidding? Jesus, woman, you're a sight for sore eyes."

She slid her bag to the floor and sat down. The obligatory droopy-eared, hangdog-faced waiter appeared, like a pallbearer at a funeral, and stood silently awaiting their order.

"Bangers and mash, fries, glass of milk," said Nora.

"Nothing stronger?" Smithback asked.

"I'm going back to work."

"So am I, but that never stopped me. I'll take a shot of that fifty-year-old Glen Grant, backed up by a steak and kidney pie."

The waiter gave a mournful dip of his head and was gone.

Smithback took her hand. "Nora, I miss you."

"Likewise. What a crazy life we lead."

"What are we *doing* here in New York City? We

should go back to Angkor Wat and live in some Buddhist temple in the jungle for the rest of our lives."

"And take a vow of celibacy?"

Smithback waved his hand. "Celibacy? We'll be like Tristan and Isolde in our own jeweled cave, making love all day long."

Nora blushed. "It was quite a shock, coming back to reality after that honeymoon."

"Yeah. Especially to find that circus ape Harriman, grinning and bobbing in my doorway."

"Bill, you're too obsessed with Harriman. The world's full of people like that. Ignore him and move on. You should see the people I have to work with at the museum. Some of them should be numbered and put in a glass case."

Their food arrived within minutes, along with Smithback's drink. He picked it up, clinked Nora's glass of milk. "Slainte."

"Chin-chin."

Smithback took a sip. Thirty-six dollars a shot and worth every penny. He watched Nora tuck into her meal. Now, there was a woman with healthy appetites—no fussy little salads for her. He recalled a certain moment that illustrated his point, back in the ruins of Banteay Chhmar, and felt an amorous stirring in his loins.

"So how are things at the museum?" he asked. "You whipping them into shape over that new show?"

"I'm only the junior curator, which means I'm mostly a whippee."

"Ouch."

"Here we are, six days from opening, and a quarter of the artifacts haven't even been mounted yet. It's a zoo. I've got only one more day to write label copy for thirty objects, and then I have to curate and organize an entire exhibit on Anasazi burial practices. And just today they said they want me to give a lecture on southwestern prehistory for the lecture series. Can you believe it? Thirteen thousand years of southwestern prehistory in ninety minutes, complete with slides." She took another bite.

"They're asking too much of you, Nora."

"Everybody's in the same boat. Sacred Images is the biggest thing to hit the museum in years. And on top of that, the geniuses that run the place have decided to upgrade the museum's security system. You remember what happened with the security system the last time they had a blockbuster exhibition? You know, Superstition?"

"Oh, God. Don't remind me."

"They don't want even the possibility of a repetition. Except that every time they upgrade the security for a new hall, they have to shut and lock the damn place down. It's impossible to get around—you never know what's going to be closed off. The bright side is that in six days it'll be over."

"Yeah, and then we'll be ready for another vacation."

"Or a stretch in a padded cell."

"We'll always have Angkor," Smithback intoned dramatically.

Nora laughed, squeezed his hand. "And how's the Duchamp story going?"

"Terrible. The homicide captain in charge is a woman named Hayward, a real ballbuster. Runs a tight ship. No leaks anywhere. I can't get a scoop to save my life."

"I'm sorry, Bill."

"Nora Kelly?"

A voice broke in, vaguely familiar. Smithback looked up to see a woman approaching their table—small, intense, brown hair, glasses. He froze in astonishment, and so did she. They stared at each other in silence.

Suddenly, she smiled. "Bill?"

Smithback grinned. "Margo Green! I thought you were living up in Boston, working for that company, what's its name?"

"GeneDyne. I was, but corporate life wasn't for me. Great money, but no fulfillment. So now I'm back at the museum."

"I had no idea."

"Just started six weeks ago. And you?"

"Wrote a few more books, as you probably know. I'm now at the *Times*. Got back from my honeymoon just a few weeks ago."

"Congratulations. Guess that means you won't be calling me Lotus Blossom anymore. I assume this is the lucky woman?"

"She sure is. Nora, meet an old friend of mine, Margo Green. Nora works at the museum, too."

"I know." Margo turned. "In fact, Bill, no offense, but I was looking for her, not you." She stretched out her hand. "Perhaps you don't remember, Dr. Kelly, but I'm the new editor of *Museology*. We met at the last departmental meeting."

Nora returned the handshake. "Of course. I read all about you in Bill's book *Relic*. How are things?"

"May I sit down?"

"To tell you the truth, we . . ." Nora's voice trailed off as Margo took a seat.

"I'll only be here for a moment."

Smithback stared. *Margo Green.* It seemed like another lifetime, it was so long ago. She hadn't changed much, except that maybe she seemed more relaxed, more confident. Still trim and athletic. She was wearing an expensive tailored suit, a far cry from the baggy L. L. Bean shirts and Levi's of her graduate student days. He glanced down at his own Hugo Boss suit. They had all grown up a little.

"I can't believe it," he said. "Two heroines from my books, together for the first time."

Margo cocked her head questioningly. "Oh, really? How's that?"

"Nora was the heroine of my book *Thunderhead.*"

"Oh. Sorry. Haven't read it."

Smithback kept smiling gamely. "What's it like to be back at the museum?"

"It's changed a lot since we were first there."

Smithback felt Nora's gaze upon him. He wondered if she assumed Margo was an old girlfriend and that perhaps there were certain salty things he'd left out of his memoirs.

"Seems like ages ago," Margo went on.

"It was ages ago."

"I often wonder what happened to Lavinia Rickman and Dr. Cuthbert."

"No doubt there's a special circle of hell reserved for those two."

Margo chuckled. "What about that cop D'Agosta? And Agent Pendergast?"

"Don't know about D'Agosta," Smithback said. "But the word around the *Times* foreign desk is that Pendergast went missing under mysterious circumstances a few months ago. Flew to Italy on assignment and never came back."

A shocked look came over Margo's face. "Really? How strange."

A brief silence settled over the table.

"Anyway," Margo resumed, turning once again to Nora, "I wanted to ask your help."

"Sure," Nora said. "What is it?"

"I'm about to publish an editorial on the importance of repatriating Great Kiva masks to the Tano tribe. You know about their request?"

"I do. I've also read the editorial. It's circulating the department in draft."

"Naturally, I've run into opposition from the museum administration, Collopy in particular. I've started contacting all the members of the Anthropology Department to see if I can build a united front. The independence of *Museology* must be maintained, and those masks must be returned. We've got to together on this as a department."

"What is it you want me to do?" asked Nora.

"I'm not circulating a petition or anything quite so overt. I'm just asking for informal support from members of the department if it comes to a showdown. A verbal assurance. That's all."

Smithback grinned. "Sure, no problem, you can always count on Nora—"

"Just a minute," Nora said.

Smithback fell silent, surprised at the sharp tone.

"Margo was speaking to me," Nora said dryly.

"Right." Smithback hastily smoothed down an unrepentant cowlick and retreated to his drink.

Nora turned to Margo with a rather chilly smile. "I'm sorry, I won't be able to help."

Smithback stared from Nora to Margo in surprise.

"May I ask why not?" Margo asked calmly.

"Because I don't agree with you."

"But it's obvious that those Great Kiva masks belong to the Tanos—"

Nora held up a hand. "Margo, I am thoroughly familiar with them and with your arguments. In one sense, you're right. They belonged to the Tano and they shouldn't have been collected. But now they belong to all of humanity—they've become a part of the human record. What's more, taking those masks out of the Sacred Images exhibition would be devastating this late in the game—and I'm one of the curators of the show. Finally, I'm a southwestern archaeologist by training. If we started giving back every sacred item in the museum, there'd be nothing left. *Everything* is sacred to Native Americans—that's one of the beautiful things about Native American culture." She paused. "Look, what's done is done, the world is the way it is, and not all wrongs can be righted. I'm sorry I can't give you a better answer, but there it is. I have to be honest."

"But the issue of editorial freedom . . ."

"I'm with you one hundred percent on that one. Publish your editorial. But don't ask me to back your arguments. And don't ask the department to endorse your private opinions."

With that, Margo stared first at Nora, then at Smithback.

Smithback grinned nervously, took another sip of his drink.

Margo rose. "Thank you for your directness."

"You're welcome."

She turned to Smithback. "It's great to see you again, Bill."

"Sure thing," he mumbled.

He watched Margo walk away. Then he realized Nora's gaze was on him.

" 'Lotus Blossom'?" she said tartly.

"It was just a joke."

"Former girlfriend of yours?"

"No, never," he replied hastily.

"You're sure about that?"

"Not even a kiss."

"I'm glad to hear it. I can't stand that woman." She turned to stare at Margo's departing figure. Then she looked back. "And to think she hasn't read *Thunderhead*. I mean, that's much better than some of the earlier stuff you wrote. I'm sorry, Bill, but that book *Relic*—well, let's just say you've matured a lot as a writer."

"Hey, what was wrong with *Relic*?"

She picked up her fork and finished her meal in silence.

Fourteen

WHEN D'AGOSTA arrived at the Omeleteria, Hayward had already taken their usual booth by the window. He hadn't seen her for twenty-four hours—she'd pulled an all-nighter at the office. He paused in the doorway of the restaurant, looking at her. The morning sunlight had turned her glossy black hair almost blue, given her pale skin the sheen of fine marble. She was industriously making notes on a Pocket PC, chewing her lower lip, brow knitted in concentration. Just seeing her sent a throb of affection through him so sharp it was almost painful.

He didn't know if he was going to be able to do this.

She looked up suddenly, as if aware of his gaze. The look of concentration vanished and a smile broke over her beautiful features.

"Vinnie," she said as he approached. "Sorry I missed your lasagna *napoletana*."

He kissed her, then took a seat opposite. "It's okay. Lasagna's lasagna. I'm worried you're working too hard."

"Nature of the business."

Just then a skinny waitress came up, placed an egg

white omelette before Hayward, started to refill her coffee cup.

"Just leave the pot, please," Hayward said.

The waitress nodded, turned to D'Agosta. "Need a menu, hon?"

"No. Give me two fried eggs, over well, with rye toast."

"I went ahead and ordered," Hayward said, taking a gulp of her coffee. "Hope you don't mind. I've got to get back to the office and—"

"You're going back?"

Hayward frowned, gave her head a single vigorous shake. "I'll rest tonight."

"Pressure from on high?"

"There's always pressure from on high. No, it's the case itself. I just can't get a handle on it."

D'Agosta watched as she tucked into her omelet, feeling the dismay grow inside him. *Unless Diogenes can be stopped, everyone close to me may die,* Pendergast had told him the night before. *Find out everything you can from Laura Hayward.* He glanced around the coffee shop, looking at the faces, looking for one bluish-white, one hazel eye. But, of course, Diogenes would be wearing contacts, disguising his most striking characteristic.

"Why don't you tell me about the case?" he asked as easily as he could.

She took another bite, dabbed at her mouth. "The autopsy results came back. No surprise there. Duchamp died of massive internal injuries resulting from his fall. Several pharyngeal bones were fractured, but the hanging itself didn't cause death: the spinal cord had not been severed and asphyxiation hadn't yet occurred. And here's the first of many weird things. The rope had been cut almost through beforehand with a very sharp blade. The killer *wanted* it to part during the hanging."

D'Agosta felt himself go cold. *My Great-Great-Uncle Maurice died in precisely the same manner . . .*

"Duchamp was initially subdued in his apartment, then tied up. There was a contusion on the left temple, but the head itself was so badly crushed in the fall we can't be certain that's what caused all the blood in the apartment. But get this: the contusion had been doctored and *bandaged,* apparently by the killer."

"I see." The case made sense to D'Agosta . . . too much sense. And he could say nothing to Hayward.

"Then the perp pushed a long desk up against the window, convinced Duchamp to climb on it, and take a running jump out the window."

"Unassisted?"

Hayward nodded. "With his hands bound behind him and a noose around his neck."

"Anyone see the perp?" D'Agosta felt a constriction in his chest; he knew who the perp was, yet he couldn't tell her directly. It was an unexpectedly difficult feeling.

"Nobody in the apartment building remembers seeing anybody unusual. There's only one possible sighting, by a basement security camera. Just a rear view of a man in a trench coat. Tall, thin. Light hair. We're having the image digitally enhanced, but the techs aren't hopeful we'll get enough to be useful. He knew the camera was there and took care passing through its field of view." She finished her coffee and poured herself another.

"We went through the victim's papers, his studio, looking for any motive," she went on. "None. Then we used his Rolodex to call up friends and acquaintances. Nobody we spoke with could believe it. A real Mister

Rogers, this guy Duchamp. Oh, and here's a bizarre coincidence. Duchamp knew Agent Pendergast."

D'Agosta froze. He didn't know what to say, how to act. Somehow, he just couldn't be phony with Laura Hayward. He felt a flush spread across his face.

"Seems they were friends. Pendergast's Dakota address was on the Rolodex. According to Duchamp's appointment book, the two had lunch three times last year, always at '21.' Too bad we can't get Pendergast's take on this from beyond the grave. Right about now I think I'd welcome even *his* help."

Suddenly, she stopped, catching sight of D'Agosta's expression. "Oh, Vinnie," she said, sliding a hand across the table and grasping his. "I'm sorry. That was a thoughtless thing to say."

This made D'Agosta feel ten times worse. "Maybe this is the crime Pendergast warned me about in his note."

Slowly, Hayward withdrew her hand. "I'm sorry?"

"Well . . ." D'Agosta stammered. "Diogenes hated his brother. Maybe he plans to revenge himself on Pendergast by killing off Pendergast's friends."

Hayward looked at him, her eyes narrowing.

"I heard there was another friend of Pendergast's killed recently. A professor in New Orleans."

"But, Vinnie, Pendergast is dead. Why kill his brother's friends now?"

"Who knows how crazy people think? All I'm saying is that, if it were my case, I'd consider it a suspicious coincidence."

"How'd you hear about this New Orleans murder?"

D'Agosta looked down, arranged his napkin on his lap. "I can't recall. I think maybe his—his secretary, Constance, mentioned it to me."

"Well, there are lots of strange aspects to the case, I'll give you that." Hayward sighed. "It's far-fetched, but I'll look into it."

The waitress reappeared with his breakfast order.

D'Agosta hardly dared meet Laura's eyes. Instead, he lifted his fork and knife and sliced into the glistening egg. A jet of yellow spurted across the plate.

D'Agosta jerked back. "Waitress!"

The woman, half a dozen booths away already, turned and walked slowly back.

D'Agosta handed her the plate. "These eggs are runny. I said over *well*. I didn't say over *easy*."

"All right, hon, hold your water." The woman took the plate and walked away.

"Ouch," Hayward said in a low voice. "Don't you think you were hard on the poor woman?"

"I *hate* runny eggs," D'Agosta said, staring into his coffee once again. "I can't stand looking at them."

There was a brief silence. "What's wrong, Vinnie?" she asked.

"This Diogenes business."

"Don't take this the wrong way, but it's time you dropped this wild-goose chase and got back on the job. It's not going to bring Pendergast back. Singleton's not going to let this go on forever. On top of that, you're not acting like yourself. Nothing like getting back to work as a way of curing the blues."

You're right, he thought. He wasn't acting like himself because he wasn't feeling like himself. It felt bad enough, not telling Hayward the truth. But it went even beyond that: here he was, pumping her for information while withholding the fact Pendergast was still alive.

He arranged his lips into what he hoped was a sheepish smile.

"I'm sorry, Laura. You're right: it's time I got back on the job. And here I am, acting cranky, when you're the one who's had no sleep. What else about the case kept you up all night?"

She glanced at him searchingly for a moment. Then she took another bite of her omelet, pushed it away. "I've never seen such a careful murder. It's not just the fact there are so few clues, but the ones we have are so damn puzzling. The only evidence left behind by the perp, other than the ropes, was some clothing fibers."

"Well, that gives you three clues to work, at least."

"That's right. The fibers, the rope, and the structure of the knots. And so far, we've come up blank on all three. *That's* what kept me away all night: that, and the usual paperwork. The fibers are of some kind of exotic wool that forensics hasn't seen before. It's in none of the local or federal databases. We've got a textile expert working on it. Same with the ropes. The material is nothing manufactured in America, Europe, Australia, the Middle East."

"And the knots?"

"They're even more bizarre. The ligature specialist— who we dragged out of bed at three, by the way—was fascinated. At first glance, they look random, massive, like some bondage fetishist gone crazy. But they're not that at all. Turns out they're expertly fashioned. Very intricate. The specialist was staggered: he said he'd never seen the knot before, that it seemed to be of a new type entirely. He went into a whole riff on mathematics and knot theory that I couldn't even begin to follow."

"I'd like to see a photograph of the knots, if I could."

She flashed him another questioning gaze.

"Hey, I was in the Boy Scouts," he said with a levity he didn't feel.

She nodded slowly. "I had this instructor at the Academy, Riderback. Remember him?"

"Nope."

"He was fascinated by knots. He used to say they were a three-dimensional manifestation of a fourth-dimensional problem. Whatever that means." She took another sip of coffee. "Sooner or later, those knots are going to help us crack this case."

The waitress came back, placing D'Agosta's eggs before him with a look of triumph. Now they were wizened-looking, almost desiccated, crisp around the edges.

Hayward glanced at the plate, a smile returning to her lips. "Enjoy," she said with a giggle.

Suddenly, his coat began to vibrate. For a moment, D'Agosta went rigid in surprise. Then, remembering the cell phone Pendergast had given him, he dug a hand into his pocket and pulled it out.

"New phone?" Hayward asked. "When'd you pick that up?"

D'Agosta hesitated. Then, rather abruptly, he decided that he just couldn't tell her one more lie.

"Sorry," he said, standing up. "Gotta go. I'll explain later."

Hayward half rose as well, a look of surprise on her face. "But, Vin—"

"Will you get breakfast?" he asked, putting his hands on her shoulders and kissing her. "I'll get the next."

"But—"

"See you tonight, sweetheart. Good luck with the case." And—holding her questioning stare with his own for a brief moment—he gave her shoulders a parting squeeze, turned, and hurriedly left the restaurant.

He glanced once more at the message displayed on the tiny cell screen:

SW Corner 77 and York. NOW.

Fifteen

THE BIG BLACK LIMO, tearing southward on York Avenue, appeared seconds after D'Agosta reached the corner. It slewed to a stop; the door flew open. Even before D'Agosta shut the door, the limo was accelerating from the curb, driver leaning on the horn, cars behind them screeching to a halt to let the big car pass.

D'Agosta turned in astonishment. A stranger sat in the seat beside him: tall, slender, well tanned, dressed in an impeccable gray suit, slim black attaché case across his knees.

"Don't be alarmed, Vincent," said the familiar voice of Pendergast. "An emergency has forced me to change my spots again. Today I am an investment banker."

"Emergency?"

Pendergast handed D'Agosta a sheet of paper, carefully sealed within layers of glassine. It read:

Nine of Swords: Torrance Hamilton
Ten of Swords: Charles Duchamp
King of Swords, Reversed: Michael Decker
The Five of Swords—?

"Diogenes is telegraphing his move in advance. Baiting me." Disguise or no disguise, Pendergast's face was as grim as D'Agosta had ever seen it.

"What are those—tarot cards?"

"Diogenes always had an interest in tarot. As you may have guessed, those cards involve death and betrayal."

"Who's Michael Decker?"

"He was my mentor when I first moved to the FBI. Before, I'd been in more, ah, *exotic* forms of government service, and he helped me make a rather difficult transition. Mike's highly placed in Quantico these days, and he's been invaluable in clearing the way for my somewhat unorthodox methods. It was thanks to Mike that I was able to get the FBI involved so quickly on the Jeremy Grove murder last fall, and he helped smooth some ruffled feathers after a small case I handled in the Midwest prior to that."

"So Diogenes is threatening another one of your friends."

"Yes. I can't raise Mike on his cell or at home. His secretary tells me he's on elevated assignment, which means they won't release any details about it—even if I were to reveal myself as a colleague. I must warn him in person, if I can find him."

"As an FBI agent, though, he must be pretty hard to get the jump on."

"He's one of the best field agents in the Bureau. I fear that would deter Diogenes not at all."

D'Agosta glanced back at the letter. "Your brother wrote this?"

"Yes. Curious: it doesn't look like his handwriting— more like a crude attempt to disguise his handwriting, rather. Far too crude, in fact, for him. And yet there's something strangely familiar about it . . ." Pendergast's voice trailed off.

"How'd you get it?"

"It arrived at my Dakota apartment early this morning. I employ a doorman there, Martyn, to take care of special things for me. He got it to Proctor, and Proctor got it to me through a prior arrangement."

"Proctor knows you're alive?"

"Yes. Constance Greene does, too, as of last night."

"What about *her*? Does she still think you're dead?"

D'Agosta didn't say the name—he didn't need to. Pendergast would know he was referring to Viola Maskelene.

"I haven't communicated with her. It would put her in grave danger. Ignorance, as painful as it is, will keep her safe."

There was a brief, awkward silence.

D'Agosta changed direction. "So your brother took this letter to the Dakota? Aren't you having the place watched?"

"Of course. Very carefully. It was delivered by a derelict. When we caught him and questioned him, he said he was paid to deliver it by a man on Broadway. His description was too vague to be of use."

The limo sheared toward the on-ramp for the FDR Drive, leaning into the turn, wheels smoking.

"You think your FBI friend will listen?"

"Mike Decker knows me."

"It seems to me that you rushing down to warn Decker is exactly what Diogenes expects."

"Correct. It is like a forced move in chess: I'm falling into a trap and there's not a thing I can do about it." Pendergast looked at D'Agosta, eyes bright even behind brown contact lenses. "We must find some way to reverse the pattern, get on the offensive. Have you learned anything more from Captain Hayward?"

"They recovered some fibers from the site. That and the ropes are the only hard evidence they've got so far. There are some other weird things about the murder, too. For example, it seems Diogenes stunned Duchamp with a blow to the head, then doctored and bandaged the injury before killing him."

Pendergast shook his head. "Vincent, I must know more. I *must*. Even the smallest, least significant detail could be critical. I have, shall we say, a connection in New Orleans who is getting me the police dossier on the Hamilton poisoning. But I have no such connection here, for the Duchamp case."

D'Agosta nodded. "Understood."

"There's another thing. Diogenes seems to be working forward, choosing his victims chronologically. That means you might soon be at risk. We worked together on my first really large-scale case on the FBI—the museum murders."

D'Agosta swallowed. "Don't worry about me."

"It seems Diogenes has begun to take pleasure in giving me advance warning. We might assume you and other potential targets are temporarily safe—at least until I receive the next message. Even so, Vincent, you must take every precaution possible. The safest thing is to go back to work immediately. Surround yourself with police, remain in the precinct house when not on call. Most important, alter all your habits—every single one. Temporarily move your residence. Take cabs instead of walking or riding the subway. Go to bed and rise at different hours. Change everything in your life that might cause you danger—or danger to those you care about. An attempt on your life could easily result in collateral damage to others, in particular Captain Hayward. Vincent, you're a good officer—I don't need to tell you what to do."

The limo came screeching to a stop. The blacktopped expanse of the East 34th Street Heliport lay directly ahead, its stubby, three-hundred-foot runway gleaming dully in the morning sun. A red Bell 206 Jet Ranger was waiting on the tarmac, rotors turning. Pendergast abruptly slipped into investment banker mode, his face relaxing, the glittering hatred and determination vanishing from his eyes, leaving behind a pleasant blandness.

"One other thing," D'Agosta said.

Pendergast turned back.

D'Agosta reached into his jacket pocket, retrieved something, held it out in a closed fist. Pendergast reached out and D'Agosta dropped into his palm a platinum medallion, slightly melted along one edge, on a chain. On one side of the medallion was the image of a lidless eye hovering over a phoenix, rising from the ashes of a fire. A crest of some sort had been stamped into the other side.

Pendergast stared at it, a strange expression passing over his face.

"Count Fosco was wearing this when I went back to his castle with the Italian police. He showed it to me, privately, as proof you were dead. You'll see the bastard engraved his own crest on the back—his final trick against me. I thought you'd want it."

Pendergast turned it over, peered at it, turned it over again.

"I took it from him the night I . . . paid him a final visit. Maybe it'll bring you good luck."

"Normally I despise luck, but at the moment I find myself in singular need of it. Thank you, Vincent." Pendergast's voice was almost too low to be heard above the revving of the rotors. He placed the medallion around his neck, tucked it into his shirt, and grasped D'Agosta's hand.

And then, without another word, he strode across the tarmac toward the waiting chopper.

Sixteen

THE CHOPPER LANDED at a corporate heliport in Chevy Chase, Maryland, where a car without a driver awaited. By nine o'clock, Pendergast was crossing into D.C. It was a cold, sunny January day, with a weak yellow sun filtering through the bare branches of the trees, leaving frost in the shadows.

In a few minutes, he was driving along Oregon Avenue, lined with stately mansions—one of Washington's most exclusive suburbs. He slowed as he passed Mike Decker's house. The tidy, brick-fronted Georgian seemed as somnolent as the rest of the neighborhood. No car was parked outside, but that in itself meant nothing: Decker ranked a car and driver when he wanted one.

Pendergast drove a block farther, then pulled over to the curb. Taking out a cell phone, he once again tried Decker's home and mobile. No answer.

Behind the row of mansions lay the wooded fastness of Rock Creek Park. Pendergast got out of the car with his attaché case and walked thoughtfully into the park. Diogenes, he felt sure, would be watching the scene and would recognize him despite his disguise—just as he felt sure he would recognize his brother, no matter what.

But he saw no one and heard nothing but the faint rush of water from Rock Creek.

He walked briskly along the fringe of the park, then darted across a driveway, crossed a garden, and came up through a hedge into Decker's backyard. The yard was deep and well tended, falling away at the rear into the dense woods of the park. There, hidden from the neighbors by thick shrubbery, he glanced up at the windows. They were closed, white curtains pulled shut. Glancing at the adjoining houses, he proceeded, with practiced casualness, across the yard and to the back door, pulling on a pair of gloves as he did so and leaving his attaché on the stoop.

Pendergast paused again, his alert eyes taking in every detail. Then, without knocking, he peered through the small window.

Decker's kitchen was modern and almost spartan in its bachelor emptiness. A folded newspaper lay on a counter beside the phone; a suit jacket had been draped over the back of a chair. On one side of the room, a door—shut—opened no doubt onto the basement stairway; on the other side, a dark corridor led into the front rooms of the house.

A shape lay on the floor of the corridor, vague in the dim light. It moved feebly, once, twice.

In an instant, Pendergast moved to pick the lock, only to find that the knob—broken—turned easily in his hand. There was a telltale cut wire: a security system had been bypassed. Nearby, the phone wire had also been snipped. He swept inside, darting toward the shape in the hall and kneeling on the broad floorboards.

A male Weimaraner lay there, eyes glassy, rear legs still twitching in slowing spasms. Pendergast ran his gloved fingers quickly over the dog's frame. Its neck had been broken in two places.

Now, rising, Pendergast reached into his pocket. When his hand appeared again, it was holding a gleaming Wilson Combat TSGC .45. Moving quickly and with utter silence, Pendergast searched the first floor of the house: wheeling around corners, gun extended, eyes darting over every surface and place of concealment. Living room, dining room, front hall, bath: all empty and still.

Next, Pendergast flew up the stairs, pausing to glance around at the upper landing. Four rooms gave onto a central hallway. Sunlight lanced in through the open doors, illuminating a few dust motes dancing lazily in the sluggish air.

Gun at the ready, he spun around the first doorway, which led into a back bedroom. Inside, the guest beds were made with almost military perfection, bedspreads tight across the mattresses and over the pillows. Beyond, the gaunt trees of Rock Creek Park were visible through the window. Everything was wrapped in a deep silence.

A faint sound came from nearby.

Pendergast froze, his hyperacute senses strained to the maximum. There had been one sound, only one: the slow outrush of air, like a languorous sigh.

He exited the back bedroom, darted across the hall, paused outside the entrance to the room opposite. Tall bookshelves and the edge of a table could be seen through the open door: a study. Here, closer, another sound could just be discerned—a fast, running patter as of a faucet improperly closed.

Tensing, gun forward, Pendergast wheeled around the door frame.

Mike Decker sat in a leather chair, facing his desk.

He was ex-military and had always endowed his movements with economy and precision, yet it was not preciseness that kept him so erect in the chair. A heavy steel bayonet had been driven into his mouth, angling down through his neck and pinning him to the headrest. The point of the old bayonet pierced all the way through the chair back, sticking out the back side, its rough edge heavy with blood. Drops fell from its tip onto the sodden carpet.

. Another low sigh sounded in Decker's ruined throat, like the collapsing of a bellows. It died into a faint, bloody gargle. The man stared sightlessly at Pendergast, white shirt stained a uniform red. Streams of blood still flowed across the table, running in slow meanders and draining, with a pattering sound, to the floor.

For a moment, Pendergast remained still, as if thunderstruck. Then he removed one glove and—leaning forward, careful not to step in the blood that had ponded beneath the chair—placed the back of his hand against Decker's forehead. The man's skin felt supple, elastic, and its surface temperature was no cooler than Pendergast's own.

Abruptly, Pendergast drew back. The house was silent—except for the steady dripping.

The sighs, Pendergast knew, were postmortem: air bleeding from the lungs as the body relaxed against the bayonet. Even so, Mike Decker had been dead less than five minutes. Probably less than three.

Yet again, he hesitated. The precise time of death was irrelevant. What was far more important was Pendergast's realization that Diogenes had waited until Pendergast entered the house *before* killing Decker.

And that meant his brother might still be here, *in this house.*

In the distance, at the threshold of hearing, came the wail of police sirens.

Pendergast swept the room, eyes glittering, searching for the slightest clue that might help him track down his brother. His eye finally rested on the bayonet—and, abruptly, he recognized it.

A moment later, his gaze fell to Decker's hands. One lay slack; the other was clenched in a ball.

Ignoring the approaching sirens, Pendergast withdrew a gold pen from his pocket and carefully teased the clenched hand open. Inside lay three strands of blond hair.

Retrieving a jeweler's loupe from his pocket, he bent forward and examined the hairs. Returning his hand back into his pocket, he exchanged the loupe for a pair of tweezers. Very carefully, he plucked every strand from the motionless hand.

The sirens were louder now.

By now, Diogenes was certainly gone. He had choreographed the scene, managed its many variables, with perfection. He had entered the house, no doubt immobilized Decker with some kind of drug, then waited for Pendergast to arrive before killing him. Chances were that Diogenes had deliberately tripped the burglar alarm *while leaving the house.*

A senior FBI agent lay dead, and the house would be picked apart in the search for clues. Diogenes would not risk sticking around—and neither could he.

He heard a screeching of tires, a confusion of sirens, as a phalanx of police cars barreled down Oregon Avenue, now just seconds from the house. Pendergast glanced back at his friend one last time, briskly wiped a trace of excess moisture from one eye, then dashed down the stairs.

The front door was now wide open, a security panel beside it blinking red. He leaped over the inert form of the Weimaraner, exited through the back door, snagged his attaché case, sprinted across the yard, and—tossing the strands of hair into a pile of dead leaves—vanished like a ghost into the shadowy depths of Rock Creek Park.

Seventeen

MARGO GREEN was the first to arrive at the museum's grand old Murchison Conference Room. As she settled into one of the old leather chairs flanking the massive nineteenth-century oak table, she took in the marvelous—but somewhat disconcerting—details: the trophy heads of now endangered species gracing the walls; the brace of elephant tusks flanking the door; the African masks, leopard, zebra, and lion skins. Murchison had done his fieldwork in Africa over a century before, and had enjoyed a career as a great white hunter alongside his more serious profession of anthropology. There was even a pair of elephant's-foot wastebaskets at opposite ends of the room. But this was a museum, and a museum must not throw anything away, no matter how politically incorrect it may have become.

Margo used the few moments of quiet before the rest of the department arrived to look through her notes and organize her thoughts. She felt a rising nervousness she seemed unable to quell. Was she doing the right thing? She'd been here all of six weeks, and now, with her very first issue of *Museology,* she was injecting herself into the midst of controversy. Why was it so important to her?

But she already knew the answer. Personally, she had to make a stand on something she believed in. And professionally, as editor of *Museology,* it was the right thing to do. People would expect the journal to comment on the issue. Silence, or a weak, waffling editorial, would be noted by all. It would set the tone of her editorship. No— it was important to show that *Museology* would continue to be relevant and topical while not fearing the controversial. This was her opportunity to show the profession that she meant business.

She went back to her notes. Because the item in question was owned by the Anthropology Department, it was the anthro curators who were most concerned. She would not get a second chance to make her case to the whole department, and she wanted to get it right.

Other curators were now drifting in, nodding to her, chatting among themselves, rattling the almost empty coffee urn, which was boiling into tar the remains of the coffee prepared that morning. Someone poured a cup, then replaced it with a clatter and a suppressed expression of disgust. Nora Kelly arrived, greeted Margo cordially, and took her seat on the opposite side of the table. Margo looked around the room.

All ten curators were now here.

The last to arrive was Hugo Menzies, chairman of the Anthropology Department since the untimely death of Dr. Frock six years before. Menzies gave Margo a special smile and nod, then took his seat at the head of the vast table. Because the bulk of *Museology* articles were on anthropological subjects, he had been appointed as her supervisor. And—she suspected—he had also been instrumental in her hiring. Unlike everybody else on staff—who favored lawyerly briefcases—Menzies carried around a classy canvas shoulder bag by John Chapman & Company, a top manufacturer of English fishing and shooting gear. At the moment, he was taking some papers out of the bag, squaring and organizing them. Next, he put on his reading glasses, adjusted his tie, and smoothed down his untidy thatch of white hair. Finally, he checked his watch, raised his lively blue eyes to the waiting group, cleared his throat.

"Glad to see you all here," he said, his voice reedy and old-fashioned. "Shall we commence?"

There was a general shuffling of papers.

"Rather than go through the usual business," he said, glancing at Margo, "let's go straight to a subject I know is on all your minds: the problem of the Great Kiva masks."

More shuffling of papers, glances at Margo. She straightened her back, kept her face neutral and composed. Deep in her heart, she believed she was right, and that helped give her the strength and conviction she needed.

"Margo Green, the new editor of *Museology*, has asked to speak to you all. As you know, the Tano Indians are requesting the return of the Great Kiva masks, a centerpiece of our upcoming show. As chairman of the department, it's my job to make a recommendation to the director on this matter: whether we give up the masks, keep them, or seek some compromise. We are not a democracy, but I can promise you your opinions will carry great weight with me. I might add that the director himself will also be seeking the advice of the board and the museum's attorneys before he makes his final decision, so mine is not the last word." He smiled, turned to Margo. "And now, Margo, would you like to take the floor?"

Margo rose, looked around the room.

"Most of you probably know I'm planning to run an editorial in the next issue of *Museology,* calling for the return of the Great Kiva masks to the Tanos. A draft of the editorial has circulated, and it's caused some consternation in the administration." She swallowed, trying to conceal the nervous flutter she could hear in her voice.

She went on to speak about the history of the masks and how they were collected, gaining confidence and poise.

"For those of you who aren't familiar with the Tano Indians," she said, "they live on a remote reservation on the New Mexico–Arizona border. Because of their isolation, they still retain their original language, religion, and customs, while living with one foot in the modern world. Less than twenty percent of the tribe identify themselves as Christian. Anthropologists believe they settled in their present area along the Tano River almost a thousand years ago. They speak a unique language, apparently unrelated to any other. I'm telling you these things because it's important to emphasize that these are not Native Americans in genotype alone, trying belatedly to recapture long-lost traditions. The Tano are one of the few tribes who have never lost their traditions."

She paused. People were listening attentively, and while she knew not all agreed with her, at least they were giving her a respectful hearing.

"The tribe is divided into moieties—that is, two religious groups. The Great Kiva Society masks are used *only* when these moieties come together for religious ceremonies in the Great Kiva—the kiva being the circular underground chamber that serves as their place of worship. They hold these great ceremonies only once every four years. They believe these ceremonies maintain balance and harmony in the tribe, in all people of the earth, and in the natural world. They believe—and I'm not exaggerating here—that the terrible wars and natural disasters of the last hundred years are due to the fact that they don't have the Great Kiva masks and have been unable to perform properly the ceremony restoring balance and beauty to the world."

She went on for another five minutes and then wrapped it up, glad that she'd been able to keep it relatively short.

Menzies thanked her, glanced around the table. "And now, let the debate begin."

There was a shuffling. Then a thin voice piped up, carrying a slightly aggrieved tone. It was Dr. Prine. The slope-shouldered curator rose to his feet. "Being a specialist in Etruscan archaeology, I don't know much about the Tano Indians, but I think the whole business has a bad odor to it. Why are the Tano suddenly so interested in these masks? How do we know the Tano won't just turn around and sell them? They must be worth millions. I'm very suspicious about their motives."

Margo bit her lip. She remembered Prine from her graduate student days: a dim bulb that had only grown dimmer with the passage of years. His life's research, she recalled, was a study of Etruscan liver divination.

"For these reasons and many others," Prine went on, "I'm strongly in favor of keeping the masks. In fact, I can't believe we're seriously considering returning them.

We bought them, we own them, and we should keep them." He sat down abruptly.

A short chubby man with a furze of red hair encircling a large bald spot rose next. Margo recognized him as George Ashton, chief curator of the Sacred Images exhibition. Ashton was a capable anthropologist, if temperamental and easily riled. And he looked riled now.

"I agree with Dr. Prine, and I take strong objection to this editorial." He turned to Margo, his eyes almost popping from his round red face, chin doubling and tripling in his excitement. "I consider it highly inappropriate that Dr. Green raised this question at this time. We're less than a week from the opening of the biggest show at the museum in years, costing almost five million dollars. The Great Kiva masks are the centerpiece of the show. If we pull those masks, there's no way the show will open on time. Really, Dr. Green, I find your timing on this matter to be *truly* unfortunate." He paused long enough to give Margo a fiery stare, then turned to Menzies. "Hugo, I propose we table this question until after the show has closed. Then we can debate it at leisure. Of course, giving back the masks is unthinkable, but for heaven's sake let's make that decision after the show."

Margo waited. She would respond at the end—if Menzies gave her the opportunity.

Menzies smiled placidly at the indignant curator. "For the record, George, I would note that the timing has nothing to do with Dr. Green—it's in response to the receipt of a letter from the Tano Indians, which was triggered by your own pre-publicity campaign for the show."

"Yes, but does she have to publish this editorial?" Ashton slashed the air with a piece of paper. "She could at least wait until after the show *closes*. This is going to create a public relations nightmare!"

"We are not in the business of public relations," said Menzies mildly.

Margo cast him a grateful look. She had expected his support, but this was more than just support.

"Public relations are a reality! We can't just sit in our ivory tower and ignore public opinion, can we? I'm trying to open a show under the most trying conditions, and I do not appreciate being undercut like this—not by Dr. Green and certainly not by you, Hugo!"

He sat down, breathing hard.

Menzies said quietly, "Thank you for your opinion, George."

Ashton nodded curtly.

Patricia Wong, a research associate in the Textile Department, stood up. "The issue, it seems to me, is simple. The museum acquired the masks unethically, perhaps even illegally. Margo demonstrates that clearly in her editorial. The Tano asked for them back. If we as a museum have any pretense to ethics, we should return them right away. I respectfully disagree with Dr. Ashton. To keep the masks for the show and display them to all the world and then return them admitting we were wrong to have them—that would look hypocritical, or at best opportunistic."

"Hear, hear," said another curator.

"Thank you, Dr. Wong," said Menzies as the woman sat back down.

And now Nora Kelly was standing up, sweeping cinnamon hair from her face, slender and tall. She looked around, poised and confident. Margo felt a swelling of irritation.

"There are two questions before us," she began, her voice low and reasonable. "The first is whether Margo has the right to publish the editorial. I think we all agree that the editorial independence of *Museology* must be preserved, even if some of us don't like the opinions expressed."

There was a general murmuring of agreement, except from Ashton, who crossed his arms and snorted audibly.

"And I am one of those who does not agree with this editorial."

Here it comes, thought Margo.

"It's more than a question of mere ownership. I mean, who owns Michelangelo's *David*? If the Italians wanted to break it up to make marble bathroom tiles, would that be acceptable? If the Egyptians decided to level the Great Pyramid for a parking lot, would that be okay? Do they own it? If the Greeks wanted to sell the Parthenon to a Las Vegas casino, would that be their right?"

She paused.

"The answer to these questions must be no. These things are owned by all of humanity. They are the highest expressions of the human spirit, and their value transcends all questions of ownership. So it is with the Great Kiva masks. Yes, the museum acquired them unethically. But they are so extraordinary, so important, and so magnificent that they cannot be returned to the Tano to disappear forever into a dark kiva. So I say: publish the editorial. Let's have the debate. But for God's sake, don't give back the masks." She paused again, thanked them for listening, and sat down.

Margo felt a redness creeping into her face. As much as she hated to admit it, Nora Kelly was formidable.

Menzies looked around, but it appeared that no one

had any more comments. He turned to Margo. "Anything further to add? Now is the time to speak."

She sprang to her feet. "Yes. I'd like to rebut Dr. Kelly."

"Please."

"Dr. Kelly has conveniently overlooked one critical point: the masks are religious objects, unlike everything else she cited."

Nora was immediately on her feet. "The Parthenon isn't a temple? The *David* isn't a figure from the Bible? The Great Pyramid isn't a sacred tomb?"

"For heaven's sakes, they're not religious objects now. No one goes to the Parthenon to sacrifice rams anymore!"

"Exactly my point. Those objects have *transcended* their original limited religious function. Now they belong to all of us, regardless of religion. Just so with the Great Kiva masks. The Tano may have created them for religious purposes, but now they belong to the world."

Margo felt the flush spread through her body. "Dr. Kelly, may I suggest that your logic is better suited to an undergraduate classroom in philosophy than a meeting of anthropologists in the greatest natural history museum in the world?"

A silence followed. Menzies slowly turned toward Margo, fixed her with his blue eyes, over which his eyebrows were drawn down in displeasure. "Dr. Green, passion in science is a marvelous quality. But we must insist upon *civility* as well."

Margo swallowed. "Yes, Dr. Menzies." Her face flamed. How had she allowed herself to lose her temper? She didn't even dare glance over at Nora Kelly. Here she was, not only creating controversy but making enemies in her own department.

There was a general nervous clearing of throats, a few whispers.

"Very well," Menzies said, his voice back to its soothing note. "I've gotten the drift of opinion from both sides, and it appears we are more or less evenly divided. At least among those with opinions. I have made my decision."

He paused, casting his eye around the group.

"I will be bringing two recommendations to the director. The first is that the editorial be published. Margo is to be commended for initiating the debate with a well-reasoned editorial, which upholds the best traditions of *Museology* journal."

He took a breath. "My second recommendation is that the masks be returned to the Tano. Forthwith."

There was a stunned silence. Margo could hardly believe it—Menzies had come down one hundred percent on her side. She had won. She sneaked a glance at Nora, saw the woman's face now reddening as well.

"The ethics of our profession are clear," Menzies went on. "Those ethics state, and I quote: 'The first responsibility of an anthropologist is to the people under study.' It pains me more than I can say to see the museum lose those masks. But I have to agree with Drs. Green and Wong: if we are to set an ethical example, we must return them. Yes, the timing is certainly awkward, and it creates an enormous problem with the exhibition. I'm sorry, George. It can't be helped."

"But the loss to anthropology, to the world—" Nora began.

"I have said what I have to say," said Menzies, just a shade of tartness entering his voice. "This meeting is adjourned."

Eighteen

ILL SMITHBACK ROUNDED a corner, stopped, then breathed a sigh of relief. There, at the far end of the corridor, lay the door to Fenton Davies's office, open and unvexed by the lingering shade of Bryce Harriman. In fact, come to think of it, Smithback hadn't seen much of Harriman at all today. As he walked toward Davies's office, a fresh spring in his step, he rubbed his hands together, feeling a delicious shudder of schadenfreude at Harriman's bad luck. To think Harriman had been so eager to get his mitts on the Dangler story. Well, he was welcome to it. In retrospect, it wasn't really much of a *Times* story, anyway: far too undignified, tending toward the burlesque. Still, Harriman—what with his recent stint at the *Post*—would probably find it right up his alley.

Smithback chuckled as he walked.

He, on the other hand, had scored a major coup by landing the Duchamp murder. It was everything a big story should be: unusual, compelling, galvanic. It was the number one topic of conversation around watercoolers all over the city: the gentle, kindly artist who—for no apparent reason—had been bound, a hangman's noose fitted around his neck, then forced out of a twenty-fourth-story window and sent crashing through the roof of one of Manhattan's fancy French restaurants. All this in broad daylight in front of hundreds of witnesses.

Smithback slowed a little as he approached Davies's office. True, those many witnesses were proving hard as hell to track down. And so far, he'd had to content himself with the police department's official line and what discreet conjectures he'd drummed out of those usually in the know, who were proving disconcertingly out of the know in this case. But the story would break open. Nora was right when she said he always came through in the end. How well she understood him. It was just a matter of working every angle, maintaining traction.

No doubt that was why Davies had summoned him: the editor was eager for more. No sweat, he'd tell Davies he was chasing down some choice leads from his confidential sources. He'd get his ass back up to Broadway and 65th. Today there wouldn't be any cops around to cramp his style. Then he'd go haunt the precinct house, talk to an old pal there, see what crumbs he could pick up. No, he corrected himself: *crumbs* wasn't the right word. Other reporters picked up crumbs, while Smithback found the cake—and ate it, too.

Chuckling at his own metaphorical wit, he paused at the secretarial station outside Davies's office. Vacant. *Late lunch,* Smithback thought. Striding forward, feeling and looking every inch the ace reporter, he breezed up, raising his hand to knock on the open door.

Davies was sitting, Buddha-like, behind his cluttered desk. He was short and perfectly bald, with fastidious little hands that always seemed to be doing something: smoothing his tie or playing with a pencil or tracing the lines of his eyebrows. He favored blue shirts with white collars and tightly knotted paisley ties. With his high, soft voice and effeminate mannerisms, Davies might look to the uninitiated like a pushover. But Smithback had learned that this was not the case. You didn't get to be an editor at the *Times* without at least a few pints of barracuda blood coursing through your veins. But his delivery was so mild it sometimes took a moment to realize you'd just been disemboweled. He played his cards close to his vest, listened more than he spoke, and one rarely knew what he was really thinking. He didn't fraternize with his reporters, didn't hang out with the other editors, and seemed to prefer his own company. There was only one extra chair in his office, and it was never occupied.

Except that today it was occupied by Bryce Harriman.

Smithback froze in the doorway, hand still raised in midknock.

"Ah, Bill." Davies nodded. "Good timing. Please come in."

Smithback took a step forward, then another. He struggled to keep his eyes from meeting Harriman's.

"Planning to file a follow-up on the Duchamp murder?" Davies asked.

Smithback nodded. He felt dazed, as if somebody had just sucker-punched him in the gut. He hoped to hell it didn't show.

Davies ran his fingertips along the edge of his desk. "What's the angle going to be?"

Smithback was ready with his answer. This was Davies's favorite question, and it was a rhetorical one: his way of letting reporters know he didn't want any grass growing under their feet.

"I was planning a local-interest angle," he said. "You know, the effect of the killing on the building, the neighborhood, friends and family of the victim. And, of course, I was planning a follow-up story on the progress of the investigation. The detective in charge, Hayward, is the youngest homicide captain in the force and a woman to boot."

Davies nodded slowly, allowing a meditative *hmmmm* to escape his lips. As usual, the response communicated nothing about what he was really thinking.

Smithback, his nervousness heightened, elaborated. "You know the drill: unnatural death comes to the Upper West Side, matrons afraid to walk their poodles at night. I'll weave in a sketch of the victim, his work, that sort of thing. Might even do a sidebar on Captain Hayward."

Davies nodded again, picked up a pen, rolled it slowly between his palms.

"You know, something that could run on the first page of the Metro Section," Smithback said gamely, still pitching.

Davies put down the pen. "Bill, this is bigger than a Metro story, the biggest homicide in Manhattan since the Cutforth murder, which Bryce here covered when he was at the *Post.*"

Bryce here. Smithback kept his face pleasant.

"It's a story with a lot of angles. Not only do we have the sensational manner of death, but we also have—as you point out—the posh location. Then we have the man himself. An artist. And the female homicide detective." He paused. "Aren't you biting off a little more than you can chew—for a single story, that is?"

"I could make it two, even three. No problem."

"No doubt you could, but then the stretched-out time frame becomes problematic."

Smithback licked his lips. He was acutely aware of the fact that he was standing and Harriman was sitting.

Davies went on. "I personally had no idea that Duchamp was, in his own quiet way, a painter of some renown. He wasn't trendy or popular with the SoHo crowd. More of a Sutton Place style of artist, a Fairfield Porter. Bryce and I were just talking about it last night."

"Bryce," Smithback repeated. The name tasted like bile in his mouth. "Last night?"

Davies waved his hand with studied nonchalance. "Over drinks at the Metropolitan Club."

Smithback felt himself stiffen. So that was how the smarmy prick had managed it. He'd taken Davies for drinks at his father's fancy club. And Davies, it seemed, like any number of editors Smithback had known, was a sucker for that kind of thing. Editors were the worst social climbers, always hanging around the fringes of the rich and famous, hoping to catch a few scraps that dropped from the table. Smithback could just imagine Davies being ushered into the cloistered fastness of the Metropolitan Club; shown to a luxurious chair in some gilded salon; served drinks by deferential men in uniform; all the while exchanging hushed greetings with various Rockefellers, De Menils, Vanderbilts—that was just the thing to turn Davies's Maplewood, New Jersey, head all the way around.

Now, at last, he glanced again in Harriman's direction. The scumbag was sitting there, one leg tucked primly over the other, looking as nonchalant as if he did this every day. He didn't bother returning Smithback's look. He didn't need to.

"We haven't just lost a citizen here," Davies went on. "We've lost an artist. And New York is a poorer place for his loss. See, Bill, you just never know who lives in that apartment next door. It could be a hot dog vendor or a sanitation worker. Or it could be a fine artist whose paintings hang in half the apartments in River House."

Smithback nodded again, frozen smile on his lips.

Davies smoothed his tie. "It's a great angle. My friend Bryce here will handle it."

Oh, God. For a bleak and terrible moment, Smithback thought he was about to be reassigned to the Dangler.

"He'll cover the society aspect of the story. He knows several of Duchamp's important former clients, he's got the family connections. They'll talk to him, whereas . . ."

His voice trailed off, but Smithback got the message: *whereas they won't talk to you.*

"In short, Bryce can give us the silk-stocking view that *Times* readers appreciate. I'm glad to see you have a handle on the cop and street angle. You keep that up."

The cop and street angle. Smithback felt his jaw muscles flex involuntarily.

"It goes without saying that you'll both share information and leads. I'd suggest regular meetings, keeping in touch. This story is certainly big enough for the both of you, and it doesn't look like it's going away any time soon."

Silence descended briefly over the office.

"Was there anything else, Bill?" Davies asked mildly.

"What? Oh, no. Nothing."

"Then don't let me keep you."

"No, of course not," Smithback said. He was practically stammering now with shock, mortification, and fury. "Thanks." And as he turned to leave the office, Harriman finally glanced in his direction. There was a smug half-smile on his shit-eating face. It was a smile that seemed to say: *See you around, partner.*

And watch your back.

Nineteen

SO HOW WAS your first day back?" Hayward asked, gamely sawing away at a chicken breast.

"Fine," D'Agosta replied.

"Singleton didn't give you a hard time?"

"Nope."

"Well, you were just out two days, which probably helped matters. He's intense—sometimes too intense—but he's a hell of a cop. So are you. That's why I know you two will get along."

D'Agosta nodded, pushed a piece of plum tomato around his plate, then lifted it to his mouth. Chicken cacciatore was the one recipe he could pull off without thinking—barely.

"This is pretty good, Vinnie. Really. I'll have to let you into the kitchen more often." And she smiled across the table.

D'Agosta smiled back. He put down his fork for a moment and just watched her eat.

She'd made a special effort to get home on time. She praised his cooking even though he'd overcooked the chicken. She hadn't even asked about his hasty departure from breakfast that morning. She was clearly making a special effort to give him some space and let him work out whatever he was working out. He realized, with a sudden upwelling of affection, that he really loved this woman.

That made what he was about to do all the harder.

"Sorry I can't do your dinner justice," she said. "It deserves to be lingered over. But I've got to rush out again."

"New developments?"

"Not really. The ligature specialist wants to brief us on the knots. Probably just a way of covering his ass—he hasn't been much help."

"No?"

"He thinks the knots are Asiatic, maybe Chinese, but that isn't narrowing it down very much."

D'Agosta took a deep breath. "Have you looked into the possibility I mentioned at the diner? That Pendergast's brother might be behind these murders?"

Hayward paused, fork halfway to her mouth. "There's so little evidence to support that theory that it verges on crank. You know I'm a professional. You have to trust me to conduct this case in the best way possible. I'll look into it when I have time."

There was nothing D'Agosta could say to this. They ate for a moment in silence.

"Vinnie," she said, and something in her tone made him look up at her again. "Sorry. I didn't mean to snap at you."

"It's all right."

She was smiling again, and her dark eyes shone in the artificial light. "Because the fact is, I'm really happy you're back on the job."

D'Agosta swallowed. "Thanks."

"This crazy posthumous case of Pendergast's has just been a distraction for you at the worst possible time. He may have been a productive agent, but he wasn't—well, *normal.* I know you were a friend of his, but I think—" She paused. "I think he had an unhealthy influence on you. And then, this request from beyond the grave, all this stuff about his brother . . . I have to tell you, I resent that."

Despite everything, D'Agosta felt a stab of irritation. "I know you never liked the guy. But he got·results."

"I know, I know. I shouldn't criticize the dead. Sorry."

The irritation was swept away by a sudden flood of guilt. D'Agosta said nothing.

"Anyway, all that's past. The Dangler case is high-profile, a great starter case. You're going to shine, Vinnie, I know you are. It'll be just like old times."

D'Agosta cut into a chicken thigh, then dropped his knife on the plate with a clatter. This was agony. He couldn't put it off any longer.

"Laura," he began. "There's no easy way to say this."

"Say what?"

He took a deep breath. "I'm moving out."

She froze, as if uncomprehending. Then a look slowly crept over her face: a look of disbelief and pain, like a child who had just been unexpectedly struck by a beloved parent. Seeing that expression, D'Agosta felt just about as bad as he'd ever felt in his life.

"Vinnie?" she asked, dazed.

D'Agosta lowered his eyes. There was a long, excruciating silence.

"Why?"

He didn't know what to say. He knew only that the one thing he could not do was tell her the truth. *Laura, honey,*

*I may be in danger. You're not a target, but I definitely
am. And by staying here, I could put you in danger, as
well.*

"Is it something I've done? Something I haven't
done?"

"No," he said immediately. He had to make up something, and with Laura Hayward, that something had better be good.

"No," he said again, more slowly. "You've been great.
It has nothing to do with you. I really care about you. It
has to do with me. Our relationship . . . maybe we started
off just a little too fast."

Hayward did not reply.

D'Agosta felt like he was walking himself off a cliff.
There was nothing he wanted more right now than to stay
with this woman—this beautiful, caring, supportive
woman. He'd rather hurt himself than her. And yet he *was*
hurting her, hurting her deeply, with every word. It was
an awful thing to do, but he had no choice. *Vincent, you
must take every precaution possible.* D'Agosta knew that
the only way to save this relationship—and, perhaps,
Laura Hayward's life—was by interrupting it.

"I just need a little space, that's all," he went on. "To
think things through. Get some perspective on my life."
The platitudes sounded hollow, and rather than continue,
he stopped short.

He sat there, waiting for Hayward to blow up, curse
him out, order him to leave. Yet there was only another
long, awful silence. Finally, he looked up. Laura was sitting there, hands in her lap, dinner growing cold, her face
pale and her eyes cast downward. Her beautiful blue-
black hair had fallen forward, covering one eye. This

wasn't the reaction he'd expected. This surprise, this hurt, was even worse than anger.

At last, she sniffed, rubbed a finger beneath her nose, pushed away her plate. Then she rose.

"I've got to get back to work," she said, so quietly D'Agosta barely heard her. He sat motionless as she brushed her hair away from her face. Then she turned and walked quickly toward the door. It wasn't until her hand was on the doorknob that she stopped, realizing she'd forgotten her coat and her briefcase. She turned, walked slowly to the closet, shrugged into her coat, picked up the case. And then she left, closing the door quietly behind her.

She did not look back.

D'Agosta sat at the dinner table for a long time, listening to the tick of the clock, to the faint street noises filtering up from below. Finally, he stood, brought the dishes into the little kitchen, threw the half-eaten dinners into the garbage, and washed up.

Then he turned and—feeling very old—headed for the bedroom to pack.

Twenty

AT THREE O'CLOCK in the morning, the boarded-up Beaux Arts mansion at 891 Riverside Drive looked asleep, perhaps even dead. But deep below the shuttered windows and double-locked doors, activity flickered in one of the basement tunnels cut into the Manhattan bedrock beneath the old house. The longest tunnel—actually a series of connected basement rooms—lay in a line due west, drilling beneath Riverside Drive and Riverside Park toward the Hudson River. At the end, a crude staircase spiraled down a natural cavity to a stone quay, where a watery tunnel led out past a small, weed-draped opening onto the river itself. More than two centuries before, the river pirate who owned the mansion's earlier incarnation had used this secret passage on nocturnal errands of mischief. Today, only a handful of people knew of the hidden entrance.

In this isolated spot, the soft lapping of oars could be heard. There was a faint plash as the green veil of weeds was lifted aside, exposing an underwater passage. It was a foggy, moonless night, and only the palest glint of light outlined a skiff as it entered the tunnel. Noiselessly, it slid forward beneath a low, rocky ceiling, easing up at last to the stone quay.

Pendergast stepped out of the skiff, tethered it to a cleat, and looked around, eyes glinting in the darkness. He remained still for several minutes, listening. Then he pulled a flashlight from his pocket, snapped it on, and headed up the staircase. At the top, he stepped out into a large room filled with wooden cases displaying weapons and armor, some modern, others dating back two thousand years. He passed through the room and into an old laboratory, beakers and retorts gleaming on long black-topped tables.

In one corner of the laboratory stood a silent, shadowy figure.

Pendergast came forward cautiously, one hand stealing toward his weapon. "Proctor?"

"Sir?"

Pendergast relaxed. "I got the signal from Constance."

"And I, in turn, got your message to meet here. But I must say I'm surprised to see you in person, sir."

"I had hoped it wouldn't be necessary. But as it happens, there's a message that I, in turn, must deliver to Constance, and it's one I felt had to be delivered in person."

Proctor nodded. "I understand, sir."

"From now on, it is *vital* that you keep a close eye on her. You know Constance, how fragile her mental condition is. How she appears on the surface is no indication at all of her true emotional state. You also know that she's been through what no other human being has. I fear that, if she is not treated with exceptional care and caution . . ."

His voice trailed off. After a moment, Proctor nodded again.

"This all couldn't have come at a worse time. I'm going to tell her that she needs to be ready at all times to return to *that* place . . . where she first hid from us. Where nobody, *nobody,* could ever find her."

"Yes, sir."

"You found the breach?"

"It has been found and sealed."

"Where was it?"

"It seems that a nineteenth-century sewer tunnel runs under Broadway, just beyond the basement fruit cellars. It has not been used for fifty years. He was able to penetrate the fruit cellars from that tunnel, knocking a hole in the pipe."

Pendergast looked at him sharply. "He didn't find the staircase leading to this sub-basement?"

"No. It seems he was in the house for only a few moments. He was there just long enough to take the item from a first-floor cabinet and leave."

Pendergast continued to look fixedly at Proctor. "You must make sure the mansion is perfectly sealed. This *cannot* be allowed to happen again. Is that clear?"

"Perfectly, sir."

"Good. Then let's go speak with her."

They passed out of the laboratory and through a series of chambers filled with glass-fronted cabinets and tall cases full of seemingly endless and impossibly eclectic collections: stuffed migratory birds, Amazonian insects, rare minerals, bottled chemicals.

At last, in a room full of butterflies, they stopped. Pendergast licked the flashlight over the ranks of display cases. Then he spoke quietly into the darkness.

"Constance?"

Only silence answered.

"Constance?" he said again, just a trifle louder.

There was a faint rustle of linen; then a woman of about twenty appeared seemingly out of nowhere. She wore a long, old-fashioned white dress with lace ruffling around the throat. Her delicate skin was very pale in the light of the flashlight.

"Aloysius," she said, embracing him. "Thank God."

For a moment, Pendergast simply held her close. Then he gently detached himself and turned away for a minute, twisting a small brass knob set into one wall. The chamber filled with faint light.

"Aloysius, what's the matter?" Her eyes—strangely wise for a face so young—grew anxious.

"I'll tell you in a moment." Pendergast placed a reassuring hand on her shoulder. "Tell me about the message."

"It arrived late this evening."

"Method of delivery?"

"It was slipped into a crack beneath the front door."

"You took the necessary precautions?"

Constance nodded. Then she reached into one of her sleeves and drew out a small ivory business card, carefully sealed inside a glassine envelope.

Pendergast took the card, turned it over. *Diogenes Pendergast* was engraved in fine copperplate on the card's face: below that, in rose-colored ink, had been written: *The Five of Swords is Smithback.*

He stared at the card for a long moment. Then he slipped it into his coat pocket.

"What does it mean?" Constance asked.

"I hesitate to tell you more. Your nerves have been strained enough already."

Constance smiled faintly. "I must say, when you walked into the library, I was sure I was seeing a—a *revenant*."

"You know my brother's plans, how he intends to destroy me."

"Yes." Constance went even paler and for a moment seemed to stagger slightly. Pendergast placed his hand on her shoulder.

She mastered herself with effort. "I'm fine, thank you. Do go on."

"He has already begun. Over the last several days, three of my closest friends have been killed." Pendergast touched his jacket pocket. "This note from Diogenes puts me on notice that William Smithback is the next target."

"William Smithback?"

"He's a reporter for the *New York Times*." Pendergast hesitated again.

"And?" Constance asked. "There's something else troubling you—I can see it in your face."

"Yes. The first three who died were all very close to me. But that isn't the case with Bill Smithback. I've known him for several years. He was involved in three cases of mine, a very effective journalist. And despite an impulsive and somewhat careerist exterior, he is a good man. What troubles me, however, is that he's more an acquaintance than a friend. Diogenes is casting his net wider than I thought. It isn't just close friends who are at risk. And that makes the situation even more difficult than I thought."

"How can I help?" Constance asked in a low tone.

"By keeping yourself absolutely safe."

"You think—?"

"That you're a possible target? Yes. And there's something more. The third man to die was Michael Decker, an old FBI associate of mine. I found Mike's body yesterday, in his Washington house. He had been killed with an old bayonet. The modus operandi was a nod to a distant ancestor of mine, who died in a very similar fashion as an officer in Napoleon's army, during the Russian campaign of 1812."

Constance shivered.

"What concerned me was the weapon itself. Constance, that bayonet came from the collections *of this very house.*"

She froze for a moment as the implications of this sank home. "The chasepot or the lebel?" she asked faintly, almost robotically.

"The chasepot. It had the initials *P.S.P.* engraved onto the quillon. Quite unmistakable."

But Constance did not reply. Her alert, intelligent eyes had sharpened, deepened, with fear.

"Diogenes has found entrance to this house. No doubt that was the message he intended to deliver to me with that particular bayonet."

"I understand."

"You're still safer within this house than without, and for now you are not in Diogenes's sights. Proctor here has found and sealed the weak point through which Diogenes entered, and as you know, this mansion has been hardened against intruders in many ways. Proctor will be ceaselessly vigilant, and he is more formidable than he looks. Still, you must be on constant guard. This is a very old and vast house. It has a great many secrets. You know those secrets better than anyone. Follow your instincts. If they tell you something is not right, melt into those recesses of the house that only you know. Be ready at a moment's notice. And until we can once again feel safe from this threat, I want you to sleep in that secret space where you first hid from me and from Wren."

At this, Constance's eyes went wide and wild. She clutched at Pendergast. "*No!*" she cried passionately. "No, I don't ever want to go back there again!"

Pendergast immediately put his arms around her. "Constance—"

"You know how it reminds me of *that* time! The dark spaces, the terrible things . . . I don't wish to be reminded, ever again!"

"Constance, *listen* to me. You'll be safe there. And I can't do what needs to be done without knowing you're safe."

Constance did not respond, and Pendergast pressed her more tightly. "Will you promise me that?"

She laid her forehead against his chest.

"Aloysius," she said, her voice breaking. "It was just a few months ago we sat in the library, upstairs. You read to me from the newspapers. Do you remember?"

Pendergast nodded.

"I was beginning to *comprehend.* I felt like a swimmer, coming to the surface after being so long underwater. I want that again. I don't want to go . . . to go *down* again. You do understand, don't you, Aloysius?"

Pendergast caressed her brown hair gently. "Yes, I understand. And everything will be as you want it, Constance. You will get better, I promise. But we must get through this first. Will you help me do that?"

She nodded.

Slowly, Pendergast lowered his arms. Then he took her

forehead between his hands and, bringing her close, kissed it gently. "I must go."

And he turned, darted back into the waiting darkness, and was gone.

Twenty-one

I T WAS QUARTER TO EIGHT when Smithback emerged from his apartment building, glanced up West End Avenue, and stretched out his hand for a taxi. A beat-up yellow cab that had been idling at the far end of the block pulled forward obediently, and Smithback got in with a sigh of regret.

"Forty-fourth and Seventh," he said. The driver—a thin, olive-skinned man with black hair and a bad complexion—muttered a few words in some unknown tongue and screeched away from the curb.

Smithback settled back, glancing out at the passing cityscape. By rights, he should still be in bed, arms around his new wife, deliciously asleep. But the image of Harriman, sitting in their editor's office with that insufferably smug look on his face, had spurred him into rising early to flog the story some more.

You'll both share information and leads, Davies had said. Hell with that. Smithback knew Harriman wasn't planning to share jack shit, and for that matter neither was he. He'd check in at the office, make sure nothing disagreeable had happened overnight, and then hit the pavement. The article he'd turned in the night before had been weak, and he had to get something better. He *had* to, even if it meant buying a damn apartment in Duchamp's building. Now, there was an idea: calling a real estate agent and posing as a prospective buyer . . .

The driver turned sharply left onto 72nd. "Hey, watch it," Smithback said. "I'm nursing a war wound back here." For once, the driver had closed the shield of Plexiglas that separated the front from the back. The cab stank of garlic, onions, and cumin, and Smithback opened the rear window. As usual, the damn thing only went down about a third of the way. Smithback's mood, already low, fell lower.

It was probably just as well he'd left the apartment ninety minutes early. Nora had been in a foul mood for several days now, getting hardly any sleep and working at the museum until well past midnight. That, plus the frosty exchange between her and Margo Green the other night at the Bones, was weighing on him heavily. Margo was an old friend and it pained him the two didn't get along. *They're too much alike,* he thought. *Strong-willed and smart.*

Ahead lay the West Side Highway and the Hudson River. Instead of turning south onto the highway and heading toward Midtown, the driver gunned the cab up the merge ramp onto the northbound lanes.

"What the hell?" Smithback said. "Hey, you're going the wrong way!"

In response, the driver jammed down harder on the accelerator, veering past blaring horns and into the far left lane.

Shit, the guy's English is worse than I thought. Smithback pounded on the heavy shield of scratched Plexiglas.

"You're going the wrong way. Okay? *The—wrong—way.* I said 44th Street. Get off at 95th and turn around!"

The driver didn't respond. Instead, he continued to accelerate, weaving in and out of lanes as he passed car after car. The 95th Street exit came and went in a flash.

Smithback's mouth went dry. *Jesus, am I being kidnapped or something?* He grabbed for the door lock, but as with most cabs the outer knob had been removed and the pull itself was engaged, sunk beneath the level of the window frame.

He renewed his frantic tattoo against the Plexiglas shield. "Stop the car!" he yelled as the cab squealed around a bend. "Let me out!"

When there was no answer, Smithback reached into his pocket and plucked out his cell phone to dial 911.

"Put that thing away, Mr. Smithback," came the voice from the front seat. "You're in good hands, I assure you."

Smithback froze in the act of dialing. He knew that voice: knew it well. But it certainly didn't belong to the Mediterranean-looking man in the front seat.

"Pendergast?" he said incredulously.

The man nodded. He was looking in the rearview mirror, scanning the cars behind them.

The fear abated—slowly, slowly—to be replaced by surprise. *Pendergast,* Smithback thought. *Oh, God. Why do I get a sinking feeling every time I run into him?*

"So the rumors were wrong," he said.

"Of my death? Most certainly."

Smithback guessed they were going at least a hundred miles an hour. Cars were flashing past, vague shapes and blurs of color.

"You mind telling me what's going on? Or why you're in disguise? You look like a fugitive from a Turkish prison—if you don't mind my saying so," he added hastily.

Pendergast glanced again in the rearview mirror. "I'm taking you to a place of safety."

This didn't immediately register. "You're taking me where?"

"You're a marked man. There's a dangerous killer after you. The nature of the threat forces me to take unusual measures."

Smithback opened his mouth to protest, then stopped. Alarm, incredulity, astonishment, mingled in equal measures within him. The 125th Street exit passed in a heartbeat.

Smithback found his voice. "A killer after me? What for?"

"The more you know, the more dangerous it will be for you."

"How do you know I'm in danger? I haven't pissed off anybody—not lately, anyway."

To the left, the North River Control Plant shot by. Glancing uneasily to his right, Smithback thought he caught the briefest glimpse of 891 Riverside Drive—ancient, shadow-haunted—rising above the greenery of Riverside Park.

The car was moving so fast now the tires barely seemed to touch the road. Smithback looked around for a seat belt, but the cab had none. Cars flashed past as if stationary. *What the hell kind of an engine does this thing have?* He swallowed. "I'm not going anywhere until I know what's going on. I'm a married man now."

"Nora will be fine. She'll be told you're on assignment for the *Times* and will be incommunicado for a while. I'll see to that myself."

"Yeah, and what about the *Times*? I'm in the middle of an important assignment."

"They will hear from a doctor of your sudden, serious illness."

"Oh, no. No way. The *Times* is a dog-eat-dog place. It doesn't matter if I'm sick or dying, I'll lose the assignment."

"There will be other assignments."

"Not like this one. Look, Mr. Pendergast, the answer is—*shit!*"

Smithback braced himself as the cab whipped around a cluster of cars, weaving across three lanes, swerving at the last moment to avoid rear-ending a lumbering truck and shooting back into the fast lane. Smithback gripped the seat, silenced by terror.

Pendergast glanced once again in the rearview mirror. Looking around, Smithback could see—four or five cars back—a black Mercedes, weaving in and out of the traffic, pacing them.

Smithback faced forward again, feeling a rush of panic. Ahead on the shoulder, an NYPD cruiser had pulled over a van and the officer was out writing a ticket. As they flew past, Smithback saw the cop whirl around in disbelief, then run back to his cruiser.

"For God's sake, *slow down*," he choked out, but if Pendergast heard him, he gave no response.

Smithback glanced back again. Despite the awful speed, the black Mercedes wasn't falling behind. If anything, it seemed to be gaining. It had heavily tinted windows, and he could not make out the driver.

Ahead were signs for Interstate 95 and the George Washington Bridge. "Brace yourself, Mr. Smithback,"

Pendergast said over the roar of the engine and the screaming of wind.

Smithback seized a door handle, planted his feet on the plastic floor mats. He was so frightened he could hardly think.

Traffic had begun to thicken as the two-lane exit approached, one stream of cars heading for the bridge and New Jersey, the other heading eastward toward the Bronx. Pendergast slowed, alternately watching the traffic ahead and the Mercedes in the rearview mirror. Then, seizing an opportunity, he sheared across all four lanes of traffic onto the right shoulder. A squeal of brakes and a torrent of angry horns erupted, Doppler-shifting lower as Pendergast jammed on the accelerator again, blasting up the narrow shoulder, sending loose trash and hubcaps flying behind them.

"Holy *shit!*" Smithback yelled.

Ahead, the shoulder narrowed, the curb of the median angling in from the right. But instead of slowing, Pendergast pushed the car relentlessly forward. The tires on the passenger side reared up onto the curb and the vehicle charged ahead at an unwieldy angle, rocking crazily back and forth, tires squealing, the stone wall of the exit perilously close at hand.

From behind came the faint wail of a siren.

Pendergast braked abruptly, then turned into a brutal, four-wheel power slide, just merging into a hole in the traffic converging on the Trans-Manhattan Expressway. He changed lanes once—so fast Smithback was thrown sideways on the seat—twice, a third time, darting back and forth, all the while accelerating. The car blasted along beneath the hulking apartments like a bullet through the barrel of a gun.

A quarter mile ahead, a sea of red lights winked back out of the gloom as traffic bunched up in the inevitable gridlock of the Cross Bronx Expressway. The right-hand lane was blocked off by orange cones, signs announcing a highway repair project that—typically—was empty and unmanned. Pendergast veered into the lane, scattering cones left and right.

Smithback glanced back. The black Mercedes was still there, no more than six cars back, pacing them despite all Pendergast could do. Much farther behind now were two police cars, lights flashing and sirens wailing.

Suddenly, Smithback was thrown to one side. Pendergast had abruptly veered onto the off-ramp for the Harlem River Drive. Instead of slowing, he maintained a speed close to a hundred miles an hour. With a shriek of stressed rubber, the car drifted sideways, its flank contacting the stone retaining wall that encircled the ramp. There was a scream of ripping steel, and an explosion of sparks flew backward.

"Son of a bitch! You're going to kill—!"

Smithback's voice was cut off as Pendergast braked violently once again. With a bucking motion, the car shot over a divider onto the opposing entrance helix to a small bridge spanning the Harlem River. The vehicle fishtailed wildly before Pendergast regained control. Then he accelerated yet again as they shot over the river and into a tangle of narrow streets leading toward the South Bronx.

Heart in mouth, Smithback glanced once again over his shoulder. Impossibly, the Mercedes was still there, farther back now but gaining once again. Even as he watched, the driver's window of the Mercedes opened and there was a sudden puff of smoke, followed by the crack of a gunshot.

With a *thunk!*, the passenger side mirror vanished in a spray of glass and plastic, annihilated by a high-caliber bullet.

"Shit!" Smithback screamed.

"Get down," Pendergast said, but Smithback was already on the floor, hands over his head.

From this position, the nightmare was even worse: unable to see anything, Smithback could only imagine the chaos of the chase, the violent changes of direction, the screeching of tires, the roar of the engine, the blaring of horns, snatches of cursing in English and Spanish. And above it all, the ever-growing wail of police sirens. Again and again, he was thrown forward against the undersupports of the front seat as Pendergast braked violently; again and again, he was thrown back as the agent accelerated.

After a few endless minutes, Pendergast spoke again. "I need you to get up, Mr. Smithback. Do so carefully."

Smithback rose, gripping the seat. The car was racing along a wide avenue through an impoverished barrio of the Bronx, darting from left to right. Instinctively, he glanced over his shoulder. In the distance, he could see the Mercedes still pacing them, swerving back and forth among slow-moving delivery vans and lowriders. Farther back were strung out at least half a dozen police cars.

"We're going to be stopping in a moment," Pendergast said. "It is imperative that you follow me out of the car as quickly as possible."

"Follow—?" Smithback was so terrorized his mind had stopped working.

"Just do as I say, please. Stay right behind me. *Right* behind me. Is that clear?"

"Yes," Smithback croaked.

Ahead, the road ended in a vast fence of barbed wire and metal pipe, interrupted only by a heavy gate directly before them. The fence enclosed at least five acres of cars, SUVs, and vans, squeezed impossibly close to one another, extending from one end of the fence to the other, a sea of vehicles, all makes and models and vintages. They were all packed so tightly not even a scooter could get between them. Atop the gate was a battered sign that read *Division of Motor Vehicles—Mott Haven Impound Facility.*

Pendergast plucked a small remote control from one pocket and punched a code onto its keypad. Slowly, the gate began to open. When Pendergast did not reduce speed, Smithback clasped the door handle again and clenched his teeth.

The car blew past the gate with an inch to spare and, with a shuddering squeal of brakes, spun sideways and stopped at the wall of cars. Without bothering to turn off the engine, Pendergast leaped out and took off, with a brusque wave for Smithback to follow. The reporter tumbled out of the backseat and dashed after Pendergast, who was already running through the maze of cars. They made directly for the rear of the facility, running and dodging through the sea of parked vehicles. Smithback could barely keep up with the agent flying along in front of him.

It was close to a half-mile sprint to the rear wall of the impound facility. At last, Pendergast stopped at the final row of vehicles, which were parked a few dozen yards in from the rear of the yard, blocked by the same heavy steel pipe fence. Taking a key from his pocket, he unlocked a battered Chevy van parked in the last row and gestured for Smithback to get in the back. Pendergast leaped behind the wheel, turned the key, and the van roared to life.

"Hold on," he said. Then he put the van in gear and shot forward, accelerating directly toward the pipe fence.

"Wait," Smithback said. "You'll never bash through that fence. We'll be—oh, *shit!*" He turned away, shielding his face from the inevitable catastrophic impact.

There was a loud clang; a brief jolt; but the van was still accelerating forward. Smithback raised his head and lowered his arms, heart pounding, and looked back. He saw that a section of the fence had been knocked away, leaving a clean rectangular hole in its place.

"The metal pipes had already been cut, then spotwelded back into place," Pendergast said by way of explanation, driving more slowly now, making a number of turns through a warren of side streets while removing his wig and wiping the stage makeup from his face with a silk handkerchief. The black Mercedes and the police cars were gone. "Help me with this."

Smithback climbed into the front seat and helped Pendergast pull off the cheap, stained brown polyester top, revealing a dress shirt and tie underneath.

"Hand me my jacket back there, if you'd be so kind."

Smithback pulled a beautifully pressed suit coat off a rack hanging behind the front seat. Pendergast slid into it quickly.

"You planned this whole thing, didn't you?" Smithback said.

Pendergast turned onto East 138th Street. "This is a case where advance preparation meant the difference between life and death."

All at once, Smithback understood the plan. "That guy who was after us—you lured him into the one place he couldn't follow. There's no way around that impound facility."

"There is a way around, yes, involving three miles of driving through congested side streets." Pendergast turned north, heading for the Sheridan Expressway.

"So who the hell was that? The man you say is trying to kill me?"

"As I said, the less you know, the better. Although I must say that the high-speed chase and the use of firearms were uncharacteristically crude of him. Perhaps he saw his opportunity evaporating and became desperate." He looked over at Smithback with a laconic expression. "Well, Mr. Smithback? Convinced?"

Smithback nodded slowly. "But why *me*? What'd I do?"

"That is, unfortunately, the very question I can't answer."

Smithback's heart was only now slowing down, and he felt as wrung out and limp as a dishrag. He'd been in tight spots with Pendergast before. Deep down, he knew the man wouldn't do something like this unless it was absolutely necessary. All of a sudden, his career at the *Times* seemed a lot less important.

"Hand me your cell phone and wallet, please."

Smithback did as requested. Pendergast shoved them in the glove compartment and handed him an expensive leather billfold.

"What's this?"

"Your new identity."

Smithback opened it. There was no money, only a Social Security card and a New York driver's license.

"Edward Murdhouse Jones?" he read off.

"Correct."

"Yes, but Jones? Come on, what a cliché."

"That's precisely why you'll have no trouble remembering it . . . Edward."

Smithback shoved the wallet in his back pocket. "How long is this going to last?"

"Not long, I hope."

"What do you mean not long? A day or two?"

No answer.

"Where the hell are you taking me, anyway?"

"River Oaks."

"River Oaks? The millionaire funny farm?"

"You are now the troubled son of a Wall Street investment banker, in need of rest, relaxation, a bit of undemanding therapy, and isolation from the hectic world."

"Hold on, I'm not checking into any mental hospital—"

"You'll find River Oaks to be quite luxurious. You'll have a private room, gourmet food, and elegant surroundings. The grounds are beautiful—pity they are buried in two feet of snow at the moment. There's a spa, library, game room, and every imaginable comfort. It's housed in a former Vanderbilt mansion in Ulster County. The director is a very sympathetic man. He'll be most solicitous, I assure you. Most important, it is *utterly secure* from the killer who is determined to end your life. I am sorry I can't tell you more, I really am."

Smithback sighed. "This director, he'll know all about me, right?"

"He's got all the information he could possibly need. You will be well treated. Indeed, you are guaranteed special treatment."

"No force-fed meds? Straitjackets? Shock therapy?"

Pendergast smiled faintly. "Nothing like that, trust me.

You'll be waited on hand and foot. An hour of counseling a day, that's all. The director is fully informed, he has all the necessary documents. I've purchased some clothes that I think will fit you."

Smithback was silent a moment. "Gourmet food, you say?"

"As much as you could wish."

Smithback sat forward. "But Nora. She'll worry about me."

"As I mentioned, she'll be led to understand you are on a special assignment for the *Times*. Given the work she's doing for the opening, she'll hardly have time to think about you at all."

"If they're after me, she'll be in danger. I need to be there to protect her."

"I can tell you that Nora is in absolutely no danger at present. However, she *will* be in danger if you remain near her. Because *you* are the target. It is for *her* sake as much as yours that you must go into hiding. The farther away you are, the safer she'll be."

Smithback groaned. "This is going to be a disaster for my career."

"Your career will suffer more from your untimely death."

Smithback could feel the lump of the wallet in his back pocket. *Edward Murdhouse Jones.* "I'm sorry, but I don't like this at all."

"Like it or not, I'm saving your life."

Smithback did not reply.

"Are we clear on that, Mr. Smithback?"

"Yes," Smithback said, with a dreadful sinking feeling.

Twenty-two

ORA KELLY TRIED to shut out the din of the exhibition hall and focus her attention on the box of sand in front of her. On one side, she had laid out the objects to be arranged: a skeleton in plasticine, along with a suite of grave goods—priceless objects in gold, jade, polychrome ceramics, bone, and carved shell. On the other side of the large box, she had set up a photograph of a real tomb, a photo taken only moments after its astonishing discovery. It was the grave of a ninth-century Mayan princess named Chac Xel, and Nora's job was to re-create it—in painstaking detail—for the Sacred Images exhibition.

As she contemplated the work, she could hear, over her shoulder, the heavy breathing from one very annoyed guard, upset at being pulled from his usual duty manning the sleepy Hall of Pelagic Birds and thrust into a manic hive of activity at the very center of the Sacred Images show. She heard the guard shift his enormous bulk and sigh theatrically as if to hurry her along.

But Nora wouldn't allow herself to be rushed. This was one of the most important exhibits in the entire exhibition. The artifacts to be arranged were extraordinarily delicate and demanded the utmost attention and care. Once again, she tried to shut out the uproar of construction, the growl of drills and the whine of Skilsaws, the shoutings back and forth, the furious comings and goings of curators, designers, and assistants. And on top of that, with the museum's security system being beefed up for the umpteenth time in preparation for the new opening, they had to drop everything and leave the exhibition now and then as sensors were installed and software tested. It was pure bedlam.

Nora refocused her attention on the sandbox in front of her. She began by arranging the bones, laying them in the sand after their original placement in the photograph. The princess had not been laid out flat, Western style; rather, her body had been bound into a mummy bundle, knees drawn up to the face, arms folded in front, the whole wrapped up like a package in beautiful woven blankets. The rotting of the bundle had caused the skeleton to fall open, spilling the bones in a crazy pattern on the floor of the tomb, which Nora carefully replicated.

Next came the placement of the objects found in the tomb. Unlike the bones, these were the real thing—and virtually priceless. She slipped on a pair of cotton gloves and lifted the largest object, a heavy pectoral in beaten electrum depicting a jaguar surrounded by glyphs. She held it up, momentarily spellbound by the dazzle of light off its golden curves. She laid it with care on the skeleton's chest. Next came a gold necklace, which she placed around the cervical vertebrae. Half a dozen gold rings were slipped onto the bony fingers. A solid-gold tiara set with jades and turquoises went atop the skull. She carefully arranged pots in a semicircle, filled with offerings of polished jade, turquoises, and glossy pieces of black obsidian. Next came a ceremonial obsidian knife, almost a foot long with many barbs, still sharp enough to make a nasty cut if not handled just so.

She paused. The last thing was the jade mask, worth millions, carved from a single flawless block of deep green nephrite jade, with rubies and white quartz set in the eyes, and turquoise teeth.

"Lady," said the guard, interrupting her reverie, "I've got a break in fifteen."

"I'm aware of that," said Nora dryly.

She was about to reach for the mask when she heard the voice of Hugo Menzies at some distance, not loud but somehow riding above the din. "Wonderful work!" he was saying. "Marvelous!"

Nora looked up to see the bushy-haired figure picking his way down the hall, stepping fastidiously across a floor strewn with electrical cables, sawdust, pieces of Bubble Wrap, and other construction detritus. The omnipresent canvas fishing bag he used instead of a briefcase was slung over one shoulder. He was shaking hands, nodding in approval, encouraging as he went along, knowing everyone's name, from the carpenters to the curators. Everyone got a nod, a smile, a word of encouragement. How different from Ashton, chief curator of this exhibition, who felt it beneath him to talk to anybody lacking a doctoral degree.

After the meeting, Nora had been furious with Menzies for coming down on Margo Green's side. But it was impossible to stay angry with a man like Menzies: he so clearly believed in what he was doing, and she'd personally witnessed so many other ways, large and small, in which he'd supported the department. No, you couldn't stay mad at Hugo Menzies.

It was a different story, though, with Margo Green.

Menzies approached. "Hello, Frank," he said to the guard, laying a hand on his shoulder. "Nice to see you here."

"You, too, sir," the guard said, straightening up and wiping the scowl off his face.

"Ahh," said Menzies, turning to Nora. "That High Classic jade mask is one of my favorite objects in the entire museum. You know how they made it so thin? Polished it down by hand with blades of grass. But I expect you already knew that."

"As a matter of fact, I did."

Menzies laughed. "Of course. What am I thinking? Excellent work, Nora. This is going to be a highlight of the show. May I watch while you place the mask?"

"Of course."

She reached down and picked it up with her white-gloved hands, not without trepidation. Carefully, she placed it in the sand above the head of the body, where it had been found, adjusting it and making sure it was secure.

"A trifle to the left, Nora."

She moved it slightly.

"Perfect. I'm glad I was in time to see that." He smiled, winked, and moved on through the chaos, leaving in his wake people who were working all the harder, if such a thing were possible. Nora had to admire his people skills.

The case was complete, but she wanted to check it one more time. She ran through the list of items, matching them to the photograph. She had only one shot to get this right: once the case was sealed under bulletproof, shatterproof glass, it wouldn't be opened until the end of the show, four months later.

As she ran the final check, for some reason her mind wandered to Bill. He'd run off to Atlantic City covering some casino story and wouldn't be back for—she realized she wasn't sure *when* he'd be back. He'd been so vague. And it had all happened so suddenly. Was this what it was like to be married to a reporter? What had happened to the murder he was covering? And wasn't he on the city desk? She supposed that a casino story in New Jersey might qualify for the city desk, but still . . . He'd sounded so strange on the telephone, so breathless, so tense.

She sighed, shook her head. It was probably for the better, given that she'd hardly been able to see him with all the craziness surrounding the opening. Everything was, as usual, behind schedule, and Ashton was on the warpath. She could hear the chief curator's voice, pitched high in querulous complaint in some far corner of the hall.

The guard issued another ostentatious sigh behind her, breaking her reverie.

"Just a minute," she said over her shoulder. "As soon as we get this sealed." She glanced at her watch. Three-thirty already. And she'd been going since six. She was going to be working at least until midnight, and every minute she wasted now was a minute of sleep lost at the end of the day.

Nora turned to the foreman, who had been nearby, waiting for this moment. "Ready to seal the case."

Soon a group of exhibition assistants, under the foreman's direction, began fitting the monstrously heavy sheet of glass over the tomb, accompanied by grunts and curses.

"Nora?"

She turned. It was Margo Green. *Bad timing, as usual.*

"Hello, Margo," she said.

"Wow. Beautiful exhibit."

Nora saw out of the corner of her eye the scowling face of the guard, the gaggle of laborers sealing up the tomb.

"Thanks. We're really under the gun here, as you can see."

"I can." She hesitated. "I don't want to take up any more of your time than I have to."

Then don't, thought Nora, trying to maintain her fake smile. She had four other cases to mount and seal. She couldn't help but watch as the workers struggled to seat the glass. If they dropped it . . .

Margo stepped closer, lowered her voice. "I wanted to apologize for my snarky comment in the meeting."

Nora straightened. This was unexpected.

"It was uncalled-for. Your points were all well taken and totally within professional bounds. I was the one who acted unprofessionally. It's just . . ." Margo hesitated.

"Just what?"

"You're so damned . . . *competent.* And articulate. I was intimidated."

Nora didn't quite know how to answer this. She looked closely at Margo, who was reddening from the effort to apologize. "You're not exactly a pushover yourself," she finally said.

"I know. We're both kind of stubborn. But stubborn is good—especially if you're a woman."

Nora couldn't help but smile, this time for real. "Let's

not call it stubbornness. Let's call it the courage of our convictions."

Margo smiled in turn. "That sounds better. Although a lot of people might call it plain old bitchiness."

"Hey," said Nora. "Bitchy is good, too."

Margo laughed. "Anyway, Nora, I just wanted to say I was sorry."

"I appreciate the apology. I really do. Thank you, Margo."

"See you around."

Nora paused, the case temporarily forgotten in her surprise, as she watched Margo's slender form make its way back through the barely controlled chaos of the exhibition.

Twenty-three

CAPTAIN LAURA HAYWARD sat in a plastic chair in the trace evidence lab on the twelfth floor of One Police Plaza, making a conscious effort not to glance at her watch. Archibald Quince, chief scientist of the fiber analysis unit, was holding forth: walking back and forth before a crowded evidence table, hands clasped behind the white lab coat one minute, then gesticulating the next. It was a rambling, repetitive tale, full of sound and fury, and yet it all came down to one easily grasped point: the man didn't have shit.

Quince paused in midstep, then turned toward her, his tall, bony frame all angles and elbows. "Allow me to summarize."

Thank God, Hayward thought. At least there was light at the end of the tunnel.

"Only a handful of fibers were recovered that were foreign to the site. A few were stuck to the ropes used to bind the victim; another was found on the couch where the victim was placed, peri-mortem. We can thus reasonably assume a fiber exchange between the murderer and the murder scene. Correct?"

"Correct."

"Since all fibers were the same—length, composition, spinning method, and so forth—we can also assume they are primary rather than secondary fiber transfers. In other words, they're fibers from the killer's clothes rather than fibers that happened to be *on* the killer's clothes."

Hayward nodded, forcing herself to pay attention. All day, as she'd gone about her work, she'd felt the strangest sensation: as if she were floating, detached, just outside her own body. She didn't know if it was due to weariness or to the shock of Vincent D'Agosta's abrupt, unexpected departure. She wished she could get mad about it, but somehow anger wouldn't come—just grief. She wondered where he was, what he was doing now. And, more urgently, she wondered how in his mind such a good thing could have suddenly gone so wrong.

"Captain?"

Hayward realized there was a question hanging in the air, unanswered. She looked up quickly. "Excuse me?"

"I said would you like to see a sample?"

Hayward rose. "Sure."

"It's an extremely fine animal fiber, one I've never seen before. We've identified it as an exceptionally rare kind of cashmere, blended with a small percentage of merino. Very, very expensive. As you'll notice, both fiber types were dyed black prior to being spun together. But take a look for yourself." Stepping back, Quince gestured toward the stereoscopic microscope that stood beside the lab table.

Hayward came forward and glanced through the oculars. Half a dozen slender black threads were displayed against a light background, sleek and glossy and very even.

Very, very expensive. Though she was still waiting for

Psych to deliver the profile, a few things about the perp were already obvious. He—or perhaps she—was very sophisticated, highly intelligent, and had access to funds.

"The dye has also proven elusive to identification. It's made from a natural vegetative pigmentation, not synthetic chemicals, but we haven't yet been able to track down the coloring agent. It's not in any database we've checked. The closest we've come is a certain rare berry grown on the mountain slopes of Tibet, used by local tribesmen and Sherpas."

Hayward stepped back from the scope. As she listened, she felt a faint frisson of recognition. She had excellent instincts, and normally that little tingle meant two pieces of a puzzle coming together. But at the moment, she couldn't imagine what those pieces might be. She was probably even more tired than she thought. She would go home, have an early dinner, then try to get some sleep.

"Despite their fineness, the fibers are very tightly woven," Quince said. "Do you know what that means?"

"An extremely soft and comfy garment?"

"Yes. But that's not the point. Such a garment doesn't shed easily. It isn't usually a donor garment. Hence the small number of fibers."

"And, perhaps, evidence of a struggle."

"My thought as well." Quince frowned. "Normally, the fact that the fabric is uncommon is important to a fiber examiner. It's helpful in identifying the suspect. But here the fabric is so uncommon it's actually proving to be the opposite. There's nothing exactly like it in any of the textile fiber databases. Then there's another odd thing: the age of the fiber."

"Which is?"

"Our tests have indicated the fabric was spun at least twenty years ago. Yet there is no evidence the clothing *itself* is old. The fibers aren't worn. There isn't the kind of fading or damage you'd expect from years of usage and dry cleaning. It's as if the fabric came off the store rack yesterday."

At last, Quince shut up. He stretched out his arms, palms up, as if in supplication.

"And?" Hayward asked.

"That's it. As I said, all our searches have come up empty. We've checked with textile mills, clothing manufacturers, everything. Foreign *and* domestic. It's the same as with the rope. This fabric seems to have been made on the moon, for all we can learn."

For all we can learn? "I'm sorry, but that's just not good enough." Fatigue and impatience gave her tone a sudden edge. "We have only a handful of evidence in this case, Dr. Quince, and these fibers are some of the most important of that evidence. You said yourself the fabric is extremely rare. If you've already checked with the mills and the manufacturers, then you should be checking with individual tailors."

Quince shrank back at this scolding. His large, moist, houndlike eyes blinked back at her, full of hurt. "But, Captain Hayward, with all the tailors in the world, that would be like looking for a needle in—"

"If the fabric's as fine as you say it is, then you'd need to contact only the most exclusive and expensive tailors. And in only three cities: New York, London, and Hong Kong."

Hayward realized she was breathing heavily and that her voice had risen. *Calm down,* she told herself.

In the uncomfortable silence that settled over the lab,

Hayward heard a throat being tactfully cleared. She glanced over her shoulder and saw Captain Singleton standing in the doorway.

"Glen," she said, wondering how long he'd been standing there.

"Laura." Singleton nodded. "Mind if we have a word?"

"Of course." Hayward turned back to Quince. "Give me a follow-up report tomorrow, please." Then she followed Singleton out into the corridor.

"What's up?" she asked as they paused in the bustling hallway. "It's almost time for Rocker's state-of-the-force meeting."

Singleton waited a moment before answering. He was dressed in a dapper chalk-stripe suit, and despite its being late afternoon, his white shirt was still as crisp as if he'd just put it on.

"I got a call from Special Agent in Charge Carlton of the New York field office," he said, motioning her to step to one side, out of the traffic. "He was following up on a request from Quantico."

"What request is that?"

"Have you heard the name Michael Decker?"

Hayward thought a moment, shook her head.

"He was a top FBI honcho, lived in a classy D.C. neighborhood. The man was murdered yesterday. Speared through the mouth with a bayonet. Nasty piece of business, and, as you can imagine, the FBI are on the case hammer and tongs. They're following up with Decker's colleagues, trying to find out if there might be any bad guys in the man's past who had a score to settle." Singleton shrugged. "It seems one of Decker's colleagues, and closest friends, was a man named Pendergast."

Hayward glanced at him abruptly. "*Agent* Pendergast?"

"That's right. You worked with him on the Cutforth murder, right?"

"He's been involved in a few priors of mine."

Singleton nodded. "Since Agent Pendergast is missing and presumed dead, Carlton asked me to check with any associates of his in the NYPD. See if he ever talked about Decker, maybe mentioned enemies the man might have had. I figured you might know something."

Hayward thought a moment. "No, Pendergast never spoke of Decker to me." She hesitated. "You might talk to Lieutenant D'Agosta, who worked with him on at least three cases going back seven years."

"That so?"

Hayward nodded, hoping that her expression remained professionally neutral.

Singleton shook his head. "The thing is, I can't find D'Agosta. He hasn't reported in since lunch, and nobody else working his case has seen him. And for some reason, we can't raise him on his radio. You wouldn't happen to know where he is, would you?" As Singleton spoke, he kept his voice studiously neutral, his eyes fixed on the people walking past them.

In that moment, Hayward realized he knew about her and D'Agosta. She felt a sudden, consuming embarrassment. *So it's not the big secret we thought it was.* She wondered how soon Singleton would learn D'Agosta had moved out.

She licked her lips. "Sorry. I've no idea where Lieutenant D'Agosta might be."

He hesitated. "Pendergast never mentioned Decker to you?"

"Never. He was the kind of guy who really kept his cards close, never talked about anyone, least of all himself. Sorry I can't be of more help."

"Like I said, it was a long shot. Let the FBI take care of their own." Now, at last, he looked directly at her. "Can I buy you a cup of coffee? We've got a few minutes before that meeting."

"No, thanks. I need to make a couple of quick phone calls first."

Singleton nodded, shook her hand, then turned away.

Hayward watched his receding form, thinking. Then, slowly, she turned the other way, preparing to head back to her office. As she did so, everything else suddenly fell away: the murmur of conversations, the people walking past; even the fresh and painful ache in her heart.

She had made the connection.

Twenty-four

WILLIAM SMITHBACK JR. paced around his sumptuous third-floor room at River Oaks. He had to admit that Pendergast was right: the place was gorgeous. His room was luxuriously furnished, albeit in a style that went out with the Victorians: dark crushed-velvet wallpaper, oversize bed with canopy, hulking mahogany furniture. Paintings in gilt frames hung on all four walls: a still life of fruit in a bowl; sunset over the ocean; a pastoral countryside of cows and hayricks. They were real oils, too, not reproductions. While nothing had been actually screwed to the floors or walls, Smithback had noticed an absence of sharp implements, and he'd had the indignity of having his belt and tie taken away upon entrance. There was also a marked absence of telephones.

He strolled thoughtfully over to the large window and stared out. It was snowing, the fat flakes ticking against the glass. Outside, in the dying light, he could see a vast lawn deep in snow, bordered with hedges and gardens—all lumps and mounds of white—and dotted with icicled statuary. The garden was surrounded by a high stone wall, beyond which stood forest and a winding road that led down the mountain to the nearest town, six miles away. There were no bars on the window, but the small, thick leaded panes looked like they'd be very difficult to break.

Just for the hell of it, he tried to push the window open. Although there was no visible lock, it refused to budge. Smithback tried a little harder. Nothing. He turned away with a shrug.

River Oaks was a huge and rambling structure, perched atop one of the lower peaks of the Catskills: the country retreat of Commodore Cornelius Vanderbilt in the days before Newport, now converted to a mental hospital for the ultra-privileged. The orderlies and nurses wore discreet black uniforms instead of the usual white, and were ready to attend to every need of the "guests." Aside from light work duty and the daily hour of therapy, he had no set schedule. And the food was fantastic: Smithback, whose work duty was in the kitchen, had learned the head chef was a Cordon Bleu graduate.

But still, Smithback felt miserable. In the few hours he'd been here, he had tried to convince himself to take it easy, that this was for his own good, that he should wallow in luxury. It was a kind of lifestyle that, under other circumstances, he'd almost welcome. He'd told himself to treat it as drama, one he could maybe turn into a book someday. It seemed incredible someone was out to kill him.

But already this personal pep talk was growing stale. At the time of his admittance, he'd still been dazed from the high-speed chase, struck dumb by the suddenness with which his life had been turned around. But now he'd had time to think. Plenty of time. And the questions—and dark speculations—just kept coming.

He told himself that at least there was no need to worry about Nora. On the drive up the New York Thruway, he'd called her himself using Pendergast's phone, making up a story about how the *Times* was sending him on an undercover assignment to Atlantic City to cover a casino scandal, rendering him incommunicado for a while. He had Pendergast's assurance Nora would be safe, and he had never known Pendergast to be wrong. He felt guilty about lying to her, but, after all, he had done it for her sake, and he could explain it all later.

It was his job that preyed most on his mind. Sure, they'd accept he was sick, and no doubt Pendergast would make it convincing. But in the meantime, Harriman would have free reign. Smithback knew that, when he finally got back after his "convalescence," he'd be lucky to get assigned even the Dangler story.

The worst of it was, he didn't even know how long he'd have to stay here.

He turned, pacing again, half mad with worry.

There came a soft knock at the door.

"What is it?" Smithback said irritably.

An elderly nurse stuck her gaunt head inside the room, raven hair pulled back in a severe bun. "Dinner is served, Mr. Jones."

"I'll be right down, thanks."

Edward Jones, troubled son of a Wall Street investment banker, in need of rest, relaxation, and a bit of isolation from the hectic world. It seemed very strange indeed to be playing Edward Jones, to be living in a place where everybody thought you were somebody else. *Especially* somebody not quite right in the head. Only Pendergast's acquaintance, the director of River Oaks—a Dr. Tisander—knew the truth. And Smithback had seen him only in passing while Pendergast was dealing with the admittance paperwork; they hadn't yet had a chance to speak privately.

Exiting his room and closing the door behind him—there were no locks on any of the guests' doors, it seemed—Smithback walked down the long hallway. His footfalls made no noise on the thick rose-colored carpeting. The corridor was of polished, figured mahogany, dark with carved moldings. More oils lined the walls. The only sound was the faint moan of the wind outside. The huge mansion seemed cloaked in a preternatural silence.

Ahead, the corridor opened onto a large landing, framing a grand staircase. From around the corner, he heard low voices. Immediately, with a reporter's instinctive curiosity, he slowed his walk.

". . . don't know how much longer I can take working in this loony bin," came a gruff male voice.

"Ah, quit complaining," came a second, higher voice. "The work's easy, the pay's good. The food's great. The crazies are nice and quiet. What the hell's wrong with that?"

It was two orderlies. Smithback, unable to help himself, stopped short, listening.

"It's being stuck out here in the middle of frigging nowhere. On top of a mountain in the dead of winter, nothing around except miles of woods. It messes with your mind."

"Maybe you should come back as a guest." The second orderly guffawed loudly.

"This is serious," came the aggrieved reply. "You know Miss Havisham?"

"Nutcase Nellie? What about her?"

"How she always claims to be seeing people who aren't there?"

"*Everyone* in this joint sees people who aren't there."

"Well, she's got *me* seeing things, too. It was early this afternoon. I was heading back up to the fifth floor when I happened to look out the staircase window. There was someone out there, I could swear it. Out there in the snow."

"Yeah, right."

"I'm telling you, I *saw* it. A dark form, moving fast in the trees. But when I looked back, it was gone."

"Yeah. And how much J.D. had you had before this?"

"None. It's like I told you, this place is—"

Smithback, who'd been edging closer and closer to the edge of the corridor, overbalanced and stumbled forward into the landing. The two men—orderlies in somber black uniforms—abruptly drew apart, their expressions dissolving into emotionless masks.

"May we help you, Mr.—Mr. Jones?" one of them said.

"No, thanks. Just on my way down to the dining room." Smithback made his way down the broad staircase with as much dignity as he could muster.

The dining room was a grand space on the second floor that reminded Smithback of a Park Avenue men's club. There were at least thirty tables within, but the room was so big it could have held dozens more comfortably. Each was covered with a crisp linen tablecloth and arrayed with gleaming—and extremely dull—silverware. Brilliant chandeliers hung from a Wedgwood-blue ceiling. Despite the elegant room, it seemed barbaric to eat dinner at 5 P.M. Guests were already seated at some of the tables, eating methodically, chatting quietly, or staring moodily at nothing. Others were shuffling slowly to their seats.

Oh, God, Smithback thought. *The dinner of the living dead.* He looked around.

"Mr. Jones?" An orderly came over, as obsequious as any maître d', with the same smirk of superiority behind the mask of servility. "Where would you care to sit?"

"I'll try that table," he said, pointing to one currently occupied by only one young man, who was buttering a dinner roll. He was flawlessly attired—expensive suit, snowy white shirt, gleaming shoes—and he looked the most normal of the bunch. He nodded to Smithback as the journalist sat down.

"Roger Throckmorton," the man said, rising. "Delighted to meet you."

"Edward Jones," Smithback replied, gratified at the cordial reception. He accepted the menu from the waiter and, despite himself, grew quickly absorbed in the long list of offerings. He finally settled on not one, but two main courses—plaice *à la Mornay* and rack of spring lamb—along with an arugula salad and plover eggs in aspic. He marked his choices on the card beside his place setting, handed the card and the menu to the waiter, then turned once again toward Mr. Throckmorton. He was about Smithback's age, strikingly good-looking, with blond hair carefully parted, and smelling faintly of expensive aftershave. Something about him reminded Smithback of Bryce Harriman; he had that same air of old money and entitlement.

Bryce Harriman . . .

With a mighty effort, Smithback drove the image from his mind. He caught the eye of the man across the table.

"So," he said, "what brings you here?" He realized only after asking the question how inappropriate it was.

But the man didn't seem to take it amiss. "Probably the same as you. I'm crazy." And then he chuckled to show he was kidding. "Seriously, I got in a bit of a scrape, and my father sent me up here for a short, ah, rest. Nothing serious."

"How long have you been here?"

"Couple of months. And what brings you here?"

"Same. Rest." Smithback cast around for a way to redirect the conversation. *What do lunatics talk about, anyway?* He reminded himself the extreme nutcases were kept in the quiet ward, located in another wing. Guests here, in the main section of the mansion, were simply "troubled."

Throckmorton placed his dinner roll on a plate, dabbed primly at his mouth with a napkin. "You just arrived today, didn't you?"

"That's right."

The waiter brought their drinks—tea for Throckmorton, a tomato juice for Smithback, who was annoyed he couldn't get his usual single-malt Scotch. His eye stole once again around the room. Everybody in the place moved so sluggishly, spoke so softly: it all seemed like a banquet in slow motion. *Jesus, I don't think I can take much more of this.* He tried to remind himself of what Pendergast had said—how he was the target of a murderer, how being here not only kept him safe, but Nora as well—yet already, even after a single day, it was getting hard to bear. Why would a dangerous killer be after him? It made no sense. For all he knew, that Mercedes, that bullet, had been meant for Pendergast, not him. Besides,

Smithback knew how to handle himself. He'd been in rough situations before—some of them really rough . . .

Once again, he forced his thoughts back to his dinner companion.

"So what do you . . . think of the place?" he asked a little lamely.

"Oh, not a bad old pile, actually." There was an amused gleam in the man's eye as he spoke that made Smithback think he might have found an ally.

"You don't get tired of all this? Of not getting out?"

"It was much nicer in the fall, of course. The grounds are spectacular. The snow is a bit confining, I'll admit, but what's there to 'get out' to, anyway?"

Smithback digested this a moment.

"So what do you do, Edward?" Throckmorton asked. "For a living."

Smithback mentally reviewed Pendergast's briefing. "My father's an investment banker. Wall Street. I work for his firm."

"My family's on Wall Street, too."

A lightbulb went on in Smithback's head. "You're not *that* Throckmorton, are you?"

The man across the table smiled. "I'm afraid so. At least, one of them. We're a rather large family."

The waiter returned with their entrées—brook trout for Throckmorton, the twin dishes of plaice and lamb for Smithback. Throckmorton looked over at Smithback's heaping portions. "I hate to see a man with no appetite," he said.

Smithback laughed. This fellow wasn't crazy at all. "I never pass up a free meal."

He raised his knife and fork and tucked into the plaice. He began to feel ever so slightly better. The food was superb. And this Roger Throckmorton seemed a decent enough guy. River Oaks might just be bearable for another day or two if he had somebody to talk to. Of course, he'd have to be careful not to blow his cover.

"What do people here do all day?" he mumbled through a mouthful of fish.

"I'm sorry?"

Smithback swallowed. "How do you pass the time?"

Throckmorton chuckled. "I keep a journal and write poetry. I try to keep up with the market, in a desultory kind of way. In good weather, I like to stroll the grounds."

Smithback nodded, speared another piece of fish. "And the evenings?"

"Well, they have billiard tables in the first-floor salon, and games of bridge and whist in the library. And there's chess—that's fun when I can find a partner. But a lot of the time I just read. Recently, I've been reading a lot of poetry. Last night, for example, I began *The Canterbury Tales.*"

Smithback nodded his approval. "My favorite bit is 'The Miller's Tale.'"

"I think mine is the General Prologue. It's full of so much hope for renewal, for rebirth." Throckmorton sat back in his chair and quoted the opening lines. "*Whan that April with his showres soote / The droughte of March hath perced to the roote.*"

Smithback cast his memory back over the prologue, managed to dredge up a few lines. "Or how about this: *Bifel that in that seson on a day, / In Southwerk at the Tabard as I lay*—"

"Fishing, with the arid plain behind me."

It took Smithback, who had turned his attention to the

lamb, a moment to register this change. "Wait a minute. That's not Chaucer, that's—"

"Out, out, brief candle!" Throckmorton sat up very stiff, almost as if at attention.

Smithback paused in the midst of forking up a piece of lamb, the smile freezing on his face. "I'm sorry?"

"Did you hear something just now?" Throckmorton had paused as if listening, head cocked to one side.

"Ah . . . no."

Throckmorton cocked his head again. "Yes, I'll take care of it right away."

"Take care of what?"

Throckmorton fixed him with an annoyed eye. "I wasn't speaking to you."

"Oh. Sorry."

Throckmorton rose from the table, dabbed primly at his lips, carefully folded his napkin. "I hope you'll forgive me, Edward, but I have a business appointment."

"Right," said Smithback, aware that the smile was still frozen on his lips.

"Yes." Throckmorton leaned over and said, in a conspiratorial whisper: "And it's a dreadful responsibility, I don't mind telling you. But when He comes calling, who are we to refuse?"

"He?"

"The Lord our God." Throckmorton straightened up, shook Smithback's hand. "It's been a pleasure. I hope we'll meet again soon."

And he walked with a jaunty step out of the room.

Twenty-five

D'AGOSTA WALKED SLOWLY through the cavernous open space of the Homicide Division, feeling self-conscious. Even though he was a lieutenant in the NYPD, and had more or less carte blanche to wander the halls of One Police Plaza as he chose, he nonetheless felt as if he were a spy within enemy territory.

I must know more, Pendergast had said. *Even the smallest, least significant detail could be critical.* It was crystal clear what he meant: he needed the file on Charles Duchamp. And it was just as clear he expected D'Agosta to get it for him.

Only it hadn't been as easy as D'Agosta initially anticipated. He'd been back on the job just two days, and he'd been forced to spend more time than expected catching up on the Dangler case. The wack-job seemed to be getting more brazen with each crime: already he'd robbed three more ATMs in the two days D'Agosta was away. And now, with the Duchamp murder, there was less manpower available for stakeouts. Coordinating the two-man teams, talking with the branch managers at the affected banks, had eaten up a lot of time. The fact was, he'd been allocating more of the work than he should have, and he was way behind on interviewing potential eyewitnesses. But always, he remembered the urgency in Pendergast's voice. There was a message in that urgency: *We have to work fast, Vincent. Before he kills again.*

And yet, though he'd wasted precious work hours poring through online records of the Duchamp murder, there was little in the wide-access database he didn't already know—or that Pendergast himself didn't have access to with his laptop. There was nothing else for it: he'd have to go get the case file.

In his left hand, he carried a small sheaf of papers: yesterday's interviews with a possible Dangler eyewitness, brought along merely as camouflage, something to hold. He glanced at his watch as he walked. Ten minutes to six. The huge room was still buzzing with activity—police officers talking together in small groups, on the phone, or, more commonly, typing at computers. Divisional offices always had 24/7 coverage, and in any precinct house, you were guaranteed to find—at any hour of the day or night—somebody at their desk, doing paperwork. Most of a cop's life was spent doing paperwork, it seemed, and nowhere was there more paperwork than in Homicide.

But D'Agosta didn't mind all the activity. In fact, he welcomed it. If anything, it helped him blend in. The important thing was that Laura Hayward would be away from *her* office. It was Thursday, and Commissioner Rocker would be holding one of his state-of-the-force meetings. Thanks to the Duchamp case, she was sure to be there.

He glanced a little guiltily toward the far end of the room. Her office was there, door wide open, desk covered with paperwork. At the sight of the desk, an electric current ran briefly through his loins. It wasn't many months ago that Laura's desk had been used for something quite different from paperwork. He sighed. But, of course, her office then had been on the floor above. And a hell of a lot had happened since—most of it bad.

He pulled his gaze away and glanced around. To his right was a series of empty desks, nameplates at their fronts and computer terminals to one side. Ahead and along the left wall were at least a dozen horizontal file cabinets, stacked from floor to ceiling. These held the files of all active homicide cases.

The good news was that Duchamp was an active case. All closed cases were kept in storage, which meant signing in and out and a host of related security problems. The bad news was that, because it *was* an active case, he had to examine the evidence right here, in front of the entire Homicide Division.

He glanced around again, still feeling ridiculously exposed. *Hesitation is what's going to do you in here, pal,* he told himself. Forcing himself to move as slowly and casually as possible, he approached the cabinets. Unlike other divisions, which sorted their cases by case number, Homicide sorted active files by victim's last name. He slowed further, eyeing the labels covertly: *DA–DE. DE–DO. DO–EB.*

Here we go. D'Agosta stopped at the appropriate cabinet, pulled out the drawer. Dozens of green hanging folders met his eye. *My God, how many active homicides are they investigating here?*

Now was the time to move quickly. Turning away from the rows of desks, he began flipping the files from left to right, pushing the name tabs with an index finger.

Donatelli, Donato, Donazzi . . . what, was it Mafia Week here in Homicide? Dowson. Dubliawitz.

Duggins.

Oh, shit.

D'Agosta paused, finger on the case file of a Randall Duggins. The one thing he hadn't wanted to consider was the possibility that the Duchamp case file wouldn't be in the cabinet.

Could Laura have it? Would she have left it on her desk when she went to meet with Rocker? Or was it perhaps with one of her detectives?

Whatever the case, he was screwed. He'd have to come back again, some other time—some other shift, so as not to arouse suspicion with the same group. But when else could he come back and still be sure Laura wouldn't be here? She was a workaholic; she could be here at almost any hour. Especially now, when she didn't have a reason to be home.

D'Agosta felt his shoulders sag. He fetched a sigh, then dropped his hand from the file to the cabinet, preparing to close it.

As he did so, he got a glimpse of the file behind Randall Duggins's. It was labeled *Charles Duchamp.*

Now, there's a break. Somebody in a hurry must have misfiled it.

D'Agosta plucked it from the cabinet and began leafing through it. The case file was much heavier than he expected. Laura had complained about the paucity of evidence. But there had to be a dozen thick documents here: fingerprint analyses and comparisons, reports of investigation, debriefing reports, interview summaries, evidence acquisition reports, toxicology and lab reports.

Leave it to Hayward to somehow document even a shitty case well.

He'd been hoping to give everything a quick once-over, return the case file, then find Pendergast and give him an oral report. But there was way too much here for that. No choice: he'd have to photocopy everything, and fast.

Once again moving as casually as possible, he slid the cabinet closed, looking left and right as he did so. A large photocopier stood in the middle of the room, but it was surrounded by desks, and, as he watched, an officer went over to use it. Taking the case file off the floor and copying it elsewhere was out of the question: too risky. But large divisions like Homicide usually had several copiers. There had to be another one close by. Where the hell was it?

There. On the far wall, close to Hayward's office, a copier sat between a bulletin board and a watercooler.

Quickly, D'Agosta approached. It was working, and it didn't require an access code to use: his luck, such as it was, still held. But he'd have to hurry: it was getting close to six, and Rocker's meeting wouldn't last much longer.

He dumped the case file on the edge of the copier, placed the Dangler paperwork on top. Just in case he was interrupted, he decided to start with the most important—the case officer's report—and work his way from there. He pulled the report from the folder and started copying.

The minutes crawled slowly by. Maybe it was the fact he had a tall stack of papers, or maybe it was because this machine was far from the desks of the homicide squad, but nobody else came up to use the machine. He made his way through the lab results, toxicology reports, fingerprint analyses, and interviews, working as fast as he could, stuffing each completed sheet beneath the Dangler paperwork.

He glanced again at his watch. It was past 6:15 now, almost 6:20. He had to get the hell out: Laura could come back at any time . . .

At that moment, a homicide lieutenant—somebody D'Agosta recognized as one of Hayward's most trusted associates—appeared at the far end of the division. That was it: his cue to leave. Finishing up the last interview report, he rearranged the files, stacked the photocopies into a crisp pile, and returned the hanging folder to the file cabinet. He hadn't copied everything, but he'd gotten the most important documents. This, along with what evidence Pendergast had obtained from New Orleans, should be a huge help. Closing the cabinet, he began making his way to the exit, once again careful to maintain an air of casualness.

The walk seemed to take forever, and at any moment he expected to see Laura appear in the doorway ahead. But at last, he gained the relative safety of the central corridor. Now it was just a question of gaining the elevator that lay directly ahead.

The corridor was relatively empty, and nobody was waiting at the elevator bank. He stepped forward, pressed the down button. Within moments, a descending elevator chimed, and he walked toward it just as the doors opened.

The elevator compartment beyond was empty except for one person: Glen Singleton.

For a moment, D'Agosta stood motionless, rooted in place with surprise. This had to be a nightmare, he decided: this kind of thing just didn't happen in real life.

Singleton gazed back at him, cool and level. "You're holding up the elevator, Vincent," he said.

Quickly, D'Agosta stepped in. Singleton punched a button and the doors whispered closed.

Singleton waited until the elevator was descending again before speaking. "I'm just coming from Rocker's state-of-the-force meeting," he said.

D'Agosta silently cursed himself. He should have known Singleton might have attended the meeting; he wasn't thinking straight.

Singleton glanced toward D'Agosta again. He didn't say anything further; he didn't need to. *And just what are you doing here yourself?* the gaze clearly said.

D'Agosta thought fast. He'd spent the last two days doing his best to avoid Singleton and this very question. Whatever he said, it had to sound believable.

"I'd heard a homicide detective might have been an inadvertent witness, post-fact, to the most recent Dangler job," he said. "I thought I'd take a minute to check it out." And he raised his sheaf of Dangler paperwork as if to underscore the point.

Singleton nodded slowly. It sounded credible, yet was just amorphous enough to allow D'Agosta some wiggle room.

"What was the detective's name again?" Singleton asked in his mild voice.

D'Agosta held his expression, careful not to betray any surprise or doubt. He thought back to the rows of empty desks he'd just passed, tried to recall the names on the nameplates. "Detective Conte," he said. "Michael Conte."

Singleton nodded again.

"He wasn't around," D'Agosta said. "Next time I'll just call."

There was a moment of silence as the elevator descended.

"You haven't heard of an FBI agent named Decker, have you?" Singleton asked.

Once again, D'Agosta had to work to keep the surprise from showing on his face. "Decker? I don't think so. Why?"

"The man was killed in his house in D.C. the other day. Seems he was good friends with Special Agent Pendergast, who I know you worked with before his disappearance. Did Pendergast ever mention Decker—any enemies he might have had, for example?"

D'Agosta pretended to think. "No, I don't think he ever did."

Another brief silence.

"I'm glad to see you're at work," Singleton went on. "Because I've been getting a few reports of items left unattended these last two days. Tasks half done, or not done at all. Jobs delegated unnecessarily."

"Sir," D'Agosta said. This was all true, but he tried to let a little righteous indignation trickle into his voice. "I'm playing catch-up as quickly as I can. There's a lot to do."

"I've also heard that, instead of working the angles on the Dangler case, you've been asking a lot of questions about the Duchamp murder."

"Duchamp?" D'Agosta repeated. "It's an unusual case, Captain. I guess I'm as curious as the next man."

Singleton nodded again, more slowly. He had a unique way of letting his expression telegraph his thoughts for him, and right now that expression was saying, *You mean a lot more curious than the next man.* But once again, he changed tack. "Something wrong with your radio, Lieutenant?"

Hell. D'Agosta had intentionally left it off that afternoon, in hopes of avoiding just such a cross-examination. He should have known this would excite even more suspicion.

"As a matter of fact, it seems to be acting kind of wonky today," he said, patting his jacket pocket.

"Better have it checked out. Or get yourself issued a new one."

"Right away."

"Is there something the matter, Lieutenant?"

The question was asked so quickly on the heels of the last one that D'Agosta was momentarily taken aback. "Sir?"

"I mean, with your mother. Is everything all right?"

"Oh. Oh, yes. The prognosis is better than I'd hoped. Thank you for asking."

"And you're okay with being back on the job?"

"Completely okay, Captain."

The elevator slowed, but Singleton still held D'Agosta's gaze. "That's good," he said. "That's good to hear. Because the truth is, Vincent, I'd rather have somebody not here at all than have him only half here. You know what I mean?"

D'Agosta nodded. "Yes, I do."

Singleton smiled faintly as the doors opened. Then he extended one hand. "After you, Lieutenant."

Twenty-six

MARGO HESITATED at the door to Menzies's office, took a deep breath, and knocked. The door was answered by Menzies himself; he'd done away with the prerogative of a secretary years before, complaining it distracted him. He smiled, nodded, and stepped aside, gesturing for her to enter.

She knew the office well. During her first stint at the museum as a graduate student, it had been the office of Menzies's predecessor, her old thesis adviser, Dr. Frock. Back then it had been stuffed with Victorian furniture, fossils, and curiosities. With Menzies, it seemed more spacious and pleasant, the dusty fossil plaques replaced by tasteful prints, the heavy old furniture retired in favor of comfortable leather chairs. A new flat-panel iMac sat in a corner. The last rays of the setting sun came through one of the west-facing windows, cutting a parallelogram of red across the wall behind Menzies's mahogany desk.

Menzies steered Margo to an armchair, then took his own seat behind the desk. He clasped his hands together and leaned forward. "Thank you for coming at such short notice, Margo."

"No problem."

"Working late, I see?"

"I've got to put *Museology* to bed this evening."

"Of course." He unclasped his hands and leaned back into the sun, his unruly white hair suddenly haloed in gold. "As you may have guessed, I asked you here because I received an answer from the board of trustees in relation to the Tano masks."

Margo adjusted herself in the armchair, tried to look confident and assertive.

He issued a long sigh. "I won't beat around the bush. We lost. The board voted to keep the masks."

Margo felt herself go rigid. "I can't tell you how sorry I am to hear that."

"I'm sorry, too. Lord knows I gave it my best shot. Collopy was not unsympathetic, but the issue hit a wall with the trustees. Most of them are lawyers and bankers who have as much knowledge of anthropology as I have of writs or currency futures. Unfortunately, the world is such that they can presume to tell us what to do, and not vice versa. Frankly, I don't find the outcome surprising in the least."

Margo could see that the usually even-tempered curator was nettled. She had been hoping that the trustees, despite all indications to the contrary, would do the right thing. It seemed so obvious to her. But then again, it wasn't even obvious to other members of her department, so how could she expect a bunch of Wall Street lawyers to understand?

Menzies leaned on the table, looking at her intently. "This puts you rather more in the hot seat than before."

"I realize that."

"There's going to be a lot of pressure on you not to publish this editorial. They'll say the decision's been made, it's done—why stir up trouble?"

"I'm publishing, anyway."

"That's what I thought you'd say. Margo, I want you to know that I'm behind you one hundred percent. But you must be realistic and expect some fallout."

"I'm ready. *Museology*'s been an independent voice in museum affairs for more than a century, and I'm not about to knuckle under—not with my first issue."

Menzies smiled. "I admire your spirit. But there's another complication I must share with you."

"And what's that?"

"The Tanos are planning a cross-country protest caravan, due to arrive at the museum the night of the opening. It isn't just to call attention to their demands, but ostensibly to 'call back the lost souls of the masks' or something along those lines. They're going to stage an all-night religious ceremony and dances on Museum Drive, directly outside the museum. The trustees received notice earlier today."

Margo frowned. "The press is going to eat it up."

"Indeed."

"The administration's going to be embarrassed."

"Undoubtably."

"The opening's going to be total chaos."

"Without question."

"God, what a mess."

"My sentiments exactly."

There was a long pause. Finally, Menzies spoke. "You do what you have to do. Academic freedom is a critical issue in these parlous times. May I venture a piece of advice?"

"Please."

"Don't speak to the press—*at all*. When they come calling, politely refer them to the editorial you wrote and tell them that's all you have to say on the matter. The museum can't fire you over the editorial, but you can bet they'll be looking for another reason. Lie low, keep your mouth shut, and don't give it to them."

Margo rose. "Dr. Menzies, I thank you more than I can say."

The man smoothed down his unruly mane and rose as well, taking Margo's hand. "You're a brave woman," he said with a smile of admiration.

Twenty-seven

A LIGHT RAP SOUNDED on the glass of the office door. Laura Hayward, who'd been peering intently at her computer screen, sat up in surprise. For a ridiculous moment, she thought it might be D'Agosta, suitcase in hand, offering to take her home. But it was just the Guatemalan cleaning lady, armed with mop and pail, smiling and nodding her head.

"Is okay I clean?" she asked.

"Sure." Hayward wheeled away from her desk to allow the woman access to her wastebasket. She glanced up at the clock: almost 2:30 in the morning. So much for getting to bed early. But all of a sudden, she found she had a lot to do—anything to avoid going back to her empty apartment.

She waited until the woman had gone, then wheeled back to the terminal, scrolling through the federal database once again. But it was really just a perfunctory check: she had what she needed, for now.

After a few more moments, she turned to her desk. Messy on the best of days, it was now awash in computer printouts, manila folders, SOC photographs, CD-ROMs, faxes, and index cards—the results of her search of recent unsolved homicides meeting certain criteria. The papers formed a vague sort of pile. On a far corner of the desk, neater and very much smaller, sat another pile containing only three folders. Each had been labeled with a name: *Duchamp. Decker. Hamilton.* All acquaintances of Pendergast. And now all dead.

Duchamp and Decker: one a friend of Pendergast, the other a colleague. Was it really a coincidence they were murdered within days of each other?

Pendergast had disappeared in Italy—under strange and almost unbelievable circumstances, as related by D'Agosta. There were no witnesses to his death, no body, no proof. Seven weeks later, three acquaintances of his were brutally murdered, one after the other. She glanced at the pile. For all she knew, there might be other victims whose connections to Pendergast she had not yet uncovered. Three was troubling enough.

What the hell was going on here?

She sat for a moment, tapping the small pile of folders restlessly. Then she pulled out the one marked *Hamilton,* opened it, reached for her phone, and dialed a long-distance number.

The phone rang seven, eight, nine times. At last, someone picked up. There was a silence so long Hayward thought she'd been disconnected. Then, heavy breathing and a slurred, sleep-heavy voice came on.

"Somebody'd better be dying."

"Lieutenant Casson? I'm Captain Hayward of the NYPD."

"I don't care if you're Captain Kangaroo. You know what time it is in New Orleans?"

"It's an hour later in New York, sir. I apologize for the

late call, but it's important. I need to ask you a few questions about one of your cases."

"Damn it all, can't it wait until morning?"

"It's the Hamilton murder. Torrance Hamilton, the professor."

There was a long, exasperated sigh. "What about it?"

"Do you have any suspects?"

"No."

"Any leads?"

"No."

"Evidence?"

"Precious little."

"What, exactly?"

"We have the poison that killed him."

Hayward sat up. "Tell me about it."

"It's as nasty as they come—a neurotoxin similar to what you find in certain spiders. Only this stuff was synthetic and highly concentrated. A designer poison. It gave our chemists quite a thrill."

Hayward tucked the phone under her chin and began to type. "And the effects?"

"Leads to brain hemorrhaging, encephalitic shock, sudden dementia, psychosis, grand mal seizures, and death. I've had a medical education from this case you wouldn't believe. Happened right in front of his class at Louisiana State University."

"Must've been quite a scene."

"You're not kidding."

"How'd you isolate the poison?"

"We didn't need to. The killer thoughtfully left us a sample. On Hamilton's desk."

Hayward stopped typing. "*What?*"

"Seems he walked, bold as brass, into Hamilton's temporary office and left it on the desk. Right while the old guy was delivering the last lecture of his life. He'd spiked Hamilton's coffee with it half an hour earlier, which means he'd been on the premises for a while. The perp left it there in plain sight, like he was sending some kind of message. Or maybe it was just a taunt to the police."

"Any suspects?"

"None. Nobody noticed anybody going in or out of Hamilton's office that morning."

"Is this information public? About the poison, I mean."

"That it was poison, yes. As to what kind, no."

"Any other evidence? Latents, footprints, anything?"

"You know how it is, the SOC team picks up a shitload of crap that has to be analyzed, hardly any of it relevant. With one possible exception: a recently shed human hair with root, enough to get a DNA reading. Doesn't match Hamilton's DNA, or his secretary's, or anyone else's who frequented the office. Kind of an unusual color—secretary said she couldn't recall any recent visitors with that hair color."

"Which was?"

"Light blond. Ultra-light blond."

Hayward felt her heart suddenly pounding in her chest.

"Hello? Are you still there?"

"I'm here," said Hayward. "Can you fax me the evidence list and the DNA data?"

"Sure can."

"I'll call your office first thing, leave my fax number."

"No problem."

"One other thing. I assume you're investigating Hamilton's past, his acquaintances, that sort of business."

"Naturally."

"Run across the name Pendergast?"

"Can't say I have. Is this a lead?"

"Take it for what you will."

"All right, then. But do me a favor—next time, call me during the day. I'm a lot more charming awake."

"You were charming enough, Lieutenant."

"I'm from the South—I suppose it's genetic."

Hayward replaced the phone in its cradle. For a long time, perhaps ten minutes, she remained motionless, staring at it. Then, slowly and deliberately, she replaced the file marked *Hamilton,* picked up the one marked *Decker,* lifted the phone again, and began to dial.

Twenty-eight

A NURSE—TALL, SLENDER, wizened, dressed in black with white shoes and stockings, a real Addams Family creation—stuck her head out from behind a mahogany door. "The director will see you now, Mr. Jones."

Smithback, who'd been cooling his heels in a long hallway on the second floor of River Oaks, jumped so fast he sent the antimacassar flying. "Thanks," he said hastily as he patted it back on the chair.

"This way." And ushering Smithback through the doorway, she began leading him down another one of the mansion's dim, ornate, and seemingly endless corridors.

It had been surprisingly difficult to secure an audience with the director. It seemed "guests" often demanded to see Dr. Tisander, usually to announce that the walls were whispering to them in French or to demand that he stop beaming commands into their heads. The fact that Smithback had been unwilling to divulge the matter he wished to see the director about had made things even more difficult. But Smithback had insisted. Last night's dinner with Throckmorton, and the stroll around the manor house that had followed—with sidelong glances at the shuffling, empty-eyed waxworks and glum-looking fossils inhabiting the library and the various parlors—had been the final straw. Pendergast's concern was all very well, but he simply couldn't face the thought of another day—or another night—in this creepy mausoleum.

Smithback had worked it all out. He'd get a hotel room in Jersey City, take the PATH train to work, stay well away from Nora until all this blew over. He could take care of himself. He'd explain it all to the director. They couldn't very well keep him here against his will.

He followed the tiny figure of the nurse down the endless corridor, passing rows of closed doors bearing gold-leaf numbers. At some point, two burly orderlies had slipped into step behind him. At last, the corridor ended in a particularly grand door bearing the single word *Director.* The nurse knocked on it, then stepped aside, gesturing for Smithback to enter.

Smithback thanked her and stepped through. Beyond lay an elegant suite of rooms dressed in dark wood, illuminated by sconces. A fire flickered in an ornate marble fireplace. Sporting prints decorated the walls. The rear wall of the main room was dominated by a bow window, which afforded a view of the wintry landscape beyond. There were no bookshelves or anything else to suggest this was the office of a hospital director, although through one of the two side doors of the suite, Smithback made out what looked like a medical library.

In the center of the room was a huge desk, surfaced in glass, with heavy, eagle-claw feet. Behind the desk sat Dr. Tisander, writing busily with a fountain pen. He looked up briefly, gave Smithback a warm smile.

"How nice to see you, Edward. Have a seat."

Smithback seated himself. For a minute or so, the only

sound in the room was the crackle of the fire, the scratch of the pen. Then Tisander placed the pen back into its desk set, blotted the paper, and set it aside. He leaned back in his heavy leather chair and smiled confidentially, giving Smithback his utmost attention.

"There, that's finished. Tell me what's on your mind, Edward. How's the adjustment to life at River Oaks?" His voice was low and mellifluous, and the kindly lines of his face were smoothed by age. He had a domed forehead, from which white hair arose in a gravity-defying leonine shock not unlike Einstein's.

Smithback noticed that the two orderlies were standing against the wall behind him.

"Can I offer you any refreshment? Seltzer? Diet soda?"

"Nothing, thanks." Smithback gestured at the orderlies. "Do they have to be here?"

Tisander gave a sympathetic smile. "One of the house rules, alas. Just because I'm the director of River Oaks doesn't mean I'm above its rules."

"Well, if you're sure they can be trusted to keep quiet."

"I have absolute confidence in them." Tisander nodded encouragingly, gestured for Smithback to proceed.

Smithback leaned forward. "You know all about me, why I'm here, I assume."

"Naturally." A warm, concerned smile lit up the director's wise features.

"I agreed to come here for protection, for my own safety. But I have to tell you, Dr. Tisander, that I've changed my mind. I don't know how much you know about this killer who's supposedly after me, but bottom line, I can take care of myself. I don't need to be here any longer."

"I see."

"I've got to get back to my job in New York at the *Times*."

"And why is that?"

Smithback was encouraged by Dr. Tisander's receptiveness. "I was working on a very important story, and if I don't get back there, I'll lose it to another reporter. I can't afford that. This is my *career*. A lot's at stake here."

"Tell me about this story you're working on."

"It's about the Duchamp murder—you know it?"

"Tell me about it."

"A killer hung an artist named Duchamp out of a highrise window, dropped him through the glass roof of a restaurant. This is one of those sensational stories that don't come along every day."

"Why do you say that?"

"The bizarre mode of death, the prominence of the victim, the fact that the killer seems to have escaped all detection—it's a super story. I *can't* let it go."

"Can you be more specific?"

"The details aren't important. I need to get out of here."

"The details are always important."

Smithback's feeling of encouragement began to evaporate. "It isn't just my job. There's my wife. Nora. She thinks I'm in Atlantic City undercover, working another story, but I'm sure she's worried about me. If I could just get out and call her, let her know I'm all right. We've only been married a few months. Surely, you understand."

"I certainly do." The director was listening with utmost sympathy and attention.

Smithback, encouraged anew, went on. "This supposed killer who's after me, I'm not concerned about him. I can look out for myself. I don't need to hide up here any longer, pretending to be some nutcase."

Dr. Tisander nodded again.

"So, anyway, that's it. Even though I was placed in here with the best of intentions, the fact is, I can't stay a moment longer." He rose. "Now, if you'd be so kind as to call for a car? I'm sure that Agent Pendergast will cover the cost. Or I'll be happy to send you a check once I get back to New York. He took away my wallet and credit cards on the way up here." He remained standing.

For a moment, the room was silent. Then the director sat forward slowly, leaned his arms on the desk, and interlaced his fingers. "Now, Edward," he began in his calm, kindly voice, "as you know—"

"And no more of this Edward business," Smithback interrupted with a flare of irritation. "The name's Smithback. William Smithback Jr."

"Please allow me to continue." A pause, another sympathetic smile. "I'm afraid I cannot accede to your request."

"This isn't a request: it's a demand. I'm telling you, I'm leaving. You can't keep me here against my will."

Tisander cleared his throat patiently. "Your care has been entrusted to us. Your family has signed papers to that effect. You've been committed here for a period of observation and treatment. We're here to help you, and to do that, we need time."

Smithback stared incredulously. "Excuse me, Dr. Tisander, but do you think we could dispense with the cover?"

"What cover might that be, Edward?"

"*I'm not Edward!* Jesus. I know what you've been told, and there's no need for this pretense any longer. I need to get back to my job, to my wife, to my *life*. I tell you, I'm not worried about any killer. I'm leaving here. Now."

Dr. Tisander's face retained its kindly, patient smile. "You are here, Edward, because you are ill. All this talk of a job with the *New York Times,* about a cover story, about being hunted by a killer—that's what we're here to help you with."

"What?" Smithback spluttered again.

"As I said, we know a great deal about you. I have a file two feet thick. The only way for you to get better is to face the truth, to abandon these delusions and fantasies, this dreamworld you inhabit. You've never had a job at the *Times* or anyplace else. You're not married. There's no killer after you."

Smithback slowly sank back into his chair, holding on to the arms for support. A terrible chill came over him. Pendergast's words on the drive up from New York City returned to him, pregnant with ominous new meaning: *The director knows all about you. He's fully informed, he has all the necessary documents.* Smithback realized that, despite what he'd assumed—despite what Pendergast implied—the director was *not* in on the deception. The "necessary documents" were probably legal papers of commitment. The full scope of Pendergast's plan to protect him lay suddenly revealed. He couldn't leave even if he wanted to. And everything he said—all his protestations and denials and talk of a killer—only confirmed what the director had learned from reading his case files: that he was delusional. He swallowed, tried to sound as reasonable and sane as possible.

"Dr. Tisander, let me explain. The man who brought me up here, Special Agent Pendergast? He gave me a false identity, put me here in order to protect me from a killer. All those papers you have are forged. It's all a ruse. If you don't believe me, call the *New York Times*. Ask them to fax up a picture of me, a description. You'll see that I'm William Smithback. Edward Jones doesn't exist."

He stopped, realizing how crazy it must all sound. Dr. Tisander was still listening to him, smiling, giving him his full attention—but now Smithback recognized the nuances of that expression. It was pity, mixed perhaps with a faint expression of that relief with which the sane view the insane. That same expression had no doubt been on his own face at dinner last night as he listened to Throckmorton talk about a business meeting with God.

"Look," he began again. "Surely, you've heard of me, read my books. I've written three best-selling novels: *Relic, Reliquary,* and *Thunderhead.* If you have them in your library, you can see for yourself. My picture's on the back of all three."

"So now you're a best-selling author as well?" Dr. Tisander allowed his smile to widen slightly. "We don't stock our library with best sellers. They pander to the lowest common denominator of reader and—worse— tend to overexcite our guests."

Smithback swallowed, tried to make himself sound the soul of sanity and reason. "Dr. Tisander, I understand that I must sound crazy to you. If you would please allow me to make one call with that phone on your desk—just one—I'll show you otherwise. I'll talk to my wife or my editor at the *Times.* Either one will immediately confirm I'm Bill Smithback. Just one call—that's all I ask."

"Thank you, Edward," said Tisander, rising. "I can see

you'll have a lot to discuss with your therapist at your next session. I have to get back to work."

"Damn you, *make the call!*" Smithback exploded, leaping to his feet and lunging for the phone. Tisander jumped back with amazing quickness, and Smithback felt his arms seized from behind by the two orderlies.

He struggled. "I'm not crazy! You cretin, can't you tell I'm as sane as you are? Make the frigging call!"

"You'll feel better once you're back in your room, Edward," the director said, settling back in his chair, composure returning. "We will speak again soon. Please don't be discouraged; it's often difficult to transition to a new situation. I want you to know that we're here to help."

"No!" Smithback cried. "This is ridiculous! This is a *travesty*! You can't do this to me—"

Howling in protest, Smithback was gently—but firmly—escorted from the office.

Twenty-nine

HILE MARGO was in the kitchen preparing dinner, Nora took a moment to look around the woman's unexpectedly large and elegant apartment. An upright piano stood against one wall, with some Broadway show tunes propped up on the music stand; next to it hung a number of nineteenth-century zoological engravings of odd animals. A set of shelves against one wall was packed with books, and a second set of shelves contained an assortment of interesting objects: Roman coins, an Egyptian glass perfume bottle, a small collection of bird's eggs, arrowheads, an Indian pot, a piece of gnarled driftwood, a fossilized crab, seashells, a couple of bird skulls, some mineral specimens, and a gold nugget—a miniature cabinet of curiosities. Hanging on the far wall was what Nora recognized as an exceptionally fine Eyedazzler Navajo rug.

It said something about Margo, Nora thought—that she was a more interesting person than she first appeared. And she had a lot more money than Nora had expected. This was no cheap apartment, and in a co-op building, no less.

Margo's voice echoed out of the kitchen. "Sorry to abandon you, Nora. I'll just be another minute."

"Can't I help?"

"No way, you relax. Red or white?"

"I'll drink whatever you're drinking."

"White, then. We're having fish."

Nora had already been savoring the smell of salmon poaching in a delicate court bouillon wafting from the kitchen. A moment later, Margo came in carrying a platter with a beautiful piece of fish, garnished with dill and slices of lemon. She set it down, returned to the kitchen, and came back with a cool bottle of wine. She filled Nora's glass and then her own, then sat down.

"This is quite a dinner," said Nora, impressed not only with the cooking but with the trouble Margo had gone to.

"I just thought, with Bill away on assignment and the show coming up, maybe you needed a break."

"I do, but I didn't expect anything quite this nice."

"I like to cook, but I rarely have the opportunity—just like I never seem to have time to meet guys." She sat down with a wry smile, brushing her short brown hair from her face with a quick gesture. "So how's the show going?"

"This is the first night in a week that I've gotten out of there before midnight."

"Ouch."

"We're down to the wire. I don't see how they're going to make it, but everyone who's been through this before swears they always pull through in the end."

"I know how that goes. I have to get back to the museum tonight as it is."

"Really?"

Margo nodded. "To put the next issue of *Museology* to bed."

"My God, Margo. Then you shouldn't be wasting time making me supper."

"Are you kidding? I had to get out of that dusty old heap, even if only for a few hours. Believe me, this is a treat for me as well." She cut a piece of salmon and served Nora, then served herself, adding some spears of perfectly cooked asparagus and some wild rice.

Nora watched her arrange the food, wondering how she could have been so wrong about a person. It was true Margo had come on rather strong in their first few encounters, brittle and defensive, but outside of the museum she seemed a different person, with a largeness of spirit that surprised Nora. Margo was trying hard to make up for her nasty comment in the staff meeting, going beyond the generous apology she had already made to treat Nora to a home-cooked dinner.

"By the way, I just wanted you to know that I'm going ahead with that editorial. It may be a lost cause, but it's just something I feel I have to do."

Nora felt a sense of admiration. Even with Menzies's support, it was a gutsy move. She herself had gone up against the museum administration, and it was no cakewalk—some of them could be extremely vindictive.

"That's awfully brave of you."

"Well, I don't know about bravery. It's sheer stupidity, really. I said I was going to do it, and now I feel like I *have* to, even though the trustees have already ruled against me."

"And your first issue, too."

"First and perhaps last."

"I meant what I said earlier. Even though I don't agree

with you, I support your right to publish. You can count on me. I think everyone in the department would agree, except maybe Ashton."

Margo smiled. "I know. And I really appreciate that, Nora."

Nora sipped the wine. She glanced at the label: a Vermentino, and a very good one. Bill, an inveterate wine snob, had taught her a lot over the last year or two.

"It's tough being a woman in the museum," she said. "While things are a lot better than they used to be, you still don't see a lot of female deans or departmental heads. And if you look at the board of trustees, well, it's basically made up of socially ambitious lawyers and investment bankers, two-thirds of them male, with little real interest in science or public education."

"It's discouraging that a top museum like this can't do better."

"It's the way of the world." Nora took a bite of the salmon. It was good, just about the best she'd tasted.

"So tell me, Nora, how did you and Bill meet? I knew him at the museum back when I was still a student. He didn't seem like the marrying sort. I was fond of him, despite everything—though I'd never let him know that. He was quite a character."

"*Fond* of him? When I first saw him, I thought he was the biggest jerk I'd ever met." She smiled at the memory. "He was in a limo, signing books in the god-awful town of Page, Arizona."

Margo laughed. "I can just see it. Funny, he tends to make a bad first impression, until you realize he's got a heart of gold . . . and the courage of a lion to match."

Nora nodded slowly, a little surprised at this insight. "It took me a while to figure that out, though, to cut through his 'intrepid reporter' pose. We're very different, Bill and I, but I think that helps in a marriage. I couldn't stand being married to someone like me—I'm way too bossy."

"Me, too," said Margo. "What were you doing in Page, Arizona?"

"That's a story. I was leading an archaeological expedition into the canyon country of Utah, and Page was our rendezvous point."

"Sounds fascinating."

"It was. Too fascinating, as it turned out. Afterwards I took a job at the Lloyd Museum."

"No kidding! So you were there when it folded?"

"It more or less folded even before it opened. Palmer Lloyd supposedly went off the deep end. But by that point I'd burned my bridges, and the upshot was I was out of work again. So I landed a job here."

"Well, the Lloyd Museum's loss is our gain."

"You mean, the diamond hall," Nora said jokingly. When the plans to open the Lloyd Museum fell apart, the New York Museum of Natural History had swooped down and—with the help of a huge donation by a wealthy patron—purchased Palmer Lloyd's world-renowned diamond collection for their own gem halls.

Margo laughed. "Don't be silly. I'm talking about you."

Nora took another sip of wine. "How about you, Margo? What's your background?"

"I worked here as a graduate student in ethnopharmacology. That was during the time of the museum murders—the ones Bill wrote up in that first book of his. Did you read it?"

"Are you kidding? One of the prerequisites of dating

Bill was reading all his books. He didn't actually *insist* on it, but the hints came thick and fast."

Margo laughed.

"From what I read," Nora said, "you've had some pretty amazing adventures."

"Yeah. Who says science is boring?"

"What brought you back to the museum?"

"After getting my doctorate, I went to work for the pharmaceutical conglomerate GeneDyne. I did it to please my mother, really: she'd desperately wanted me to go into the family business, which I absolutely refused to do. Working for GeneDyne, making lots of money in a corporate environment, was like throwing her a bone. Poor Mom. She liked to say she couldn't fathom why I wanted to spend my life studying people with bones through their noses. Anyway, the money was great, but the corporate world just wasn't to my liking. I guess I'm not a team player—or an ass-kisser. Then one day Hugo Menzies called. He knew of my earlier work at the museum, and he'd come across some of my GeneDyne research papers on traditional Khoisan medicine. He wondered if I'd ever consider coming back to the museum. The position at *Museology* had just opened up and he wanted me to apply. So I did, and here I am." She pointed to Nora's plate. "Seconds?"

"Don't mind if I do."

Margo placed another piece of salmon on her plate, took a little more for herself. "I don't suppose you've heard about the Tano cross-country march," she said, eyes on her plate.

Nora looked up sharply. "No. Nothing."

"The museum is trying to keep it under wraps, hoping it won't come off. But I think that since you're one of the curators of the show, you should know about it. The Tanos have begun a sort of protest caravan from New Mexico to New York to ask for the return of those masks. They plan to set up in front of the museum the night of the opening, perform dances, sing songs, and hand out leaflets."

"Oh, no," Nora groaned.

"I managed to speak to the leader of the group, a religious elder. He was a very nice man, but he was also extremely firm about what they were doing and why. They believe there's a spirit inside each mask, and the Tanos want to placate them—to let them know they haven't been forgotten."

"But on opening night? It'll be a disaster."

"They're sincere," Margo said gently.

Nora glanced at her, a retort already on her lips. Then she softened. "I suppose you're right."

"I really did try to talk them out of it. Anyway, I only mention this because I figured you might appreciate a heads-up."

"Thanks." Nora thought for a moment. "Ashton's going to have a shit-fit."

"How can you stand working with that man? What a dork."

Nora burst out laughing, amazed at Margo's directness. It was, of course, true. "You should see him these days, running around the exhibition, yelling at everyone, waving his hands, the wattle on his forearms flapping back and forth."

"Stop! I don't want to picture it."

"And then Menzies comes through, and with a quiet word here and a nod there, he gets more accomplished in five minutes than Ashton does in a whole morning."

"Now, there's a lesson in management." Margo pointed at Nora's glass. "Another?"

"Please."

She filled up both their glasses, then raised hers. "Too bad Menzies's soft-spoken approach doesn't yet work for us women. So here's to you and me, Nora, kicking ass in that fossilized pile."

Nora laughed. "I'll drink to that."

And they clinked glasses.

Thirty

IT WAS EXACTLY TWO in the morning when Smithback cracked open the door of his room. Holding his breath, he glanced out through the narrow gap. The third-floor corridor was deserted and dark. Easing the door open still farther, he ventured a look in the other direction.

Deserted, as well.

Smithback closed the door again, leaned against it. His heart pounded in his chest, and he told himself it was because he'd been waiting so long for this moment. He had lain in bed for hours, feigning sleep, all the while putting the finishing touches on his plan. Earlier in the evening, there had been the occasional hushed footfall outside; around eleven, a nurse had looked in on him and—seeing him motionless in bed—left him to sleep. Since midnight, there had been no sound at all outside the door.

Smithback grasped the door handle again. It was time to put his plan into action.

After his outburst with the director, Smithback had been summoned to dinner that evening as usual. He was shown to a seat and given a menu as if nothing had happened—it seemed that delusional outbursts were par for the course at River Oaks. After dinner, he'd put in his requisite hour of work detail in the kitchen, returning perishable goods to the walk-in refrigerators of the rambling kitchen complex on the mansion's first floor.

It was while on duty Smithback had managed to purloin a key to the basement.

Though he'd worked only two shifts, Smithback already had a pretty good sense of how the kitchen operated. Deliveries came in through a loading dock in the back of the mansion, and were then brought through the basement and up into the kitchen. Security at River Oaks was a joke: half the kitchen staff seemed to have keys to the basement, from the head chef on down to the dishwashers, and the door was always being unlocked, opened, and relocked during working hours. When the sous chef had gone down to get a piece of equipment, Smithback seized his chance and—when nobody was looking—pocketed the key that had been left in the lock. The chef had come back up, grunting under the weight of a vertical broiler, the key completely forgotten.

It had been that easy.

Now Smithback tensed, preparing to open his door again. He was wearing three shirts, a sweater, and two pairs of pants, and was sweating profusely. It was a necessary precaution: if everything went according to plan, he had a long, cold ride ahead of him.

While on duty in the kitchen, he'd learned that the first food service truck arrived at the loading dock at 5:30 A.M. If he could make his way through the basement, wait until the truck arrived, and then sneak into its rear compartment just before it departed, nobody would be the wiser. Two hours or more would pass until his absence was discovered—and by then he'd be well on his way back to New York, beyond the grasp of Dr. Tisander and his legion of creepy, black-uniformed nurses.

He cracked the door open again. Deathly silence. He opened it wider, then slipped out into the corridor and closed it noiselessly behind him.

He glanced over his shoulder, then began making his way cautiously down the corridor toward the landing, keeping close to the walls. He stood little chance of being spotted: the chandeliers were dimmed and their amber pools of light faint. The landscapes and portraits hanging on the walls were dark, indistinguishable rectangles. The soft carpeting was a river of maroon so deep it looked almost black.

It was the work of five minutes to reach the landing. Here the light was a little brighter and he hung back, listening for the sound of footsteps on the stairway. He took a step, then another, listening intently.

Nothing.

Gliding forward, hand on the banister, Smithback made his way down, ready to dart back up the stairs at the first sign of an encounter. Reaching the second-floor landing, he retreated to a dark corner, crouching behind a sideboard. Here he paused to reconnoiter. The landing widened into four corridors: one leading to the dining room, another to the library and west parlor, the others to treatment areas and administrative offices. This floor seemed as silent and deserted as the first, and Smithback, encouraged, began creeping out.

From down the administrative hallway came the sound of a closing door.

Quickly, he darted back to his hiding place, crouched down, and waited.

He heard a key turning in a lock. Then, for perhaps a

minute, nothing more. Had somebody been locking himself *inside* an office? Or out?

He waited another minute. Still nothing.

Just as he was gathering himself to rise again, someone came into view from the darkness of the administrative corridor: an orderly, walking slowly, hands clasped behind him. The man was looking from left to right as he strolled, as if checking that all doors were properly closed.

Smithback shrank back farther into the darkness behind the sideboard, not moving, not even breathing, as the man walked across the far side of the landing and vanished down the corridor leading to the library.

Smithback waited, motionless, another five minutes. Then, keeping low, he made his way down the staircase to the first floor.

Here it seemed even gloomier. After making sure nobody was in sight, Smithback darted down the wide corridor that led to the kitchen.

It was the work of thirty seconds to reach the heavy double doors. Taking one last look over his shoulder, he pushed against the door, preparing to back into the kitchen.

The door didn't budge.

Smithback turned to face it, pressed harder.

Locked.

Shit. This was something he hadn't anticipated: a door that was never locked during the day.

He sounded his pocket for the basement key, hoping against hope it would open the kitchen door as well. No luck.

He glanced over his shoulder again, disappointment and a rising despair flooding over him. It had been such a good plan. And he'd been so close to getting out. To be thwarted like this . . .

Then he paused. There might—just *might*—still be a chance.

Cautiously, he made his way back to the landing. He peered up, straining for any sound, but the velvety darkness remained silent. Noiselessly, he crept up the stairway to the second floor, flitted across the landing, and entered the dining room.

The vast, ghostly space seemed sepulchral in its stillness. A few bars of pale moonlight slanted in through tall windows, bathing the room in an eerie, almost phosphorescent illumination. Smithback threaded his way quickly between the tables—already laid for breakfast—until he reached the rear. Here, a decorative partition ran parallel to the wall, concealing the service ports and waiters' stations behind. Smithback ducked behind the partition and—now in deeper darkness—moved carefully toward his destination: the dumbwaiter, covered by a four-by-three-foot metal panel set into the back wall.

Slowly, careful to make no noise, Smithback grasped the metal panel and pulled it open. Inside was an empty shaft. A heavy rope, mounted to a pulley mechanism on the chute's ceiling, vanished in inky depths below.

Smithback couldn't help but smile.

During his kitchen duty, he'd seen gray tubs of silverware and dirty dishes come down from the dining room via this same dumbwaiter. Now, with any luck, it would carry a very different cargo.

There were a series of buttons beside the access panel, used to raise and lower the dumbwaiter. Smithback peered at them in the faint illumination, then reached out to press the up button. He'd bring the thing up from the kitchen, clamber in, and descend . . .

Then he froze. The motor would make a lot of noise in the stillness. And there was the faintest chance somebody might still be inside the kitchen: the last thing he wanted was to betray his presence.

Leaning forward, he grasped the heavy rope, gave one or two exploratory tugs, and then—with a grunt—began to haul upward with all his might.

It took ages to hoist the dumbwaiter from the kitchen below. By the time he was done, Smithback was gasping and puffing, his triple layer of shirts soaked in sweat. He paused to rest a moment and look around. Still nobody.

Returning his attention to the dumbwaiter, he clambered inside, squeezing his long limbs into its narrow confines. He pulled the access panel closed behind him.

Utter darkness.

Sitting inside the dumbwaiter, knees up around his ears, Smithback realized there was no easy way to lower the device. Then he discovered that, by placing his hands against the front wall of the chute and exerting upward pressure, he could force the dumbwaiter down, inch by inch. It was blind, sweaty, exhausting work, but in a few minutes he felt his hands brushing against the steel frame of another access panel. He'd reached the first floor—and the kitchen.

He paused a moment, despite the stifling, claustrophobic space, to listen. Hearing nothing, he pushed open the panel.

The kitchen was empty. The only light came from the emergency exit signs, which threw a faint crimson light over the sprawling space.

Smithback climbed out, worked the kinks out of his

limbs, and looked around. There, set into a far wall, was the door to the basement.

He stiffened with excitement. *Almost there.* Nothing could stop him now. River Oaks might be able to incarcerate slack-jawed wackos like Roger Throckmorton, but it couldn't hold the likes of William Smithback.

The kitchen was a strange mélange of old and new. The soot-blackened walk-in fireplace was flanked by professional stainless-steel mixers large enough to hold a family. Long bunches of braided garlic cloves, peppers, and fines herbes hung from the ceiling: the head chef was a native of Brittany. The granite countertops gleamed with ranks of cookware. Dozens of top-quality German carving knives sat behind locked frames of steel and meshed glass.

But Smithback had eyes for only one thing: the heavy wooden door set in the far wall. He quickly walked over to it, unlocked it. A stone stairway led down into a well of darkness.

Gingerly, Smithback stepped down, careful not to slip on the clammy stone. He closed and locked the door behind him, shutting out the pale red glow of the exit signs and plunging the stairwell into utter darkness. He made his way downward with exquisite care, counting steps as he went.

At the twenty-fourth step he reached bottom.

He stopped to look around. But there was nothing to see: the surrounding blackness was, if anything, even more complete. The air smelled of mold and damp. For the first time, it occurred to him that he should have nicked a flashlight, made some discreet inquiries about the layout of the basement and the route to the loading dock. Maybe he should put this escape attempt off for a day or two, go back to his room, and try again another night . . .

He pushed these thoughts away. It was too late to go back: he could never force the dumbwaiter back up to the dining room. Besides, his job was at stake. And he wanted, *needed,* to talk to Nora. He had three hours until the first delivery of the morning: that was more than enough time to find his way.

He took a deep, steadying breath, then another, suppressing a faint susurrus of fear. Then, arms stretched out before him, he began to move slowly forward, sliding one foot ahead, then the other. After about a dozen steps, he made contact with a brick wall running perpendicular to his position. He turned right and began moving again, a little more quickly now, one hand brushing the wall.

There was another sound, Smithback realized, in addition to his steps: the low pattering and squeaking of rats.

His foot came in sudden contact with something on the floor, squat and heavy and immovable. He pitched forward, saving himself at the last minute from sprawling. He rose, rubbed his shin with a curse, then felt forward with his hands. Some kind of a slop sink, bolted to the brick face, barred his way. He moved carefully around it, then continued forward. The squeaking of rats died away, as if the rodents were fleeing at his approach.

The wall to his left ended abruptly, leaving him once again marooned in the black.

This was crazy. He needed to think this out.

Mentally, he went over what he knew of the layout of the mansion. As he reviewed his twistings and turnings from the base of the stairs, it seemed to him the rear must lie to the left.

The moment he turned, he saw it: a pinpoint glimmer

in the distance. It was the faintest smudge of light, a mere attenuation of black, but he made for it with the greediness of a drowning man for terra firma. As he walked, it seemed to recede before him, miragelike. The floor level rose, then fell again. At last, as he drew close, he could see that the illumination was set at eye level: a set of small green display panels fastened to an automatic thermostat of some kind. They threw a faint glow over a strange room: groined and vaulted in dressed limestone, it contained a half dozen steam boilers of polished brass and copper. They dated back to the mid-nineteenth century, at least, and had been retrofitted to the thermostat controls by bundles of colored wires. The giant boilers hissed and rumbled softly, almost as if snoring in rhythm to the sleeping mansion they warmed.

Over the sound of the boilers came again the scampering and squeaking of rats.

And then, quite distinctly, the clump of a boot on stone.

Smithback whirled around. "Who is it?" he blurted out, his voice echoing among the vaults and boilers.

No answer.

"Who's there?" Smithback said a little louder. And, as he took a slow step backward, the only response was the thudding of his heart.

Thirty-one

𝔐 ARGO MADE THE final correction to the last page of the bluelines for *Museology* and laid the proof aside. *I'm probably the only editor in the country who still works with hard copy,* she thought to herself. She settled back into her chair with a sigh and glanced at the clock: 2 A.M. exactly. She yawned, stretched, the old oaken chair creaking in protest, and rose.

The offices of *Museology* were located in a stuffy set of rooms half a flight up from the fifth floor, jammed under the eaves of the museum's west wing. A dirty skylight provided illumination during the day, but now the skylight was a rectangle of black, and the only light came from a feeble Victorian lamp that sprouted from the ancient desk like an iron mushroom.

Margo slipped the corrected bluelines into a manila envelope and wrote a quick note to the journal's production manager. She would drop them off at the museum's printing office on her way out. The journal would be printed first thing in the morning, and by noon proof copies would be going out by hand to the museum's president, the dean of science, Menzies, and the other department heads.

She shivered involuntarily, experiencing a moment of self-doubt. Was it really her duty to mount this crusade? She loved working again at the museum—she could see herself working here happily for the rest of her life. Why mess it up?

She shook her head. It was too late now, and besides, it was something she had to do. With Menzies behind her, it was doubtful they'd fire her.

She climbed down the metal stairs and entered the enormous fifth-floor corridor, stretching four city blocks, said to be the longest horizontal corridor in all of New York City. She walked along its length, heels clicking on the marble floor. At last, she stopped at the elevator, pressed the down button. A rumble sounded in the bowels of the building as the elevator rose. After about a minute, the doors opened.

She stepped in and pressed the button for the second floor, admiring as she did so the once-elegant elevator, with its nineteenth-century brass grille and fittings and its ancient bird's-eye-maple paneling, much scarred by time and use. It creaked and groaned its way back down, then stopped with a jolt, the doors rumbling open again. She made her way through a succession of old, familiar museum halls—Africa, Asian Birds, Shells, the Trilobite Alcove. The lights in the cases had been turned off, which gave them a creepy aspect, the objects inside sunken in shadow.

She paused in the gloom. For a moment, memories of a terrible night seven years earlier threatened to return. She pushed them aside and quickened her step, arriving at the unmarked door to the printing division. She slipped the bluelines into the slot, turned, then made her way back through the echoing, deserted galleries.

At the top of the second-floor stairs, she paused. When she spoke to the Tano elder, he'd told her that, if the masks *had* to be displayed, they must be placed facing in the proper directions. Each of the four masks embodied the spirit of a cardinal direction: as a consequence, it was critical that each faced its respective direction. Any other arrangement would threaten the world with chaos—or so the Tanos believed. More likely, it would threaten the museum with even more controversy, and that was something Margo was most anxious to avoid. She had forwarded the information to Ashton, but Ashton was overworked and snappish, and she had little faith he'd carried it out.

Instead of descending the stairs to the employee security entrance, Margo turned left, heading for the Sacred Images entrance. In a few moments, she arrived. The door to the exhibition had been designed to look like the portal to an ancient Hindu tomb of the Khmer style, the carved stone lintels depicting gods and demons engaged in a titanic struggle. The figures were in violent motion: flying apsaras, dancing Shivas, gods with thirty-two arms, along with demons vomiting fire and cobras with human heads. It was unsettling enough that Margo stopped, wondering if it wouldn't be better to call it a night and do this errand in the morning. But tomorrow the hall would be a madhouse again, and Ashton would be there, impeding her and—in the wake of her editorial—perhaps even denying her access.

She shook her head ruefully. She couldn't just give in to the demons of the past. If she walked away now, her fears would have won.

She stepped forward and slid her magnetic card through the reader beside the entrance door; there was a soft click of well-oiled steel disengaging, and the security light went green. She pushed the door open and entered, carefully closing it behind her and making sure the security LED returned to red.

The hall was silent and empty, lit softly by exterior spots, the cases dark. Two o'clock was too late for even the most dedicated curator. The air smelled of fresh lumber, sawdust, and glue. Most of the exhibits were in place, with only a few remaining unmounted. Here and there a curatorial cart stood loaded with objects not yet in place. The floor was strewn with sawdust, lumber, pieces of Plexiglas, and electrical wires. Margo looked around, wondering how they could possibly open in three days. She shrugged, glad the opening was Ashton's problem and not hers.

As she walked through the initial room of the exhibition, her curiosity rose despite the sense of unease. Last time, she'd been looking for Nora and hadn't bothered to pay much attention to the surroundings. Even in its unfinished state, it was clear this was going to be an exceptionally dramatic exhibit. The room was a replica of the burial chamber of the ancient Egyptian queen Nefertari, located in the Valley of the Queens in Luxor. Instead of depicting the unlooted tomb, the designers had reconstructed what the tomb might have looked like just *after* being looted. The enormous granite sarcophagus had been broken into several pieces, the inner coffins all stolen. The mummy lay to one side, a gaping hole in its chest where the looters had cut it open to steal the gold and lapis scarab that lay next to the heart as a promise of eternal life. She paused to examine the mummy, carefully protected by glass: it was the real McCoy, the label identifying it as belonging to the actual queen herself, on loan from the Cairo Museum in Egypt.

She continued to read the label, her mission temporarily forgotten. It explained that the tomb had been robbed not long after the queen's burial by the very priests who had been assigned to guard it. The thieves had been in mortal dread of the power of the dead queen and had tried to destroy that power by smashing all her grave goods in order to purge the objects of their sacred power. As a result, everything not stolen had been smashed and was lying about helter-skelter.

She ducked under a low stone archway, its dark surfaces busy with graven images, and found herself suddenly plunged underground into the early Christian catacombs beneath Rome. She was in a narrow passageway cut into the bedrock. Loculi and arcosolia radiated outward in several directions, niches in their sides packed with bones. Crude inscriptions in Latin graced some of the niches, along with carved crosses and other sacred Christian imagery. It was disturbingly naturalistic, down to the models of rats scampering around the bones.

Ashton had gone for the sensational, but Margo had to admit it was effective. This would definitely pack in the crowds.

She hastened on into a completely different space that depicted the Japanese tea ceremony. There was an orderly garden, the plantings and pebbled walkway in meticulous order. Beyond lay the *sukiya*, the tea room itself. It was a relief to enter this open, orderly space after the claustrophobia of the catacombs. The tea room was the living embodiment of purity and tranquillity, with its polished wood, paper screens, mother-of-pearl inlays, and tatamis, along with the simple accouterments of the ceremony: the iron kettle, the bamboo dipper, the linen napkin. Even so, the emptiness of it, the deep shadows and dark spaces, started to unnerve Margo again.

Time to wrap up this errand and get out.

She walked briskly through the tea room and wound her way deeper into the exhibition, passing an eclectic parade of exhibits including a dark Indian funerary lodge, a hogan filled with Navajo sand paintings, and a violent Chukchi shamanistic rite in which the shaman had to be physically chained to the ground to keep his soul from being stolen by demons.

She finally arrived at the four Kiva Society masks. They stood in a glass case in the center of the room, mounted on slender rods, each facing in a different direction. Around the circular walls had been painted a magnificent depiction of the New Mexico landscape, and each mask faced one of the four sacred mountains that surrounded Tanoland.

Margo gazed at them, awestruck anew by their power. They were amazingly evocative masks, severe, fierce, and yet at the same time overflowing with human expression. Although they were close to eight hundred years old, they looked modern in their formal abstraction. They were true masterpieces.

She glanced at her notes, then walked to the nearest wall map to orient herself. Then she moved around the central display, checking each mask—and was surprised to find that they were, in fact, facing the correct directions. Ashton, for all his bluster, had gotten it right. In fact, she grudgingly had to admit he'd put together an outstanding exhibition.

She stuffed the notes back in her purse. The silence,

the dimness, was starting to get to her. She'd take in the rest of the show some other time, in broad daylight, when the halls were bustling with people.

She had just turned to retrace her steps when she heard a loud clatter, like a board falling, in the next room.

She jumped, heart suddenly pounding in her ears. A minute passed with no further sound.

Her heart slowing again, Margo advanced to the archway and peered into the dimness of the exhibit beyond. It was a depiction of the interior of Arizona's haunting House of Hands Cave, painted by the Anasazi a thousand years ago. But the room was empty, and the quantity of cut lumber still lying around indicated that what she'd heard was just a propped-up board which had finally gotten around to falling.

She took a deep breath. The watchful stillness, the spookiness of the exhibition, had finally gotten to her. That was all. *Don't think about what happened before. The museum's changed since then, changed utterly.* She was probably in the safest place in New York City. The security had been upgraded half a dozen times since the debacle seven years ago. This latest system—still being finalized—was the best money could buy. Nobody could get into this hall without a magnetic key card, and the card reader recorded the identity of each person who passed through, as well as the time.

She turned again, preparing to walk back out of the exhibition, humming to herself as a defense against the silence. But before she had even crossed the exhibit, she was stopped again by the clatter of lumber—this time from the room ahead of her.

"Hello?" she called out, her voice unnaturally loud in the quiet hall. "Somebody there?"

There was no answer.

She decided it must be the guard making his rounds, tripping over loose boards. In the old days, the guards, having discovered the tanks of grain alcohol preservative stored in the Entomology Department, were sometimes found drunk at night. *I guess some things never change.*

Once again, she headed back in the direction of the entrance, wending her way through the dark exhibits, walking briskly, her heels making a reassuring *click-click* on the tiled floor.

With a sudden *snap!*, the exhibition was plunged into blackness.

An instant later, the emergency lights came to life, rows of fluorescent tubes set in the ceiling, popping and humming as they winked on, one by one.

Once again, she tried to calm her wildly beating heart. This was silly. It wasn't the first time she'd been in the museum during a power failure; they happened all the time in the old building. There was nothing, absolutely nothing, to worry about.

She had barely taken another step when she heard yet another clatter of lumber, this time from the room she had just passed through. It sounded almost deliberate—as if someone were deliberately trying to spook her.

"Who's there?" she asked, whirling around, suddenly angry.

But the hall behind her—a crimson-painted crypt arrayed with the cruel trappings of a black mass—was empty.

"If this is some kind of joke, I don't appreciate it."

She waited, tense as a spring, but there was no sound.

She wondered if it was just a coincidence: another board falling on its own, the exhibition settling down after a hectic day. She reached into her handbag, feeling around for something she might use as a weapon. There was nothing. In years past, following the trauma of the museum killings and their aftermath, she had taken to keeping a pistol in her bag. But this was a habit she'd dropped when she left the museum and went to work for GeneDyne. Now she cursed herself for letting down her guard.

Then she spied a box cutter, sitting on a worktable on the far side of the exhibit. She ran to it, snatched it up, and—holding it out aggressively before her—resumed her walk toward the entrance.

Another clatter, this one louder than the others, as if someone had tossed something.

Now Margo was sure there was someone else with her in the exhibition: someone deliberately trying to scare her. Was it possible it was somebody who objected to her editorial and was now trying to intimidate her? She'd find out from security who else had been in the hall and report them immediately.

She broke into a trot. She passed through the Japanese tea room and had just entered the looted Egyptian tomb when there was another sharp *snap!* This time the emergency lights went out and the windowless hall was plunged into total blackness.

She halted, almost paralyzed by sudden fear and a chilling sense of déjà vu as she recalled a similar moment in another exhibition, years earlier, in this same museum.

"Who is it?" she cried.

"It's just me," a voice said.

Thirty-two

MITHBACK FROZE, all senses on high alert. He looked left and right, eyes straining in the greenish dark. But there was no sound; no figure rushing toward him, black upon black.

Must be my imagination, he thought. The creepy place was enough to give anybody the heebie-jeebies.

Much as he hated to leave the faint light of the boiler room, he knew he had to move on. He needed to find the loading dock and—just as important—a good hiding place nearby. If the last ten minutes were any indication, it might take him a while.

He waited a good five minutes, listening, making sure the coast was clear. Then he crept back out of the vast room and, turning, began making his way toward what he thought must be the back of the mansion. The pale light faded away and he once again slowed his pace, putting his arms out in front of him, shuffling his feet gingerly so as not to bark his shins a second time.

He paused. Was that another sound? Was somebody down here with him?

Heart still hammering uncomfortably in his chest, he stopped to wait again. But he heard nothing but the faint squeak of mice and, after another minute, resumed his slow progress.

Suddenly, his hands encountered another wall: rough stone, slick with moisture. Following it to the right, he encountered a perpendicular wall, with what felt like a steel door bolted into it. His fingers probed along the jamb until they found the handle. He seized it, turned.

The handle refused to move.

Taking a deep breath, he yanked with all his might. No good: the thing wouldn't budge.

With a curse, he went back along the wall in the other direction. After about twenty paces, the wall ended and his hands groped once again on open space. He turned the corner, then stopped, his heart in his throat.

There was a sudden glow of light ahead, framing a turn in the corridor. Someone had just turned on the lights up ahead. Or had they been on all this time?

Smithback paused, frozen with indecision. That was the way he had to go, he was sure of it, and the light was welcoming. But was anyone waiting up there for him?

He crept forward, keeping close to the wall, and peered around the corner.

The corridor ahead was lit by a string of dim bulbs hanging from the ceiling. They were few and far between, and the light they shed was feeble, but at least he'd be able to see where he was going. Best of all, the corridor was empty. Nobody had turned on the lights, Smithback decided—they'd been on all along. He just hadn't noticed them at first. Or maybe he'd been too far away to catch their light.

He walked slowly down the stone corridor. On both sides, ancient doors lay open, yawning gulfs of barely penetrable murk. He paused to look into a few. A wine cellar, rows of bottles and heavy oaken kegs covered in dense cobwebs. An old storage room, wooden file cabinets bursting with yellowing documents. A billiard room, the felt of its table torn and curled. Just what you'd expect in a manor house that had been converted into an insane asylum for the rich.

Smithback walked on, confidence returning. It was a good plan. The basement couldn't go on forever. He had to be getting near the loading dock. He *had* to . . .

There it was again: that nagging sensation he was being stalked; that someone was deliberately trying to conceal the sound of their footsteps with his own.

He stopped abruptly. He couldn't be certain, but he thought he'd heard the sound of an interrupted tread, as if someone in the darkness behind had frozen in the act of taking a step. He wheeled. The corridor, at least the lighted part, stretched empty behind him.

Smithback licked his lips. "Pendergast?" he tried to say, but his throat was thick and dry and his tongue didn't want to work. Just as well, because he knew in his gut there *was* somebody back there, and it wasn't Pendergast; oh, God, no, it wasn't Pendergast . . .

He began walking forward again, heart pounding furiously. Suddenly, the pools of faint light were no longer a godsend. They were treacherous, revealing . . . And he was suddenly terribly certain somebody *had* turned on the lights, the better to see him with.

There is a killer after you. A supremely dangerous killer of almost supernatural ability . . .

He fought against the instinct to run. Panic wasn't the answer here. He needed to think this through. He needed to find a dark corner, a place where he could hide. But first he had to be sure. Absolutely sure.

He passed quickly beneath another bulb and into the interval of darkness beyond. He slowed his pace, trying to get the timing right. Then, tensing, he turned abruptly.

Behind, a dark form—cloaked, strangely muffled—shrank back from the light into the dark oblivion of the basement.

At this sight, expected yet unutterably awful, Smithback's failing nerves deserted him. He turned and ran like a frightened rabbit, tearing down the corridor, heedless of any hidden obstacles to his escape.

The sound of heavy boots closing in from behind spurred him on.

Lungs burning, Smithback tore down the corridor, beyond the last of the hanging bulbs and back into absolute, endless, protective darkness . . .

And then something cold and unyielding slammed up against him, stopping him dead. A savage pain tore through his head and chest; white light exploded in his skull; and, as consciousness fled away and he sank to the ground, his last impression was of a clawlike grasp, hard as steel, fastening onto his shoulder.

Thirty-three

HO?" Margo almost shrieked, holding the box cutter toward the sound, swinging it back and forth. "Who is it?"

"Me."

"Who is 'me' and what the hell do you want?"

"I'm looking for an honest man . . . or woman, as the case may be." The voice was small and almost effeminate in its exactitude.

"Don't you come near me," she cried, brandishing the box cutter in the blackness. She tried to calm her pounding heart and focus. This was no joker: she sensed instinctively that this man was dangerous. The emergency lights would come back on shortly; they must—it was automatic. But as the seconds ticked by, she felt her terror continue to escalate. Had the man himself cut the emergency backup? It didn't seem possible. What was going on?

Struggling to master herself, she inched forward as silently as possible, sliding her feet along the floor, stepping carefully over objects as she encountered them, poking the box cutter out in different directions. She had a vague idea of where the entrance was, and for now the man seemed to have shut up—perhaps as confounded by the darkness as she was. She reached the far wall and began feeling her way along it. Then her hands encountered the cool steel of the security door. With a flood of relief, she felt for the handle, found the card reader, pulled her card from her bag, and swiped it through.

Nothing.

As quickly as it had come, the relief ebbed away, replaced by a dull, pounding fear. *Of course:* the magnetic lock was electric and the power was off. She tried opening the door, rattling the knob and throwing her weight against it, but it didn't budge.

"When the power goes off," came the thin voice, "the security system locks everything down. You can't get out."

"Get close to me and I'll cut you!" she cried, spinning around and putting her back to the door, brandishing the box cutter at the darkness.

"You wouldn't want to do that. The sight of blood leaves me faint . . . faint with pleasure."

In the clarity of her fear, Margo realized that she had to stop responding. She had to go on the offensive. She fought to control her breathing, control her fear. She had to do something unpredictable, surprise him, turn the tables. She took a noiseless step forward.

"What does the sight of blood do to you, Margo?" came the gentle whisper.

She inched toward the voice.

"Blood is such a strange substance, isn't it? Such a perfect, exquisite color, and so teeming with life, packed with all those red and white cells and antibodies and hormones. It's a living liquid. Even spilled on a dirty museum floor, it lives on—at least for a time."

She took another step toward the voice. She was very close now. She braced herself. Then, in one desperate motion, she sprang forward and brought the box cutter around in a slashing arc; it contacted something and ripped through it. As she jumped back, she heard a stumbling noise, a muffled sound of surprise.

She waited, tensing in the blackness, hoping she'd opened up an artery.

"Brava, Margo," came the whispery voice. "I'm impressed. Why, you've ruined my greatcoat."

She began circling the voice again, intending to strike a second time. She had *him* on the defensive now. If she could wound him, preoccupy him, she'd buy herself enough time to run back into the exhibition. If she could do that, put half a dozen rooms between herself and this evil, disembodied voice, he'd never find her in the blackness. She could wait for the guards to make their next set of rounds.

There was a low, breathy chuckle. The person seemed to be circling her at the same time. "Margo, Margo, Margo. You didn't really think you'd *cut* me?"

She lunged again, her arm sweeping only air.

"Good, good," came the voice with another dry chuckle. The chuckle went on and on, hanging in the blackness, circling slowly.

"Leave me alone or I'll kill you," said Margo, surprised at how calm her voice sounded.

"What spunk!"

Instantly, Margo tossed her purse toward his voice, heard it strike, and followed up with a lightning-fast slash that met with just enough resistance to let her know she'd struck home.

"My, my, another good trick. You are far more formidable than I had supposed. And now you *have* cut me."

As she turned to run, she felt, rather than heard, a sudden movement; she threw herself sideways, but the man seized her wrist and—with one terrible twist that cracked her bones—sent the box cutter flying. She cried out, struggling despite the unbearable pain shooting up her arm. He twisted again and she screamed, lashing out with her foot, landing a punch with her free hand, but the man pulled her up against him in a brusque, horrid movement that almost caused her to faint from the pain to her broken wrist. His hand was like a steel manacle around her arm, and his hot breath, smelling faintly of damp earth, washed over her.

"You *cut* me," he whispered.

With a hard shove, he released her, stepping back. Margo fell to her knees, close to blacking out from shock and pain, holding her shattered wrist close against herself, trying to gather her wits, to determine where in the darkness the box cutter had fallen.

"Although I am a cruel man," came the voice, "I will not let you suffer."

There was another swift movement, like the rush of a giant bat above her. And then she felt a stunning, searing blow from behind that dropped her to the ground. And as she lay there, she realized, with a sense of strange disbelief, that he had driven a knife into her back; that she'd been given a mortal blow. Yet still she clawed the floor, trying to rise, the sheer force of her will bringing her to her knees. It was no use. Something warm was running down her arm now, running onto the floor, as a different kind of blackness rushed in on her from all sides. The last thing she heard, coming from a great distance as if in a dream, was a final astringent chuckle . . .

Thirty-four

LAURA HAYWARD WALKED quickly through the museum's Great Hall, the early morning light casting parallel banners through its tall bronze windows. She strode through the bands of light with purpose, as if the physical act of walking would somehow prepare her for what was to come. Beside her, almost skipping to keep up, was Jack Manetti, head of museum security. Behind them followed a silent but swift phalanx of NYPD homicide detectives and museum personnel.

"Mr. Manetti, I'm assuming the exhibition has a security system. Correct?"

"State-of-the-art. We're just completing a full overhaul."

"Overhaul? Wasn't the exhibit alarmed?"

"It was. We've got redundancies built into each zone. Strange thing is, no alarm went off."

"Then how'd the perp get in?"

"At this point, we have no idea. We've compiled a list of everyone who had access to the exhibition space."

"I'll want to talk to them all."

"Here's the list." Manetti pulled a printout from his jacket pocket.

"Good man." Hayward took it, scanned it, handed it to one of the detectives behind her. "Tell me about the system."

"It's based on magnetic keys. The system keeps track of everyone coming and going after hours. I have a register of that, as well." He handed her another document.

They rounded the corner of the Hall of Ocean Life. Hayward walked past the great blue whale, hanging ominously from the ceiling, without even a glance.

"Any key cards reported missing?"

"No."

"Can they be duplicated?"

"I'm told it's impossible."

"Someone could have borrowed a card, perhaps?"

"That's possible, although as of now all cards except the victim's are accounted for. I'll be looking into that specific question."

"So will we. Of course, the perp might be a museum employee with prior access."

"I doubt it."

Hayward grunted. She doubted it herself, but you never knew—she'd seen more than her share of certifiable lunatics wandering around this old pile. As soon as she'd heard about this case, she'd asked to be assigned, despite still being busy with the Duchamp murder. She had a theory—no, call it more of a premonition—that the two were connected. And if she was right, it was going to be big. Very big.

They passed through the Hall of Northwest Coast Indians, then stopped before the oversize portal leading to the Sacred Images exhibition. The door itself was open but taped off, and beyond, Hayward could hear the murmurings of the SOC team working the scene. "You, you,

and you"—she jabbed her finger at detectives in turn—
"pass the tape with me. The rest wait here and keep back
the curious. Mr. Manetti? You come, too."

"When Dr. Collopy arrives—?"

"This is a crime scene. Keep him out. I'm sorry."

Manetti didn't even argue. His face was the color of
putty and it was pretty clear he hadn't even had time for
his morning cup of coffee.

She ducked under the police tape, nodded to the waiting sergeant, signed his clipboard. Then she entered the
foyer of the exhibition, moving slower now, far more deliberate. SOC and forensics would have already gone
over ingress and egress, but it was always good to keep
an eye open.

The truncated group wound its way through the first
room, past almost completed exhibits, stepping over the
odd piece of lumber, and then into the exhibition's second
room: the scene of the crime itself. Here a chalk outline
delineated where the victim had fallen. There was quite a
lot of blood. The SOC photographer had already docu-
mented the scene and was awaiting any special requests
Hayward, as the investigating officer, might have. Two
members of the SOC team were still on their hands and
knees with tweezers.

She eyed the scene almost fiercely, her eye roving over
the central pool of blood, across various splatters, bloody
footprints, smears. She gestured to Hank Barris, the senior SOC officer. He rose, put away his tweezers, came
over.

"What a damn mess," she said.

"The paramedics worked on the victim for a while."

"The murder weapon?"

"A knife. It went with the victim to the hospital. You know, you can't pull it out—"

"I'm aware of that," snapped Hayward. "Did you see the original scene?"

"No. The EMTs had already messed it up by the time I arrived."

"ID on the victim?"

"Not that I know of, at least not yet. I could call the hospital."

"Any witnesses to the original scene?"

Barris nodded. "One. A technician named Enderby. Larry Enderby."

Hayward turned. "Bring him in."

"In here?"

"That's what I said."

A silence ensued while Hayward looked around, body completely still, her dark eyes the only thing moving. She scrutinized the blood splatters, making rough estimates of trajectories, speed, and origin. Slowly, a general picture of the crime began to come together in her mind.

"Captain? Mr. Enderby is ready."

Hayward turned to see a surprisingly young, pimply man with black hair and a ninety-eight-pound-weakling physique. A T-shirt, a Mets cap worn backward, and a pair of ratty jeans completed the picture.

At first, she thought his high-tops were dyed red, until she saw them closer.

A policeman ushered him forward.

"You were the first to find the victim?"

"Yes, ma'am . . . I mean . . . Officer." He was already flustered.

"You may call me Captain," she said gently. "What's your position at the museum, Mr. Enderby?"

"I'm a systems technician, grade one."

"What were you doing in the hall at three A.M.?"

The voice was high and quavery, ready to break. *Always the timidest who find the deadest,* Hayward remembered her former professor of forensic psychology at NYU joking. Hayward swallowed, tried to make her voice sympathetic. It wouldn't do to have Enderby crack up.

"Checking the install of the new security system."

"I see. Was security up and running in the hall?"

"Mostly. We're running some updated software routines, and there was a glitch. My boss—"

"His name?"

"Walt Smith."

"Proceed."

"My boss sent me down to see if the power had been cut."

"Was it?"

"Yeah. It was. Someone had cut a power cable."

Hayward glanced at Barris.

"We know about it, Captain. It appears the perp cut the cable to kill the emergency lights, the better to ambush the victim."

"So what is this new security system?" she asked, turning back to Enderby.

"Well, it's multilayered and redundant. There are motion sensors, live video feeds, crisscrossing infrared laser beams, vibration sensors, and air pressure sensors."

"Sounds impressive."

"It is. For the past six months, the museum's been upgrading the security in each hall, one after another, to the latest version of the system."

"What does that involve?"

Enderby took a deep breath. "Interfacing with the security contractors, reconfiguring the monitoring software, running a test bed, that sort of thing. All on a rigid schedule calibrated to an atomic satellite clock. And it has to happen at night, when the museum's closed."

"I see. So you came down here to check the power failure and found the body."

"That's right."

"If you can manage it, Mr. Enderby, could you look at the scene here and describe for me exactly how the victim was lying?"

"Well . . . the body . . . the body was lying just as it's outlined, one arm thrown out like you see. There was an ivory-handled knife sticking out of the small of the back, buried to the hilt."

"Did you touch or try to remove the knife?"

"No."

Hayward nodded. "The victim's right hand, was it open or closed?"

"Ah, it seems to me it was open." Enderby swallowed painfully.

"Bear with me, Mr. Enderby. The victim was moved before the photographer arrived, so all we have is your memory."

He wiped his brow with the back of his hand.

"The left foot: turned in or out?"

"Out."

"And the right?"

"In."

"Are you sure?"

"I don't think I'll ever forget. The body was kind of twisted a little."

"How so?"

"Kind of lying facedown, but with the legs almost crossed."

The act of talking seemed to be helping Enderby get a grip on himself. He was turning out to be a good witness.

"And the blood on your shoes? How'd that happen?"

Enderby stared at his shoes, eyes widening. "Oh. I . . . I rushed over and tried to help."

Hayward's respect for the young man went up a notch. "Describe your movements."

"Let's see . . . I was standing there when I saw the body. I stopped, ran over. I knelt, felt for a pulse, and I guess that's when I . . . stepped in the blood. I got blood on my hands, too, but I washed that off."

Hayward nodded, adding those facts to her mental reconstruction.

"Any pulse?"

"I don't think so. I was hyperventilating, it was hard to tell. I don't really know how to read a pulse too well. First I rang security—"

"On a house phone?"

"Yes, around the corner. Then I tried mouth-to-mouth, but within a minute, a guard arrived."

"The guard's name?"

"Roscoe Wall."

Hayward nodded to one of the detectives to note this.

"Then the paramedics came. They basically pushed me away."

Hayward nodded. "Mr. Enderby, if you could just step aside with Detective Hardcastle for a few minutes, I might have more questions."

She returned to the first room of the exhibition, looked around, then walked slowly back. A thin scattering of sawdust on the floor, despite having been stirred up, retained traces of the struggle. She bent to examine the small sprays of blood. A mental splatter analysis helped finalize her general understanding of what had happened. The victim had been ambushed in the first exhibit room of the hall. Perhaps he'd even been followed from the opposite end of the exhibition—there was a rear door, she'd been told, although it had been found secured and locked. It looked like they had circled each other for a moment. Then the killer grabbed the victim, twisted him sideways; struck him with the knife while moving fast in a lateral motion . . .

She closed her eyes a moment, visualizing the choreography of murder.

Then she reopened them, zeroing in at a tiny spot, off to one side, that she'd noticed in passing on her initial circuit of the room. She walked over and stood looking down at it: a drop of blood about the size of a dime, a quiet little drop that appeared to have fallen vertically, from a stationary subject, from a height of about five feet.

She pointed at it. "Hank, I want this entire drop taken out, floorboard and all. Photograph it in situ first. I want DNA on it, *yesterday*. Run it against all the databases."

"Sure thing, Captain."

She looked around, her eyes traveling on a tangent from the chalk outline, through the lone drop of blood, to the far wall. There she saw a large dent in the new wooden floor molding. Her eyes sharply narrowed. "And Hank?"

He looked up.

"I think you might find the victim's own weapon behind that exhibit case."

The man rose, walked over, peered behind.

"I'll be damned."

"What is it?" Hayward asked.

"A box cutter."

"Blood?"

"Not that I can see."

"Bag it and run every test in the book. And run it against that spot you just took out. You'll find a match, I'll bet my last dollar."

As she stood there, somehow unwilling to take her eyes off the scene, another thought occurred to her. "Bring Enderby back."

A moment later, Detective Hardcastle returned, Enderby in tow.

"You said you gave the victim mouth-to-mouth?"

"Yes, Captain."

"You recognized him, I assume."

"Her, not him. Yes, I did."

"Who was it?"

"Margo Green."

Hayward stiffened, as if coming to attention. "Margo Green?"

"Yes. I understand she used to be a graduate student here. Anyway, she'd returned to be editor of . . ."

His voice faded into the background. Hayward was no longer listening. She was thinking back half a dozen years to the subway murders and the famous Central Park riot, when she was a lowly T.A. cop, and to the Margo Green she had met back then—the young, feisty, and deeply courageous woman who'd risked her life and helped crack open the case.

What a shitty world it was.

Thirty-five

MITHBACK SAT GLUMLY in the same chair he had occupied the day before, feeling an unpleasant sense of déjà vu. The same fire seemed to be flickering in the ornate marble fireplace, lending a faint perfume of burning birchwood to the air; the same sporting prints decorated the walls; and the same snowy landscape presented itself through the bow windows.

Worse, the same director sat behind his gigantic desk with the same pitying, condescending smile on his well-shaven face. He was giving Smithback the reproachful-stare treatment. Smithback's head still throbbed painfully from running full tilt into a cement wall in the dark, and he felt deeply humiliated for panicking at the footsteps of a mere orderly. And he also felt like a real jerk for thinking he could beat the security system in such a ham-handed way. All he had accomplished was to confirm the director's opinion that he was a nutcase.

"Well, well, Edward," said Dr. Tisander, clasping his veined hands together. "That was quite an escapade you had last night. I do apologize if orderly Montaney gave you a start. I trust you found the medical care at our infirmary satisfactory?"

Smithback ignored the patronizing question. "What I want to know is, why was he sneaking around after me like that in the first place? I could've been killed!"

"Running into a wall? I *hardly* think so." Another genial smile. "Although you were lucky to avoid a concussion."

Smithback didn't respond. The dressing on the side of his head tightened uncomfortably whenever he moved his jaw.

"I *am* surprised at you, Edward. I thought I'd already explained it to you: just because we don't *appear* to have security doesn't mean we don't *have* security. That's the whole purpose of our facility. The security is unobtrusive, so that our guests don't feel uncomfortable."

Smithback felt irritated by the word *guest*. They were inmates, pure and simple.

"We followed your nocturnal perambulations via the infrared beams you interrupted and the motion sensors you moved past. It wasn't until you actually penetrated the basement that orderly Montaney was dispatched to tail you unobtrusively. He followed protocol to the letter. I imagine you thought you'd escape on one of the food service trucks; that's usually what they try first."

Smithback felt like leaping up and wrapping his hands around the good doctor's neck. *They? I'm not crazy, you idiot!* But he didn't. He realized now what an exquisite catch-22 he was in: the more he insisted he was sane, the more excited he became, the more he validated the doctor's opinion to the contrary.

"I just want to know how much longer I'm going to be here," he said.

"That remains to be seen. I must say, this escape attempt does not lead me to think your departure will be any time soon. It shows resistance on your part to being helped. We can't help you until we have your cooperation, Mr. Jones. And we can't release you until we've helped you. As I am fond of saying, *you* are the most important person in your cure."

Smithback balled his fists, making a supreme effort not to respond.

"I have to tell you, Edward, that another escape attempt will result in certain changes to your domestic arrangements that might not be to your liking. My advice is, accept your situation and work with us. Right from the beginning, I have sensed an unusual amount of passive-aggressive resistance on your part."

That's because I'm as sane as you are. Smithback swallowed, tried to muster an obsequious smile. He needed to be a lot more clever if he was going to escape, that much was clear.

"Yes, Dr. Tisander. I understand."

"Good, good! Now we're making progress."

There *had* to be a way out. If the Count of Monte Cristo could escape the Château d'If, William Smithback could escape from River Oaks.

"Dr. Tisander, what do I have to do to get out of here?"

"Cooperate. Let us help you. Go to your sessions, devote all your energies to getting better, make a personal commitment to cooperate with the staff and orderlies. The only way anyone leaves here is carrying a document with my signature release on it."

"The only way?"

"That's correct. I make the final decision—based, of

course, on expert medical and, if necessary, legal advice."

Smithback looked at him. "Legal?"

"Psychiatry has two masters: medicine and law."

"I don't understand."

Tisander was clearly getting into his favorite subject. His voice took on a pontifical ring. "Yes, Edward, we must deal with legal as well as medical issues. Take yourself, for instance. Your family, who love you and are concerned for your welfare, have committed you here. That's a legal as well as a medical process. It is a grave step to deprive a person of his freedom, and due process must be followed with utter scrupulousness."

"I'm sorry . . . did you say my *family*?"

"That's right. Who else would commit you, Edward?"

"You know my family?"

"I've met your father, Jack Jones. A fine man indeed. We all want to do what's right for you, Edward."

"What'd he look like?"

A puzzled expression crossed Tisander's face, and Smithback cursed himself for asking such an obviously crazy question. "I mean, when did you see him?"

"When you were brought here. He signed all the requisite papers."

Pendergast, Smithback thought. *Damn him.*

Tisander rose, held out his hand. "And now, Edward, is there anything else?"

Smithback took it. The germ of an idea had seeded itself in his mind. "Yes, one thing."

Tisander raised his eyebrows, the same condescending smile on his face.

"There's a library here, isn't there?"

"Of course. Beyond the billiard room."

"Thank you."

As he exited, Smithback caught a glimpse of Tisander settling back down at his enormous claw-footed desk, smoothing his tie, his face still wearing a self-satisfied smile.

Thirty-six

A WATERY WINTER LIGHT was fading over the river as D'Agosta reached the old door on Hudson Street. He paused for a moment, taking a few deep breaths, trying to get himself under control. He'd followed Pendergast's complicated instructions to the letter. The agent had moved yet again—he seemed determined to keep one step ahead of Diogenes—and D'Agosta wondered, with a dull curiosity, what disguise he had assumed now.

Finally, having composed himself and taken one last look around to make sure there was no one near, he tapped on the door seven times and waited. A moment later, it was opened by a man who, from all appearances, was a derelict in the last stages of addiction. Even though D'Agosta knew this was Pendergast, he was startled—once again—by the effectiveness of his appearance.

Without a word, Pendergast ushered him in, padlocked the door behind him, and led him down a dank stairwell to a noisome basement room filled by a large boiler and heating pipes. An oversize cardboard carton piled with soiled blankets, a plastic milk crate with a candle and some dishware, and a neat stack of tinned food completed the picture.

Pendergast swiped a rag from the floor, exposing an iMac G5 with a Bluetooth wireless Internet connection. Beside it lay a well-thumbed stack of papers: the photocopied case file that D'Agosta had purloined from headquarters, along with other reports that, D'Agosta assumed, were from the police dossier on the Hamilton poisoning. Clearly, Pendergast had been studying everything with great care.

"I . . ." D'Agosta didn't quite know how to begin. He felt rage take hold once again. "That bastard. That son of a *bitch*. My God, to murder Margo—"

He fell silent. Words just couldn't convey the shaking fury, turmoil, and disbelief he felt inside. He hadn't known Margo was back in New York, let alone working at the museum, but he'd known her well in years past. They'd worked together on the museum and subway murders. She'd been a brave, resourceful, intelligent woman. She hadn't deserved to go out like this: stalked and killed in a darkened exhibition hall.

Pendergast was silent as he rapped at the computer keyboard. But his face was bathed in sweat, and D'Agosta could see that was not part of the act. He was feeling it, too.

"Diogenes lied when he said Smithback would be the next victim," D'Agosta said.

Without looking up, Pendergast reached into the crate and pulled out a ziplock bag with a tarot card and a note inside, handing it to D'Agosta.

He glanced at the tarot card. It depicted a tall, orange brick tower, being struck by multiple bolts of lightning. It was afire, and tiny figures were falling from its turrets toward the grass far beneath. He turned his attention to the note.

Ave, frater!

Since when did I ever tell you the truth? One would think after all these years you'd have learned by now I am a skillful liar. While you were busy hiding the braggart Smithback—and I commend you for your cleverness there, for I haven't yet found him—I was free to plot the death of Margo Green. Who, by the way, put up a most spirited struggle.

Wasn't it all so very clever of me?

I'll tell you a secret, brother: I'm in a confessional mood. And so I will name my next victim: Lieutenant Vincent D'Agosta.

Amusing, what? Am I telling the truth? Am I lying again? What a delicious conundrum for you, dear brother.

I bid you, not *adieu,* but *au revoir.*

Diogenes

D'Agosta handed the note back to Pendergast. He felt a strange sensation in his gut. It wasn't fear—no, not fear at all—but a fresh groundswell of hatred. He was shaking with it.

"Bring the motherfucker on," he said.

"Have a seat, Vincent. We have very little time."

It was the first thing Pendergast had said, and D'Agosta was silenced by the deep seriousness in his voice. He eased himself down onto a crate.

"What's with the tarot card?" he asked.

"It's the Tower, from *El Gran Tarot Esotérico* variant of the deck. The card is said to indicate destruction, a time of sudden change."

"No kidding."

"I've spent all day compiling a list of potential victims and making arrangements for their protection. I've had to call in virtually every favor I'm owed, which will have the unfortunate collateral effect of blowing my cover. Those I have dealt with have promised to keep things to themselves, but it's only a matter of time before the news will come out that I'm alive. Vincent, take a look at this list."

D'Agosta leaned over and looked at the document on the screen. On it were a lot of names he recognized, along with many others he didn't know.

"Is there anyone else you feel should be on here?"

D'Agosta stared at the list. "Hayward." The thought of her sent a twinge through his gut.

"Hayward is the one person I know whom Diogenes will certainly *not* target. There are reasons for this that I cannot yet explain to you."

"And what about . . ." D'Agosta hestitated. Pendergast was an extremely private person and he wondered how he would react to him mentioning *her* name. "Viola Maskelene?"

"I have thought a great deal about her," he said in a low tone. He looked down at his white hands. "She's still on the island of Capraia, which in many ways is a perfect fortress for her. It's almost impossible to get to, involving several days' travel. There's only one small harbor, and a stranger—no matter how disguised—would be instantly noted. Diogenes is here in New York.

He can't reach her quickly, nor would he ever operate with a proxy. And finally"—his voice dropped—"Diogenes can know nothing of my—my *interest* in her. No one else in the world but you is aware of that. As far as Diogenes is concerned, she's simply a person I interviewed once with regard to a violin. On the other hand, if I were to take steps to protect her, it might actually alert Diogenes to her existence."

"I can see that."

"So in her case I have opted to leave things as is."

He unclasped his hands. "I have taken steps to protect the others, whether they like it or not. Which brings us to the most difficult question: what about you, Vincent?"

"I'm not going into hiding. As I said, bring him on. I'll be the bait. I'd rather die than run like a dog from Margo's killer."

"I'm not going to argue with you. The risk you're taking is enormous—you know that."

"I certainly do. And I'm prepared for it."

"I believe you are. Margo's attack was patterned after the murder of a spinster aunt of mine, who was stabbed in the back with a pearl-handled letter opener by a disgruntled servant. It's still possible that there's evidence from the scene of the attack that can help lead us to Diogenes—I'll need your help there. When word of my continuing existence reaches the police, there is going to be a serious problem."

"How so?"

Pendergast shook his head. "When the time comes, you'll understand. How long you choose to stay with me is, of course, up to you. At a certain point, I intend to take the law into my own hands. I would never entrust Diogenes to the criminal justice system."

D'A   sta nodded brusquely. "I'm with you all the way."

"The worst is yet to come. For me, and especially for you."

"That bastard killed Margo. End of discussion."

Pendergast placed a hand on his shoulder. "You're a good man, Vincent. One of the best."

D'Agosta did not respond. He was wondering at Pendergast's enigmatic words.

"I've arranged for all who might be likely targets of Diogenes to go to ground. That is phase one. And this brings us to phase two: stopping Diogenes. My initial plan failed utterly. It has been said: 'When you lose, don't lose the lesson.' The lesson here is that I cannot defeat my brother alone. I assumed that I knew him best, that I could predict his next move, that with enough evidence I could stop him myself. I've been proven wrong—devastatingly so. I need help."

"You've got me."

"Yes, and I'm grateful. But I was referring to another kind of help. *Professional* help."

"Like what?"

"I'm too close to Diogenes. I'm not objective, and I'm not calm—especially now. I have learned the hard way that I don't understand my brother and never have. What I need is an expert psychological profiler to create a forensic model of my brother. It will be an extraordinarily difficult task, as he is a psychologically unique individual."

"I know of several excellent forensic profilers."

"Not just any will do. I need one who is *truly excep-*

tional." He turned and began scribbling a note. "Go to the Riverside Drive house and give this to my man Proctor, who will pass it on to Constance. If this individual exists, Constance will find him."

D'Agosta took the note, folded it into his pocket.

"We're almost out of time: two days until January 28."

"Any idea yet what the date could mean?"

"None, except that it will be the climax of my brother's crime."

"How do you know he isn't lying about the date, too?"

Pendergast paused. "I don't. But instinct tells me it's real. And at the moment, that's all I have left: instinct."

Thirty-seven

WHIT DEWINTER III hunched over his fifteen-pound calculus textbook in the bowels of the Class of 1945 Library at Phillips Exeter Academy. He was staring at a formula made entirely of Greek letters, trying to pound it into his muddy brain. The midterm was in less than an hour and he hadn't even memorized half the formulas he'd need. He wished to hell he'd studied the night before instead of staying up so late, smoking weed with his girlfriend Jennifer. It had seemed like a good idea at the time . . . Stupid, so stupid. If he failed this test, his B in calculus would drop to a C, he'd have to go to UMass instead of Yale, and that would be it. He'd never get into medical school, he'd never have a decent job, he'd end up living out his miserable life in a split-level in Medford with some cow of a wife and a houseful of squalling brats . . .

He took a deep breath and dived once again into the tome, only to have his concentration broken by a raised voice from one of the nearby carrels. Whit straightened up. He recognized the voice: it was that sarcastic girl in his English lit class, the Goth with retro purple hair . . . Corrie. Corrie Swanson.

"What's your problem? Can't you see I'm studying here?" the voice echoed loudly across the sleek atrium of Academy Library.

Whit strained and failed to catch the calm, murmured answer.

"Australia? Are you *nuts*?" came the raised reply. "I'm in the middle of midterms! What're you, some kind of pervert?"

A couple of shushes came from students studying nearby. Whit peered above the edge of his carrel, glad for the diversion. He could see a man in a dark suit leaning over a carrel a few dozen yards away.

"*He* told you that? Yeah, right, let's see some ID."

More murmuring.

"All right, hey, I believe you, and I'm all for a beach vacation. But right now? You've *got* to be kidding."

More talk. More shushes.

"Okay, *okay*. All I can say is, if I fail biology, it'll be Pendergast's fault."

He heard a chair scraping and saw Corrie Swanson rise from the carrel and follow the man in the suit. He looked like Secret Service, all buttoned down, square jaw, dark glasses. He wondered what kind of trouble Corrie was in now.

Whit watched her pass, her trim behind twitching invitingly in a slinky black dress with pieces of metal jingling from it, her purple hair falling in a thick cascade down her back, grading almost to black at the ends. Damn, she was cute, just as long as he didn't try to take her home to Father. The old man would kill him for dating a girl like that.

Whit turned his throbbing eyeballs back to the formula for finding the radius of curvature for a function of two variables, but it remained all Greek to him. Literally. The damn formula had so many squiggly letters it could be the first line of the *Iliad,* for all he knew.

He groaned again. His life was about to end. And all because of Jennifer and her magic bong . . .

A light snow had fallen on the white clapboard house that stood on the corner of Church Street and Sycamore Terrace in the quiet Cleveland suburb of River Pointe. The whitened streets were broad and silent, the streetlights casting pools of yellow light across the nocturnal landscape. The distant whistle of a train added a melancholy note to the silent neighborhood.

A shadow moved behind a shuttered window in a second-story gable—a figure in a wheelchair—barely outlined in the soft blue light that emanated from the depths of the room. Back and forth the figure went in silent pantomime, busy at some unknown task. Inside the room, metal racks stood from floor to ceiling, packed with electronic equipment: monitors, CPUs, printers, terabytes of hard drives, units for the remote seizure of computer screen images, cellular telephone scanner-interceptors, wireless routers, NAS devices, and Internet port sniffers. The room smelled of hot electronics and menthol.

The figure rolled this way and that, a single withered hand tapping keyboards, pressing buttons, turning dials, and punching keypads. Slowly, one by one, the units were being powered down, shut off, closed out. One by one, the lights went off, LAN and broadband connections were cut, screens went dark, hard drives spun down, LEDs winked out. The man known in the underground hacking community by the single name of Mime was shutting himself off from the world.

The last light to go off—a large blue flat-panel LCD—plunged the room into darkness.

Mime rested when he was finished, breathing in the unaccustomed darkness. He was now completely cut off from the outside world. He knew that, blacked out like this, he could not be found. Still, the information that had reached him from the man known as Pendergast, one of only two people in the world he trusted implicitly, made him uneasy.

Mime had not been cut off in many years from the vast torrents of data that washed over his house like an invisible ocean. It was a cold, lonely feeling.

He sat brooding. In a minute, he would turn to an entirely new set of controls, and new lights would come on in the room: the lights from a battery of video camera monitors and security readouts from a surveillance system set up around and within his house. It was a protective measure that had been installed years before, but that had never been needed. Until now.

Mime breathed in the darkness, and—for the first time in his life—he was afraid.

Proctor carefully locked the door to the great shuttered mansion at 891 Riverside Drive, looked around, then slipped into the waiting Hummer. The building was shut up tightly, every potential breach or entry point carefully sealed. Constance was still within, hiding in the secret spaces that had shielded her in the past, spaces that not even he—not even Pendergast—knew about. She had supplies, an emergency cell phone, medication: everything she needed.

Proctor accelerated from the curb, easing the enormous armored vehicle around the corner, moving south on Riverside Drive. Out of habit, he glanced in his rearview mirror to see if he was being followed. There was no evidence of it, but—as Proctor well knew—the lack of evidence of being followed was not evidence of a lack of being followed.

At the corner of 95th and Riverside, he slowed as he approached an overflowing public trash receptacle; as he passed, he tossed into it a sack of greasy, congealed McDonald's french fries almost completely coated with solidified ketchup. Then he accelerated onto the on-ramp to the West Side Highway, where he headed north, keeping to the speed limit and checking his mirrors frequently. He continued up through Riverdale and Yonkers to the Saw Mill River Parkway, then the Taconic, then I-90, and then I-87 and the Northway. He would drive all night and much of the next morning, until he reached a certain small cabin on a certain small lake twenty-odd miles north of St. Amand l'Eglise, Quebec.

He glanced to his right, where an AR-15 lay on the seat, fully loaded with 5.56mm NATO rounds. Proctor almost hoped he was being followed. He'd like nothing more than to teach the fellow a lesson he'd never forget as long as he lived—which in any case would not be long, not long at all.

As the sky paled and a dirty dawn broke across the Hudson River, and a freezing wind whipped scraps of newspaper down the empty streets, a lone derelict, shuf-

fling along Riverside Drive, paused at an overflowing
garbage can and began rummaging about. With a grunt of
satisfaction, he extracted a bag of half-frozen McDonald's french fries. As he stuffed them greedily into his
mouth, his left hand deftly pocketed a small piece of
paper hidden in the bottom of the bag, a paper with a few
lines written in a beautiful, old-fashioned script:

There is only one man in the world who meets your
particular requirements:
Eli Glinn of Effective Engineering Solutions
Little West 12th Street, Greenwich Village,
New York

Thirty-eight

A BRILLIANT MOON, huge and intensely white, seemed to gild the vast expanse of sea far, far below. Looking out her window, Viola Maskelene could see a long white wake like a pencil laid across the burnished water, at the head of which was an enormous ocean liner, looking like a toy boat from 33,000 feet. It was the *Queen Mary,* she thought, on its way to New York from Southampton.

She gazed at it, feeling the enchantment of it, imagining the thousands of people below on that great ship in the middle of the ocean, eating, drinking, dancing, making love—an entire world on a ship so small it seemed she could hold it in her hand. She watched until it vanished on the far horizon. Funny how she'd flown at least a thousand times and still it was such an exciting experience for her. She glanced at the man across the aisle, dozing over his copy of the *Financial Times,* having never once looked out the window. That was something she couldn't understand.

She settled back in her seat, wondering how to amuse herself next. This was the second leg of her journey from Italy, having changed planes in London, and she'd already read her book and flipped through the trashy in-flight magazine. The first-class cabin was almost empty, and as it was almost 2 A.M. London time, what few passengers shared the cabin were asleep. She had the flight attendant to herself. She caught the woman's eye.

"Can I be of assistance, Lady Maskelene?"

She winced at the use of her title. How in the world did they all seem to know? "Champagne. And if you don't mind, please don't call me Lady Maskelene. It makes me feel like an old bag. Call me Viola instead."

"My apologies. I'll bring the champagne right away."

"Thanks ever so."

While Viola waited, she rummaged in her purse and withdrew the letter she had received at her house on the Italian island of Capraia three days before. It already showed signs of being opened and closed one too many times, but she read it again, anyway.

My dear Viola,

This letter will no doubt come as a shock to you, and for that I'm sorry. I find myself in the same position as Mark Twain in having to announce that the reports of my death are much exaggerated. I am alive and well, but I was forced to go underground due to an exceptionally delicate case I have been working on. That, combined with certain recent events in Tuscany with which you are no doubt acquainted, created the unfortunate impression among my friends and colleagues that I was dead. For a time, it was useful for me not to correct that impression. But I *am* alive, Viola—though I experienced a situation that put me as close to death as a human being can get.

That terrible experience is the reason for this letter. I realized during those dreadful hours of near-death how short life is, how fragile, and how we must none of us let slip those rare opportunities for happiness. When we met by chance on Capraia scant hours before that experience began, I was taken by surprise—and so, if you'll pardon my saying so, were you. Something happened between us. You made an indelible impression on me, and I entertain hopes that I made a not dissimilar impression on you. I would therefore like to invite you to stay with me in New York for ten days, so that we may get to know each other better. To see, in effect, if indeed that impression is as indelible, and as favorable, as I strongly believe it to be.

At this, Viola had to smile; the old-fashioned, somewhat awkward wording was so like Pendergast that she could almost hear his voice. But the fact was, this *was* an extraordinary letter, unlike any she had ever received. Viola had been approached by many different men in many different ways, but never quite like this. *Something happened between us.* It was true. Even so, most women would be surprised and even shocked to receive an invitation like this. Somehow, even on one meeting, Aloysius already knew her well enough to understand that such a letter would not displease her. On the contrary . . .

She returned her attention to the letter.

If you accept this admittedly unconventional invitation, please arrange to be on the January 27 British

Airways Flight 822 from Gatwick to Kennedy. *Do not tell anyone why you are coming.* I will explain when you get here; suffice to say that, if word of your visit got out, it could even now endanger my life.

When you arrive at Kennedy, my dear brother, Diogenes, will meet you at the luggage carousel.

Diogenes. She found herself smiling, remembering how Aloysius had said on Capraia that eccentric names ran in his family. He wasn't kidding—who would ever name their child Diogenes?

You will recognize him instantly because of his strong resemblance to me—except that he sports a neatly trimmed beard. What is most striking about him is that, due to a childhood accident, he has eyes of two different colors: one hazel, the other a milky blue. He will carry no sign and he, of course, does not know what you look like, so you will have to find him yourself. I wouldn't trust you with anyone less than my brother, who is utterly discreet.

Diogenes will escort you to my cottage out on Long Island, in a little town on Gardiners Bay, where I will be waiting for you. This will allow us several days in each other's company. The cottage is well equipped but rustic, with a splendid view of Shelter Island across the bay. You will naturally have your own chambers, and we will comport ourselves with propriety—unless, of course, circumstances dictate otherwise.

At this, Viola giggled out loud. He was so old-fashioned, and yet here he was, basically propositioning her in a way that wasn't even subtle—but managing to do it tastefully, with the driest sense of humor.

In three days following your arrival, the case I've been involved in will conclude. We will then emerge and I will once again show myself to the living, with (I trust) you on my arm. We will proceed to enjoy a splendid week of theater, music, art, and culinary exploration in New York City before your return to Capraia.

Viola, I beg you again, tell no one of this. Please give me your answer by old-fashioned telegram to the following address:

A. Pendleton
15 Glover's Box Road
The Springs, NY 10511

and sign it, "Anna Livia Plurabelle."

You will make me very happy if you accept my invitation. I know I am not very clever with sentiment and flowery phraseology—that is not my way. I will save further demonstrations of affection for when we meet in person.

Sincerely,
Aloysius

Again, Viola had to smile. She could almost hear Pendergast, with his elegant but rather severe air, speaking the sentences. Anna Livia Plurabelle, indeed; nice to know that Pendergast wasn't above tossing in a witty literary allusion, and an esoteric, highbrow one at that. How appealing he was; she fairly tingled with the thought of seeing him again. And the faint whiff of danger he alluded to in the letter simply added spice to the adventure. Once again, she couldn't help but reflect on how odd it was she seemed to know him so well after spending only that one afternoon together. She had never before believed in that nonsense about soulmates, about love at first sight, about matches made in heaven. But somehow . . .

She folded up the letter and took out the second one. It was a telegram, and it read simply:

```
Delighted you are coming! Con-
firmed my brother will meet
you. I know I can trust you to
be discreet. Fondly, A.X.L.P.
```

She carefully put both letters back into her handbag and sipped the champagne, her mind drifting back to that meeting on Capraia. She remembered how she had been digging manure into her vineyard when she saw a man in a black suit approaching, picking his way gingerly among the clods, accompanied by an American policeman in mufti. It was such an odd sight it had almost made her laugh. They had called out to her, thinking she was a peasant laborer. And then they'd drawn closer and she had looked at Pendergast's strange and beautiful face for the first time. Nothing like that sudden, queer feeling had happened to her before. She could read the same experience in his face, despite his efforts to conceal it. It had been a short visit—an hour's talk over glasses of white wine on her terrace overlooking the sea—and yet her mind had returned again and again to that afternoon, as if something momentous had happened.

Then there was that second visit—by D'Agosta alone, his face wan and troubled, and his terrible news of Pendergast's death. It wasn't until that awful moment that she had realized just how much she'd looked forward to seeing Agent Pendergast again—and how certain she had somehow been that he would figure in the rest of her life.

How dreadful that day had been. And how joyful things had become, now that she'd received his letter.

She smiled, thinking about seeing him again. She loved intrigue. She had never shied away from anything life had thrown at her. Her impulsiveness had gotten her into trouble on occasion, but it had also given her a colorful and fascinating life she wouldn't trade for anything. This mysterious invitation was like something out of the romance novels she used to devour in her early teen years. A weekend in a cottage hidden away on Long Island, with a man who fascinated her like no other, followed by a whirlwind week in New York City. How could she refuse? She certainly didn't have to sleep with him—he was the very soul of a gentleman—although just the thought brought an electric tingle that caused her to blush . . .

She finished off the champagne, which was excellent, as it always was in first class. She sometimes felt guilty about flying first class—it seemed elitist—but on a transatlantic flight, it was so much more comfortable. Viola was used to discomfort from her many years digging up tombs in Egypt, but she had never seen any sense in being uncomfortable for its own sake.

She checked her watch. She'd be landing at Kennedy in just over four hours.

It would certainly be interesting to meet this brother of Pendergast's—this Diogenes. You could tell a lot about a person by meeting his brother.

Thirty-nine

D'AGOSTA FOLLOWED Pendergast's downtrodden form as the agent shambled around the corner of Ninth Avenue onto Little West 12th Street. It was nine o'clock in the evening and a bitter wind was blowing hard off the Hudson River. The old meatpacking district—sandwiched into a narrow corridor south of Chelsea and north of Greenwich Village—had changed in the years D'Agosta was away. Now hip restaurants, boutiques, and technology start-ups were sprinkled among the wholesale meat distributors and commercial butcheries. It seemed like a hell of a place for a forensic profiler to hang up his shingle.

Halfway down the block, Pendergast halted before a large twelve-story warehouse that had seen better days. The steel-mesh windows were opaque with age, and the lower stories were caked with soot. There was no sign of any kind, no name, nothing to announce the existence of any firm within beyond a weathered sign painted directly onto the old brick which read *Price & Price Pork Packing Inc.* Below that was an oversize entrance for truck deliveries, closed and barred, and a smaller door beside it with an unlabeled buzzer. Pendergast's finger went up to it and gave it a jab.

"Yes?" a voice asked immediately from the adjoining speaker grille.

Pendergast murmured something and there was the sound of an electronic lock disengaging. The door opened into a small white space, empty save for a tiny camera mounted high on the rear wall. The door closed behind them with a faint click. They stood there, facing the camera, for thirty seconds. Then an almost invisible door in the rear wall slid back. Pendergast and D'Agosta walked down a white corridor, then stepped into a dim room—an amazing room.

The lower floors of the warehouse had been gutted, leaving a large, six-story shell. Ahead, the sprawling main floor was a maze of display tables, hulking scientific equipment, computer workstations, and intricate models and dioramas, all cloaked in shadow. D'Agosta's attention was drawn to a gigantic table displaying what appeared to be a model of the ocean floor somewhere around Antarctica, cut away to show sub-seafloor geology, along with what looked like a strange volcano of some kind. There were other intricate models, including one of a ship packed with mysterious-looking ROVs, scientific equipment, and military hardware.

A voice sounded from the shadows. "Welcome."

D'Agosta turned into the dimness and saw a figure in a wheelchair approaching between two rows of long tables: a man with closely cropped brown hair and thin lips set above a square jaw. He wore an unassuming but well-cut suit and controlled the wheelchair with a small joystick operated by a black-gloved hand. D'Agosta realized that one of the man's eyes must be glass, because it conveyed none of the fierce gleam of its mate. A purple scar ran down the right side of his face, from hairline to jaw, giving the illusion of a dueling wound.

"I am Eli Glinn," he said, his voice low, mild, and neutral. "You must be Lieutenant D'Agosta and Special Agent Pendergast." He stopped the wheelchair and extended his hand. "Welcome to Effective Engineering Solutions."

They followed him back between the tables and past a small greenhouse, its grow-lamps flickering eerily, then got into an elevator cage that took them up to a fourth-floor catwalk. As he followed the wheelchair down the catwalk, D'Agosta felt a twinge of doubt. Effective Engineering Solutions? Mr.—not Dr.—Eli Glinn? He wondered if, despite her vaunted research skills, Constance Greene had made a mistake. This didn't look like any forensic profiling consultant he had ever seen before— and he had dealt with quite a few.

Glinn glanced back, ran his good eye over D'Agosta's uniform. "You might as well turn off your radio and cell phone, Lieutenant. We block all wireless signals and radio frequencies in this building."

He led the way into a small conference room decorated in polished wood, closed the door, then gestured for them to be seated. He wheeled himself to the far side of the lone table, where a gap between the charcoal-colored Herman Miller chairs was clearly reserved for him. A thin envelope lay on the table before him; otherwise, the spotless table was empty. Leaning back in the wheelchair, he fixed them both with a penetrating gaze.

"Yours is an unusual request," he said.

"Mine is an unusual problem," Pendergast replied.

Glinn eyed him up and down. "That is a rather effective disguise, Mr. Pendergast."

"Indeed."

Glinn folded his hands. "Tell me the nature of your problem."

Pendergast glanced around. "Tell me the nature of your company. I ask because all this"—he gestured—"does not look like the office of a forensic profiler."

A slow, mirthless smile stretched the features of the man's face, distorting and inflaming the scar. "A fair question. Effective Engineering Solutions is in the business of solving unique engineering problems and performing failure analysis."

"What kind of engineering problems?" Pendergast asked.

"How to neutralize an underground nuclear reactor in a certain rogue Middle Eastern state being used to produce weapons-grade fuel. The analysis of the mysterious and sudden loss of a billion-dollar classified satellite." He twitched a finger, a small gesture that carried surprising weight, so motionless had the man been up to that point. "You'll understand if I don't go into details. You see, Mr. Pendergast, 'failure analysis' is the other side of the engineering coin: it is the art of understanding how things fail, and thus preventing failure before it happens. Or finding out why failure occurred *after* it happens. Sadly, the latter is more common than the former."

D'Agosta spoke. "I still don't get it. What does failure analysis have to do with forensic profiling?"

"I'm getting to that, Lieutenant. Failure analysis begins and ends with psychological profiling. EES realized long ago that the key to understanding failure was understanding exactly how human beings make mistakes. Which is

the same as understanding how human beings make decisions in general. We needed *predictive power*—a way to
predict how a given person would act in a given situation.
We therefore developed a muscular proprietary system for
psychological profiling. It currently runs on a grid-powered
supercomputer of IBM eServer nodes. We do psychological profiling better than anyone else in the world. And I do
not tell you this by way of salesmanship. It's a simple
fact."

Pendergast inclined his head. "Most interesting. How is
it I have never heard of you?"

"We do not generally wish to be known—beyond, that
is, a small circle of clients."

"Before we begin, I must be assured of discretion."

"Mr. Pendergast, EES makes two guarantees. First,
utter discretion. Second, guaranteed success. Now, please
tell me your problem."

"The target is a man named Diogenes Pendergast—my
brother. He disappeared over two decades ago, after con-
triving to stage his own false death. He seems to have vanished off the face of the earth—at least officially. He's not
in any government databases, beyond a death certificate
which I know to be forged. There are no adult records of
him at all. No address, no photos, nothing." He removed
a thick manila folder from his coat and placed it on the
table. "Everything I know is in here."

"How do you know he's still alive?"

"We had a curious encounter last summer. It's in the report. That, and the fact he has turned into a serial killer."

Glinn gave a slow nod.

"From a young age, Diogenes hated me, and he's made
it his life's work to destroy me. On January 19 of this year,
he finally put his plan into action. He has begun murder-

ing my friends and associates, one by one, and taunting me with my inability to save them. He's killed four so far. For the last two, he's mocked me with notes ahead of time, naming the victim—the first time correctly, and the second time as a ruse to make me protect the wrong person. In short, I have utterly failed to stop him. He claims to be targeting Lieutenant D'Agosta here next. Again, the summaries of the homicides are in that folder."

D'Agosta saw Glinn's good eye gleam with new interest. "How intelligent is this Diogenes?"

"As a child, his I.Q. was tested at 210. That was, incidentally, after he had scarlet fever, which altered him permanently."

Glinn raised an eyebrow. "Are we dealing with organic brain damage?"

"Not likely. He was strange before the fever. The illness seems to have focused it, brought it to the fore."

"And this is why you need me. You need a complete psychological, criminal, and behavioral analysis of this man. Naturally, because you are his brother, you are too close to him—you cannot do it yourself."

"Correct. Diogenes has had years to plan this. He's been three steps ahead of me all the way. He leaves no clues at his crime scenes—none that are unintentional at least. The only way to stop him is to anticipate what he'll do next. I must stress this is an emergency situation. Diogenes has threatened to complete his crime tomorrow, January 28. He named this day as the culmination of all his planning. There is no telling how many more lives are in jeopardy."

Glinn opened the folder with his good hand and began leafing through it, scanning the pages. "I cannot produce a profile in twenty-four hours."

"You *must.*"

"It's impossible. The earliest I can do it—assuming I drop all other work and focus solely on this—is seventy-two hours from now. You have come to me too late, Mr. Pendergast. At least too late for the date your brother named. Not too late, perhaps, to take effective action afterwards." He gave his head a curious tilt as he eyed Pendergast.

The agent was very still for a moment. "So be it, then," he said in a low voice.

"Let's not waste any more time." Glinn put a hand on the folder before him and slid it across the table. "Here is our standard contract. My fee is one million dollars."

D'Agosta rose from his chair. "A million bucks? Are you crazy!"

Pendergast stilled him with a wave of his hand. "Accepted." He took the folder, opened it, scanned the contract rapidly.

"At the back," said Glinn, "you'll find our standard disclaimers and warranties. We offer an absolute, unconditional guarantee of success."

"This is the second time you've mentioned that curious guarantee. How do you define 'success,' Mr. Glinn?"

Another ghostly smile lingered on Glinn's face. "Naturally, we cannot guarantee that you will apprehend Diogenes. Nor can we guarantee to stop him from killing. That lies in your hands. Here's what we do guarantee. First: we will give you a forensic profile of Diogenes Pendergast that will accurately elucidate his motive."

"I already know his motive."

Glinn ignored this. "Second: our forensic profile will have *predictive* power. It will tell you, within a limited range of options, what Diogenes Pendergast's next actions will be. We offer follow-up services — if you have specific questions about the target's future actions, we will run them through our system and provide you with reliable answers."

"I question whether that's possible with any human being, let alone someone like Diogenes."

"I do not wish to bandy philosophical questions with you, Mr. Pendergast. Human beings are disgustingly predictable, and this is as true of psychopaths as it is of grandmothers. We shall do what we say."

"Have you ever failed?"

"Never. There is one assignment that remains — shall we say — open."

"The one involving the thermonuclear device?"

If Glinn was surprised by this question, he did not show it. "What thermonuclear device is that?"

"The one you are designing downstairs. I saw several equations on a whiteboard relating to the curve of binding energy. On a nearby table lay a paper with the design for machining a piece of H.E. that could only be used to compress a core."

"I shall have to speak to my chief engineer about his carelessness with regard to our other project."

"I also see you're developing a genetically engineered plant mosaic virus. Does that also relate to that other project?"

"We offer the same guarantee of confidentiality to our other clients that we offer you. Shall we return to the subject of Diogenes? In particular, the question of his motive."

"Not quite yet," said Pendergast. "I do not speak frivolously. Your entire manner — your speech, your movements, your very intensity, Mr. Glinn — speaks of someone with an overriding obsession. I have also noted that, at least if the scar on your face is an indication, your injuries are recent. When I weigh that with what I saw downstairs, I find myself growing concerned."

Glinn raised his eyebrows. "Concerned?"

"Concerned that a man such as you, wrestling with a problem far greater than my own, wouldn't be able to devote his full attention to mine."

Glinn remained very still, not answering. Pendergast looked across the table at him, equally motionless.

A minute went by, then two, without either man speaking. Watching, waiting, D'Agosta grew increasingly alarmed. It was as if the two men were fighting a duel, waging a battle of turn and counterturn, all without speaking or even moving.

Suddenly, without preamble, Glinn began to speak again in the same calm, neutral voice. "If you ever decide to leave the FBI, Mr. Pendergast, I believe I could find a place for you here. There is no obsession on my part, however—only the simple fulfillment of our guarantee of success. You see, we don't make that guarantee just for our clients: we make it for ourselves. I intend to complete that other project successfully, although the original client is no longer in a condition to appreciate it. That project involves a severe seismic dislocation at a certain site in the South Atlantic that requires a, ah, nuclear adjustment. And that is more than you need to know. It is true that I am taking on your little problem chiefly because I find myself embarrassed for funds. However, I will devote *all my energy* to seeing your project through, because to fail would mean having to return your money and to suffer personal humiliation. And, as I said, EES does not fail. Clear enough?"

Pendergast nodded.

"And now, let us return to your brother's motive—the fountainhead of his hatred. Something happened between you and him, and I must know what it is."

"It's all described in that folder. He always hated me. The final straw was when I burned my brother's journals."

"Tell me about it."

"I was fourteen, and he was twelve. We had never gotten along. He was always cruel and strange—much more so after the scarlet fever."

"When was that?"

"When he was seven."

"Are there any medical records?"

"None. He was treated by the private family physician."

"Proceed."

"One day I came across his journals, which were filled with the most vile things ever put on paper—abominations beyond the reach of any normal mind. He'd been keeping them for years. I burned them—and that was the precipitant. Some years later, our home burned, and our parents died in the fire. I was away at school, but Diogenes saw it all, heard their cries for help. That drove him over the edge."

A cold smile played at the corners of Glinn's lips. "I think not."

"*You* think not?"

"I have no doubt that he was jealous of you and that the destruction of his journals infuriated him. But that happened far too late to produce such a deep, pathological, obsessive hatred. Nor can a mere bout with scarlet fever create hatred out of thin air. No, Mr. Pendergast: this hatred stems from *something else* that happened between you and your brother at a much earlier age. *That* is the information we lack. And you are the only person who can supply it."

"Everything of relevance that happened between me and my brother is in that file, including our recent encounter in Italy. I can assure you there is no single incident, no smoking gun, which explains his hatred."

Glinn picked up the file, leafed through it. Three minutes passed, then five. Then Glinn put the folder down. "You're right. There is no smoking gun here."

"Just as I said."

"It's quite possible you've repressed it."

"I repress nothing. I have an exceptional memory going back to before my first birthday."

"Then you are deliberately withholding something."

Pendergast went very still. D'Agosta watched the two men, surprised. He had never seen anyone challenge Pendergast in quite this way before.

As he eyed Pendergast, Glinn had become, if possible, even more expressionless. "We can't proceed without this information. I need it, and I need it now." He glanced at his watch. "I'm going to call in several of my trusted associates. They'll be here within the hour. Mr. Pendergast, there's a small room with a bed behind that door in the back; please make yourself comfortable and await further instructions. Lieutenant, your presence here is no longer required."

D'Agosta looked at Pendergast. For the first time in his memory, the agent's face wore a look of something like apprehension.

"I'm not going anywhere," D'Agosta said immediately, irritated at Glinn's arrogance.

Pendergast smiled thinly, shook his head. "It's all right,

Vincent—much as I loathe the idea of rummaging around in my past for something that probably doesn't exist, I see the necessity for doing so. I will meet you back at our pre-arranged place."

"Are you sure?"

Pendergast nodded. "And never forget: you are the one named next by Diogenes. January 28 is less than three hours away. Vincent: be *transcendentally* cautious."

Forty

$\mathcal{L}$AURA HAYWARD PACED the small room like a
caged lioness, glancing frequently at the ugly
clock behind her desk. She felt that, if she
didn't work off her nervous energy, she would explode.
And since she couldn't leave her office, she paced.

She had spent almost the entire evening organizing the
evidence from the Duchamp and Green killings, and
cross-comparing it to evidence she had cajoled, pried,
and bludgeoned out of the New Orleans and D.C. police
departments. She had cleared her cork wall of all other
cases and had divided it into four cantons, one for each
homicide: Professor Torrance Hamilton on January 19;
Charles Duchamp on January 22; Special Agent Michael
Decker on January 23; and Dr. Margo Green on January
26. There were micrographs of fibers and hair, photographs of knots and footprints, abstracts of the M.E. reports, blood splatter analyses, photographs of the murder
scenes and weapons, fingerprint reports, diagrams showing ingress and egress where determined, along with an
embarrassment of other evidence, relevant or not. Push-
pins with colored strings drew red, yellow, green, and
blue connections among the evidence. And there were a

surprising number of connections: while the M.O.'s were all quite different, there was no doubt in Hayward's mind the same person had committed all four homicides.

No doubt.

Sitting on the middle of her desk was a thin report, just in, from the top guy in the forensic profiling division. He had confirmed that the homicides were psychologically consistent and could have been committed by the same perp. What's more, he had prepared a profile of the killer. It was startling, to say the least.

D.C. and New Orleans didn't know it yet; the FBI didn't know it yet; not even Singleton or Rocker knew it yet: but they were dealing with a serial killer. A meticulous, intelligent, methodical, cool, and utterly insane serial killer.

She spun, strode, spun again. As soon as she showed Rocker that she'd connected the cases, the shit would hit the fan. The FBI, already involved because of Decker's murder, would descend like a ton of bricks. There would be an earthquake of publicity—serial killers always garnered big headlines. But a serial killer like *this* was totally unheard of. She could almost see the screaming 72-point headline in the *Post*. The mayor would get involved, maybe even the governor. It was going to be a mess. A god-awful mess.

But she couldn't call Rocker until she had the last piece of evidence, the last piece of the puzzle. The smoking gun. She was going to get raked over the coals, no matter what. The political fallout would be terrible. It was important she had all her ducks in a row—that was the only thing that could save her ass.

A timid rap came on the door, and she halted midstride. "Come in," she said.

A man holding a manila envelope poked his head in.

"Where've you been? I was supposed to have this report two hours ago!"

"I'm sorry," the man stammered, taking a few tentative steps inside the office. "As I explained on the phone, we had to run the match three times because—"

"Never mind. Just give me the report, please."

He held it out from a distance, almost as if fearful of being bitten.

"You got a DNA match?" she asked, taking the report.

"Yes. A pair of beautiful matches, blood from the box cutter and the spot on the floor. Both from the same individual, not the victim. But here's the problem: the DNA wasn't in any of the FBI criminal or juvenile databases, so we did like you asked and ran it against all the DNA databases. When we finally did get a match, it was in a federal database, and we had a major problem because of confidentiality issues and . . . well . . ." He hesitated.

"Go on," Hayward said as gently as she could.

"The reason I had to run the program three times was to be absolutely sure about this match. This is explosive stuff, Captain. We can't afford to be wrong."

"And?" Hayward could hardly breathe.

"You aren't going to believe this. The DNA matched one of the Bureau's top agents."

Hayward breathed out. "I believe it. God help us, I believe it."

Forty-one

Eli GLINN WAITED in his small private office on the fourth floor of the Effective Engineering Solutions building. It was a sober room, containing only a table, several computers, a small bookshelf, and a clock. The walls were painted gray, and there was nothing of a personal nature in the office, save for a small photograph of a stately blonde woman wearing the uniform of a ship's captain, waving from what appeared to be the bridge of a tanker. A line from a W. H. Auden poem was handwritten beneath.

The office lights had been turned off, and the only illumination came from a large flat-panel monitor, which carried a high-definition digital feed from an office in the basement of the EES building. The video feed showed two people: the subject, Pendergast, with EES's psychological specialist, Rolf Krasner, who was preparing the subject for questioning.

Glinn observed the slender figure of Pendergast with interest. The man's insight into Glinn's own psychology, his extraordinary ability to pick out and interpret a few details scattered about a room which itself was a very morass of detail, had nearly unnerved Glinn—and, in a curious way, deeply impressed him.

While still watching the proceedings on the monitor, the audio turned off, he turned again to the folder Pendergast had given him. Although unimportant in the larger scheme of things, Pendergast's case was not without its points. For example, there was the near mythical Cain and Abel relationship between these two extraordinary brothers. For Pendergast *was* extraordinary—Glinn had never before met a man whose intellect he could respect as equal to his own. Glinn had always felt somewhat alienated from the mass of humanity—and yet here was a man he could, in the revolting parlance of the present age, *identify* with. That Pendergast's brother appeared to be even more intelligent, and yet utterly malevolent, Glinn found even more intriguing. This was a man so consumed by hatred that he had devoted his life to the object of his hatred, not unlike a man under the spell of obsessive love. Whatever lay at the bottom of that hatred was something perhaps unique in human experience.

Glinn glanced back at the monitor. The chitchat was over and Rolf Krasner was getting down to business. The EES psychologist combined a disarmingly friendly air with consummate professionalism. You could hardly believe that this cheerful, round-faced, unassuming man with the Viennese accent could be considered a threat. Indeed, at first glance, he seemed about the most unthreatening personality imaginable—until you saw him in action. Glinn knew just how effective that Jekyll and Hyde strategy could be with an unsuspecting subject.

On the other hand, Krasner had never had a subject like this one.

Glinn leaned over and switched on the audio feed.

"Mr. Pendergast," Krasner was saying cheerily, "is there anything I can get you before we begin? Water? A soft drink? A double martini?" A chuckle.

"Nothing, thank you."

Pendergast appeared ill at ease, as well he should. EES had developed three different modes of interrogation, each for a particular personality type, along with an experimental fourth mode to be used only on the most difficult, resistant—and intelligent—subjects. After they had read through Pendergast's folder and discussed the situation, there was no argument over which mode would be used. Pendergast would be only the sixth person to undergo this fourth type of interrogation. It had never failed.

"We use some of the techniques of good, old-fashioned psychoanalysis," Krasner said. "And one of them is that we ask you to lie down on a couch, out of view of the questioner. Would you please make yourself comfortable?"

The figure lay down on the richly brocaded couch and folded his white hands on his chest. Except for the ragged clothes, he looked alarmingly like the corpse at a wake. *What a fascinating creature this man is,* Glinn thought as he moved his wheelchair closer to the monitor.

"Perhaps you recognize the office we're in, Mr. Pendergast?" Krasner said, bustling about, getting ready.

"I do. Number 19 Berggasse."

"Exactly! Modeled after Freud's own office in Vienna. We even managed to acquire some of his African carvings. And that Persian carpet in the center also belonged to him. Freud called his office *gemütlich*, which is an almost untranslatable German word meaning agreeable, comfortable, cozy, friendly—and that is the atmosphere we have strived to create. Do you speak German, Mr. Pendergast?"

"German is not one of my languages, much to my regret. I should have liked to read Goethe's *Faust* in the original."

"A marvelous work, vigorous and yet poetic." Krasner took a seat on a wooden stool out of Pendergast's view.

"Do you employ the free-association methods of psychoanalysis?" Pendergast asked dryly.

"Oh, no! We've developed a technique all our own. It's very straightforward, actually—no tricks, no dream interpretations. The only thing Freudian about our technique is the office decor." He chuckled again.

Glinn found himself smiling. The fourth interrogation mode used tricks—they all did—but, of course, the subject wasn't supposed to see them. Indeed, this fourth mode seemed like pure simplicity itself . . . on the surface. Highly intelligent people could be fooled, but only with the greatest of care and subtlety.

"I'm going to help you through some simple visualization techniques, which will also involve questioning. It's simple and there is no hypnosis involved. It's just a way to induce a calm and focused mind, receptive to questioning. Does that suit you, Aloysius? May I call you by your first name?"

"You may, and I am at your disposal, Dr. Krasner. I am only concerned that I may not be able to give you the information you desire, because I do not believe it exists."

"Do not concern yourself with that. Simply relax, follow my instructions, and answer the questions as best you can."

Relax. Glinn knew this was about the last thing Pendergast would be able to do, once Krasner got started.

"Wonderful. Now I'm going to turn down the lights. I will also ask you to close your eyes."

"As you wish."

The lights dimmed to a faint diffuse glow.

"Now we will allow three minutes to pass in silence," said Krasner.

The minutes crawled by.

"Let us begin." Krasner's voice had taken on a hushed, velvety tone. Another long silence, and then he resumed.

"Breathe in slowly. Hold it. Now let it out even more slowly. Again. Breathe in, hold, breathe out. Relax. Very good. Now, I want you to imagine you are at your favorite place in all the world. The place where you feel most at home, most comfortable. Take a minute to place yourself there. Now turn around, examine your surroundings. Sample the air. Take in the scents, the sounds. Now, tell me: What do you see?"

A momentary silence. Glinn leaned still closer to the monitor.

"I am on a vast green lawn at the edge of an ancient beechwood forest. There is a summerhouse at the far end of the lawn. There are gardens and a millhouse to the west, where a brook flows. The lawn sweeps up to a stone mansion, shaded by elms."

"What is this place?"

"Ravenscry. The estate of my Great-Aunt Cornelia."

"And what is the year and season?"

"It is 1972, the ides of August."

"How old are you?"

"Twelve."

"Inhale the air again. What scents can you smell?"

"Freshly cut grass, with a faint overlay of peonies from the garden."

"What are the sounds?"

"A whip-poor-will. The rustle of beech leaves. The distant murmur of water."

"Good. Very good. Now I want you to rise. Rise off the ground, let yourself float . . . Look down as you rise. Do you see the lawn, the house, from above?"

"Yes."

"Now rise further. One hundred feet. Two hundred. Look down again. What do you see?"

"The great sprawling house, the carriage house, the gardens, lawns, millhouse, trout hatchery, arboretum, greenhouses, the beechwood forest, and the drive winding to the stone gates. The encircling wall."

"And beyond that?"

"The road to Haddam."

"Now. Make it night."

"It is night."

"Make it day."

"It is day."

"Do you understand that you are in control, that all this is in your head, that none of this is real?"

"Yes."

"During this process, you must always keep that in mind. You are in control, and none of what is happening is real. It is all in your mind."

"I understand that."

"Below, on the lawn, put the members of your family. Who are they? Name them, please."

"My father, Linnaeus. My mother, Isabella. My Great-Aunt Cornelia. Cyril, the gardener, working to one side . . ."

There was a long pause.

"Anyone else?"

"And my brother. Diogenes."

"His age?"

"Ten."

"What are they doing?"

"Standing around just where I put them." The voice sounded dry and ironic. Glinn could see very well that Pendergast was maintaining an ironic detachment and would attempt to do so as long as possible.

"Put them in some kind of typical activity," Krasner went on smoothly. "What are they doing now?"

"Finishing tea on a blanket spread out on the lawn."

"Now I want you to drift down. Slowly. Join them."

"I am there."

"What are you doing, exactly?"

"Tea is over and Great-Aunt Cornelia is passing a plate of petits fours. She has them brought up from New Orleans."

"Are they good?"

"Naturally. Great-Aunt Cornelia has the highest standards." The tone of Pendergast's voice was laden with irony, and Glinn wondered just who this Great-Aunt Cornelia was. He glanced down at an abstract attached to Pendergast's file, flipped through it, and came to the answer of his question. A chill crept up his spine. He quickly shut the file—right now that was a distraction.

"What kind of tea did you take?" asked Krasner.

"Great-Aunt Cornelia will only drink T. G. Tips, which she has sent over from England."

"Now look around the blanket. Look at everyone. Gaze around until your eyes come to rest on Diogenes."

A long silence.

"What does Diogenes look like?"

"Tall for his age, pale, with very short hair, eyes of two

different colors. He is very thin and his lips are overly red."

"Those eyes, look into them. Is he looking at you?"

"No. He has turned his head away. He does not like to be stared at."

"Keep staring at him. Stare hard."

A longer silence. "I have averted my eyes."

"No. Remember, you control the scene. Keep staring."

"I don't choose to."

"Speak to your brother. Tell him to rise, that you wish to speak to him in private."

Another, longer silence. "Done."

"Tell him to come with you to the summerhouse."

"He refuses."

"He cannot refuse. You control him."

Even through the monitor, Glinn could see that a small sheen of sweat had appeared on Pendergast's brow. *It's beginning,* he thought.

"Tell Diogenes that there is a man waiting for him in the summerhouse who wants to ask you both some questions. A Dr. Krasner. Tell him that."

"Yes. He will come to see the doctor. He is curious that way."

"Excuse yourselves and walk to the summerhouse. Where I am waiting."

"All right."

A brief silence. "Are you there?"

"Yes."

"Good. Now, what do you see?"

"We're inside. My brother is standing here, you're here, I'm here."

"Good. We shall remain standing. Now, I will ask you and your brother some questions. You will relay your brother's answers to my questions, since he cannot speak to me directly."

"If you insist," said Pendergast, a touch of irony returning to his voice.

"*You* control the situation, Aloysius. Diogenes cannot evade answering, because it is you who is really answering for him. Are you ready?"

"Yes."

"Tell Diogenes to look at you. To *stare* at you."

"He won't."

"*Make* him. With your mind, make him do it."

A silence. "All right."

"Diogenes, I am now speaking to you. What is your first memory of your older brother, Aloysius?"

"He said he remembers me drawing a picture."

"What is the picture?"

"Scribbles."

"How old are you, Diogenes?"

"He says six months."

"Ask Diogenes what he thinks of you."

"He thinks of me as the next Jackson Pollock."

That ironic tone again, thought Glinn. This was one very resistant client.

"That would not normally be the thought of a six-month-old baby."

"Diogenes is answering as a ten-year-old, Dr. Krasner."

"Fine. Ask Diogenes to keep looking at you. What does he see?"

"He says nothing."

"What do you mean, nothing? He isn't speaking?"

"He spoke. He said the word *nothing*."

"What do you mean by the word *nothing*?"

"He says, 'I see nothing that is not there and the nothing that is.' "

"Excuse me?"

"It's a quotation from Wallace Stevens," said Pendergast dryly. "Even at ten, Diogenes was partial to Stevens."

"Diogenes, when you say 'nothing,' does that mean you feel your brother, Aloysius, is a nonentity?"

"He laughs and says the words are yours, not his."

"Why?"

"He is laughing harder."

"How long will you be at Ravenscry, Diogenes?"

"He says until he goes back to school."

"And where is that?"

"St. Ignatius Loyola on Lafayette Street, New Orleans."

"How do you like school, Diogenes?"

"He says he likes it as much as you would like being shut up in a room with twenty-five mental defectives and a middle-aged hysteric."

"What is your favorite subject?"

"He says experimental biology . . . on the playground."

"Now I want you, Aloysius, to ask Diogenes three questions, which he must answer. You must make him answer them. Remember, you are in control. Are you ready?"

"Yes."

"What is your favorite food, Diogenes?"

"Wormwood and gall."

"I want a straight answer."

"That, Dr. Krasner, is the one thing you will never get from Diogenes," said Pendergast.

"Remember, Aloysius, that it is *you* who are actually answering the questions."

"And with great forbearance, I might add," said Pendergast. "I am doing all I can to suspend my disbelief."

Glinn leaned back in his wheelchair. This wasn't quite working. Clients resisted, some with every fiber of their being, but not quite like this. Irony was the ultimate resistance—he had never before seen it so skillfully employed. And yet Glinn felt a shiver of self-recognition: Pendergast was a man who was hyperaware of himself, unable ever to step outside of himself, to let go, to lower, even for an instant, the elaborate defensive mask he had created to place between himself and the world.

Glinn could understand a man like that.

"All right. Aloysius, you are still in the summerhouse with Diogenes. Imagine you have a loaded pistol in your hand."

"Fine."

Glinn sat up, a little startled. Krasner was already moving to what they termed phase two—and very abruptly. Clearly, he, too, realized this session needed to be jump-started.

"What kind of pistol is it?"

"It's a gun from my collection, a Signature Grade 1911 .45 ACP by Hilton Yam."

"Give it to him."

"It would be most unwise to give a pistol to a ten-year-old, don't you think?" Again, that ironic, amused tone.

"Nevertheless, do it."

"Done."

"Tell him to point the gun at you and pull the trigger."

"Done."

"What happened?"

"He's laughing uproariously. He didn't pull the trigger."

"Why not?"

"He says it's too soon."

"Does he intend to kill you?"

"Naturally. But he wants . . ." His voice trailed off.

Krasner pounced. "What does he want?"

"To play with me for a while."

"What kind of play?"

"He says he wants to pull off my wings and watch what happens. I am his ultimate insect."

"Why?"

"I don't know."

"Ask him."

"He's laughing."

"Grab him and demand an answer."

"I would prefer not to touch him."

"*Grab him.* Get physical. Force him to answer."

"He's still laughing."

"Hit him."

"Don't be ridiculous."

"*Hit him.*"

"I won't carry on with this charade."

"Take the gun away from him."

"He's dropped the gun, but—"

"Pick it up."

"All right."

"Shoot him. Kill him."

"This is utterly absurd—"

"Kill him. Do it. You've killed before; you know how to do it. You *can* and you *must* do it."

A long silence.

"Did you do it?"

"This is an asinine exercise, Dr. Krasner."

"But you *did* imagine it. Didn't you? *You imagined killing him.*"

"I imagined no such thing."

"Yes, you did. You killed him. You imagined it. And now you are imagining his dead body on the ground. You see it because you cannot *help* but see it."

"This is . . ." Pendergast's voice trailed off.

"You see it, you can't *help* but see it. Because I am telling you to, you are seeing it . . . But wait—he's not yet dead . . . He moves, he still lives . . . He wants to say something. With his last dying strength, he beckons you closer, says something to you. *What did he just say?*"

A long silence. Then Pendergast answered dryly, "*Qualis artifex pereo.*"

Glinn winced. He recognized the quotation but could see that Krasner did not. What should have been a breaking point for Pendergast had suddenly turned into an intellectual game.

"What does that mean?"

"It's Latin."

"I repeat: what does it mean?"

"It means 'O, what an artist dies with me!' "

"Why did he say that?"

"Those were Nero's last words. I believe Diogenes was speaking facetiously."

"You have killed your brother, Aloysius, and now look on his body."

An irritated sigh.

"This is the second time you have done it."

"The second time?"

"You killed him once before, years ago."

"Pardon me?"

"Yes, you did. You killed whatever goodness was in him; you left him a hollow shell filled with malice and hatred. You did something to him that murdered his very soul!"

Despite himself, Glinn found he was holding his breath. The gentle, soothing tones were long gone: Dr. Krasner had slipped into phase three, once again with unusual swiftness.

"I did no such thing. He was born that way, empty and cruel."

"No. *You killed his goodness!* There is no other possible answer. Don't you see, Aloysius? The hatred Diogenes feels for you is mythological in its immensity. It cannot have sprung from nothing; energy can neither be created nor destroyed. *You* created that hatred, *you* did something to him that struck out his heart. All these years, you have repressed this terrible deed. And now *you* have killed him again, literally as well as figuratively. What *you* must face, Aloysius, is that you are the author of your own fate. *You* are at fault. *You did it.*"

Another long silence. Pendergast lay on the couch, unmoving, his skin gray, waxlike.

"Now Diogenes is rising. He is looking at you again. I want you to ask him something."

"What?"

"Ask Diogenes what you did to him to make him hate you so."

"Done."

"His answer?"

"Another laugh. He said, 'I hate you because you are you.' "

"Ask again."

"He says that is reason enough, that his hatred has

nothing to do with anything I did, it simply exists, like the sun, moon, and stars."

"No, no, *no*. What is it that you did, Aloysius?" Krasner's voice was once again gentle, but it had great urgency. "Unburden yourself of it. How terrible it must be to carry that weight on your shoulders. Unburden yourself."

Slowly, Pendergast arose from the couch, swinging his legs over the side. For a moment, he sat motionless. Then he passed a hand across his forehead, looked at his watch. "It is midnight. It is now January 28, and I am out of time. I can't be bothered with this exercise anymore."

He stood and turned to Dr. Krasner. "I commend you on your valiant effort, Doctor. Trust me, there's nothing in my past that would justify Diogenes's conduct. In the course of my career studying the criminal mind, I have come to realize a simple truth: some people are born monsters. You can elucidate their motives and reconstruct their crimes—but you cannot explain the evil within them."

Krasner looked at him, great sadness in his face. "There's where you're wrong, my friend. Nobody is born evil."

Pendergast held out his hand. "We shall differ, then." Then his eyes turned directly toward the hidden camera, startling Glinn. How could Pendergast know where it was?

"Mr. Glinn? I thank you, too, for your effort. You should have plenty in that folder to complete the job at hand. I can help you no further. Something terrible will happen today, and I must do everything in my power to stop it."

And he turned and walked briskly from the room.

Forty-two

THE MANSION AT 891 Riverside Drive lay above one of the most complex geological areas of Manhattan. Here, beneath the litter-strewn streets, the bedrock of Hartland schist yielded to a different formation, the Cambrian Manhattan. The gneiss of the Manhattan Formation was particularly faulted and contorted, and riddled with weak areas, cracks, and natural tunnels. One such weak area, several centuries ago, had been enlarged to form the passage from the mansion's sub-basement to the weed-choked shore of the Hudson River. But there were other tunnels, older and more secret, that burrowed beneath the mansion into dark and unknown depths.

Unknown to all, that is, but one.

Constance Greene moved slowly through one of these tunnels, descending with practiced ease into the blackness. Though she held a torch in one slim hand, it was not lit: she knew these deep and hidden spaces so well that light was not necessary. The passage was frequently narrow enough to allow her to follow both walls with her outstretched hands. Though the tunnel was of natural rock, the ceiling was tall and quite regular, and the floor was even enough to appear almost like steps fashioned by man.

But only Constance had ever walked this way before.

Until a few days ago, she had hoped never to come here again. It was a reminder of the old times—the bad times—when she had seen things no living being should ever have to witness. When *he* had come, with violence and murder, and had taken from her the only human being she had known, a man who was like a father to her. *The murderer* had upended the ordered world she had grown so used to. She had fled here then, into the chill recesses of the earth. For a time, it seemed, sanity itself also fled, under the shock.

But her mind had been too carefully trained, over too many years, to ever become fully lost. Slowly, slowly, she came back. Once again, she grew interested in the ways of the waking, the living; once again, she began creeping back up to her old home, her world, the mansion at 891 Riverside. That was when she began watching the man named Wren and—finally—revealed herself to the kindly old gentleman.

Who, in turn, had brought her to Pendergast.

Pendergast. He had reintroduced her to the world, helped her move out of a shadowy past into a brighter present.

But the work was not yet done. All too well, she was aware of that tenuous line still separating her from instability. And now *this* had happened . . .

As she walked, Constance bit her lip to keep back a sob.

But it shall be all right, she tried to tell herself. *It shall be all right.* Aloysius had promised her so. And he could do anything, it seemed; even rise from the dead.

She had made a promise to him as well, and she would keep it: to spend her nights here, where not even Diogenes Pendergast could ever find her. She would keep her promise, despite the dreadful weight this place, and its memories, placed on her heart.

Ahead, the passage narrowed, then split into two. To the right, the tunnel kept corkscrewing down into darkness. To the left, a narrower way led off horizontally. Constance chose this passage, following its twists and turns for a hundred yards. Then she stopped and, at last, turned on the lamp.

Its yellow light revealed that the passage widened abruptly, dead-ending in a small, snug chamber, perhaps ten feet by six. Its floor was covered by an expensive Persian carpet, taken from one of the basement storage rooms of the mansion above. The lines of the bare rock walls were softened by reproductions of Renaissance paintings: Parmigianino's *Madonna with the Long Neck,* Giorgione's *Tempest,* half a dozen others. A cot was set into the rear of the niche, and a small table lay at one side. Works by Thackeray, Trollope, and George Eliot were stacked neatly beside Plato's *Republic* and St. Augustine's *Confessions.*

It was much warmer here, belowground. The air smelled, not unpleasantly, of rock and earth. Yet the relative warmth, the small attempts at domesticity, afforded Constance little comfort.

She set the lamp upon the table, sat down before it, and glanced to one side. There was a recess in the rock face here, perhaps three feet above the level of the floor. She pulled a leather-bound book from it: the most recent volume of a diary she had kept in the old days, when she had been the ward of Pendergast's ancestor.

She opened the diary and turned its pages over slowly,

thoughtfully, until she reached the final entry. It was dated July of the previous year.

Constance read the entry once, then again, brushing away a stray tear as she did so. Then, with a quiet sigh, she replaced the diary into the recess, beside its mates.

Forty-two other volumes, identical in size and shape, stood there. While the closer volumes looked quite new, the ones farther along the recess grew increasingly cracked and worn with age.

Constance sat there, looking at them, her hand resting pensively on the edge of the niche. The movement had pulled back the material of her sleeve, exposing a long row of small, healed scars on her forearm: twenty or thirty identical marks, lined up precisely in parallel with one another.

With another sigh, she turned away. Then she extinguished the light and—saying a brief prayer to the close and watchful darkness—she stole toward the cot, turned her face to the wall, and lay down, eyes open, preparing herself as best she could for the nightmares that would inevitably come.

Forty-three

VIOLA MASKELENE PICKED UP her luggage at the international arrivals carousel at Kennedy Airport, engaged a luggage porter to load it onto a cart, and followed it through customs. It was after midnight, and the wait was brief; the bored official asked her a few desultory questions, stamped her U.K. passport, and ushered her through.

A small crowd of people was waiting at the arrivals area. She paused, scanning the crowd, until she noticed a tall man in a gray flannel suit standing at the fringe. She recognized him instantly, so uncanny was the resemblance to his brother, with his high smooth forehead, aquiline nose, and aristocratic bearing. Just seeing a person with such a close resemblance to Pendergast made her heart accelerate. But there were differences, too. He was taller and less wiry, a little more heavily built perhaps; but his face was sharper, the cheekbones and bony ridges around the eyes more pronounced, all of which, taken together, gave his face a curiously asymmetrical feeling. His hair was ginger-colored and he sported a thick, neatly trimmed beard. But the most startling difference was in his eyes: one was a rich hazel green, the other a glaucous blue. She wondered if he was blind in the pale eye—it looked dead.

She smiled, gave him a quick wave.

He, too, broke into a smile and came walking over with a languid step, his hands outstretched. He grasped her hand in both of his, hands cool and soft. "Lady Maskelene?"

"Call me Viola."

"Viola. I'm charmed." His voice had much of his brother's buttery southern tones, yet although his manner of speech was almost as languorous as his walk, his words were very precisely enunciated, as if bitten off at the ends. It was an unusual, almost strange combination.

"A pleasure to meet you, Diogenes."

"My brother has been quite mysterious about you, but I know he's anxious to see you. Is this your luggage?" He snapped his fingers and a porter came rushing over. "See that this lady's luggage is brought to the black Lincoln parked just outside," Diogenes told him. "The trunk is open." A twenty appeared in his hand as if by magic, but the man was so captivated by Viola that he barely saw it.

Diogenes turned back to Viola. "And how was your trip?"

"Bloody awful."

"I'm sorry I couldn't suggest a more convenient flight. It's been rather a hectic time for my brother, as you know, and the logistics of arranging the meeting were a bit daunting."

"No matter. The important thing is that I'm here."

"Indeed it is. Shall we go?" He offered her his arm and she took it. It was surprisingly strong, the muscles hard as steel cables, very different from the soft, languid impression his movements gave.

"There'd be no mistaking you for anyone but Aloysius's brother," she said as they walked out of the baggage claim area.

"I'll take that as a compliment."

They went through the revolving doors into a blast of cold air. A dusting of fresh snow glittered on the sidewalks beyond the covered walkway.

"Brrr!" Viola said, recoiling. "When I left Capraia, it was a balmy twenty degrees. This is barbaric!"

"That would be twenty degrees Celsius, of course," said Diogenes with a wink. "How I envy you, able to live there year-round. My car." He opened the door for her, then went around, waited for the skycap to close the trunk, then slipped in the other side.

"I don't actually live there year-round. Normally at this time of year, I'm in Luxor, working on a dig in the Valley of the Nobles. But this year, with the blasted state of the Middle East, I ran into some permit problems."

Diogenes accelerated smoothly from the curb and merged into the traffic headed for the airport exit. "An Egyptologist," he said. "How fascinating. I myself spent some time in Egypt, a junior member of the von Hertsgaard expedition."

"Not the one that went into Somalia looking for the diamond mines of Queen Hatshepsut? The one where Hertsgaard was found decapitated?"

"The very one."

"How exciting! I'd love to hear about it."

" 'Exciting' is certainly one way to describe it."

"Is it true that Hertsgaard may have found the Hatshepsut mines just before he was murdered?"

Diogenes laughed quietly. "I sincerely doubt it. You know how these rumors get started. What I find more interesting than those mythical mines is the very real Queen Hatshepsut herself—the only female pharaoh—but, of course, you know all about her, I'm sure."

"Fascinating woman."

"She claimed legitimacy by saying that her mother slept with the god Amon and that she was the issue. How does that famous inscription go? *Amon found the queen sleeping in her room. When the pleasant odors that proceeded from him announced his presence she awoke. He showed himself in his godlike splendor, and when he approached the queen she wept for joy at his strength and beauty and gave herself to him.*"

Viola was intrigued: Diogenes seemed to be as much of a polymath as his brother.

"So tell me, Viola. What kind of work are you doing in the Valley of the Nobles?"

"We've been excavating the tombs of several royal scribes."

"Find any treasures—gold or, even better, jewels?"

"Nothing like that. They were all robbed in antiquity. We're after inscriptions."

"What a marvelous profession, Egyptology. It seems my brother appreciates interesting women."

"I hardly know your brother, to tell you the truth."

"That will change this week, I have little doubt."

"I'm looking forward to it." She laughed a little self-consciously. "Actually, I still can't believe I'm here. This whole trip is such a . . . a caprice. So *mysterious*. I love mysteries."

"So does Aloysius. It seems you two are made for each other."

Viola felt herself coloring. She quickly changed the

subject. "Do you know anything about this case he's been working on?"

"It's been one of the most difficult of his career. Fortunately, it's almost over. Today, in fact, will come the denouement—and then he'll be free. The case involves a serial killer, a truly insane individual, who for various obscure reasons has conceived a deep hatred for Aloysius. He's been killing people and taunting my brother with his inability to catch him."

"How *terrible*."

"Yes. My brother was forced to go underground so abruptly in order to conduct his investigation that it gave everyone the impression he'd been killed."

"I thought he was dead. Lieutenant D'Agosta told me as much."

"Only I knew the truth. I helped him after that Italian ordeal, nursed him back to health. I saved his life, if I may be allowed a moment of self-congratulation."

"I'm so glad he has a brother like you."

"Aloysius has few real friends. He's very old-fashioned, somewhat forbidding, a bit standoffish. And so I've tried to be his friend as well as his brother. I'm so glad he found you. I was so worried about him after that dreadful accident with his wife in Tanzania."

Wife? Tanzania? Suddenly, Viola found herself wanting very much to ask what had happened. She resisted: Aloysius would tell her in good time, and she had always had the English abhorrence of prying into someone else's personal life.

"He hasn't really found me yet. We're just the most casual of new friends, you know."

Diogenes turned his strange, bicolored eyes to her and

smiled. "I believe my brother is already in love with you."

This time Viola colored violently, feeling a sudden mixture of excitement, embarrassment, and foolishness. *Stuff,* she thought. *How could he be in love with me after one meeting?*

"And I have reason to believe you are in love with him."

Viola managed a careless laugh, but she was tingling all over with the strangest sensation. The car hurtled through the frosty night. "This is all *far* too premature," she finally managed to say.

"While Aloysius and I are much alike, I do differ from him in terms of directness. Forgive me if I've embarrassed you."

"Think nothing of it."

The Long Island Expressway stretched ahead, a snowy alley of darkness. It was almost one o'clock in the morning and there were few cars on the road. Flakes of snow were drifting down, whipping up and over the windshield of the car as they hurtled along.

"Aloysius was always the indirect one. I could never tell what he was thinking, even when he was a boy."

"He does seem a bit inscrutable, I suppose."

"Very inscrutable. Rarely does he ever reveal his real motivations for doing things. For example, I've always believed he devoted himself to public service to make up for some of the black sheep in the Pendergast line."

"Really?" Viola's curiosity was piqued again.

An easy laugh. "Yes. Take Great-Aunt Cornelia, for example. Lives not far from here, at the Mount Mercy Hospital for the Criminally Insane."

Curiosity was replaced by surprise. "Criminally insane?"

"That's right. Every family has its black sheep, I suppose."

Viola thought of her own great-grandfather. "Yes, that's true."

"Some families more than others."

She nodded, glanced over, found Diogenes looking at her, quickly lowered her eyes.

"I think it adds interest, *spice,* to a family lineage. Much better to have a murderer for a great-grandfather than a shopkeeper."

"A rather unique point of view." Diogenes might be a little odder than first impressions indicated, but he was certainly amusing.

"Any interesting criminals in your ancestry?" Diogenes asked. "If you don't mind me prying."

"Not at all. No criminals, exactly, but I did have an ancestor who was one of the great violin virtuosi of the nineteenth century. He went insane, froze to death in a shepherd's hut in the Dolomites."

"Exactly my point! I felt sure you would have some interesting ancestors. No dull accountants or traveling salesmen in your lineage, eh?"

"Not that I know of."

"Actually, we *did* have a traveling salesman in our own ancestry—contributed greatly to the Pendergast fortune, in fact."

"Really?"

"Indeed. He concocted a quack medicine by the name of Hezekiah's Compound Elixir and Glandular Restorative. Started by selling it from the back of a wagon."

Viola laughed. "What a funny name for a medicine."

"Hilarious. Except it consisted of a deadly combination of cocaine, acetanilid, and some rather nasty alkaloid botanicals. It caused uncounted numbers of addictions and thousands of deaths, including that of his own wife."

The laughter died in Viola's throat. She felt a twinge of uneasiness. "I see."

"Of course, nobody knew back then of the dangers of drugs like cocaine. You can't fault Great-Great-Grandfather Hezekiah for that."

"No, of course not."

They fell silent. The light snow continued to fall, the flakes drifting out of the dark sky, a glitter flashing through the headlights—and then were gone.

"Do you think there's such a thing as a criminal gene?" asked Diogenes.

"No," said Viola. "I think that's rubbish."

"Sometimes I wonder. There have been so many in our own family. There was Uncle Antoine, for example, one of the truly great mass murderers of the nineteenth century. Killed and mutilated almost a hundred workhouse girls and boys."

"How awful," murmured Viola.

The feeling of uneasiness grew stronger.

Diogenes gave an easy laugh. "The English transported their criminals to the colonies—Georgia and then Australia. They figured it would purge the Anglo-Saxon race of the criminal classes, but the more criminals they transported, the higher the crime rate became."

"Crime obviously had a lot more to do with economic conditions than genetics," said Viola.

"You think so? True: I would not have wanted to be poor in nineteenth-century England. In my view, the real criminals back then were the titled classes. Less than one

percent of the people owned more than ninety-five percent of the land. And with the enclosure laws, the English
lords could evict their tenant farmers, who flocked to the
cities and either starved or turned to crime."

"True," Viola murmured. It seemed Diogenes had forgotten that she came from those titled classes.

"But here in America, it was different. How would you
explain the fact that criminals run in some families like
blue eyes or blond hair? In every generation, the Pendergast family seems to have produced a killer. After Antoine, let's see . . . There was Comstock Pendergast,
famed mesmerist, magician, and mentor of Harry Hou-
dini. He killed his business partner and the man's poor
family, and then committed suicide. Cut his own throat
twice. Then . . ."

"Pardon?" Viola realized that she was unconsciously
gripping the door handle.

"Oh, yes. Twice. The first time he didn't quite get it
deep enough, you see. I guess he didn't relish the thought
of bleeding slowly to death. Myself, I wouldn't mind
dying a slow death by exsanguination—I hear it's rather
like going to sleep. I would have plenty of time to admire
the blood, which has such an exquisite color. Do you like
the color of blood, Viola?"

"Excuse me?" Viola felt panic well up within her.

"Blood. The color of a fine ruby. Or vice versa. I personally find it to be the most compelling color there is.
Some might call me eccentric, but there it is."

Viola tried to quell her feelings of fear and uncertainty.
They were now far from the city, and the dark night
rushed by, only a few lights on in the darkened neighbor-
hoods they passed, barely visible from the highway.

"Where are we going?" she asked.

"To a little place called the Springs. A charming cottage on the shore. It's about two more hours."

"And Aloysius is there?"

"Of course. Dying to see you."

This whole trip was a colossal mistake, she could see that now. Another foolish, impulsive decision. She'd been caught up in the heady romance of it, in the relief of learning Pendergast was still alive. But the truth was, she hardly knew the man. And this brother of his . . .

Suddenly, the thought of spending two more hours in a car with him was unthinkable.

"Viola," came the soft voice, "I'm sorry. Are you all right?"

"Fine. Just fine."

"You look worried."

She took a deep breath. "To tell you the truth, Diogenes, I'd prefer to stay in New York tonight. I'm more tired than I realized. I'll see Aloysius when he comes to town."

"Oh, no! He'll be *crushed.*"

"I can't help that. If you would, please turn the car around? Really, I'm terribly sorry for the sudden change of mind, but this will be best. You've been very kind. Please take me back to New York."

"If that's what you want. I'll have to get off at the next exit to reverse direction."

She felt a wave of relief. "Thank you. I'm really awfully sorry for putting you to all this trouble."

The exit soon came: Hempstead. The car slowed, exited. It approached the stop sign at the top of the exit ramp and cruised to a stop. There were no cars in sight and Viola sat back, hand still unconsciously clutching the door handle, and waited for Diogenes to proceed.

But he didn't proceed. And then, suddenly, she smelled the queerest chemical odor.

She turned quickly. "What is—?"

A hand holding a bunched cloth clamped itself over her mouth while an arm lashed around her neck with lightning speed and wrenched her brutally down to the seat. She was pinned, the stinking cloth jammed mercilessly over her nose and mouth. She struggled, trying to breathe, but it was as if a door of darkness had just opened before her: against her will, she leaned forward, falling and falling into darkness, and then the world went blank.

Forty-four

THE WINTRY SCENE could not have been more bleak: a thin snow had fallen on the cemetery the night before, and now a bitter wind blew through the bare trees, rattling the branches and sending wisps of snow whipping across the frozen ground. The grave itself looked like a black wound in the earth, surrounded by bright green Astroturf laid on the snow, with a second Astroturf carpet laid over the pile of dirt. The coffin rested beside the hideous hole, strapped to a machine that would lower it into the grave. Huge bouquets of fresh flowers stood about, jittering in the wind, adding a surreal fecundity to the frozen scene.

Nora could not take her gaze from the coffin. Wherever she turned, she always seemed drawn back to it. It was a highly polished affair, with brass handles and trim. Nora couldn't accept that her friend, her new friend, lay inside. Dead. How terrible to think that, just a few days before, she and Margo had been enjoying dinner together in Margo's apartment, chatting about the museum.

That same night she had been murdered.

And then, yesterday, the very disturbing, very urgent call from Pendergast . . .

She shivered uncontrollably, took a few deep breaths. Her fingers were freezing even through her gloves, and her nose felt like it had lost all sensation. She was so cold that she thought the tears might freeze on her face.

The minister, dressed in a long black down coat, was reading Rite One of the Burial of the Dead from the Book of Common Prayer, his voice sonorous in the freezing air. A large crowd had turned out—amazingly large when you considered the weather. An enormous quantity of people had come from the museum. Margo had clearly made a large impression even during her short tenure there: but then, she had also been a graduate student there years before. Standing near the front was the museum's director, Collopy, with a stunningly beautiful wife even younger than Nora. Most of the Anthropology Department had showed up, except for those who were supervising the desperate last-minute work on the Sacred Images show: the opening gala was this evening. She herself should have stayed at the show, but she would never have forgiven herself if she'd missed Margo's funeral. There was Prine, bundled up like an Eskimo and dabbing at his bright red nose with a cotton handkerchief; the security director, Manetti, looking genuinely stricken, probably feeling that Margo's death had been a personal failure. Her eye roamed the crowd. A quietly weeping woman stood at the front, supported on either side by ushers: no doubt Margo's mother. She had Margo's light brown hair, her same fine features and slim build. She seemed to be the only member of Margo's family—and Nora remembered Margo saying at dinner that she was an only child.

A particularly strong gust of wind rattled through the cemetery, temporarily overwhelming the minister's voice. Then it returned: "Into thy hands, O Lord, we commend thy servant Margo, our dear sister, as into the hands of a faithful Creator and most merciful Savior, beseeching thee that she may be precious in thy sight . . ."

Nora bent against the bitter wind and drew her coat tighter as she listened to the sad, soothing words. She wished with all her heart that Bill was there with her. The bizarre telephone call from Pendergast—and it *was* Pendergast, she had no doubt—had left her shaken. Bill's life threatened, and he in hiding? And now her own life in danger? It all seemed incredible, frightening, as if a dark cloud had descended on her world. And yet the evidence was directly in front of her. Margo was dead.

A humming noise broke her black reverie. The machine was lowering Margo's coffin into the grave with a grinding of gears and the whirring of a motor. The minister's voice raised slightly as the coffin descended. Making the sign of the cross with an upraised hand, he read the last words of the service. With a faint thump, the coffin came to rest, and then the minister invited Margo's mother to throw in a clod of dirt. She did so, and some others followed, the frozen clods making a disturbingly hollow sound as they struck the coffin lid.

Nora felt as if her heart would break. Her friendship with Margo, which had gotten off to such a bad start, had just begun to blossom. Her death was a tragedy in the truest sense of the word—she was so brave, so full of conviction.

The service over, the crowd began to drift back toward the narrow cemetery lane where their cars waited, frosty breath rising in the air. Nora checked her watch: ten o'clock. She had to get back to the museum immediately, to work on the final preparations for the opening.

As she turned to leave, she saw a man dressed in black approach obliquely; a few more moments and he had fallen into step beside her. He looked haggard with grief, and she wondered if Margo didn't have other close relatives, after all.

"Nora?" came the low voice.

Nora was startled. She paused.

"Keep walking, please."

She kept walking, feeling mounting alarm. "Who are you?"

"Agent Pendergast. Why are you out in the open after my warning?"

"I have to live my life."

"You can't live a life if you've lost it."

Nora sighed. "I want to know what's happened to Bill."

"Bill is safe, as I explained. It is you I'm worried about. You're a prime target."

"Target of what?"

"I can't tell you that. What I can tell you is that you must take steps to protect yourself. You should be afraid."

"Agent Pendergast, I *am* afraid. Your call scared me half to death. But you can't expect me to drop everything. As I told you, I've got an opening I've got to prepare for tonight."

A sharp, exasperated exhalation. "He's killing everyone around me. He will kill you, too. And then you'll miss not only your opening but the rest of your life."

The voice, far from the honeyed drawl she remembered, was tense and urgent.

"I *have* to take the risk. I'll be in the museum the rest of the day, under high security in the exhibit. And then I'll be at the opening tonight, surrounded by thousands."

"High security did not stop him before."

"Who is this *him*?"

"As I've said, to tell you more would only put you at greater risk. Oh, Nora, *what* must I do to *protect* you?"

She faltered, shocked at the near despair in his voice. "I'm sorry. Look, it's just not in my nature to run and hide. I've worked too long for this opening. People are counting on me. Okay? Tomorrow—let's take this up again tomorrow. Just not today."

"So be it." The anonymous figure turned away— strange how little he looked like the Pendergast Nora remembered—melted into the dark clusters of people walking toward their cars, and was gone.

Forty-five

D'AGOSTA PAUSED at the door of Hayward's office, feeling almost afraid to knock. The painful memory of their first encounter in her office came into his mind unbidden, and he forced it away with great effort, rapping more loudly than he intended.

"Come in." The very sound of her voice caused his heart to pause. He grasped the handle, pushed open the door.

The office looked very different. Gone were the various piles of paper, the pleasant, controlled untidiness. Now it was severe in its organization—and it was clear Hayward was working, living, and breathing a single case.

And there she was, standing behind her desk, her short, slim figure in a neat gray suit with captain's bars on the shoulder, looking directly at him. The look was so intense D'Agosta found himself almost pushed back by it.

"Have a seat." The voice was coldly neutral.

"Listen, Laura, before we begin, I just want to say—"

"Lieutenant," came the crisp response. "You've been

summoned here on police business, and anything you might have to say of a personal nature is inappropriate."

D'Agosta looked at her. This was unfair. "Laura, please . . ."

Her face softened, but only for a moment, and she spoke in a low voice. "Vincent, don't do this to me or to yourself. Especially not now. I have something very, very difficult to show you."

This stopped D'Agosta.

"Please take a seat."

"I'll stand."

Brief silence while she stared at him. Then she spoke again. "Pendergast is alive."

D'Agosta felt himself go cold. He hadn't known why she'd summoned him, hadn't even dared to guess—but this was the last thing he'd expected. "How did you find out?" he blurted.

Her face tightened with anger. "So you *did* know."

Another tense silence. Then she reached down and picked up a piece of paper, drew it in front of her. D'Agosta could see it was a list of handwritten notes. What was this about? He had never seen Laura so wound up.

"On January 19, Professor Torrance Hamilton was poisoned in front of a lecture hall of two hundred students in his class at Louisiana State University and died about an hour later. The only useful evidence uncovered from the crime scene, some black fibers found in his office, is analyzed in this report." She dropped a slim folder on her desk.

D'Agosta glanced at it but did not pick it up.

"The report states that the fibers were from a very costly cashmere-merino blended-wool fabric made for only a few years in the 1950s in a factory outside Prato, Italy. The only place it was sold in America—the *only* place— was a small shop on Rue Lespinard in New Orleans. A shop patronized by the Pendergast family."

D'Agosta felt a sudden hope. Was it possible, after all, that she believed him? That she'd checked into Diogenes? "Laura, I—"

"Lieutenant, *let me finish*. My forensic team searched Pendergast's apartment in the Dakota—at least the rooms we could get into—and took fiber samples. In addition, we found two dozen identical black suits in a closet. The suits and the fibers all came from the same source: those bolts of cashmere-merino wool, dyed black. This is a virtually unique fiber. There can be no mistake."

D'Agosta felt a very strange sensation crawl up his spine. He suddenly had a premonition of where this might be going.

"On January 22, Charles Duchamp was hung from his apartment building on 65th and Broadway. Again, the crime scene was unusually clean. However, our forensic team did recover a few more of the same black fibers that were found at the Torrance homicide. In addition, the rope used to hang Duchamp was woven of a rare type of gray silk. We ultimately learned it is a special type of rope used in Buddhist religious ceremonies in Bhutan. The monks tie these silk ropes into incredibly complex knots for meditative and contemplative purposes. These are unique knots, found nowhere else in the world."

She paused, laid down a photograph of the rope that hung Duchamp, showing the knot, smeared with blood. "That particular knot is known as *Ran t'ankha durdag,* 'the tangled path to hell.' It has come to my attention that

Special Agent Pendergast spent time in Bhutan studying with the very monks who make these knots."

"There's a simple answer—"

"Vincent, if you interrupt me one more time, I'll have you muzzled."

D'Agosta fell silent.

"The next day, on January 23, FBI Special Agent Michael Decker was murdered in his house in Washington, D.C., stabbed through the mouth with an antique Civil War bayonet. This crime scene was equally clean. The forensic team recovered fibers from the same bolt of cashmere-merino wool found at the Hamilton poisoning." She laid another report before D'Agosta.

"At around two o'clock in the morning of January 26, Margo Green was fatally stabbed in the New York Museum of Natural History. I've gone over the museum's personnel lists, and she was the last person to enter the exhibition hall. But she also checked out of the hall—the murderer must have used her card to leave. This crime scene wasn't nearly as clean as the others. Green was a formidable opponent, and she put up a struggle. She defended herself with a box cutter and wounded her assailant. Blood not belonging to the victim was recovered from the scene, both on the box cutter—which had been imperfectly wiped clean—and from a single spot on the floor." She paused. "The DNA tests came back late last night."

She picked up a piece of paper and, with a snap, dropped it, too, in front of D'Agosta. "Those are the results."

D'Agosta couldn't bring himself to look. He knew the answer already.

"That's right. Special Agent Pendergast."

D'Agosta knew better than to say anything.

"Which brings me to motive. All these people had something in common—they were close acquaintances of Pendergast. Hamilton was Pendergast's language tutor in high school. Duchamp was Pendergast's closest—and perhaps only—childhood friend. Michael Decker was Pendergast's mentor at the FBI. He's one of the main reasons Pendergast has even *survived* in the FBI, after all the trouble his unorthodox methods got him into. And finally—as you well know—Margo Green was a close friend of Pendergast's from two cases dating back several years, the museum murders and the subway killings.

"All this evidence, all these tests, have been checked and rechecked. There can be no mistake. Special Agent Pendergast is a psychopathic killer."

D'Agosta had gone cold. He realized now why Diogenes had saved Pendergast the way he did, why he'd helped nurse him back to life after what had happened in the Castel Fosco. It wasn't enough just to murder his brother's friends. No—he would also frame him for the crimes.

"And now *this*," Hayward said. She showed him another report. It was bound in plastic, and the title was visible:

Psychological Profile
Hamilton/Duchamp/Decker/Green Killer
Behavioral Science Unit
Federal Bureau of Investigation, Quantico

"I didn't tell them that I suspected one of their own. I just told them we thought the crimes might be connected and asked them to draw up a profile. Because of the

Decker killing, I got it back in twenty-four. Go ahead and read it if you want, but here's the short version. The killer is a highly educated male with at least four years of post-graduate education. He's an expert chemist. He's thoroughly familiar with forensic and police procedure and he probably once worked, or still works, in law enforcement. He has a broad knowledge across a range of subjects in science, literature, math, history, music, and art—in short, he is a Renaissance man. His I.Q. lies in the 180 to 200 range. His age is probably between thirty and fifty. He is well traveled and probably multilingual. He is likely ex-military. He is a person of considerable financial means. He is very adept at disguises."

She looked D'Agosta in the eye. "This remind you of anyone, Vincent?"

D'Agosta didn't reply.

"Those are the outward details. Now comes the psych analysis." She paused, finding the place in the report. "The killer is a self-controlled and controlling person. He's extremely well organized, neat, and places a high premium on logic. He represses any outward show of emotion and rarely, if ever, confides in anyone. He has few, if any, real friends and has difficulty forming relationships with the opposite sex. This individual probably suffered a difficult childhood, with a cold, controlling mother and a distant or absent father. His family relationships were not close. There will probably be a history of mental illness or crime in the family. As a young boy, he suffered a crippling emotional trauma involving a close family member—mother, father, or sibling—that he has spent the rest of his life compensating for. He is deeply suspicious of authority, considers himself intellectually and morally superior to others—"

"What a load of psychobabble!" D'Agosta exploded. "It's all twisted up. This isn't the way he is at all!"

He stopped abruptly. Hayward was looking at him with raised eyebrows.

"So you *do* recognize this person."

"Of course I recognize him! But this is a twisting of who he really is. Pendergast didn't murder those people. He was framed. The evidence, the blood, was planted. His brother, Diogenes, is the killer."

Another long silence. "Go on," she said, her tone neutral.

"After Pendergast's ordeal in Italy, when we all thought he was dead, Diogenes took him to a clinic to recover. He was sick, drugged. It must have allowed Diogenes plenty of opportunity to harvest all the forensic evidence he needed to frame Pendergast—hair, fibers, blood. It's *Diogenes*. Don't you see? He's hated Pendergast all his life, he's been planning this for years. He sent Pendergast a taunting letter saying he was going to commit the perfect crime and naming the date—today."

"You're not going to lay this crazy theory on me again, Vincent—"

"It's my turn to talk. Diogenes wanted to commit a crime even more horrible than killing his brother. He wanted to kill everyone his brother loves but leave his brother alive. Now it seems he's also framing his brother for those same crimes—"

D'Agosta stopped. She was looking at him with an expression of pity bordering almost on pain.

"Vinnie, you remember how you told me to look into Diogenes? Well, I did. I had a hell of a time tracing him, but here's what I found." She opened a folder, took out yet another document, and slid it in front of him. It was stamped and embossed and notarized.

"What is it?"

"A death certificate. Of Diogenes Dagrepont Bernoulli Pendergast. He was killed twenty years ago in a car accident in the U.K."

"A forgery. I saw a letter from him. I know he's alive."

"What makes you think *Pendergast* didn't write the letter?"

D'Agosta stared at her. "Because I *saw* Diogenes. With my own eyes."

"Is that so? Where?"

"Outside Fosco's castle. When we were being chased. He had eyes of two different colors, just like Cornelia Pendergast told us."

"And how do you know it was Diogenes?"

D'Agosta hesitated. "Pendergast told me."

"Did you speak to him?"

"No. But I saw a picture of him as a child, just recently. It was the same face."

A long silence followed. Hayward reached down and picked up the forensic profile again. "There's something else in here. Read it." She pushed a piece of paper over to him.

```
The target subject may manifest symptoms
of a rare form of multiple personality
disorder, a variant of Munchausen syn-
drome by proxy, in which the subject acts
out two separate, diametrically opposite
roles: that of killer and of investiga-
tor. In this unusual condition, the
killer may also be a law enforcement of-
```

ficer assigned to the case or an investigator connected to the case. In another
variant of this pathology, the killer is
a private citizen who initiates his own
investigation into the killings, often
making apparently brilliant discoveries
of evidence that law enforcement has
overlooked. In both variants, the killer
personality leaves minute clues for the
investigator personality to discover,
such discoveries often made apparently
through extraordinary powers of observation and/or deduction. The killer personality and investigator personality are
not aware of each other's existence on a
conscious level, although much cooperation is noted on the subconscious, pathological level.

"Bullshit. Munchausen by proxy is about somebody
wanting attention. Pendergast goes *out of his way* to
avoid the limelight. This doesn't describe Pendergast.
You know the guy, you've worked with him. What does
your gut tell you?"

"You don't want to know what my gut tells me." Her
dark eyes were scrutinizing him. "Vinnie, you know why
I'm sharing this information with you?"

"Why?"

"For one thing, because I think you're in terrible danger. Pendergast is a crazy son of a bitch and he's going to
kill you next. I know he will."

"He won't kill me because he isn't the killer."

"The Pendergast you know isn't even *aware* he's the
killer. He believes in this Diogenes. He genuinely thinks

his brother is still alive and that you two are going to find him. It's all part of the pathology mentioned here." She slapped the report. "There's the other personality of his . . . Diogenes. Who exists within the same body. That personality you haven't met yet. But you will . . . *when he kills you.*"

D'Agosta couldn't even find the words to respond.

"I don't know. Maybe I shouldn't have told you all this." Her voice hardened. "You don't have a right to know any of this after how royally you've screwed up. I went out on a ten-mile limb for you, got you a great position on the force—and you betrayed my trust, you rejected my . . ." She paused, breathing hard, recovering her composure.

Now D'Agosta felt a flash of real anger. "I betrayed *you*? Listen, Laura: I *tried* to talk with you about this. I tried to explain. But you pushed me away, saying I was obsessing over someone's death. How do you think that felt? Or how do you think I feel now, listening to you say how naive I am, how gullible, trusting Pendergast like this? You've seen my casework in the past, you know what I'm capable of. Why do you think I'm so wrong now?"

The question hung in the air.

"This isn't the time or place for that discussion," Hayward replied after a moment. Her tone had grown quiet and businesslike. "And we're straying from the point."

"And what, exactly, is the point?"

"I want you to bring Pendergast in."

D'Agosta stood rooted in place, thunderstruck. He should have seen it coming.

"Bring him in. Save yourself. Save your career. If he's innocent, let him have his day in court."

"But the evidence against him is overwhelming—"

"That's right. It's damning as hell. And you didn't even see the half of it. But that's the way our system works: bring him in and let him face a jury of his peers."

"Bring him in? How?"

"I've got it all worked out. You're the only man he trusts."

"You're asking me to betray him?"

"*Betray?* My God, Vinnie, *the man's a serial killer.* Four innocent people are dead. And there's another thing you seem to be overlooking. Your actions to date—keeping Pendergast's existence secret, lying to me, lying to Captain Singleton—border on obstruction of justice. Now that you know Pendergast is a fugitive—that's right, a warrant for his arrest has already been sworn out—any further actions on your part to protect him will amount to criminal obstruction and accessory after the fact. You're already in deep shit, and this is the only way you're going to get out of it. You bring him in, or you go to jail. It's that simple."

For a long moment, D'Agosta said nothing. When he spoke, his voice sounded dead, wooden, even in his own ears. "Give me a day to think it over."

"A day?" She looked at him incredulously. "You've got ten minutes."

Forty-six

$\mathcal{V}$IOLA WOKE WITH a splitting headache. For a moment, she stared blankly, uncomprehendingly, at the frilled top of a canopied bed rising above her. And then it all came back: the drive along the dark highway, the increasingly bizarre comments by Pendergast's brother, the sudden attack . . .

She fought down a rising wave of panic, lying still, concentrating only on her breathing, trying not to think of anything at all.

Finally—when she felt she was master of herself—she sat up slowly. Her head reeled, and dark spots danced across her vision. She closed her eyes. When at last the throbbing had subsided a little, she opened her eyes once again and looked around the room.

It was a small bedroom with rose-patterned wallpaper, some old Victorian furniture, and a single barred window. Moving carefully—for the sake of both her headache and silence—she swung her legs over the bed and stood unsteadily on the floor. Quietly, she reached for the door handle and gave it a turn, but, as she expected, it was locked. A second twinge of panic was suppressed more quickly than the first.

She went to the window and looked out. The house was set a few hundred yards back from a marshy bay. Beyond a line of scraggly dunes, she could see a pounding line of surf and a dark ocean flecked with whitecaps. The sky was a metal gray and, with the instinct of somebody who had spent many nights under the open sky, she sensed it was morning. On both the right and the left, she could just make out a pair of ramshackle beach houses, their windows boarded up for the season. The beach was empty.

She reached through the bars and tapped on the glass. It seemed to be unusually blue and thick—perhaps unbreakable. And soundproofed, too—at least, she could not hear the surf.

Still moving slowly, and making every effort to be silent, she walked into a small adjoining bathroom. Like the bedroom, it was old-fashioned and neat, with a sink, a claw-footed tub, and another small window, also barred and paned in the same oddly thick glass. She turned on the tap and out came a gush of water, which quickly went from cold to piping hot. Shutting it off, she returned to the bedroom.

She sat back down on the bed, thinking. It was all so unreal, so utterly bizarre, it was impossible to comprehend. That the person who had picked her up was Pendergast's brother, she had absolutely no doubt—in many ways, he was practically a twin of the man. But why had he kidnapped her like this? What were his intentions? And, most important: what on earth was Pendergast's role in it? How could she have been so wrong about him?

But then, when she thought back to their brief meeting on the island of Capraia last fall, she realized how strange it all was. Perhaps word of his tragic death had made her romanticize their lone encounter and made it seem more than it really was. And then that letter, with its news that Pendergast was still alive, and its romantic, impulsive request . . .

Impulsive. That was the word. Once again she had allowed her impulsiveness to get her into trouble—and this time it looked like deadly serious trouble.

Was it possible that D'Agosta was in on it, too? That the entire story of Pendergast's death had been a sham, part of some complex plot to lure her here? Was this some kind of sophisticated kidnapping network? Or were they holding her for ransom? The more she thought about this complete and utter dog's breakfast, the more she felt fear giving way to anger and outrage. But even that emotion she repressed. Better to direct her energies toward escape.

She went back into the bathroom and made a quick inventory: plastic comb, toothbrush, toothpaste, water glass, clean towels, washcloth, shampoo. She reached down and picked up the glass. It was heavy and cold, real glass.

She turned it over thoughtfully in her hands. A sharp piece would make a weapon, but it could also double as a tool. Escape through the windows was out of the question, and no doubt the door would be reinforced and secure. But this was an old house, and the walls would probably be plaster and lath beneath the wallpaper.

She took a towel, wrapped it tightly around the glass, and gave it several sharp taps on the edge of the sink until it broke. She unwrapped the towel: as she'd hoped, the glass had broken into several large pieces. She took the sharpest, walked back into the bedroom, and approached the opposite wall. Careful to minimize noise, she stuck the pointed edge into the wallpaper and gave an exploratory thrust.

It immediately slipped, taking with it a piece of the wallpaper. She saw, to her dismay, the glint of metal underneath. With her fingernails, she caught the cut edge of wallpaper and peeled it back, revealing a smooth, cold expanse of steel.

A chill went up her spine. And in that moment, a knock came at the door.

She started, then quickly climbed back into the bed, pretending to be asleep.

The knock came again, and a third time, and then she heard the scrape of a key in the lock. The door creaked open. She lay there, eyes closed, shard of glass concealed beside her body.

"Dear Viola. I know you have been up and about."

Still she lay there.

"I see you have already discovered I've decorated your room in metal. Now, please sit up and stop this tiresome charade. I have something important to tell you."

Viola sat up, anger returning. A man stood in the doorway whom she did not recognize, although the voice was unmistakably that of Diogenes.

"Forgive my unusual appearance; I am dressed for the city. To which I am headed in a few minutes."

"In disguise, it seems. You fancy yourself a right Sherlock Holmes."

The man bowed his head.

"What do you want, Diogenes?"

"I have what I want—you."

"Whatever for?"

The strange man gave a broad smile. "What do I want with you? Frankly, I could care less about you, except for one thing: you aroused the interest of my brother. I heard your name pass his lips just once, no more. It piqued my curiosity. Luckily, your name is unique, your family is prominent, and I was able to find out a great deal—a *great* deal—about you. I suspected tender feelings on your part for my brother. When you responded to my letter, I knew my hunch was right, and that I had landed a prize beyond compare."

"You're an ass. You don't know anything about me."

"My dear Viola, rather than worrying about what I know, you should be worrying about two things you *don't* know—and should. First, you need to know that you cannot get out of this room. The walls, floor, ceiling, and door are made of riveted ship's hull steel. The windows are two layers of unbreakable, soundproof, bulletproof glass. The glass is one-way, which means that you can see out but those outside—and there will not be any— cannot see in. I tell you this only to save you trouble. There are books in the bookcase, drinking water from the tap, and some hard candies in the bottom drawer of the bureau for you to suck on."

"My, you've gone to a lot of trouble and expense. Boiled sweets, even."

"Indeed."

"*Indeed.*" She mocked his courtly drawl. "You said you had two things to tell me. What's the second?"

"That you must die. If you believe in a supreme being, be sure to resolve any unfinished business you have with Him. Your death will take place tomorrow morning, at the traditional time: dawn."

Almost without intent, Viola laughed: an angry, bitter laugh. "If you could only hear what a pompous ass you sound! *You will die at dawn.* How histrionic."

Diogenes took a step back, a frown passing fleetingly over his face before neutrality returned. "What a sprightly vixen you are."

"What have I done to you, you bloody nutter?"

"Nothing. It is what you did to my brother."

"I did *nothing* to your brother! Is this some kind of sick joke?"

A dry chuckle. "It is indeed a sick joke, a *very* sick joke."

Anger and frustration burned away her fear. Viola slowly tightened her grip on the shard of glass. "For such a revolting man, you seem insufferably pleased with yourself."

The dry chuckle died off. "My, my. We certainly have a sharp tongue this morning."

"You're crazy."

"I have no doubt that, by the standards of society, I am clinically insane."

Viola's eyes narrowed. "So you're a follower of the Scottish psychiatrist R. D. Laing."

"I follow nobody."

"So you believe, in your ignorance. Laing said, 'Mental illness is the sane response to an insane world.' "

"I commend the gentleman—whoever he is—for his insight. But my dear Viola, I don't have all day to exchange pleasantries—"

"My *dear* Diogenes—if only you knew just how boorish you sound." She put on a deadly accurate imitation of his languid accent. "How *dreadfully* sorry I am that we can't continue this *charming* conversation. You and your feeble attempts at breeding."

There was a silence. Diogenes had lost his smile, but if other thoughts were going through his head, they did not express themselves on his face. Viola was amazed at the depth and clarity of her own anger. She was breathing fast, and her heart was going like mad in her chest.

Diogenes finally sighed. "You are as chattery as a monkey and almost as smart. If I were you, I'd be a little less garrulous and face your end with dignity, as befits your station."

"My station? Oh my God, don't tell me you're another of those American poons who get their willy up meeting some red-nosed baronet or doddering old viscount. I should have known."

"Viola, *please*. You're getting overexcited."

"Wouldn't you be a little overexcited if you had been lured overseas, drugged and kidnapped, locked in a room, and threatened—"

"Viola, *ça suffit!* I will be back in the wee hours of the morning to carry out my promise. Specifically, I will cut your throat. Twice. In honor of our Uncle Comstock."

She suddenly stopped. The fear had come back in full force. "Why?"

"Finally, a sensible question. I am an existentialist. I carve my own meaning out of the suppurating carcass of this rotting universe. Through no fault of your own, you have become part of that meaning. But I do not feel sorry for you. The world is abrim with pain and suffering. I simply choose to direct the festivities instead of offering myself up as another witless victim. I take no pleasure in the suffering of others—except one. *That* is my meaning. I live for my brother, Viola; he gives me strength, he gives me purpose, he gives me life. He is my salvation."

"You and your brother can go to hell!"

"Ah, dear Viola. Didn't you know? This *is* hell. Except that you are about to gain your release."

Viola leaped off the bed and rushed at him, shard raised, but in the blur of an instant she found herself pinned to the floor. Somehow Diogenes now lay on top of her, his face inches from hers, his breath, sweetly smelling of cloves, in her face.

"Good-bye, my lively little monkey," he murmured, and kissed her tenderly on the lips.

And then, in one swift, batlike movement, he rose and was gone, the door slamming behind him. She flung herself on it but it was too late: there was the sound of oiled steel sliding into steel, and the door felt as cold and unyielding as a bank vault.

Forty-seven

D'AGOSTA DIDN'T NEED a day to consider Hayward's offer; he didn't even need ten minutes. He walked straight out of the building, pulled out the cell phone Pendergast had given him, and asked for an emergency meeting.

A quarter of an hour later, as he stepped out of a cab at the corner of Broadway and 72nd, the memory of his encounter with Laura was still raw. But he told himself he couldn't think about that right now. He had to bury his personal feelings until the crisis was over—assuming, that is, it would ever be over.

He walked east down 72nd. Ahead, in the distance, he could see Central Park, the brown trees skeletal in the January chill. At the next intersection, he stopped and pulled out the cell phone again. *Call me again once you reach Columbus and 72nd*, Pendergast had said. D'Agosta was only a block away from Pendergast's apartment at the Dakota. Could he possibly be at home? It seemed outrageous, given the circumstances.

He flipped open the phone, dialed the number.

"Yes?" came the voice of Pendergast. In the background, D'Agosta could hear the tapping of keys.

"I'm at the corner," he replied.

"Very good. Make your way unobserved to 24 West 72nd. The building is mixed residential and commercial. The entrance is locked during working hours, but the receptionist habitually buzzes in anyone who looks normal. Take the stairs to the basement and locate the door marked *B-14*. Make sure you are alone. Then knock slowly, seven times. Have you got that?"

"Got it."

The line went dead.

Putting the phone away, D'Agosta crossed the street and continued toward the park. Up ahead, at the far corner, he could see the crenellated, sand-colored bulk of the Dakota. It looked like something out of a Charles Addams cartoon. At its base, beside a huge Gothic entrance, was a doorman's sentry box. Two cops in uniform loitered nearby, and three squad cars were parked along Central Park West.

It seemed the cavalry was already in place.

D'Agosta slowed his pace, keeping as near as he could to the building fronts, a wary eye on the police.

Twenty-four West 72nd Street was a large brownstone structure halfway down the block. He glanced around again, saw nobody suspicious, rang the buzzer, gained admittance, and quickly ducked inside.

The lobby was small and dark, the walls covered with dingy-looking gray marble. D'Agosta nodded to the receptionist, then made his way down the staircase at the rear of the lobby. There was a single basement hallway, with metal doors set into the cinder-block walls at regular intervals. It was the work of sixty seconds to find the door marked *B-14*. He glanced around once again, then rapped on the door seven times, as instructed.

For a moment, silence. Then, from within, the sound of a bolt being slid back. The door opened and a man wearing the black and white uniform of a doorman appeared. He glanced up and down the hall, then nodded to D'Agosta and ushered him inside.

To his surprise, D'Agosta found himself, not in a room, but in a very narrow hallway—barely more than a crawl space—that ran on ahead into darkness. The doorman switched on a flashlight, then led the way along the corridor.

It seemed to go on forever. The walls changed from cinder block, to brick, to plaster, then back to brick again. At times, the corridor widened; at others, it grew so narrow it almost brushed against D'Agosta's shoulders. It jogged left a few times, then right. At one point, they emerged into a tiny courtyard, little more than an air shaft, and D'Agosta could see a small patch of blue sky far above. It felt like being at the base of a chimney. Then they climbed a short stairway, the doorman opened another door with a large, old-fashioned key, and they entered yet another narrow corridor.

At length, the corridor dead-ended at a small service elevator. The doorman pulled back the brass grillwork, unlocked the elevator door with a different key, and motioned for D'Agosta to step in. The man stepped in behind D'Agosta, closed the grille and the elevator door, then grasped a large, circular handle in one wall. With a protesting chuff, the elevator creaked upward.

The ancient door was windowless, and D'Agosta had no idea how many floors they ascended: he guessed four or five. The elevator stopped of its own accord and the doorman opened its door. As the bronze grille was pulled back, D'Agosta saw a short passageway beyond, leading to a single door. The door was open, and Pendergast stood within it, once again clad in his habitual black suit.

D'Agosta paused, staring at him. Ever since his surprise reappearance, the man had appeared in some disguise or other—his face or clothing, or more usually both, dramatically altered—and it gave D'Agosta a strange chill to see his old friend as he really was.

"Vincent," Pendergast said. "Do come in." And he led the way into a small, almost featureless room. There was an oaken dresser and a leather sofa along one wall, and a worktable along another. Four iMac laptops were lined up on the worktable, along with some NAS devices and what looked to D'Agosta like a network hub. There were two doors in the rear of the room; one was closed, and the other opened onto a small bathroom.

"*This* is your Dakota apartment?" D'Agosta asked in disbelief.

A wan smile appeared on Pendergast's face, then disappeared again. "Hardly," he said, closing the door. "My apartment is on the floor above this one."

"Then what's this place?"

"Think of it as a bolt-hole. A rather high-tech bolt-hole. It was set up last year on the advice of an Ohio acquaintance of mine, in case his services were temporarily unavailable."

"Well, you can't stay here. The cops are crawling all over the entrance to the Dakota. I've just come from Laura Hayward's office, and she's got a red-hot suspect."

"Me."

"And how in *hell* did you learn that?"

"I've known it for some time." Pendergast's eyes darted from monitor to monitor as his hands flew over the keys. "When I came upon the murder scene of my friend

Michael Decker, I found several strands of hair clutched in his hand. Blond hair. My brother's hair is not blond: it's a gingery red. Immediately, I realized that Diogenes's plan was even more 'interesting' than I'd suspected. Not only did he plan to kill everyone close to me—he planned to frame me for their murders."

"But what about the notes Diogenes wrote you? Don't they indicate he's alive?"

"No. Recall the odd handwriting, the handwriting I said was strangely familiar? That was my handwriting, but altered just enough so it would appear—to a handwriting expert, anyway—that I was trying to disguise it."

D'Agosta took a moment to digest this. "Why didn't you tell me?"

"I saw no reason to burden you with all this before it was necessary. When I saw those hairs, it was perfectly clear to me that Diogenes would have salted the other crime scenes with false evidence as well. I'm sure, during my convalescence in Italy, he stocked up on all the physical evidence he needed, taken from my person, including my blood. It was only a matter of time before they connected me to the killings. I had hoped I'd have a little more time than this. Hayward did a commendable job."

"That's not all. Laura asked me to set you up. I walked out on that one. They've sworn out a warrant on you. You can't stay here."

"On the contrary, Vincent, I must stay here. It's the only place with the resources I need on short notice. And it is a bit like Poe's purloined letter—the last place they expect to find me is at home. The police presence is a mere formality."

D'Agosta stared at him. "So *that's* how you knew

Diogenes wouldn't target Laura. She's the one investigating Duchamp's murder. He was banking on her suspecting you."

"Precisely. Now, pull up a chair and let me show you what I'm doing." Pendergast waved his hands toward the four laptops.

"These computers are tapped in parasitically to the city's web of street corner surveillance cameras, along with a couple of major private systems—ATMs and banks, for example." He pointed at one of the screens, which was currently subdivided into a dozen small windows: in each window, black-and-white video feeds of sidewalks, street intersections, and toll plazas were zipping by in accelerated reverse motion.

"Why?"

"I'm convinced Diogenes's final crime is going to take place in or around Manhattan. And you cannot move around a city like New York these days without being photographed, taped, or otherwise surveyed dozens of times every hour."

"But Diogenes is disguised."

"To most, yes. Not to me. You can disguise your appearance, but you can't disguise everything—your mannerisms, the way you walk, even the way you blink your eyes. Diogenes and I are very alike physically. I've videotaped myself, and now I'm running image-recognition and pattern-recognition algorithms against these video-in-various-states-of-motion feeds." He waved at another of the laptops. "As you can see, I'm concentrating particularly on feeds near the Dakota and the intersections around the Riverside Drive mansion. We know Diogenes has been to the mansion, and he has probably been here as well. If I can locate him, acquire an image print, I can track him backwards and forwards visually from that point, try to find a pattern in his movements."

"Wouldn't that need more computing horsepower than you'd find at a small university?"

"Hence the wiring closet." And Pendergast reached over and opened the closed door. Inside, stacked from floor to ceiling, were rack-mounted blade servers and RAID arrays.

D'Agosta whistled. "You understand all this shit?"

"No. But I know how to use it."

Pendergast swiveled to look at him. Although his skin was paler than D'Agosta had ever seen it, the agent's eyes glittered with a dangerous brightness. He had the manic energy, the deceptive second wind, of somebody who had not slept in several days.

"Diogenes is *out* there, Vincent. He's lurking somewhere in this myriad of data streams. To commit his ultimate crime, he's going to have to surface. And that's my chance—my last, my *only* chance—to stop him. This room is the only place anymore where I have access to the technology that can accomplish that." More clattering of keys. "The acquaintance I spoke of just now, the one in Ohio? He would be far better suited to this job than I. But he has been forced to make himself invisible for . . . for reasons of his own protection."

"Laura isn't the type to wait around. They're probably already coming after you."

"And no doubt you, too."

D'Agosta said nothing.

"They've searched my apartment, they've probably searched the Riverside Drive house. As for this little warren . . . well, you saw yourself that I have a private exit from the Dakota. Even the doormen here don't know about it. Only Martyn, who you just met."

He paused in his typing. "Vincent, there is something you must do."

"What's that?"

"You'll go straight to Laura Hayward, say that you'll cooperate in every way, but that I seem to have disappeared and that you've no idea where I am. There's no need for you to damage your career any further over this."

"I already told you, I'm with you all the way."

"Vincent, I am *demanding* that you leave."

"Hey, Aloysius?"

Pendergast looked at him.

"Up yours."

He saw Pendergast's eyes were upon him. "I won't forget this, Vincent."

"Never mind."

The agent went back to his work. Ten minutes passed, twenty—and then Pendergast suddenly stiffened.

"A hit?"

"I believe so," Pendergast said. He was staring intently at one of the computers, playing a grainy image over and over, forward and backward.

D'Agosta looked over his shoulder. "Is that him?"

"The computer believes so. And I do, as well. It's odd, though—the image isn't taken from outside the Dakota, as I'd expected. It's about six blocks north, outside of—"

At that moment, a low chime sounded from a box on the table. Pendergast turned toward it quickly.

"What's that?" D'Agosta asked.

"It's Martyn. It seems there's somebody to see me."

D'Agosta tensed. "Police?"

Pendergast shook his head. He leaned toward the box, depressed a switch.

"A bicycle messenger, sir," came the voice. "He has an envelope for you."

"You've asked him to wait?"

"Yes."

"And the police are unaware of his presence?"

"Yes, sir."

"Bring him up. Take the usual precautions." Pendergast took his finger from the switch and straightened. "Let's see what this is about." His tone was casual, but his face looked drawn.

They walked down the short hallway to the elevator. A minute passed without a word being exchanged. Then, from below, the elevator gave a clank and began to rise. Shortly, the brass grille was drawn back and two figures emerged: the doorman D'Agosta had met earlier and the bicycle messenger, a slim Hispanic youth wearing a scarf and a heavy jacket. He held an oversize envelope in one hand.

Looking at the package, Pendergast's pale face went gray. Wordlessly, he reached into a pocket of his black jacket, withdrew a pair of medical gloves, and drew them on. Then he took a twenty-dollar bill from his wallet and gave it to the messenger.

"Would you mind waiting here a few moments, please?" he asked.

"I guess," the messenger said, looking suspiciously at the gloves.

Pendergast took the envelope, exchanged a private look with the doorman. Then, nodding to D'Agosta, he strode quickly back into the room.

"Is it from Diogenes?" D'Agosta asked, closing the door behind them.

Pendergast didn't respond. Instead, he spread a sheet of white paper on the desk, laid the envelope on top of it, and examined it carefully. It was unsealed, the rear flap loosely fastened by twisted red thread. Pendergast gave the thread a brief, close scrutiny. Then he unwound it and carefully upended the envelope.

A small sheet of folded paper fell out, followed by a lock of glossy dark hair.

Pendergast drew in his breath sharply. In the room, it sounded explosively loud. Quickly, he knelt and opened the folded sheet.

The paper was a beautiful, hand-pressed linen, with an embossed coat of arms at its top: a lidless eye over two moons, with a lion couchant. Beneath, written in tobacco-colored ink with a fountain pen or quill, was a date: January 28.

D'Agosta realized it was identical to the note Pendergast had received a few months earlier, at the mansion on Riverside Drive. Unlike that note, however, this one had more written upon it than just a date. His eye fell to the words below:

She's very spirited, brother. I can see why you like her.

Savor this token as earnest of my claim: a lock of her lovely hair. Savor it also as a memento of her passing. If you caress it you can almost smell the sweet air of Capraia.

Of course, I could be lying about everything. This lock could belong to someone else. Search your heart for the truth.

Frater, ave atque vale.

"Oh, my . . ." D'Agosta said. The words were cut off as his throat closed up involuntarily. He glanced over at the agent. He was sitting on the floor, gently stroking the lock of hair. The look on his face was so terrible D'Agosta had to turn away.

"It could be a lie," he said. "Your brother's lied before."

Pendergast did not answer. There was a brief and awful silence.

"I'll go question the messenger," D'Agosta said, not daring to look back.

Exiting the room, he walked down the corridor to the elevator. The messenger was there, waiting, watched over by Martyn.

"NYPD," he said, briefly showing his badge. Everything had slowed down, as in a nightmare. He felt curiously heavy, as if he could barely move his limbs. He wondered if this was what it was like to be in shock.

The youth nodded.

"Who gave you the package to deliver?"

"Somebody in a cab dropped it off at our service."

"What did the passenger look like?"

"It was just the cabbie. There was no passenger."

"What kind of vehicle, exactly?"

"Typical yellow cab. From the city."

"Did you get a name or medallion number?" Even as he asked the question, D'Agosta knew it wouldn't matter whether the kid had gotten one or not; no doubt Diogenes had covered his trail.

The messenger shook his head.

"How were you paid?"

"The driver paid fifty bucks. Said his instructions were to get a messenger to deliver the package to a Dr. Pendergast, 1 West 72nd Street. In person, if possible. And not to talk to anybody but Dr. Pendergast or the doorman."

"Very well." D'Agosta got the youth's name and employer. Then he took Martyn aside, asking him to make sure the cops didn't stop the messenger as he left the building. The strange feeling of heaviness had not left him. He walked back down the corridor to the small room.

Pendergast did not look up at his entrance. He was still sitting on the floor, hunched forward, the lock of hair placed before him. One hand rested on each knee, palm inward, each thumb forming a small circle with the middle finger. The bereft, grief-stricken expression on his face had disappeared, and in its place was utter impassivity. He did not move, did not blink, didn't even seem to breathe. He looked to D'Agosta as if he were a million miles away.

Maybe he is, D'Agosta thought. *Maybe he's meditating or something. Or maybe he's just trying to keep himself sane.*

"The messenger knew nothing," he said as gently as he could. "The trail's too well covered."

Pendergast did not acknowledge this. He remained motionless. His face had lost none of its pallor.

"How the hell did Diogenes find out about Viola?" D'Agosta burst out.

Pendergast spoke almost robotically. "For the first week, while in Diogenes's care, I was raving. Delirious. It's possible I mentioned her name. Nothing escapes Diogenes—nothing."

D'Agosta sank into a nearby chair. Right now, he didn't think he cared if Laura Hayward, a dozen FBI agents, and an army corps came storming into the apartment. They could lock him up and throw away the key. It wouldn't make any difference. Life was shit.

The two sat in the room, motionless, silent, as half an hour ticked by.

Then, without warning, Pendergast leaped to his feet, so suddenly that D'Agosta's heart turned over in his chest.

"She would have traveled under her own name!" he said, eyes glittering intently.

"What?" D'Agosta said, rising himself.

"She wouldn't have come if he'd asked her to use a pseudonym or arranged for a false passport. And she must have just arrived; he wouldn't delay the note—he wouldn't have had time!"

He raced toward the nearest laptop and began typing furiously. Within twenty seconds, the typing stopped.

"Here she is!" he cried.

D'Agosta raced to look at Pendergast's screen:

```
Folkestone DataCentre      PROPRIETARY
SQL Engine 4.041.a         & CONFIDEN-
TIAL

    Passenger Manifest Lookup


    Results of inquiry follow

    One record(s) found:
```

```
BA-0002359148
Maskelene, Lady Viola
British Airways Flight 822
Departed: London Gatwick LGW, 27 Jan-
uary, 11:54 P.M. GMT
Arrived: Kennedy Intl JFK, 28 Janu-
ary, 12:10 A.M. EST
```

End of Inquiry

———————————————————————————————

Pendergast turned away from the screen. His entire being seemed to crackle with energy, and his eyes—before so empty and distant—were on fire.

"Come, Vincent—we're off to JFK. Every minute we waste, the trail grows colder." And without another word, he dashed out of the room and down the hall.

Forty-eight

*I*T WAS LIKE the old days, D'Agosta thought grimly: Pendergast in his black suit, racing along the streets of New York City in his Rolls. Except that, really, it wasn't like the old days at all. Pendergast was a hunted man, and D'Agosta himself was in such deep shit he'd need a decompression chamber when he surfaced—assuming he ever surfaced at all.

The Rolls pulled up to the curb at Terminal 7 Arrivals. Pendergast leaped out, leaving the vehicle running. A Port Authority policeman was strolling along the curb, and Pendergast swooped down on him.

"Federal Bureau of Investigation." He passed his gold shield in front of the officer briefly, then closed it up and slid it back into his suit.

"What can I do for you, sir?" the officer responded, instantly intimidated.

"We're here on an investigation of the utmost importance. Can I ask you to watch my vehicle, Officer?"

"Yes, sir." The man practically saluted.

Pendergast strode into the terminal, black coat flapping behind him. D'Agosta followed him to baggage claim security. Within, a heavyset guard was listening patiently to a man in a suit shouting angrily about a stolen bag.

Again, Pendergast opened his badge, "Special Agent Pendergast, Federal Bureau of Investigation. My associate, Vincent D'Agosta, NYPD."

"Well, it's about time!" the man cried angrily. "My wife's *extremely valuable* jewelry—"

"*Never* put valuable jewelry in check-in luggage," said Pendergast smoothly, linking his arm in the man's and propelling him to the door and out, then stepping quickly back and shutting and locking it.

"You make it look so easy," said the guard with a grin.

"Is there an Officer Carter on duty?" said Pendergast, his eye just flitting over the man's identification badge.

"That's me. Randall Carter. What can I do for you?"

"I was told you were the best man to handle my problem."

"Really?" The man's face lit up. "Who—?"

"We need to review some security videotapes from last night. Just after midnight. It's a matter of great urgency."

"Yes, sir, let me just call the director of security."

Pendergast shook his head wonderingly. "Didn't they tell you this was already cleared?"

"It is? I didn't know. Funny they didn't send down an S.C. . . ."

"Well," Pendergast interrupted briskly, "I'm glad they at least had the sense to send me to you. You think for yourself; you're not one of those bureaucratic types." He suddenly leaned into the man's face and grasped his shoulder. "Are you wearing body armor, Officer?"

"Body armor? We're not required . . . Hey, but why—?"

"We'd better get going."

"Yes, sir." The officer needed no more persuasion. He hustled to the back of his office and unlocked a security door.

Down a beige corridor, past another locked door, and D'Agosta found himself in a large computer room festooned with monitors playing back live video feeds from all over the terminal. A few security guards were sitting around a cafeteria-style table drinking coffee, while a thin, irritated technician rapped away on a keyboard in one corner.

"These gentlemen need to see some video," Carter said to the technician.

"Moment," said the technician.

"No, *now.* This man's FBI and it's a matter of grave importance."

The technician got up, expelling an irritated hiss. "Right. Let's see the S.C." He held out his hand.

"It's been cleared. You got my okay on that."

A roll of the eyes. "So what do you want?"

Pendergast stepped up. "British Airways Flight 822 arrived here from Gatwick just after midnight. I want the security videotapes of the carousel where that flight's luggage arrived and, *most important,* I need to review the feed from the greeting area just beyond customs clearance."

"Have a seat. This might take a while."

"I'm afraid I don't have a while."

"Give me a break. I'll do what I can, but don't hold your breath."

Pendergast broke into a gentle smile. Seeing that smile, D'Agosta felt himself tense up instinctively.

"You're Jonathan Murphy, are you not?" Pendergast asked in his honeyed voice.

"So you can read an ID card. Bravo."

"I believe in the carrot-and-stick method of doing things, Jonathan," Pendergast said, still pleasantly. "Get me those videotapes in five minutes and you will receive a ten-thousand-dollar reward from the FBI's Public Incentive and Reward Program, also known as PIRP. No doubt you've heard of it. On the other hand, fail to get me that videotape and I'll put a red security flag in your file, which will mean that you'll never work at another airport, or any other secured site, in the country again. Now, which is it to be: carrot or stick?"

A silence. The security guards were nudging each other and grinning. Clearly, the technician wasn't popular.

Murphy smirked. "I'll take the ten grand."

"Excellent."

The technician sat down again and went to work with a vengeance, fingers hammering at the keys. D'Agosta watched as numbers scrolled frantically across the CRT.

"We don't use videotapes anymore," he said. "We have everything stored digitally, on-site. The ganged feeds use up an entire terabyte of our RAID-1 array every . . ."

Suddenly, he stopped bashing at the keyboard. "Okay. The flight arrived at ten minutes after midnight, gate 34. Let's see . . . It takes about fifteen minutes, on average, to go through pre-customs and walk to the carousel . . . I'll cue up to twelve-twenty, just to be safe."

A video sprang to life on Murphy's screen. Pendergast bent forward, scrutinizing it intently. D'Agosta peered over his shoulder. He could see the international baggage area, an empty carousel turning.

"I'll nudge up the speed until people start arriving," Murphy said.

Now the carousel turned much faster. The seconds spun by, in fast motion, at the bottom of the screen. Shortly, people began arriving at the carousel, looking for their luggage. Murphy tapped a set of keys, slowing the video down to normal speed.

"That's her!" Pendergast whispered urgently, pointing at the screen.

D'Agosta made out the slender form of Viola Maskelene, carrying a small bag. She approached the carousel, pulled her ticket out of the bag, examined the baggage claim checks, then crossed her arms to wait.

For a minute, Pendergast just stared at the image. Then he spoke again. "Switch to the greeting area, please. Same time frame."

The technician typed in some more commands. The image of the baggage area disappeared, replaced by the waiting area outside customs. It was sparsely populated, a few knots of people standing around restlessly, waiting to meet arrivals.

"*There*," said Pendergast.

A man stood off to one side, tall, slender, dressed in a dark overcoat. He had gingery hair, and he was looking around the room rather languidly, peering into various corners. His eye turned and stopped, fixed on the security camera.

D'Agosta had to stop himself from taking an instinctual step back. The man was staring right at them. His face was tan and angular and he had a closely trimmed beard, one eye milky blue, the other hazel. D'Agosta recognized him instantly as the man he had seen on the slopes above Castel Fosco in Italy that fateful day not two months earlier.

The man nodded formally at the camera, raised his hand just a little, and tipped a wave. His lips moved as if in speech.

D'Agosta glanced at Pendergast. His face was white—with rage.

Pendergast turned to the technician. "Back that up and print it out, there—when the man waves."

"Yes, sir."

A moment later and the computer printer was humming. Pendergast ripped the color image out and stuffed it in his pocket.

"Fast-forward, please, until a lady comes out and greets him."

Once again, the images on the screen scurried briefly in accelerated motion, slowing again when Viola emerged. Diogenes approached with two outstretched hands and a large smile. D'Agosta watched breathlessly as the two exchanged what appeared to be pleasantries; then Diogenes waved a bill and a skycap came rushing over. They turned and headed toward the door, the skycap following with Viola's bags.

Pendergast pointed at the screen. "Who's that skycap?"

Carter, the security officer, squinted at the screen. "Looks like Norm. Norman Saunders."

"Is he still on?"

Carter shook his head. "Couldn't say."

"He goes off at eight," one of the other guards said. "But sometimes he works overtime."

The figures disappeared out the glass doors.

"Go to the curbside camera."

"Right."

More rapping of keys. The scene abruptly changed again. There was Diogenes striding toward a dark Lincoln. He grasped the door handle, opened the door for Viola, helped her in. He waited for the skycap to close the trunk; then he walked around the car and got into the driver's seat.

The car pulled away, accelerating into the darkness beyond, and was gone.

"Back up," said Pendergast, "and get me a print of the car. When the door is open, please: I want to see the interior. And another print when the car's pulling away, so we can get a make on the plate."

A moment later, the computer was spitting out the images, which Pendergast immediately thrust into his jacket. "Good. Now we're going to find Saunders."

"If he's here, he'll be at the east carousels," Carter said.

"Thank you." Pendergast turned to go.

"So," said the technician, "how do I collect my ten grand?"

Pendergast paused. "Ten thousand dollars? Just for doing your job? A ridiculous idea."

To much muffled laughter and shaking of heads, they left the room. "If Saunders is on, he'll be over by baggage," said Carter. "I'll show you."

Several flights had recently arrived, and streams of travelers were crowding into baggage claim. All carousels were running full-bore, packed with luggage, and skycaps were coming and going busily.

Carter stopped one of them. "Saunders take an extra shift?"

The man shook his head. "He's off until midnight."

Looking past the skycap, D'Agosta noticed four Port Authority cops on the landing above the baggage claim concourse, scanning the crowd. Immediately, he nudged Pendergast. "I don't like that."

"Neither do I."

Carter's radio went off and he grabbed it.

"We better get the hell out of here," murmured D'Agosta.

They began walking briskly toward the exit.

"Hey!" came a distant shout. "Wait!"

D'Agosta glanced back to see the officers spilling into the crowd, pushing their way through. "You two! Wait!"

Pendergast broke into a run, darting through the throngs of people and heading back out to the curb. The P.A. cop was still beside the idling Rolls, talking on his radio. Pendergast shot past him, and D'Agosta half jumped, half tumbled into the passenger seat. The man's protest was lost in the roar of the big engine and the tremendous screech of rubber as the Rolls shot away from the pickup area at high speed.

As they accelerated onto the JFK Expressway, Pendergast pulled the printouts from his suit coat.

"Boot up my laptop, there in the carrier, and do a make on a Lincoln Town Car, New York license 453A WQ6. Radio the milepost 11 toll plaza on the Van Wyck Expressway and talk someone into reviewing the security tapes for between twelve-thirty and one A.M., going both east and west."

"What about us?"

"We're going east."

"East? You don't think he took her into the city?"

"That's exactly what I *do* think he did. But given that

Diogenes seems to be able to anticipate what I think, I'm going east—to the far end of the island."

"Right."

"Another thing: we're going to need to trade down." And Pendergast abruptly pulled off the airport expressway into the returns lot of a Hertz office, steered the big car into an empty spot, and killed the engine.

D'Agosta looked up from the laptop. "What, rent something?"

"No. Steal something."

Forty-nine

ONCE AGAIN, Smithback entered the gracious confines of Dr. Tisander's office, a load of textbooks under one arm. It was eight o'clock, well past the barbaric 5:30 P.M. dinner hour of River Oaks. He found the psychiatrist seated behind his desk, but this evening the usual look of genteel condescension was marred by an irritated flash in the eyes.

"Edward," Dr. Tisander said. "Although I am extremely busy, I am happy to give you five minutes of my undivided attention."

Smithback seated himself without an invitation and thumped the load of books onto the man's desk.

"I've been thinking about something you said in our conversation the day before yesterday," he began. "You told me: 'It is a grave step to deprive a person of his freedom, and due process must be followed with total scrupulosity.' "

"I may have said something like that, yes."

"You said exactly that. It made me curious to know just what that process is."

Tisander nodded condescendingly. "You seem to have found our library to your satisfaction."

"Very much so. In fact, I found exactly what I was looking for."

"How nice," said Tisander, feigning interest while taking a surreptitious glance at his watch.

Smithback patted the top book. "The laws of New York State regarding the involuntary commitment of the mentally ill are among the strictest in the nation."

"I am well aware of that. It's one reason why we have so many homeless people on the street."

"It isn't enough for a family to sign the documents in order to commit someone against his will. There's a whole process involved."

Another sage nod from Tisander.

"Isn't it true, for example, that a judge has to declare the person non compos mentis?"

"Yes."

"And even a judge cannot make that declaration unless two conditions are met. Do you recall those two conditions, Dr. Tisander?"

This time the psychiatrist gave a genuine smile, delighted to show off his erudition. "I certainly do. The person is either a danger to himself—mentally or physically—or a danger to society."

"Right. In the first case, suicide ideation or an actual attempt must usually be present, which must be attested to by a signed letter from a doctor. In the case of a person being a danger to society, it's usually necessary for the person to have been arrested."

"You *have* been busy, Edward," said Tisander.

"And then, *after* the declaration of non compos mentis, there must be a psychiatric evaluation recommending involuntary commitment."

"All standard procedure. Now, Edward, it's after eight, and it isn't long until lights-out, so if you'd—"

Smithback pulled one of the books from the pile. "I'll be done in a minute."

Tisander rose, squaring papers on his desk. "If you make it quick." He nodded imperceptibly, and an orderly emerged from the shadows near the door.

Smithback hastily pulled a sheet of paper from the book and handed it over the desk. "I drew up a list of documents that must, by law, be in my file."

Tisander took the list, scanned it with a frown. "A judge's declaration. A suicide-attempt report—signed by a doctor—or an arrest record. A psychiatric evaluation." He read them off. "I've no doubt they're all there. Now, Edward, it's time."

The orderly advanced.

"One other thing," Smithback said.

"*Thank* you, Edward." A note of exasperation had crept into Tisander's orotund voice.

"A question. That psychiatric evaluation that must be in the file—who administers it?"

"We do. Always. Surely, Edward, you remember the interview and tests you took on admittance."

"There's where you blew it, Tisander." Smithback dropped the heavy tome back on the desk, for effect. "It says right in here—"

"Jonathan?"

The orderly appeared at Smithback's elbow, a hulking presence. "This way, Mr. Jones."

"—by law," Smithback went on loudly, "the psychiatric evaluation can't be done by anyone on the staff of the admitting institution."

"Rubbish. Show Mr. Jones to his room, Jonathan."

"It's *true*!" Smithback cried as the orderly took his arm. "Back in the fifties, a young man was committed by his family in collusion with the asylum. They stole his inheritance. In the aftermath, a law was passed stating the evaluation had to be done by an independent psychiatrist. Check it out. Page 337, *Romanski v. Reynauld State Hospital*!"

"This way, Mr. Jones," said the orderly, propelling him firmly across the Persian carpet.

Smithback dug in his heels. "Tisander, when I get out, I'm going to sue River Oaks and you personally. If you can't produce that independent evaluation, you'll lose the suit—and it'll cost you dearly."

"Good *night*, Edward."

"I'll make it my mission in life! I'll dog you like the Furies dogged Orestes. I'll take away everything you have, your job, your reputation, this whole pile. As you know, I'm as rich as Croesus. Check my file. I know *for a fact* you cut that corner! There's no independent evaluation, and you know it!"

Smithback felt himself being dragged bodily toward the door.

"Shut the door on your way out, will you, Jonathan?" Dr. Tisander said.

"Tisander?" Smithback raised his voice. "Can you afford to make this mistake? You'll lose the whole enchilada, you son of a—!"

Jonathan shut the door to the office. "Come on, Jones," he said, giving Smithback a gentle push down the hall. "Give it a rest."

"Get your hands off me!" Smithback cried, struggling.

"Hey, man, I'm just doing my job," said the orderly calmly.

Smithback relaxed. "Right. Sorry. I imagine it's about as much fun working here as it is being a 'guest.' "

The orderly released him and Smithback dusted off his jacket. "All right, Jonathan," he said, mustering a feeble smile. "Escort me back to my cage. I'll work up a new angle tomorrow."

Just as they were turning the corner, Tisander's voice came echoing down the hall. "Jonathan? Bring Mr. Jones back."

Jonathan paused. "Looks like you get another hearing."

"Yeah, right."

As they turned back toward Tisander's office, Smithback heard the low voice of the orderly behind him. "Good luck."

Smithback entered the office. Tisander was standing behind the desk, his figure rigid. Smithback saw his own file open on the director's desk. Next to it was the book he'd indicated—opened to page 337.

"Sit down," Tisander said tersely. He nodded at the orderly. "You can wait outside."

Smithback took a seat.

"You think you're a clever fellow," Tisander said. All the phony good humor and condescension was gone. His face was now as hard and gray as a boiled potato.

"I was right," Smithback murmured, more to himself than to Tisander.

"A sheer technicality. There isn't a psychiatric hospital in the state that does independent evaluations. I don't think anyone's even aware of this ridiculous law. But under the circumstances, I can't afford to keep you here."

"You're damn right you can't afford it. I'll sue your ass from here to Albany—"

Tisander closed his eyes and held up a hand. "Mr. Jones, *please*. Our intention was to help you, but I'll be damned if I'll let some spoiled brat undo all the good I've built up over the years. Frankly, you're not worth it."

"So I'm free?"

"As soon as I write up the decommitment papers. Unfortunately, it's almost lockdown. You won't be able to leave until six A.M. tomorrow."

"Tomorrow?" Smithback echoed, almost afraid to believe his ears.

"Believe me, I'd love to get rid of you now. Jonathan?"

The orderly came back in.

"Mr. Jones is to be discharged in the morning. See to it he's given every consideration until then."

They exited the office, and as soon as the door closed, Smithback grinned. "Jonathan, I'm outta here."

Jonathan high-fived him with a big smile. "Man, how'd you do it?"

Smithback shrugged. "Sheer brilliance."

Fifty

ORA KELLY PAUSED on the corner of 77th Street and Museum Drive, looking northward. The great Romanesque entrance to the museum was lit up with spotlights, a five-story banner touting the opening hung on the facade. Below, the drive was packed with the usual New York chaos of limos and black Mercedes, disgorging patrons and celebrities in furs and black tie to successive waves of flashes. The inevitable red carpet had been rolled down the granite steps, which were roped off as if at a movie premiere, to keep back the press and the uninvited.

The whole spectacle made her sick.

Margo Green had been brutally murdered just two days ago and buried this very morning—yet it was as if the museum had already dismissed and forgotten her. Nora wondered what would happen if she just turned around and went back to her apartment; but she already knew the answer: she might as well kiss her career goodbye. She was supposedly one of the stars of this show, as George Ashton had made all too clear to her. The show must go on.

Taking a deep breath, and pulling her woolen coat

more tightly about her shoulders, she started forward. As she drew closer, she noticed a commotion off to one side. A group of short, heavyset men dressed in buckskins and wrapped in decorated blankets was standing in a circle, beating drums and chanting—some waving bundles of smoking sagebrush. After a moment of incomprehension, she suddenly realized what it was all about: the Tano protesters had arrived. She could see Manetti, the security director, talking with them and gesturing, flanked by a couple of NYPD cops and some museum guards. It seemed the commotion had begun to attract the attention of the guests, and some of them were coming over to see what was happening.

"Excuse me!" Nora pushed her way through some gawkers, ducked under the velvet rope, stuck her museum badge in the face of a protesting guard, and approached the group of Indians. At that very moment, a beautiful young woman came sweeping up: a star or starlet of some kind, judging by the trail of paparazzi that followed in her wake.

"This is private property," Manetti was saying to what Nora assumed was the leader of the Tanos. "We don't object to your protesting, but you have to do it down there, on the sidewalk—"

"Sir," the leader began in a quiet voice, "we are not protesting, we are praying—"

"Whatever. This is private property."

The celebrity waded in. With a jolt, Nora recognized her as movie star Wanda Meursault, tall, exotic, and vaguely foreign, rumored to be in line for best actress at the upcoming Academy Awards.

"Hold on! Why shouldn't these people have a right to pray?" she demanded to a dozen simultaneous flashes. A thicket of boomed mikes came swinging around to capture every deathless word that might drop from her lips, and TV lights fired up.

Instantly, Nora saw a P.R. disaster in the making.

"I'm not saying they can't pray," Manetti said, exasperation strong in his voice. "All I'm saying is that this is *private property*—"

"These Native Americans are *praying*." Meursault turned and asked, as an afterthought: "Why are you praying?"

"We're praying for our sacred masks, locked in a case in the museum," the leader said.

"They've *locked up* your *sacred* masks?" The actress's face bloomed in mock horror.

The cameras zeroed in.

Something had to be done—and fast. Nora shoved forward, pushing aside a policeman and jostling Manetti to one side.

"Hey, just a minute," the security director began.

"Nora Kelly, assistant curator of the exhibition," Nora explained to the cop, dangling her badge before every official face within reach. She turned to the security director. "I'll handle this, Mr. Manetti."

"Dr. Kelly, these people are trespassing on museum property—"

"I know that. I'll *handle* it."

Manetti fell silent. Amazing, Nora thought, how quickly a sharp tone and an air of authority—an authority she didn't have—could turn the tables.

She turned to the Tano leader, startled to see he was old, at least seventy. The calmness and dignity in his face was remarkable. This wasn't the young, angry activist she had imagined. The other men were equally aged, all somewhat rotund, wrapped in Pendleton wool blankets. The old VW bus they'd arrived in, a real junker, was parked illegally on Museum Drive and would no doubt soon be towed.

"*Y'aah shas słił dz'in nitsa,*" she said to the man.

The leader stared at her dumbfounded. "*Y'aah shas,*" he said hastily, as if remembering himself. "How—?"

"I spent some time at Tano Pueblo," said Nora. "That's all I know of your language, so please don't try to reply!" She smiled and held out her hand. "Nora Kelly, one of the curators of the show. I believe I spoke to one of your colleagues."

"You spoke to me."

"Then you must be Mr. Wametowa."

The old man nodded.

"How can I help you?" Nora asked.

"They want to pray!" Meursault shouted from the sidelines.

Nora ignored her, keeping her attention on Wametowa.

"We're praying to the masks," he said. "That's all we're asking, to speak to our masks."

"Speak to the masks?"

"Yes. To reassure them that we're here, that we care about them, that they haven't been forgotten."

Nora could see Manetti rolling his eyes.

"That's *so* beautiful," said Meursault, turning her head to better expose her profile to the cameras. Another dozen flashes went off.

"We believe the masks are alive, that they have a spirit. They've been alone and away from us for a long time. We've come to bless them, comfort them."

Suddenly, Nora realized just what the solution was.

She pretended to think for a moment. She knew, from

her brief week at Tano Pueblo back in her graduate student days, that they viewed any decision arrived at quickly as a poor decision. "This doesn't seem like a good place to do that," she said at last.

"That's just what I was saying—" Manetti began.

Nora paid no attention. "I wonder if there might be a better place . . ."

"There is," Manetti said. "Down there on the sidewalk."

Nora flashed a look at Manetti.

"We would like to be closer to our masks, not further," said Wametowa.

"Why don't you come in, then?" Nora asked.

"They won't let us."

"Come in as my guests. I'll take you to the masks right now, so you can speak to them in private—*before* the unveiling of the hall."

"Dr. Kelly, are you crazy?" Manetti protested.

The Tano elder stared at her a minute. Then his broad, ancient face broke into a radiant smile. He gave a dignified bow. "*Eesha łat dził.* You are a human being, Miss Nora."

"Bravo!" cried Meursault.

"I won't permit this," the security director said.

"Mr. Manetti, I'll take full responsibility."

"You can't just bring these people into the hall before the ribbon cutting—that's impossible!"

"Nothing's impossible. In fact, this is the way it *should* be." She turned to the Indians. "Would you gentlemen like to follow me?"

"We'd be happy to," said the Tano.

Meursault linked her arm with the startled old Indian's and they marched forward behind Nora, the crowd of press and onlookers surging behind. "Make way for the Tano elders!" Meursault cried. "Make way!" Her sequined dress shimmered under the lights, her face radiant at seizing so brilliantly the center of attention.

Like magic, the crowd parted as they mounted the red-carpeted steps. The Tanos began softly chanting and beating their drums again as they passed through the Rotunda and entered the Hall of the Heavens, and Nora found herself facing a line of gala partygoers who had fallen rapt at the sight of Native Americans marching toward the hall. No doubt they all thought the procession was part of the program. The mayor came forward, sensing, like Meursault, an opportunity.

Manetti followed behind, his face red but his mouth shut, obviously realizing it would be counterproductive to continue the argument in front of the whole city.

Now Collopy came rushing forward from the greeting line. "Nora! What in the world?"

She bent toward him and whispered quickly. "The Tanos would like to have a private moment with the masks alone, before the ribbon cutting."

"Whatever for?"

"To pray for and bless the masks. That's all."

Collopy frowned. "Nora, this is not the time. *Surely,* this can wait!"

Nora looked straight into his eyes. "Dr. Collopy. Please trust me on this. I know the Indians of the Southwest well, I've lived and worked among them for years. They're not here to cause you trouble or public embarrassment. They just want a little private time with their masks. By the time the ceremony's over, they'll be gone. And the whole situation will be defused. This is the very best way to handle things, and I know if you give it *care-*

ful consideration, you'll agree." She dropped her voice even further. "It also happens to be a great public relations opportunity."

Collopy looked at Nora, his patrician face wide with astonishment. Then he looked at Manetti. Finally, he turned toward the waiting Tanos. He cleared his throat and smoothed his hair, his brow wrinkled in thought.

And then suddenly, his face broke into a welcoming smile. He reached out his hand toward the Tano leader. "Welcome! Mr. . . . ?"

"Wametowa."

"Of course! Welcome! The museum is delighted to receive you and your group as representatives of the Tano people. I understand you've come a long way to see the Great Kiva masks."

"Two thousand miles."

A murmur went up in the crowd. The cameras were whirring.

"We are so glad you could make it. This is a special honor for the museum and for me personally."

The press was eating it up. Nora felt a huge relief: it was going to turn out all right.

"Our security director, Mr. Manetti, will take you into the hall to, ah, visit with the masks in private. Mr. Manetti? You can handle the security zones a tad ahead of schedule, I'm sure. And leave them alone while they pray."

"Yes, sir."

"Will half an hour suffice?" Collopy asked the leader.

"Yes, thank you," replied the Tano elder.

"Splendid! Afterwards, you're all invited to join the festivities, Mr. Wem, ah, Wem . . ."

"Wametowa."

"Excellent! Is there anything else we can do?"

"For now, this will suffice." The Tanos nodded, looking around and nodding to one another. "To tell you the truth, we didn't expect to be treated with this kind of respect."

"Nonsense! We're delighted to have you!" Collopy turned toward the cameras, having fully recovered his composure. "The museum thanks the Tano people for the privilege of being allowed to share these remarkable masks with the rest of the world."

Meursault began the clapping and soon the hall was thundering with applause, the television cameras capturing every detail.

Nora watched Manetti lead the group of Indians down the corridor, speaking into a two-way radio as he did so. Then she turned, walked to the nearest chair she could find, and collapsed in it. She couldn't believe she'd spoken to the museum director like that. Her knees felt like rubber.

In a detached, almost weary way, it occurred to her how fitting an elegy this was for Margo. It had been so important to her, this issue of the masks and the Tanos' sovereignty over them. Seeing these Indians ushered into the exhibition with solicitousness and respect would have made her very happy.

Suddenly, a cold glass of champagne appeared before her. She looked up in surprise to see Hugo Menzies standing behind her, resplendent in a magnificent shawl-collared tuxedo, his flowing white hair combed back, face beaming.

He took Nora's hand, placed the cold glass into it, patted her on the back, and sat down. "Did anyone ever tell you what a genius you are?" He chuckled. "That was the most dashing publicity coup it has been my privilege to witness."

Nora shook her head. "It could have been a publicity disaster."

"It *would* have been a disaster if you hadn't been on the scene. But not only did you handle the Tanos, but you made the museum look downright benevolent. Brilliant, just brilliant." He practically chortled with pleasure, his eyes sparkling. Nora had never seen him so animated.

She took a slug of champagne. It had been the week from hell, with Bill threatened and in hiding, Margo's murder, the stress of the opening, the warnings from Pendergast . . . But right now she was too tired and exhausted to feel any fear. All she wanted to do was go home, double-lock the door, and crawl into bed. Instead, she had to endure hours of speechifying, mingling, and forced gaiety.

Menzies placed a gentle hand on her shoulder. "When this is all over, I'd like you to take a week's vacation. You deserve it."

"Thanks. I wish I could begin now."

"Three more hours."

Nora held up her glass. "Three more hours," she said, and took another gulp of champagne.

A string ensemble struck up Haydn's *Emperor* Quartet as the crowd began to move toward the food tables. They were loaded with blini *au caviar,* prosciutto, rare French and Italian cheeses, mounds of crusty baguettes, crudités, fresh oysters on beds of crushed ice, cold lobster tails, smoked sturgeon—the works. Other tables groaned with wines and champagne, and every third person seemed to be a waiter rushing about with a silver tray loaded with drinks and food.

"Nora," said Menzies, "you must circulate."

She groaned. "God help me."

"Come on. We'll face the ravening hordes together."
He took her arm and they began making their way slowly
through the crowd. Nora found that she was greeted at
every turn by congratulators, peppered with questions
from the press. Her stunt with the Tanos had apparently
gone down exceptionally well, everyone assuming it had
been long planned.

When at length she returned to their assigned table,
she found that several other members of the department
were there, including Ashton, the show's chief curator. As
the serious eating got under way, Collopy, flanked by his
young wife, mounted the podium and gave a short, witty
speech.

Then it was time for the cutting of the ribbon. Nora,
Menzies, Ashton, and a few other curators lined up at the
podium while Collopy, wielding the gigantic pair of scis-
sors used for such occasions, went to the ribbon and
made a hash of trying to cut it. When it was finally accomplished, a cheer went up and the huge doors leading
to the Sacred Images exhibition swung open. Smiling and
nodding, Menzies, Nora, and the rest of the Anthropology
Department led the way, the partygoers following in an
excited crush behind.

It took about half an hour to reach the far end of the
hall, propelled along by the mass of people behind them.
Nora felt a shudder as she passed through the room
Margo had been murdered in, but, of course, all trace of
the crime scene had been removed and nobody but her
even seemed aware of it. As she moved farther and farther beyond the scene of the murder, Nora felt the horror

replaced by a quiet sense of pride. She could hardly believe they'd managed to pull it off.

Menzies stayed close beside her, occasionally murmuring compliments on the cases she had curated or arranged. The Tanos had come and gone, leaving some bits of turquoise, pollen, and cornmeal on the top of the mask case, which everybody took care to leave in place. At last, when they reached the final hall, Menzies turned to Nora and bowed.

"I do believe we have done our duty." He smiled, face twinkling. "And now you may beat a discreet retreat home. I, unfortunately, have some work to do upstairs in my office. Let's talk next week about that vacation I owe you."

He bowed again and Nora, with relief, turned to make her way to the nearest exit—and home.

Fifty-one

FOR PERHAPS THE FIFTIETH time in the last two days, Larry Enderby had made up his mind to quit, get the hell out of the museum.

It wasn't enough that he worked in a windowless basement room in the Museum of Natural History, the spookiest damn place in all of New York City. He couldn't get the horror of what he'd found two days ago out of his head. They hadn't even given him a frigging day off, offered him counseling, or even thanked him. It was like he didn't count. It was like *she* didn't count, the way they just moved right ahead with the exhibition as if nothing had happened.

Margo Green. He didn't know her well, but she'd gone out of her way to be nice to him the few times they'd met. Which was more than he could say for most of the curators and all the administrators. It was just the way the museum treated everybody below a certain level: hired help.

But, if he could admit it to himself, Enderby was mainly disgruntled because the museum had chosen this exact time—during the biggest party in five years—to switch over yet *another* museum hall to the new security system. So, instead of scarfing down caviar and champagne with the beautiful people two flights up, they were down there in the basement once again, toiling over software subroutines. Sure, they'd been invited to the party, like everyone else in the museum. That just added insult to injury.

He rolled back from the computer console with an exaggerated sigh.

"Holding up?" Walt Smith, project manager for the museum's security upgrade, asked from behind a nearby monitoring screen.

Smitty had been unusually gentle since Enderby's discovery, two days before. Everyone was tiptoeing around him, like somebody had died in his family.

"How about a short break to check out the party?" Enderby asked him. "I wouldn't mind a few of those cocktail shrimp."

Smitty shook his head. He held a BlackBerry in one hand and a cell phone in the other. "I don't think that's going to be possible, Larry. Sorry."

"Come on, Smitty," Jim Choi, the software engineer, said from the far side of the diagnostic display unit. "Just give us half an hour. You'd be surprised how many shrimp I can ingest in half an hour. The party's almost over, they'll run out of food soon."

"You know we can't alter the schedule. The Astor Hall's just like any other, one more on the list. What, we're going to sneak the hands of the atomic clock back five minutes, maybe nobody will notice?" Smitty laughed at his own miserable joke.

Choi rolled his eyes. Smitty was not known for his rapier-like wit.

Enderby watched the goatee on Smith's chin waggle

up and down as he laughed. It was a straggly little thing, seemingly attached by only a few hairs, and Enderby half hoped it might fall off one of these days. Despite Enderby's general irritation, he had to admit Smitty wasn't a bad guy to work for. He'd worked his way up through the ranks and, despite being only thirty-five, was as Old Museum as they came. A real stickler, relatively humorless, but as long as you were a conscientious worker and did your job, he looked out for you. It wasn't Smitty's fault the museum bigwigs were demanding that the new security system be fully installed and operational, yesterday.

Smitty stood up and walked across the room, past racks of computer workstations and servers, to a bank of six dozen small CCTV monitors mounted in the far wall. Most of the monitors showed black-and-white still lifes of empty museum hallways and display cases. Half a dozen in the lower right corner, however—the video feeds from the Hall of the Heavens, where the opening party was going on—were a riot of movement. From his terminal, Enderby watched the little images dance and jitter their way across the screen with a heavy heart. Upstairs, the museum's slope-shouldered, mouth-breathing curators were rubbing elbows with starlets and nymphets; and here he was, toiling in this cave like some troglodyte. True, it could be worse—he could be working in the "Pit," the museum's Central Security Office, which was twice as large but unpleasantly hot and crammed full of even more screens and keyboards than this Advanced Technology Center. Worse, but not much worse.

Smitty was squinting at his BlackBerry. "Okay, set to initialize the final test?"

Nobody replied.

"I'll take that as a yes." He turned back to his console, tapped briefly on the keyboard. "Astor Hall," he intoned, "final fail-safe test of the security upgrade, January 28, 8:28 P.M."

Jeez, he always makes it sound like it's Mission Control in here, Enderby thought. He glanced over at Jim Choi, who once again rolled his eyes.

"Larry, what's the status of the legacy system?" Smitty asked.

"Looks good."

"Jim, give me an update on the laser grid in the Astor Hall."

A brief tapping of keys. "Ready to go," Choi said.

"Then let's run the low-level diagnostics."

There was a brief silence as both Smitty and Choi ran independent tests. Enderby, whose job was to monitor the behavior of the preexisting security system as the updated laser security system was brought online, stared at his monitor. This was probably the fortieth hall they'd converted to the new system. And for each conversion, there were a hundred steps to perform: on-site analysis, system architecture, coding, installation . . . He could be making three times his salary in some slick start-up in Palo Alto, with stock options to boot. And he probably wouldn't stumble over any bodies in the middle of the night, either.

Smitty looked up from his keyboard. "Jim, what's your checksum?"

"It's 780E4F3 hex."

"I concur. Let's proceed." Smitty picked up a phone, dialed.

Enderby watched without interest. He knew Smitty

was calling the boys in the Pit, giving them a heads-up that the switchover was about to happen, just a reminder in case some newbie went apeshit when he saw the hiccup on their screens. It was always the same. The old system would be disabled; there would be a ninety-second period in which the new system was initialized and the "handshake" performed; then a final twenty-minute test of the new system would follow, to ensure the installation was correct and that it had been brought online successfully. Twenty minutes in which they had nothing to do but twiddle their thumbs. Then, at last, the new system would become fully operational and the old system put in backup mode. He fetched a huge yawn. As he did so, his stomach grumbled unhappily.

"Central Security?" Smitty was saying into the phone. "Who is this, Carlos? Hey, it's Walt Smith in ATC. We're activating the lasers in the Astor Hall. We'll be initializing in about five minutes. Right. I'll call back once the handshake's complete."

He put the phone down, then looked back at Enderby. "Hey, Larry," he said gently.

"What?"

"Just how much time did Choi there say he needed to consume that trawler-load of shrimp?"

"I told you," Choi piped up. "Thirty minutes."

Smitty leaned forward, resting his arm on the console. "Tell you what. If we can get this initialization done and the twenty-minute test phase started, I'll give you fifteen. *Including* the time it'll take us to get there and back again."

Enderby sat up. "On the level?"

Smitty nodded.

Choi grinned widely. "You just purchased yourself a boy."

"Good. Then let's see how fast we can get through this checklist." And Smitty turned back to his terminal.

Fifty-two

HUGO MENZIES INSERTED his key into the staff elevator and rode it from the second to the fifth floor. Exiting the elevator, he strolled meditatively down the long, polished corridor. The curatorial offices lay on either side: old oaken doors with panels of frosted glass, each bearing the name of a curator in old-fashioned gold-leaf lettering, even those most recently appointed. Menzies smiled, already feeling a nostalgia for the old pile and its quaint traditions.

He paused before his own office door, opened it, and entered just long enough to pick up the canvas satchel that accompanied him almost everywhere. Then he closed and locked the door and continued his stroll to the farthest end of the hall, where there was an unmarked door. He unlocked it, stepped into the stairwell beyond, descended two flights, and exited into a dark, deserted hall—the Hall of Northwest Coast Indians. It was one of the oldest halls in the museum, a true gem of late-nineteenth-century museology, and it smelled of old cedar and smoke. Transformation masks, totem poles, slate bowls gleamed in the dark recesses. Menzies paused to inhale the air with delight. Then he walked briskly through the deserted hall and several others, finally arriving at a large metal door bearing the legend *The Astor Hall of Diamonds*.

His eye dwelled lovingly on the door in all its brushed-steel splendor, taking special note of the two video cameras on either side, staring down at him like beady black eyes—except, as he knew, they were currently not functioning. He smiled again, then removed a large round watch from his vest pocket and gazed at it. Although in shape it resembled a pocket watch, it was, in fact, a modern digital stopwatch. On its face, numbers were counting down with enormous rapidity, at an accuracy to the thousandths of a second.

The watch was reading time signals from the same satellite that the museum's security system used.

He waited until the watch signaled a certain point in time with a soft beep. Menzies immediately put the watch away, stepped rapidly to the door, placed his ear against it, and then quickly swiped a magnetic card through the reader. The door did not open; instead, a small eye-level window shot open, revealing a retinal optical scanner.

Menzies bowed his head, popped two soft contact lenses out from his eyes and into a waiting plastic container, then stepped up to the optical reader. A quick bar of light passed across his face; there was a moment's stillness, and then a soft click announced the disengagement of the lock. He stepped through the door into the hall beyond, the door automatically closing behind him.

With a rapidity of movement marvelous for his advanced age, Menzies knelt, opened his satchel, and got to work. First he reached up and, with a sharp tug, removed his leonine thatch of white hair, shoved the wig into the satchel, then reached into his mouth and pulled out five molded rubber cheek and chin pieces. This act alone caused an astonishing transformation in the shape and apparent age of his face. Another pair of quick tugs took off the bushy eyebrows and a few small blemishes, liver spots, a mole.

Next, still kneeling, the man removed more than a dozen small dental mirrors from the satchel, mounted on bizarre little stands in a variety of odd shapes and sizes, all made of beautifully hand-machined brass. Next came an array of black objects wired together, a stack of thin Mylar sheets, several small cutting tools, exotic-looking metal instruments, and a flat of sticky pads, each the size and shape of a lentil.

When these had been arranged on the floor with military precision, the man waited, still crouching, unmoving, stopwatch again in his hands. He raised his head once to look at the hall in front of him. It was dark—utterly dark—without even the slightest gleam announcing its extraordinary contents. The darkness was part of the security, because the only electromagnetic radiation in the hall after closing was invisible infrared and far-infrared wavelengths. Even the myriad laser beams crisscrossing the hall were infrared, undetectable to the naked eye. But he did not need light: he had rehearsed this many hundreds of times, in an exact duplicate of this room which he had constructed himself.

The watch gave another soft beep, and the man exploded into movement. With the speed of a ferret, he darted about the room, placing the dental mirrors in precisely fixed and calibrated locations, each mirror turned to the precise angle.

In two minutes, he was done and back in his place by the door, breathing slowly and regularly, watch in hand.

Another soft beep indicated the laser beams had gone back on—each one now redirected to a different path, running around the outer walls instead of crisscrossing the hall itself. This rotating series of laser grids was one of the features of the new security system. No doubt the technicians in the basement were congratulating themselves on another successful test.

Again, the man waited, looking at his watch. Another soft beep and he was up again, this time carrying the Mylar sheets, which he stuck over the video camera lenses which had been placed in numerous strategic locations. The Mylar sheets, clear to the naked eye, were actually etched with holographs which responded strongly to infrared light, and which reproduced the precise scene that the infrared video cameras were pointed at—minus, of course, the man. When the video cameras came back on, they would see the same boring scene they had seen before. Only it would not be real.

Again, like a cat, the man retreated to his safe corner. Again, he waited until the stopwatch beeped another soft warning.

This time he scurried around the perimeter of the hall, setting a sleek black box in each corner, connected by wires to a small power pack. These were powerful radar guns of the type used by state police, modified to jam the museum's new infrared Doppler radar system, said to be so sensitive it could detect the motion of a cockroach across the carpeting.

Once the radar jammers were in place and active, the man straightened up, dusted his knees, and gave a low, dry chuckle. Movements now almost languid, he removed a flashlight from the satchel, turned it on, and played the dull green beam about the hall—a precise wavelength of green light chosen because none of the sophisticated electromagnetic sensors in the hall could see it.

The man strolled casually to the center of the hall where a square, four-foot pillar had been constructed, on top of which was set a thick Plexiglas box. He bent down and looked in the box. Resting inside on thick satin was the dark form of a heart-cut diamond of extraordinary, almost incredible size: Lucifer's Heart, the museum's prize gem, which had been called the most valuable diamond in the world. It was certainly the most beautiful.

A fine place to start.

With a small cutting tool, the man opened a hole in the Plexiglas. Then, with a series of slender tools machined precisely for this purpose and some of the tiny, sticky pads, he reached in and removed the diamond, being careful to prevent the trigger pin under the diamond from rising. Another deft movement placed a large glass marble on the same stand, which would keep the pin depressed.

The man held the diamond in his hand, shining the flashlight up through it for a moment. In the green light it looked black and dead, without color, almost like a piece of coal. But the man was not perturbed: he knew that a red diamond under green light always looked black. And this diamond was red—or more precisely, a rich cinnamon, but without a trace of brown. It was the only diamond of its color in the world. Blue diamonds were created by boron or hydrogen trapped in the crystal matrix, green diamonds by natural radiation, yellow and brown diamonds by nitrogen, and pink diamonds by the presence of microscopic lamellae. But this color? Nobody knew.

He held it up and peered through it to the flashlight below. He could see his own eyes reflected and multiplied by the diamond's facets, creating a surreal kaleidoscope of eyes and more eyes, hundreds of them, staring every which way inside the gem. He moved the gem back and forth, from eye to eye, enjoying the spectacle.

And the strangest thing of all was that the eyes were of different colors: one hazel, the other a milky, whitish blue.

Fifty-three

LARRY ENDERBY SAT at his console in the Advanced Technology Center, puffing slightly. The hollowness in his stomach had gone, replaced with an uncomfortable bloated feeling. He felt like a frigging suckling pig, to tell the truth. He belched, let out his belt a notch. All that was missing was the shiny red apple for his mouth.

He glanced over at his co-workers, Walt Smith and Jim Choi. Smitty—who, true to his nature, had acted with restraint—was staring at a bank of monitors, no worse for wear. The same couldn't be said for Choi, who was slumped at his terminal, a glazed expression on his face. During the fifteen minutes Smitty had allotted, Choi had indeed shown a remarkable ability to bolt down jumbo shrimp and glasses of champagne. Enderby had given up counting shrimp at sixty-two.

He eased up another bolus of air, then patted his stomach gingerly. They'd gotten to the food table just in time: the feeding frenzy was almost over. There was a dribble of caviar on his shirtfront, and he flicked it away with a fingernail. But that fourth glass of champagne he'd chugged at the last moment had probably been a mistake.

He just hoped he could keep it together for the rest of his shift. He glanced up at the clock: only another hour. They'd verify that the Astor Hall's upgraded security system was fully operational, then go through the procedure of mothballing the old system. No sweat: he'd done it dozens of times before, he could probably do it in his sleep.

A low chime sounded. "That's it," Smitty said. "Twenty minutes." He glanced over at Choi. "What's the status of the Astor Hall system?"

Choi blinked a little blearily at his screen. "Test completed without incident." His eye swept the cluster of video feeds. "Hall looks fine."

"Error logs?"

"None. The system's nominal."

"And the beam modulation?"

"Every five minutes, as programmed. No deviation."

Smitty walked over to the wall of monitors. Enderby watched as he peered at the video feeds devoted to the Astor Hall of Diamonds. He could see case after case of the precious gems, gleaming faintly in the infrared light. There was no movement, of course: once the laser beams were activated after lockdown, not even guards were permitted in the high-security exhibition halls.

Smitty grunted his approval, then walked over to his monitoring station and picked up the internal phone. "Carlos? It's Walt in the ATC. We've completed the twenty-minute shakedown of the Astor Hall laser grid. How'd it look from Central Security?" A pause. "Okay, good. We'll get the standard scheduling online and mothball the prior."

He hung up the phone and glanced over at Enderby. "The Pit says that everything's five by five. Larry, put it to bed. I'll help Jim finalize the automation routines for the laser grid."

Larry nodded and pulled his chair closer to the console. Time to put the old security system in backup mode. He blinked, wiped the back of a hand across his mouth, then began typing in a series of commands.

Almost immediately, he sat back. "That's strange."

Smitty looked over. "What is?"

Enderby pointed at an LED screen sitting on the side of his workstation. A single red dot glowed in its upper left corner. "When I rolled back the first zone into standby mode, the system gave me a code red."

Smitty frowned. A "code red" was the legacy system's alarm setting. In the Astor Hall, this would have been activated only when a diamond was removed from its setting. "What zone was that?"

"Zone 1."

"What's it contain?"

Enderby turned to a separate console, accessed the accession and inventory database, typed in a SQL query. "Just a single diamond. Lucifer's Heart."

"That's right in the center of the room." Smitty walked over to the bank of video monitors, peered at one closely. "Looks fine to me. We're dealing with some kind of software glitch here."

He glanced back toward Enderby. "Roll back zone 2."

Enderby typed a few more commands into his primary terminal. Immediately, a second red dot glowed into view on the LED screen. "That's giving me a code red, too."

Smitty walked over, a worried look coming onto his face.

Enderby stared at the screen. His mouth was dry, and the alcohol haze was dissipating fast.

"Do a global rollback," Smitty said. "All zones in the hall."

Enderby took a deep breath, then typed a short sequence on his keyboard. Immediately, he was flooded with dismay.

"Oh, no," he breathed. "No."

The little LED screen on Enderby's desk had just blossomed into a Christmas tree of red.

For a moment, there was a shocked silence. Then Smitty waved his hand dismissively.

"Let's not have a cow here. What we've got is a software glitch. Incompatibility between the new system and the old probably crashed the legacy system. Must've happened when we pulled it off-line. Nothing to get excited about. Larry, shut down the old system, one module at a time. Then reboot from the backup master."

"Shouldn't we report to Central?"

"What, and make ourselves look like idiots? We'll report *after* we've solved the problem."

"Okay. You're the boss." And Enderby began to type.

Smitty mustered a weak grin and gestured at the video screens of the empty hall, the diamonds glittering within their cases. "I mean, hey—take a look. Does the hall look robbed to you?"

Enderby had to chuckle. Maybe Smitty was acquiring a sense of humor, after all.

Fifty-four

D'AGOSTA MOVED THROUGH the channels on the portable police-band radio he'd pulled from the Rolls, searching for more official chatter about him and Pendergast. Their appearance at Kennedy had set off an APB across the entire length of Long Island, from Queens to Bridgehampton. The Rolls had been impounded at the rental lot, and in time the authorities had identified the Toyota Camry they'd stolen, and put out an advisory on that, as well. They'd managed to evade several roadblocks established on the Long Island Expressway by keeping to back roads and taking their cues from the radio advisories.

They were in a net, and the net was drawing tighter.

Still, Pendergast searched, stopping at one all-night service area after another, refusing to give up—and yet to D'Agosta it seemed a hopeless task, the kind of last-resort, brute-force police work that soaked up man-hours and rarely yielded results. It was a numbers game in which the numbers were just too damn big.

Pendergast screeched into an all-night service area at Yaphank, which looked just like the two dozen others they had already visited: glassed-in front, sickly green fluorescent lights beating back the bitter darkness. At some point, D'Agosta mused, they were going to get an attendant who had heard about the APB. And that would be it.

Yet again, Pendergast leaped out of the Camry like a cat. The man seemed to burn with a fierce, inextinguishable flame. They'd been at it more than twelve hours straight, and during all that time spent alternately searching and evading, he'd said few words not directly related to the game at hand. D'Agosta wondered how long the agent could keep it up.

Pendergast was into the little store and in the sleepy attendant's face before the man could even rouse himself from his cozy chair behind the counter, where he'd apparently been watching a martial arts movie.

"Special Agent Pendergast, FBI," he said in his usual cool voice, which somehow managed to convey menace without being offensive, as he passed his shield across the man's field of view. At the same time, D'Agosta reached over and snapped off the television, creating a sudden, unnerving silence.

The man's chair legs clunked down on the floor as he hastily righted himself. "FBI? Sure, yeah, right. What can I do for you?"

"When do you go on shift?" Pendergast asked.

"At midnight."

"I want you to look at these." He removed the prints he had collected at Kennedy, held one in front of the attendant. "Have you seen this man? He would have come in last night, sometime between one and three."

The attendant took the photo, screwing up his face. D'Agosta watched carefully, relaxing slightly. Clearly, the guy knew nothing of the APB. He glanced out toward the dark highway. It was almost four in the morning. It was only a matter of time. They weren't ever going to get a lead, this was needle-and-haystack stuff. The police would find them, and . . .

"Yeah," the guy said. "I saw him."

The air in the tiny store went electric.

"Look at this photo as well, please." Pendergast passed the man a second image. "I want you to be sure." He spoke quietly, but his body was tense as a coiled spring.

"That's him again," the man murmured. "I remember those funny eyes, kind of freaked me out."

"Did you see this car?" Pendergast murmured, showing him a third image.

"Well, I can't say I remember that. He did the self-serve, you know?"

Pendergast took back the photographs. "And your name is—?"

"Art Malek."

"Mr. Malek, can you tell us if anyone was with him?"

"He came into the store alone. And like I said, I didn't go out, so I really can't say if there was anybody in the car. Sorry."

"That's all right." Pendergast returned the photos to his jacket and drew still closer. "Now, tell me exactly what you remember from the time this man arrived to the time he left."

"Well . . . it was last night, like you said, must have been close to three in the morning. There wasn't anything unusual about it—he pulled up, filled the car himself, came in to pay."

"Cash."

"Right."

"Did you notice anything else about him?"

"Not really. Had a funny accent, kind of like yours. No offense," Malek added hastily. "In fact, he looked kind of like you."

"What was he wearing?"

A labored effort to remember. "All I can remember is a dark overcoat. Long."

"Did he do anything else but pay?"

"Seems to me he wandered about the aisles a bit. Didn't buy anything, though."

At this, Pendergast stiffened. "I assume you have security cameras in the back aisles?"

"Sure do."

"I'd like to see the tapes from last night."

The man hesitated. "The system recycles them on a thirty-hour loop, and it gets erased as—"

"Then please stop the security system *now*. I must see the tape."

The man almost jumped to comply, hastening into a back office.

"Looks like we've finally got a lead," said D'Agosta.

The pair of eyes Pendergast turned on him seemed almost dead. "On the contrary. Diogenes hoped we would find this place."

"How do you know?"

Pendergast didn't answer.

The man came huffing out of the back room with a videotape. Pendergast ejected the movie from the VCR and shoved in the security tape. A ceiling-level shot of the tiny store came into view, a time and date stamp in the bottom left corner. Pendergast punched the rewind button, stopped, rewound again. Within a minute, he'd located the 3 A.M. time stamp for January 28. Next, he cued it back another half hour to allow for a margin of error. Then they began watching the tape at accelerated speed.

The black-and-white picture quality was poor. The aisles of the convenience store glowed and flickered on the screen. Now and then a huddled shape raced through on fast-forward, like a pinball, bounced around grabbing things off shelves, then disappeared again.

Suddenly, Pendergast jabbed the play button, slowing it to a normal pace as yet another dark figure entered the screen. The figure strolled down the aisle, its eyes—differing shades of gray—seeking out and fixing on the security camera.

It was Diogenes. A smile spread over his face as he casually reached into his pocket and withdrew a piece of paper. He unfolded it and nonchalantly held it up to the camera.

BRAVO, FRATER! TOMORROW, CALL AT 466
AND ASK FOR VIOLA.
THIS WILL BE OUR LAST COMMUNICATION.
MAY OUR NEW LIVES BEGIN! VALEAS.

"Four six six?" said D'Agosta. "That's not a legit emergency number . . ."

Then he stopped. It was not a telephone number, he realized, but an address. Four sixty-six First Avenue was the underground entrance at Bellevue that led to the New York City Morgue.

Pendergast rose, ejected the tape, and put it in his pocket.

"You can keep that," said the attendant helpfully as they left.

Pendergast slipped behind the wheel, started the Camry, but did not move. His face was gray, his eyes half lidded.

There was a terrible silence. D'Agosta could think of nothing to say. He felt almost physically ill. This was even worse than at the Dakota—worse because, for the last twelve hours, they'd had hope. Slender, but hope nevertheless.

"I'll check the police band," he said stiffly. It was a pointless gesture, just something to keep himself busy. And even police chatter about the APB was preferable to the dreadful silence.

Pendergast didn't respond as D'Agosta turned on the radio.

A burst of frantic, overlapping voices poured from the speaker.

Instinctively, D'Agosta glanced out the window. Had they been spotted? But the roads around the service area were deserted.

He leaned forward and changed the frequency. More frantic voices.

"What the hell?" D'Agosta punched the button, changed the frequency again and again. Almost half the available channels were taken up, and the talk wasn't about them. Something big, it seemed, was going down in the city. As he listened, trying to figure out what it was, he became aware that Pendergast was listening, too, suddenly totally alert.

The talk on the current channel was about the Museum of Natural History, a theft of some kind. It seemed the Astor Hall of Diamonds had been hit.

"Go to the command-and-control channel," Pendergast said.

D'Agosta dialed it in.

"Rocker wants you to sweat the techies," a voice was saying. *"This was an inside job, that much is clear."*

D'Agosta listened in disbelief. Rocker at four in the morning? This must be gigantic.

"They got 'em all? Including Lucifer's Heart?"

"Yup. And see who knew the specs on the security system, get a list, move through it fast. Museum security, too."

"Got that. Who's the insurer?"

"Affiliated Transglobal."

"Jeez, they're going to shit bricks when they learn about this."

D'Agosta, glancing at Pendergast, was shocked at the rapt expression on his face. Strange how, at this moment of ultimate crisis, he could become so fixated on something that had no bearing on the problem at hand.

"The museum's president is on his way. And they've gotten the mayor out of bed. You know how he'll crucify anybody who lets him get behind the curve on a major—"

"Someone knocked off the diamond hall," said D'Agosta. "I guess that's why we've been temporarily upstaged."

Pendergast said nothing. D'Agosta was taken aback by the look on his face.

"Hey, Pendergast," he said. "You okay?"

Pendergast turned his pale eyes toward him. "No," he whispered.

"I don't get it. What's this got to do with anything? It's a diamond heist—"

"Everything." And then the FBI agent looked away, out into the winter darkness. "All these brutal killings, all

these mocking notes and messages . . . nothing more than a smoke screen. A cruel, cold-blooded, sadistic smoke screen."

He tore away from the curb and headed back into the neighborhood they had just passed through.

"Where are we going?"

Instead of answering, Pendergast jammed on the brakes, pulling up in front of a split-level house. He pointed to an F150 pickup parked in the driveway. *For Sale* was written on the windshield in soap.

"We need a new vehicle," he said. "Get ready to move the radio and laptop into that truck."

"Buy a car at four A.M.?"

"A stolen car is reported too quickly. We need more time."

Pendergast got out of the car and strode up the short concrete walk. He rang the bell, rang it again. After a minute, the lights on the second floor came on. A window scraped open, and a voice shouted down: "What do you want?"

"The pickup—it's operational?"

"Hell, pal, it's four in the morning!"

"Will hard cash help get you out of bed?"

With a muttered curse, the window shut. A moment later, the porch light came on and a corpulent man in a bathrobe appeared at the door. "It's three thousand. And it works good. Got a full tank of gas, too."

Pendergast reached into his suit, removed a book of cash, peeled off thirty hundreds.

"What's going on?" the man asked a little blearily.

Pendergast pulled out his badge. "I'm with the FBI." He nodded at D'Agosta. "He's NYPD."

Balancing the radio and laptop under one arm, D'Agosta removed his shield.

"We're working an undercover narcotics job. Be a good citizen and keep this to yourself, all right?"

"Sure thing." The man accepted the cash.

"The keys?"

The man disappeared, came back a moment later with an envelope. "The title's in there, too."

Pendergast took the envelope. "An officer will be by shortly to take care of our previous vehicle. But don't say anything about the car or about us, not even to another police officer. You know how it is with undercover cases."

The man nodded vigorously. "Sure do. Hell, the only books I read are true crime."

Pendergast thanked the man and turned away. A minute later, they were inside the truck, accelerating from the curb.

"That should buy us a few hours," Pendergast said as he raced back in the direction of the Montauk Highway.

Fifty-five

IOGENES PENDERGAST drove slowly, without hurry, through the bleak winter townscapes along the Old Stone Highway: Barnes Hole, Eastside, Springs. Ahead, a traffic light turned red, and he coasted to a stop at the intersection.

He eased his large head to the left, to the right. A wintry potato field stretched to one side, frozen and dusted with snow. At its edge stood a dark wood of bare trees, branches etched in white. The world was black and white and it had no depth: it was flat, like a nightmare confection of Edwin A. Abbott. *Fie, fie how franticly I square my talk . . .*

The light moved down, indicating it had turned green, and Diogenes slowly depressed the accelerator. The car nosed forward and swung right onto Springs Road as he turned the wheel, letting it slide through his hands as the car straightened out. He increased the pressure on the accelerator, easing off as the vehicle approached the speed limit. More gray potato fields passed on his right, beyond which stood several rows of gray houses, and beyond that, the Acabonack Marshes.

All gray, exquisite gray.

Diogenes reached to the dash and turned the heater vent several clicks to the right, increasing the flow of warmth into the glass, steel, and plastic compartment that enclosed his body. He felt neither triumph nor vindication, only a curious kind of emptiness: the sort that came with the achievement of a great thing, the completion of a long-planned work.

Diogenes lived in a world of gray. Color did not enter his world, except fleetingly, when he least expected it, coming in from the corner of his eye like a Zen koan. Koan. Ko. Koan ko. *Ko ko rico, ko ko rico* . . .

Long ago, his world had attenuated to shades of gray, a monochromatic universe of shape and shadow, where true color had vanished even from his waking dreams. No, not quite. Such a statement would be dissembling, melodrama. There *was* a final repository of color in his world, and it was there, in the leather satchel beside him.

The car moved down the empty road. No one was out.

He could tell, from a shifting of the monochromatic landscape around him, that night was relinquishing its hold on the world. Dawn was not far away. But Diogenes had little use for sunlight, just as he had little use for warmth or love or friendship or any of the countless things that nourished the rest of humanity.

As he drove, he played back, in meticulous detail, the events of the night before. He went over every last action, motion, statement, taking pleasure in satisfying himself that he had made no errors. At the same time, he thought of the days ahead, mentally ticking off the preparations he would have to make, the tasks he'd need to perform, the great journey he would make—and, *aber natürlich,* the journey's end. He thought of Viola, of his brother, of his childhood, multithreaded multiplexing waking daydreams that seemed more real than the present. Unlike the other bags of meat and blood that made up his species, Diogenes mused, he could process several disparate trains of thought simultaneously in his head.

The Event which had robbed Diogenes of color had also stolen his ability to sleep. Full oblivion was denied him. Instead, he drifted, he lay on his bed in a world of waking dreams: memories of the past, conflagrations, conversations, conflations, certain animals poisoned and dying with exquisite restraint, racked bodies on splintered roods, a hair shirt fashioned from nerve ganglia, a mason jar of fresh blood—the disconnected images from his past played on the screen of his mind like a magic-lantern show. Diogenes never resisted them. Resistance would be futile, and futility itself was, of course, to be resisted. He let the scenes drift in and out as they would.

All this would change. The great wheel would come around, because he—after all—was about to break a butterfly upon a wheel. The thing that had preyed upon his mind would at long last be exorcised. His revenge on his brother was all but complete.

As he drove, Diogenes let his thoughts drift back almost thirty years. At first—after *it* had happened—he had lost himself in the inner maze of his mind, wandering as far from reality and sanity as it was possible to go, while even a small part of him remained prosaic, quotidian, able to interact with the outside world, whose true nature now—thanks to the Event—stood revealed to him.

But then—slowly, very slowly—insanity alone lost its power to shelter. It was no longer a comfort, even a bitter one. So he came back, but he was like a diver who had gone too deep, run out of air, and rushed to the surface only to be racked by the bends.

That was the worst moment of all.

And yet it was at this very moment, as he balanced on the cruel knife-edge of reality, that he comprehended there *was* a purpose waiting for him back in the real world. A double purpose: a reckoning and a reclamation. It would take decades of planning. It would be, in his own self-referential world, a work of art: the masterpiece of a lifetime.

Why then Ile fit you.

And so Diogenes did return to the world.

He knew now what kind of place it really was and what kind of creatures inhabited it. It was not a lovely world, no, not a lovely world at all. It was a world of pain and evil and cruelty, walked on by vile creatures of piss and excrement and bile. But his newfound purpose, the end toward which he had bent all his intellect, made such a world *just* bearable. He became a chameleon par excellence, hiding everything, *everything,* behind a fast-changing skin of disguise, prevarication, misdirection, irony, cool detachment.

At times, when his will threatened to crumble, he found that certain temporary pastimes were enough to divert him, to haul him up from the deeps. The emotion that sustained him some might call hatred, but for him it was the mead that nourished him, that gave him superhuman patience and a fanatic's attention to detail. He found he could live not merely a double life or a triple life, but in fact could assume the very personalities and lives of half a dozen invented people, in several different countries, as the needs of his work of art required.

Some of the personalities he had assumed years, even

decades before, as he laid the complex groundwork of his master plan.

Ahead, an intersection. Diogenes slowed, turned right.

Night was relinquishing its hold on the world, but Suffolk County still slept. It gave Diogenes comfort to know that his brother, Aloysius, was not one of those sunken in voluptuous or erotic stupefaction. Nor would Aloysius sleep well again: ever. Just now he would be growing fully conscious of the dimensions of what he, Diogenes, had done to him.

His plan had the power and functional perfection of a well-oiled bear trap. And now Aloysius was caught in its jaws, awaiting the arrival of the hunter and the merciful bullet to the brain. Only, Diogenes would show no such mercy.

His eyes strayed back to the satchel on the passenger seat. He had not opened it since filling it hours before. The transcendental moment, when he looked at—or rather *into*—the diamonds at leisure had almost arrived. The moment of freedom, of release, he had so long yearned for.

For only through the intense, brilliant, refracted light issued by a deeply colored diamond could Diogenes escape, if only for a moment, his black-and-white prison. Only then could he recapture that faintest and most sought-after of his memories—the essence of color. And of all the colors he most longed for, red was his overriding passion. Red in all its myriad manifestations.

Lucifer's Heart. That was where he would begin and where he would end. The alpha and the omega of color.

Then there would be Viola to take care of.

The instruments had all been cleaned, polished, honed, and stropped to their sharpest edges. Viola would take some time. She was a *grand cru* wine that merited being taken up from the cellar, brought to room temperature, uncorked, and allowed to breathe—before being enjoyed, one exquisite sip after another, until nothing was left. She had to suffer—not for her sake, but for the marks it would leave on her body. And no one would be better able to interpret those marks than Aloysius. They would induce a suffering in him equal to, if not exceeding, the pain they caused the body's owner.

Perhaps he would start with a re-creation, in the cottage's damp stone basement, of the scene depicted in *Judith and Holofernes*. That had always been his favorite painting of Caravaggio's. He'd stood in front of it for hours, at the Galleria Nazionale d'Arte Antica in Rome, rapt in admiration: the lovely little furrow of determination on Judith's brow as she did the knifework; the way she kept every part of her body, save her bare hands and arms, away from the messy work in progress; the bright strong cords of blood that slashed diagonally across the bedsheets. Yes, that would make a fine start. Perhaps he and Viola could even study the painting together, before he got to work. Judith and Holofernes. With the roles reversed, of course, and the addition of a pewter bleeding bowl so that none of the precious nectar would be lost . . .

Diogenes passed through the empty village of Gerard Park. Gardiners Bay appeared ahead of him, a dull cold sheet of zinc broken by the dark outlines of distant islands. The car eased right onto Gerard Drive, Acabonack Harbor on one side, the bay on his left. Less than a mile more now. As he drove, he smiled faintly.

"*Vale, frater,*" he murmured in Latin. "*Vale.*"

Viola had pulled the chair up to the barred window, and she watched the first streak of light creep over the black Atlantic—a smudge of dirty chalk—with a sense of surreal detachment. It was like a nightmare she couldn't wake from, a dream as real and vivid as it was senseless. What scared her most of all was the realization of just how much trouble and expense Diogenes had gone to in creating this prison cell—riveted steel walls, floor, and ceiling, a steel door with a tumbler lock from a safe, not to mention the unbreakable windows, the special plumbing and wiring. It was as secure as a cell in the highest security prison—maybe more so.

Why? Was it really possible that, with dawn approaching, she had mere minutes to live?

Yet again, she forced this useless speculation from her mind.

She had long since concluded that escape was impossible. A great deal of thought had gone into constructing her prison, and her every effort to seek a way out had been anticipated and blocked. He had been gone all night—at least that's what the utter silence seemed to tell her. From time to time, she had banged and screamed on the door, at one point striking a chair against it again and again until the chair had come apart in her hands. No one had come.

The smear of chalk took on a faintly bloody tinge: a lurid glow over the heaving Atlantic. A ferocious wind dotted the dark ocean with dim flecks of whitecaps. Wisps of frozen snow—or was it sand?—whipped along the ground.

Suddenly, she sat up, abruptly alert. She had heard the faint muffled sound of a door opening. She rushed to her own door, pressed an ear against it. The very faintest of sounds came from below: a footfall, the closing of a door.

He was back.

She felt a sudden surge of fear and glanced across the room toward the window. The limb of the sun was just now climbing above the gray Atlantic, and just as quickly rising into a black bar of storm cloud. He had made it a point to arrive just at dawn. In time for the execution.

Viola curled her lip. If he thought he was going to kill her without a struggle, he was sorely mistaken. She would fight him to the death . . .

She swallowed, realizing how foolish her bravado was, aimed against a man who would surely have a gun and know exactly how to use it.

She fought against a sudden, panicky hyperventilation. A strange set of conflicting feelings rose within her: on the one hand, an urgent, instinctive desire for survival at whatever the cost; on the other, an ingrained need to die—if death, in fact, was near—with dignity, not with screaming and struggling.

There were more sounds and, without thinking, she immediately lay down on the floor to listen at the tiny space between the door and the threshold. The sounds were still faint and muffled.

She rose and ran into the bathroom, tore the toilet paper from its receptacle, unraveled it with a fierce shake of her hand, and pulled the cardboard tube free. Then she ran back to the door frame, pressing one end of the tube to her ear and squeezing the other end up against the long crack of the jamb.

Now she could hear much better: the rustle of clothing, the setting down of several things, the sound of a latch being undone.

There was a sudden, sharp intake of breath. Next, a long, long silence. Five minutes passed.

Then came a strange and terrible sound: a low, agonized keening, almost like the warning moan of a cat. It rose and fell in singsong fashion before suddenly ascending in volume to become a shriek of pure, undistilled, absolute anguish. It was inhuman, it was the shriek of the living dead, it was the most horrifying sound she had ever heard—and it came *from him.*

Fifty-six

THE CAB PULLED UP in front of the Times Building. Smithback impatiently signed the credit card receipt—the fare was $425—paying with the card he'd picked up at his apartment. He handed the slip back to the cabbie, who took it with a frown.

"Where's the tip?" the driver said.

"Are you kidding? I could've flown to Aruba for what I just paid you."

"Look, pal, I got gas, insurance, expenses up the wazoo—"

Smithback slammed the door and ran into the building, sprinting for the elevator. He would just touch base with Davies, let his boss know he was back in town, make sure his job wasn't on the line—and then head straight to the museum and Nora. It was quarter after nine: she hadn't been at the apartment, and he assumed she'd already left for work.

He punched the button for the thirty-third floor and waited while the elevator rose with maddening slowness. At last, it arrived, and he exited the car and jogged down the hall, pausing outside Davies's door just long enough to catch his breath and smooth down the unruly cowlick that always seemed to pop up at the worst possible time.

He took a deep breath, gave the door a polite rap.

"It's open," came the voice.

Smithback stepped forward into the doorway. Thank God: Harriman wasn't anywhere in sight.

Davies glanced up from his desk. "Bill! They told me you were at St. Luke's, practically at death's door."

"I made a quick recovery."

Davies looked him over, his eyes veiled. "Glad to see you looking so fat and happy." He paused. "I take it you'll be providing us with a note from your doctor?"

"Of course, of course," Smithback stammered. He assumed Pendergast could fix that, as he seemed able to fix everything else.

"You picked a convenient time to disappear." Davies's voice was laced with irony.

"I didn't pick it. It picked me."

"Have a seat."

"Well, I was just on my way—"

"Oh, I beg your pardon—I didn't realize you had a pressing engagement."

On hearing the icy tone in the voice, Smithback decided to sit down. He was dying to see Nora, but it wouldn't pay to piss off Davies any more than he already had.

"Bryce Harriman was able to take up the slack during your recent indisposition, both on the Duchamp killing and that other one up at the museum, since the police are now saying they're linked—"

Smithback sat forward in the chair. "Excuse me. Did you say a murder up at the museum? What museum?"

"You really have been out of it. The New York Museum of Natural History. A curator was murdered there three days ago—"

"*Who?*"

"Nobody I'd heard of. Don't worry about it, you're long off that story—Harriman's taken it over." He snapped up a manila envelope. "Here's what I've got for you, instead. It's a big story, and I'll be frank with you, Bill: I feel a certain trepidation entrusting it to someone in shaky health. I'd have considered passing it on to Harriman, too, only he's got a lot on his plate as it is and he was already in the field when the news broke twenty minutes ago. There was a big robbery at the museum last night. Seems it's a busy place these days. You're the one with contacts there, you wrote that book on the place— so it's your story, despite my feelings of concern."

"But who—?"

He shoved the envelope at Smithback. "Somebody cleaned out the diamond hall last night while a big function was under way. There's going to be a press conference at ten. Your credentials are in there." He glanced at his watch. "That's half an hour, you better get moving."

"About the killing at the museum," Smithback said again. "Who was it?"

"Like I said, nobody important. A new hire named Green. Margo Green."

"*What?*" Smithback found himself gripping the seat, reeling. It was impossible. Impossible.

Davies gazed at Smithback with alarm. "Are you all right?"

Smithback rose on shaking legs. "Margo Green . . . *murdered?*"

"Do you know her?"

"Yes." Smithback barely got the word out.

"Well, better that you're not handling the story, then," said Davies briskly. "Reporting on a subject too close to you, my old editor used to say, is like trying to be your own lawyer: you've got a fool for a lawyer and a fool for a—hey! Where're you going?"

Fifty-seven

As Nora turned the corner from Columbus Avenue onto West 77th Street, she immediately realized something big had happened at the museum. Museum Drive was packed with police vehicles, unmarked cars, and scene-of-crime vans, these in turn surrounded by television vans and a seething crowd of reporters.

She checked her watch—it was quarter to ten, usually a time when the museum was still waking up. Her heart quickened: had there been another killing?

She walked briskly down the service drive to the employee entrance. The police had already cleared a path for arriving museum employees and were pushing back an increasingly unruly crowd of rubberneckers. Apparently, whatever happened had already been reported on the morning news, as the crowds were swelling even as she watched. But because of the opening the night before, she'd overslept and hadn't had time to listen to the radio.

"Museum employee?" one cop asked.

She nodded, pulling out her badge. "What's going on?"

"Museum's closed. Go over there."

"But what—?"

The cop was already shouting at someone else, and she found herself propelled toward the security entrance, which seemed to be mobbed with museum security. Manetti, the security director, was there, gesturing frantically at a pair of hapless guards.

"All arriving staff to the roped area on the right!" one of the guards shouted. "Have your badges ready!"

Nora saw George Ashton in the milling crowd of arriving employees and grabbed his arm. "What's happened?"

He stared at her. "You must be the only one in the city who doesn't know."

"I overslept," she said testily.

"This way!" a policeman bawled. "Museum employees this way!"

The velvet ropes that had blocked off the gawkers and press from the gala the night before were now being put to a second use, this time to funnel museum staff to a holding area near the security entrance, where guards were checking IDs and calming irate employees.

"Someone hit the Astor Hall last night," said Ashton breathlessly. "Cleaned it out. Right in the middle of the party."

"Cleaned it *out*? Even Lucifer's Heart?"

"Especially Lucifer's Heart."

"How?"

"Nobody knows."

"I thought the Astor Hall was impregnable."

"So they said."

"Move back and stay to the right!" a cop yelled. "We'll have you inside in a moment!"

Ashton grimaced. "Just what I need the morning after five glasses of champagne."

More like ten, Nora thought wryly as she recalled Ashton's slurred ramblings of the previous evening.

Police and museum guards were checking IDs, questioning each employee, then moving them to a second penned area just before the security entrance.

"Any suspects?" Nora asked.

"None. Except that they're convinced the burglars had inside help."

"IDs!" a cop bawled in her ear.

She fished in her purse again and showed her ID. Ashton did the same.

"Dr. Kelly?" The cop had a clipboard. Another pulled Ashton aside.

"May I ask a few quick questions?"

"Fire away," Nora said.

"Were you at the museum last night?"

"Yes."

He marked something down.

"What time did you leave?"

"About midnight."

"That's all. Step over there and, as soon as we can, we'll open the museum and you can go to work. We'll be in touch with you later to schedule an interview."

Nora was shunted to the second holding area. She could hear Ashton's raised voice behind her, demanding to know why he hadn't been read his rights. The curators and staff waiting around her beat their hands in the cold, their breath filling the air. It was a gray day and the temperature hovered just below freezing. Voices were raised in complaint all around.

Nora heard a commotion from the street and looked.

The press had suddenly surged forward, cameras juggling on shoulders, boom mikes swinging. Then she saw the reason: the museum doors had swung open. The museum's director, Frederick Watson Collopy, appeared, flanked by Rocker, the police commissioner. A phalanx of uniformed policemen stood behind them.

Immediately, the press erupted in a clamor of shouted questions and waved hands. It was the start, it seemed, of a press conference.

At that same moment, she saw a frantic movement off to one side. She turned toward it. It was her husband, fighting through the crowd, shouting frantically and trying to reach her.

"Bill!" She rushed forward.

"Nora!" Smithback plowed through a milling crowd of hangers-on, sent a beefy museum security guard sprawling, hopped the velvet ropes, and muscled his way through the museum employees. "Nora!"

"Hey, where's that guy going?" A policeman struggled to intercept him.

Smithback cut through the last of the crowd and almost ran into Nora, enveloping her in a bear hug and lifting her bodily off the ground.

"Nora! God, did I miss you!"

They hugged, kissed, hugged again.

"Bill, what happened to you? What's that bruise on the side of your head?"

"Never mind about that," Smithback replied. "I just heard about Margo. Was she really killed?"

Nora nodded. "I went to her funeral yesterday."

"Oh my God. I can't believe it's true." He wiped savagely at his face, and Nora saw that his eyes were leaking tears. "I can't believe it."

"Where were you, Bill? I was so worried!"

"It's a long story. I was locked in an insane asylum."

"*What?*"

"I'll tell you about it later. I've been worried about you, too. Pendergast thinks there's a maniac killer wandering around, knocking off all his friends."

"I know. He warned me. But it was right before the opening—there was nothing I could—"

"This man's not supposed to be here," a museum guard interrupted, stepping between them. "This is for museum employees only—"

Smithback swung around to respond, but they were interrupted by the shriek of feedback on an improvised P.A. system. A moment later, Commissioner Rocker stepped up to the mike and asked for silence—and, miraculously, got it.

"I'm with the *Times*," said Smithback, scrounging some paper out of his pocket and fumbling for a pen.

"Here, use mine," Nora said, her arm still around his waist.

The crowd was silent as the police commissioner began to speak.

"Last night," Rocker began, "the Astor Hall of Diamonds was burglarized. At this point, the scene-of-crime teams are still on the site, along with some of the best forensic experts in the world. Everything that can be done is being done. It's too early for leads or suspects, but I promise you, as new developments arise, we will keep the press informed. I'm sorry I can't give you more, but it's still very early in the investigation. I will say this: it was an extremely professional job, obviously planned long in advance, by technologically sophisticated thieves who appear to have been intimately familiar with the museum's security system, and who used the distraction of last night's opening gala to their advantage. It will take a while to analyze and understand how they penetrated the museum's security. That's about all I have to say for the present. Dr. Collopy?"

The museum's director stepped forward, standing straight, trying to put the best face on things—and failing. When he spoke, a tremor underlay his words.

"I want to reiterate what Commissioner Rocker just said: all that can possibly be done is being done. The truth is, most of the diamonds stolen are unique and would be instantly recognizable to any gem dealer in the world. They cannot be fenced in their present form."

A murmur of unease went up at the implication they might be recut.

"My fellow New Yorkers, I know what a great loss this is to the museum and to the city. Unfortunately, we just don't know enough yet to be able to say who might have done it, or why, or what their intentions are."

"What about Lucifer's Heart?" someone shouted from among the press.

Collopy seemed to stagger. "We're doing all we can, I promise you."

"Was Lucifer's Heart stolen?" another shouted.

"I'd like to turn the floor over to the museum's public affairs director, Carla Rocco—"

A barrage of shouted questions followed and a woman stepped forward, holding up her hands. "I'll take the questions when there's silence," she said.

The clamor subsided and she pointed. "Ms. Lilienthal of ABC, your question?"

"What about Lucifer's Heart? Is it gone?"

"Yes, it was among the diamonds taken."

A turbulent murmur followed this unsurprising revelation. Rocco held up her hands again. "Please!"

"The museum claimed their security was the best in the world!" a reporter shouted. "How did the thieves get through?"

"We're analyzing it as we speak. Security is multilayered and redundant. The hall was under constant video surveillance. The thieves left behind a mass of technical equipment."

"What kind of technical equipment?"

"It'll take days, maybe weeks, to analyze."

More shouted questions. Rocco pointed to another reporter. "Roger?"

"How much is the collection insured for?"

"One hundred million dollars."

A murmur of awe.

"What's it *actually* worth?" the reporter named Roger persisted.

"The museum never put a value on it. Next question to Mr. Werth from NBC."

"What's Lucifer's Heart worth?"

"Again, you can't put a value on it. But let me *please* emphasize that we expect to recover the gems, one way or another."

Collopy stepped forward abruptly. "The museum's collection consists mostly of 'fancy' diamonds—that is, colored ones—and most are unusual enough to be recognizable from color and grade alone. That's especially true of a diamond like Lucifer's Heart. There's no other diamond in the world with its deep cinnamon color."

Nora watched as Smithback stepped over the velvet cord and into the group of press, waving his hand.

Rocco pointed to him, squinted. "Smithback, from the *Times*?"

"Isn't Lucifer's Heart considered the finest diamond in the world?"

"The finest *fancy* diamond, yes. At least that's what I've been told."

"So how are you going to explain this to the people of New York? How are you going to explain the loss of this unique gemstone?" His voice was suddenly shaking with emotion. It seemed to Nora that all the anger Smithback felt at Margo's death, and at his enforced separation from her, was being channeled into his question. "*How* could the museum have allowed this to happen!"

"No one *allowed* this to happen," said Rocco defensively. "The security in the Astor Hall is the most sophisticated in the world."

"Apparently, not sophisticated enough."

More chaos and shouting erupted. Rocco waved her hands. "Please! Let me speak!"

The roar died to an uneasy rumble.

"The museum *deeply regrets* the loss of Lucifer's Heart. We understand its importance to the city and, indeed, to the country. We're doing all we can to recover it. Please be patient and give the police time to do their work. Ms. Carlson of the *Post*?"

"This is for Dr. Collopy. Not to put too fine a point on it, but you were holding that diamond in trust for the people of New York, to whom it really belongs. How do you, personally, as the head of the museum, intend to bear responsibility for this?"

The rumble was rising again. But it suddenly died away as Collopy held up his hands. "The fact is," he said, "any security system devised by man can be defeated by man."

"That's a rather fatalistic view," Carlson continued. "In other words, you're admitting the museum can't ever guarantee the security of its collections."

"We certainly *do* guarantee the security of our collections," Collopy thundered.

"Next question!" Rocco called. But the reporters had latched onto something and weren't going to let go.

"Can you explain what you mean by 'guarantee'? The greatest diamond in the world has just been stolen and you tell us its security was guaranteed?"

"I can explain." Collopy's face swelled with anger.

"There's a bit of cognitive dissonance floating around here!" Smithback shouted.

"I make that statement because Lucifer's Heart *was not among the diamonds stolen!*" Collopy cried.

There was an astonished silence. Rocco turned and looked at Collopy in amazement, as did Rocker himself.

"Excuse me, sir," Rocco began.

"Silence! I'm the only person in the museum privy to this information, but under the circumstances I don't see any point in keeping the information back any longer. The stone on display was a replica, a real diamond artificially colored by radiation treatments. The *true* Lucifer's Heart has *always* been safely locked in a vault at the museum's insurance company. The gem was too valuable to put on display—our insurance company wouldn't allow it."

He raised his head, a glitter of triumph in his eyes. "The thieves, whoever they are, stole a *fake.*"

A roar of questions followed. But Collopy simply mopped his brow and retreated.

"This press conference is over!" shouted Rocco, to no effect. "No more questions!"

But it was clear, from the frantic hands and the shouts, that it was not over, and that there were many, many more questions to come.

Fifty-eight

OURS PASSED AS THEY drove through one deserted beach town after another. Dawn had swelled into a dismal day, bitterly cold, with a knife-edged wind whipping out of a pewter sky. D'Agosta was still listening, moodily, to the police radio. He was growing increasingly concerned: the police chatter concerning them had abruptly dropped off—not just because of the gem heist, although that filled most of the channels, but because they'd probably switched to more secure channels that couldn't be monitored from their portable police-band radio.

It was becoming obvious to him they had reached the end of the line. Hitting more convenience stores was hopeless—with a full tank of gas, Diogenes would have no further reason to stop. Their previous score in Yaphank had only confirmed what Diogenes wanted them to know—that he had gone east and that Viola would shortly be dead. Beyond that, nothing. D'Agosta felt sick for Pendergast: it was hopeless, and he knew it.

Still, they soldiered on, stopping at motels, marts, all-night diners, each time exposing themselves to the possibility of being spotted and arrested.

What few scraps D'Agosta had managed to glean from the radio had been disheartening. Bolstered by a new and strong federal presence, the police were rapidly closing in. New roadblocks had been erected, and local authorities were on full alert. Inevitably, they'd learn about the purchase of the pickup truck. Unless Pendergast had something truly clever up his sleeve, their free-range hours were numbered.

The pickup swerved abruptly and D'Agosta clutched the roof handle as Pendergast screeched into a small parking lot, coming to a halt in front of a twenty-four-hour Starbucks. Beyond lay a public parking lot and, beyond that, the gray, rolling Atlantic.

They sat for a moment while the police radio, still tuned to the museum theft, droned on. Some kind of press conference was in session, being broadcast over one of the public channels.

"No way they stopped here," said D'Agosta.

"What I'm after is a wireless hot spot." Pendergast opened the laptop, booted it up. "No doubt there's one inside. I'll use a sniffer to find an open port, tap into the Net that way. I left my pattern-recognition software running at the Dakota. Perhaps it has something more to tell us."

D'Agosta watched morosely as Pendergast tapped on the keyboard. "Would you be so kind as to order us some coffee, Vincent?" he asked without looking up.

D'Agosta got out of the truck and entered the Starbucks. When he returned a few minutes later with a couple of lattes, Pendergast had moved into the passenger seat and was no longer typing.

"Anything?"

Pendergast shook his head. Slowly, he sat back, closed his eyes.

D'Agosta eased himself into the driver's seat with a sigh. As he did so, he noticed a police cruiser turning into the parking lot. It slowed as it passed them, then halted at the far end of the lot.

"Shit. That cop's running our plates."

Pendergast didn't respond. He sat motionless, eyes closed.

"That's it. We're screwed."

Now the cruiser eased into a three-point turn at the end of the lot and headed back toward them.

Pendergast opened his eyes. "I'll hold the drinks. See what you can do about getting him off our tail."

Instantly, D'Agosta slammed the truck into drive and peeled out, fishtailing past the cruiser and onto the road paralleling the boardwalk. The cruiser snapped on its lights and siren, accelerating behind them.

They tore along the dune road. Moments later, D'Agosta heard another siren, this one coming from somewhere ahead.

"The beach," said Pendergast, gingerly balancing the lattes.

"Right." D'Agosta shifted into 4WD, spun the wheel, and bashed through the railing onto the boardwalk. The truck rumbled across the uneven wooden planks, hit the railing on the far side, and was briefly airborne as it made the two-foot drop to the sand.

In a moment, they were racing along the beach, just beyond the surf. D'Agosta glanced back to see the squad cars in the sand, still following.

They were going to have to do better.

He accelerated further, tires spinning up jets of damp

sand. Ahead, he could see an area of dunes, one of the many preserves along the South Shore. He swerved into it, broke down another wooden fence, and hit the scrubby dunes at forty. It was clearly a large preserve, and he had no idea where he was going, so he angled the truck into the roughest-looking section, where the brush was heaviest and the dunes highest, covered with a scattering of scrubby pines. No way the cruisers could follow them in here.

Suddenly, Pendergast sat up, like the snapping of a steel spring.

D'Agosta bashed through some more heavy brush, then glanced into the rearview mirror. Nothing. The cruisers had been stopped, but D'Agosta knew their respite was only temporary. All the police stations along the South Shore had beach patrol buggies—he knew, he used to drive one, in another life just a few months back. They were still in deep shit and he'd have to find some other way to—

"Stop the truck!" Pendergast said abruptly.

"No way, I've got to—"

"*Stop!*"

Something in the tone caused D'Agosta to jam on the brakes. They swerved wildly, stopping beneath the shadow of an overhanging dune. He killed the lights and the engine at the same time. This was crazy. They'd left a set of tracks any idiot could follow.

The radio was still on the press conference, and Pendergast was listening intently.

"*. . . always been safely locked in a vault at the museum's insurance company. The gem was too valuable to put on display—our insurance company wouldn't allow it.*"

Pendergast turned to D'Agosta, a look of astonishment and sudden, fierce hope lighting up his face.

"That's *it*!"

"What?"

"Diogenes finally made a mistake. This is the opening we need." He had his cell phone out.

"I wish to hell I knew what you were talking about."

"I'm going to make some calls. As of now, you have but one vital task, Vincent: *get us back to Manhattan.*"

The faint sound of a siren came up from behind the screen of dunes.

Fifty-nine

SMITHBACK SLOWLY SHUT his cell phone, stunned by the bizarre call he had just received. He found Nora looking at him curiously. They had finally opened the museum's staff entrance and employees were streaming past them, rushing to gain the warmth of indoors.

"What is it, Bill?" she asked. "Who was that?"

"Special Agent Pendergast. He managed to track me down on this loaner cell phone I picked up at the *Times*."

"What'd he want?"

"I'm sorry?" He felt dazed.

"I said, what did he want? You look shell-shocked."

"I've just had a most, um, extraordinary proposal put to me."

"Proposal? What are you talking about?"

Smithback roused himself and grasped Nora's shoulder. "I'll tell you about it later. Look, are you going to be okay here? I'm worried about your safety, with Margo dead and all these warnings of Pendergast's."

"The safest place in New York City is inside that museum right now. There must be a thousand cops in there."

Smithback nodded slowly, thinking. "True."

"Listen, I do have to go to work."

"I'm coming in with you. I've got to talk to Dr. Collopy."

"Collopy? Good luck."

Smithback could already see a large, angry crowd of reporters being kept from the museum by a string of policemen and guards. No one was getting in but employees. And Smithback was well known—all too well known—to the guards.

He felt Nora put an arm around his shoulder. "What are you going to do?"

"I've got to get inside."

Nora frowned. "Does this have to do with that call of Pendergast's?"

"It sure does." He looked into her green eyes, his gaze wandering over her copper hair and freckled nose. "You know what I'd really like to do . . ."

"Don't tempt me. I have a ton of work to do. Today's the public opening of the exhibition—assuming we ever open again."

Smithback gave her a kiss and a hug. He started to break away but found that Nora wouldn't release him.

"Bill," she murmured in his ear, "thank God you're back."

They held each other a few moments more, then Nora slowly let her arms fall away. She smiled, winked, then turned and walked into the museum.

Smithback watched her disappearing form. Then he shouldered his way into the crowd of employees lined up outside the door, bypassing the thicket of reporters who had been shunted off to one side. All the employees had their IDs out, and the crowd was thick. Police and museum guards were checking everybody's identification: it was going to be a bitch getting in. Smithback thought a moment, then pulled out his business card and scribbled a short note on the back.

When his turn came to pass through the security barrier, a guard barred his way. "ID?"

"I'm Smithback of the *Times*."

"You're in the wrong place, pal. Press is over there."

"Listen to me. I have a *very urgent and private* message for Dr. Collopy. It must be delivered to him immediately, or heads will roll. I'm not kidding. Yours, too"—Smithback glanced at the guard's nameplate— "Mr. Primus, if you don't deliver it."

The guard wavered, a look of fear in his eyes. The museum administration had not made life easy in recent years for those on the bottom, fostering a climate of fear more than family. Smithback had used this fact before, to good effect, and he hoped it would work again.

"What's it about?" the guard named Primus asked.

"The diamond theft. I have private information."

The guard seemed to waver. "I don't know . . ."

"I'm not asking you to let me in. I'm asking you to deliver this note directly to the director. Not to his secretary, not to anyone else—just to him. Look, I'm not some schmuck, okay? Here are my credentials."

The guard took the press pass, looking at it doubtfully.

Smithback pressed the message into his hand. "Don't read it. Put it in an envelope and deliver it personally. Trust me, you'll be glad you did."

The guard hesitated a moment. Then he took the card and retreated to the security office, reappearing a few moments later with an envelope. "I sealed it in here, never looked at it."

"Good man." Smithback scribbled on the envelope:

"For Dr. Collopy, extremely important, to be opened immediately. From William Smithback Jr. of the *New York Times*."

The guard nodded. "I'll see it's delivered."

Smithback leaned forward. "You don't understand. I want *you* to deliver it personally." He glanced around. "I don't trust any of these other bozos."

The guard flushed, nodded. "All right." Envelope in hand, he disappeared down the hall.

Smithback waited, cell phone in hand. Five minutes passed. Ten.

Fifteen.

Smithback paced in frustration. This was not looking good.

Then his phone gave a shrill ring. He opened it quickly.

"This is Collopy," came the patrician voice. "Is this Smithback?"

"Yes, it is."

"One of the guards will escort you to my office immediately."

A scene of controlled chaos greeted Smithback as he approached the grand, carved oaken doors of the director's office. Outside was a confabulation of New York City police, detectives, and museum officials. The door was shut, but as soon as Smithback's escort announced him, he was shown inside.

Collopy stood pacing before a great row of curved windows, hands clasped behind his back. Beyond the windows lay the wintry fastness of Central Park. Smithback recognized the security director, Manetti, along with several other museum officials standing before Collopy's desk.

The museum director noticed him, stopped pacing. "Mr. Smithback?"

"That's me."

Collopy turned to Manetti and the other officials. "Five minutes."

He watched them leave, then turned to Smithback. He was gripping the card in one hand, his face slightly flushed. "Who's behind this *outrageous* rumor, Mr. Smithback?"

Smithback swallowed. He had to make this sound good. "It's not exactly a rumor, sir. It came from a confidential source which I can't reveal. But I made a few calls, checked it out. It seems there might be something to it."

"This is intolerable. I've got enough to worry about without *this*. It's just some crank speculation, best ignored."

"I'm not sure that would be wise."

"Why? You're not going to publish unsubstantiated calumnies like this in the *Times,* are you? My assertion that the diamond is safe at our insurance company ought to be enough."

"It's true the *Times* doesn't publish rumors. But as I said, I've got a reliable source that claims it's true. I can't ignore that."

"Bloody *hell*."

"Let me pose a question to you," Smithback said, keeping his voice the soul of reasonableness. "When was the last time you personally saw Lucifer's Heart?"

Collopy shot him a glance. "It would have been four years ago, when we renewed the policy."

"Did a certified gemologist examine it at the time?"

"No. Why, it's an unmistakable gemstone . . ." Collopy's voice trailed off as he realized the weakness of his remark.

"How do *you* know it was the genuine article, Dr. Collopy?"

"I made a perfectly reasonable assumption."

"That's the crux of it, isn't it, Dr. Collopy? The truth is," Smithback continued gently, "you don't know for a fact that Lucifer's Heart is still in the insurance company vault. Or, if a gemstone is there, whether it's the real one."

"This is an absurd spinning of a conspiracy theory!" The director set off pacing again, hands balled up behind his back. "I don't have time for this!"

"You wouldn't want to let a story like this get out of control. You know how these things tend to assume a life of their own. And I do have to file my article by this evening."

"Your article? What article?"

"About the allegations."

"You publish that and my lawyers will eat you for breakfast!"

"Take on the *Times*? I don't think so." Smithback spoke mildly and waited, giving Collopy plenty of time to think things out to the inevitable, preordained conclusion.

"*Damn* it!" Collopy said, spinning on his heel. "I suppose we'll just have to bring it out and have it certified."

"An interesting suggestion," said Smithback.

Collopy paced. "It'll need to be done publicly, but under tight security, of course. We can't just invite every Tom, Dick, and Harry in to watch."

"May I suggest that all you really need is the *Times*? The others will follow our lead. They always do. We're the paper of record."

Another turn. "Perhaps you're right."

Another pace across the room, another turn. "Here's what I'm going to do. I'm going to get a gemologist to certify that the stone held by our insurance company is, in fact, Lucifer's Heart. We'll do it right there, at Affiliated Transglobal Insurance headquarters, under the tightest security. You'll be the only journalist there and, damn it, you'd better write an article that will scotch those rumors once and for all."

"*If* it's genuine."

"It'll be genuine or the museum will end up owning Affiliated Transglobal Insurance, so help me God."

"What about the gemologist? He'd have to be independent, for credibility."

Collopy paused. "It's true we can't use one of our own curators."

"And his reputation will obviously need to be unimpeachable."

"I'll contact the American Council of Gemologists. They could send one of their experts." Collopy walked to the desk, picked up the phone, and made several calls in rapid succession. Then he turned back to Smithback.

"It's all arranged. We'll meet at the Affiliated Transglobal headquarters, 1271 Avenue of the Americas, forty-second floor, at one o'clock precisely."

"And the gemologist?"

"A fellow named George Kaplan. Said to be one of the best." He glanced at Smithback. "Now, if you'll excuse me, I've got a lot to do. See you at one." He hesitated. "And thank you for your discretion."

"Thank you, Dr. Collopy."

Sixty

D'AGOSTA LISTENED to the sirens coming across the dunes. They grew louder, receded, then grew louder again. From his days with the Southampton P.D., he recognized the tinny sound as coming from the cheap units mounted on the dune patrol buggies.

They'd sat here in the shadow of a sand dune, hiding, assessing the situation, at least five minutes. If he remained on the beach, there was no way their truck was going to escape dune buggies. And yet if he went back on the street, he'd be nabbed immediately, now that they knew his approximate location, vehicle, and license plate.

They were now near Southampton, D'Agosta's old stomping ground, and he knew the lay of the land, at least in general terms. There had to be a way out. He would just have to find it.

He started the truck, popped the emergency brake.

"Hold on to your seat," he said.

Pendergast, who had apparently finished making a string of cell phone calls, glanced over. "I am in your hands."

D'Agosta took a deep breath. Then he gunned the engine, the pickup digging out of the hollow and climbing the side of a dune, shooting huge jets of sand behind them. They plunged into another depression, wound around several dunes, then climbed diagonally up the flank of an especially large one that separated them from the mainland. As they topped it, D'Agosta got a backward glimpse of several patrol buggies scooting along the hard sand a quarter mile back, with at least two others in the dunes themselves, no doubt following their tracks.

Shit. They were closer than he'd expected.

D'Agosta jammed the pedal to the floor as the pickup topped the dune. For a moment, they were airborne. Then they landed on the far side, bottoming out in the loose sand, churning and grinding their way through a patch of dense brush. The preserve ended, and the path ahead was blocked by several grand Hampton estates. As he fought with the wheel, D'Agosta quickly arranged the local topography in his head. If they could just get past the estates, he knew, Scuttlehole marsh lay beyond.

The dunes leveled out and he bashed the truck through a slat fence, emerging onto a narrow road. On the far side was a high boxwood hedge, surrounding one of the great estates. He tore alongside the hedge, and where the road curved up ahead, he saw what he was looking for—a sclerotic patch in the foliage—and he veered off, aiming directly for it. The pickup truck hit it at forty, bashed through the hedge, tearing off both mirrors in the process, and then they were accelerating across a ten-acre lawn, a huge Georgian mansion on the left, a gazebo and covered pool on the right, the way beyond blocked by an Italian rose garden.

He flashed past the pool at speed, ripped through the rose garden, nicked the arm off a sculpture of some naked woman, and crashed through a raised vegetable bed that lay beyond. Up ahead, like a green wall, stood another unbroken line of hedge.

Pendergast looked back through the rear window of the pickup truck, a pained expression on his face. "Vincent, you're cutting quite a swath," he said.

"They can add nude statue molestation to my growing list of crimes. For now, though, you'd better brace yourself." And he accelerated toward the hedge.

They hit it with a shuddering crash that nearly stopped the vehicle dead. The engine coughed and sputtered, and for a moment D'Agosta feared it would die. But they fought their way out the far side of the hedge, still running. Across another narrow road, he could see a split-rail fence and, beyond that, the marshes surrounding Scuttlehole Pond.

For the past couple of weeks it had been cold—very cold. Now D'Agosta was going to find out if it had been cold enough.

He tore along the road until he found a break in the fence, then pointed the truck through it and went off-road again. He was forced to slow down as he wound through the sparse jack-pine forest that surrounded the marsh. He could still hear the sirens coming faintly from behind. If he had gained ground cutting through the estate, it was precious little.

The stunted pines gradually gave way to marsh grass and sandy flats. Ahead, he could see the dead stalks of cattail and yellow marsh grass. The pond itself seemed lost in the gray light.

"Vincent?" Pendergast said calmly. "You're aware there's a body of water ahead?"

"I know."

The pickup accelerated over the frozen verge of the marsh, the wheels sending shards of crackling ice skittering away on either side like a wake. The speedometer edged back up to thirty, then thirty-five, then forty. For what he was about to do, he was going to need all the speed he could get.

With a final slapping sound, the cattails scattering in their wake, the pickup truck was on the ice.

Pendergast gripped the door handle, the lattes forgotten. "Vincent—?"

The truck was moving fast across the ice, breaking it as they went with a machine-gun chatter. D'Agosta could see in his rearview mirror that the ice was cracking and shattering behind them, some pieces even flung up and skittering away, black water slopping up. The sound of fracturing ice boomed across the lake like the reports of cannon.

"The idea is they won't be able to follow us," said D'Agosta through clenched teeth.

Pendergast didn't answer.

The far shore, lined with stately homes, steadily approached. The truck felt almost like it was floating now, rising up and down like a powerboat on the continuously breaking crust of ice.

D'Agosta could feel he was losing momentum. He applied just a little more gas, being careful to ease down slowly on the accelerator. The truck roared, wheels spinning, the crackle and snap of ice growing louder.

Two hundred yards. He gave it more gas, but it just spun the wheels faster.

The amount of power being transferred from the wheels to the slick surface was steadily decreasing. The truck jerked, bounced, slowed, and began to slew sideways as the craquelure of failing ice spread out from them in all directions.

This is no time for half measures. D'Agosta jammed the pedal to the floor once again as he spun the wheel. The engine screamed, the truck accelerating, but not quite enough to stay ahead of the horrible disintegration of ice.

One hundred yards.

The engine was now screaming like a turbine, the truck still yawing sideways, moving now on inertia alone.

The far shore was close, but the truck was slowing with every passing second. Pendergast had scooped up the laptop and police radio under his arm, and seemed to be preparing to open his door.

"Not yet!" D'Agosta gave the wheel a sharp check, just enough to straighten out the truck. The nose, the heavier part, was still up, and as long as it stayed that way . . .

With a horrible sinking sensation, the front of the truck began to settle. There was a moment of breathless suspension. And then it nosed down sharply and slammed into the forward edge of ice, stopping the truck cold.

D'Agosta flung open the door and launched himself into the freezing water, clutching at the breaking edge of ice, gripping it, hauling himself up onto a jagged floe. He scrambled away crablike onto solid ice as the bed of the pickup truck swung upward vertically, the back wheels still spinning off watery slush—and then as he watched, the truck plunged straight down with a rush of forced air, slopping him with a wave of icy water, cakes of broken ice dancing and churning in its wake.

After the truck had vanished, there, on the far side of the gaping hole, stood Pendergast, standing on the ice as if he'd merely stepped out of the truck, computer and radio tucked under one arm, black coat dry and unruffled.

D'Agosta rose unsteadily to his feet on the groaning ice. They were a mere dozen yards from shore. He glanced back but the dune buggies had not yet appeared on the shore of the pond.

"Let's go."

In a moment, they reached the shore and hid themselves behind a raised dock. The buggies were just arriving, their yellow headlights piercing the bitter gray air. The story that met their eyes was evident enough: a long, broken path of heaving ice that led most of the way across the lake to a gaping hole, littered with broken chunks of ice. A slick of gasoline was slowly rising and spreading in rainbow patterns.

Pendergast peered across the lake from between the slats of the dock. "That, Vincent, was a most ingenious maneuver."

"Thanks," D'Agosta said through chattering teeth.

"It will take them a while to determine that we're still alive. Meanwhile, shall we see what the neighborhood has to offer in the way of transportation?"

D'Agosta nodded. He had never been so cold in his life. His hair and clothes were freezing, and his hands burned with the cold.

They crept up along the hedges of one of the great houses—all summer "cottages," currently shut up for the winter. The driveway was empty, and they moved around the side of the house and looked in the garage window.

There sat a vintage Jaguar on blocks, the wheels stacked in the gloom of one corner.

"That should do," Pendergast murmured.

"Garage's alarmed," D'Agosta managed to say.

"Naturally." Pendergast glanced around, found a wire tucked behind a drainpipe, followed it to the garage door, and in a few minutes had found the alarm plate coupling.

"Very crude," he said, jamming a stray nail behind the plate and prying it loose, being careful not to cut the connection. Then he picked the lock on the garage door, raised it a foot, and they slid underneath.

The garage was heated.

"Warm yourself, Vincent, while I get to work."

"How in hell did you avoid going in the water?" D'Agosta said, standing directly on top of the heating vent.

"Perhaps my timing was better." Taking off his coat and jacket and rolling up his crisp white sleeves, Pendergast set the four tires in place, jacked up one end of the car, slipped the tire on and bolted it, then followed the same procedure for the other three wheels.

"Feeling warmer?" he asked as he worked.

"Sort of."

"Then if you don't mind, Vincent, open the hood and connect the battery." Pendergast nodded toward a toolbox that sat in one corner.

D'Agosta pulled out a wrench, opened the hood, connected the battery, checked the fluid levels, and examined the engine. "Looks good."

Pendergast kicked away the final block and jacked down the last wheel. "Excellent."

"No one to call the cops about a stolen car."

"We shall see. Although the area seems deserted for the winter, there's always the danger of a nosy neighbor. This 1954 Mark VII saloon is not an inconspicuous vehicle. Now for the moment of truth. Please get in and help me start her."

D'Agosta clambered into the driver's seat and waited for instructions.

"Foot on the accelerator. Choke out. Gear in neutral."

"Check," D'Agosta said.

"When you hear the engine turn, give it a bit of gas."

D'Agosta complied. A moment later, the car roared to life.

"Ease off the choke," Pendergast said. He walked over to the alarm box, glanced around, picked up a long wire, attached it to both metal plates in the alarm, then opened the door. "Take her out."

D'Agosta eased the Jag out. Pendergast shut the garage door and got into the rear of the vehicle.

"Let's get the heat on in this baby," said D'Agosta, fiddling with the unfamiliar controls as he drove onto the street.

"You do that. Pull over and let it run for a few minutes. I am going to lie down, and . . . ho, what's this?" He held up a loud sports jacket checkered in various shades of light green. "A stroke of luck, Vincent! Now you look the part."

D'Agosta drew off his sodden coat and tossed it on the floor, putting on the sports jacket instead.

"How becoming."

"Yeah, right."

At that moment, Pendergast's cell phone rang. D'Agosta watched as the agent plucked it from his pocket.

"Yes," Pendergast said. "I understand. Yes, excellent. Thank you." And he hung up.

"We have three hours to get to Manhattan," he said, checking his watch. "Do you think you can manage it?"

"You bet." D'Agosta hesitated. "Now, you want to tell me who that was and what the heck you've been up to?"

"That was William Smithback."

"The journalist?"

"Yes. You see, Vincent, at last—at long, long last—we might have been given a break."

"How do you figure that?"

"Diogenes was the person who robbed the Astor Hall last night."

D'Agosta turned to stare at him. "Diogenes? You sure?"

"Undoubtedly. He's always had an obsession with diamonds. All these murders were just a horrible distraction to keep me busy while he planned his *real* crime: the robbing of the diamond hall. And he chose to take Viola last, to ensure my maximal distraction during the robbery itself. Vincent, it *was* a 'perfect' crime, after all, in a spectacular, public sense—not one aimed simply at myself."

"So what makes this a break for us?"

"What Diogenes didn't know—couldn't know—was that the finest gem of all, no doubt the one he most wanted, wasn't on display. He didn't steal Lucifer's Heart: he stole a fake."

"So?"

"So I'm going to steal the real Lucifer's Heart for him and make a trade. Is the motor warmed up? Let's get back to New York—there's no time to waste."

D'Agosta eased the car away from the curb. "I've seen you pull a few rabbits out of your hat, but how in the hell are you going to steal the world's greatest diamond on the spur of the moment? You don't know where it is, you don't know anything about its security."

"Perhaps. But as it happens, Vincent, my plans are already in motion." And Pendergast patted the pocket where his cell phone was.

D'Agosta kept his eyes on the road. "There's a problem," he said in a quiet voice.

"What's that?"

"We're assuming that Diogenes still has something to trade."

There was a brief silence before Pendergast spoke. "We can only pray that he does."

Sixty-one

LAURA HAYWARD WALKED briskly up the steps of the Lower Manhattan Federal Building, Captain Singleton at her heels. Singleton was, as usual, dressed nattily: camel's-hair topcoat, Burberry scarf, thin black leather gloves. He hadn't said much on the ride downtown, but that was okay: Hayward hadn't felt much like talking.

It had been barely twenty-four hours since D'Agosta walked out of her office and away from her ultimatum, but it might as well have been a year. Hayward had always been an exceptionally levelheaded person, but as she walked into the Federal Building, she had an almost overpowering sense of unreality. Maybe none of this was happening, maybe she wasn't on her way to an urgent FBI briefing, maybe Pendergast wasn't the most wanted criminal in New York and D'Agosta his accomplice. Maybe she'd just wake up and it would be January 21 again, and her apartment would still smell of Vinnie's overcooked lasagna.

At the security checkpoint, Hayward showed her shield, checked her weapon, signed the clipboard. There wasn't going to be a happy ending. Because if D'Agosta wasn't Pendergast's accomplice, he would be Pendergast's victim.

The conference room was large, paneled in dark wood. Flags of New York and the United States drooped from brass flagpoles on both sides of the entryway, and color photos of various government types lined the walls. A huge oval table dominated the room, surrounded with leather chairs. The coffee urn and the table heaped with donuts and crullers, a staple of NYPD departmental meetings, was absent. Instead, a pint bottle of spring water had been placed before each chair.

Unfamiliar men and women in dark suits were standing around in knots, talking quietly among themselves. As Hayward and Singleton entered, the groups began making their way quickly toward the chairs. Hayward chose the nearest seat and Singleton sat down beside her, removing his gloves and scarf. There was no place to hang their stuff, and as a result they were the only two people in the room wearing coats.

At that moment, a tall, stocky man walked into the conference room. Two shorter men followed on his heels, like obedient hounds. Each of the two carried a brick of red folders under his arm. The tall man stopped for a moment, glancing around the table. Unlike the rest of the faces in the room, pallid from the New York winter, his was sunburned. It wasn't the even, artificial tan you got from a salon: this man had spent long hours working someplace sunny and hot. His eyes were small, narrow, and pissed-off.

He walked to the head of the table, where three seats had been left empty, and took the middle one. His two retainers sat to his right and his left.

"Good morning," the man said in an abrasive Long Island accent at odds with the sunburn. "I'm Special Agent in Charge Spencer Coffey, and with me are Special Agents Brooks and Rabiner. With their assistance, I'll be leading the search for Special Agent Pendergast."

The man seemed to spit out the final word, and as he said it, the anger spread from his eyes to his entire face.

"The facts as we know them so far are these: Pendergast is a primary suspect in four homicides, one in New Orleans, one in D.C., and two here in New York. We have DNA and fiber evidence from all four sites, and we're co-operating with local authorities in an effort to gather more."

Singleton shot Hayward a meaningful look. Coffey's idea of "cooperation" had been a phalanx of FBI agents swooping down on her office, grilling her men, and taking whatever evidence struck their fancy. Ironic how her own request for the Quantico profile had aroused Coffey's interest in the first place.

"Clearly, we're dealing with a mentally unbalanced individual—the psych profile confirms it. There is a high probability he is planning additional homicides. He was last spotted yesterday afternoon at Kennedy Airport, where he eluded security guards and police officers, stole a rental car, and drove away. He abandoned his own vehicle at the rental lot—a Rolls-Royce."

A low murmur went around the room at this, punctuated by several scoffs and dark looks. Pendergast must have made more than his share of enemies during his tenure with the FBI.

"There have been unconfirmed sightings of Pendergast at several convenience stores and gas stations in Nassau and Suffolk counties, last night and this morning. We're following up on those now. Pendergast is traveling with another man, believed to be NYPD lieutenant Vincent D'Agosta. And I've just had news of a high-speed chase in the vicinity of Southampton. Preliminary eyewitness accounts from the officers involved would seem to ID Pendergast and D'Agosta."

Hayward shifted uncomfortably in her chair. Singleton stared straight ahead.

"We have teams searching Pendergast's 72nd Street apartment and his New Orleans town house as we speak. Any information we discover that might shed light on his future movements will be passed down the line to you. We're setting up a command-and-control structure that will allow for quick dissemination of new information. This is going to be a very fluid situation, and we have to be ready to revise our strategy accordingly."

Coffey nodded to his retainers, and they stood up and began walking around the table, passing out the red folders. Hayward noticed that neither she nor Singleton received one. She'd assumed this was to be a working meeting, but it appeared that Special Agent in Charge Coffey already had his own ideas about how to handle the case and neither needed nor wanted input from anybody else.

"You'll find your initial instructions and assignments in these folders. You will be working in teams, and each team will be assigned six field agents. Our immediate priority is to determine Pendergast's movements over the last twenty-four hours, look for patterns, set up checkpoints, and draw in the net until we have him. We don't know why he's running around Long Island, stopping at convenience stores and gas stations: those we've interviewed indicate he's been looking for someone. I'll be expecting hourly verbal reports from each team, made either to me directly or to Special Agents Brooks and Rabiner."

Coffey stood up heavily, sweeping the table with his angry gaze. "I'm not going to sugarcoat this. Pendergast is one of our own. He knows all the tricks of the trade. Even though it seems we've got him pinned down on eastern Long Island, he could still elude us. That's why we're throwing the entire resources of the Bureau into this. We need to nail this bastard, and quickly. The reputation of the Bureau's at stake."

He surveyed the table again. "Any questions?"

"Yes," Hayward said.

All eyes turned toward her. She hadn't intended to speak, but the word had just tumbled out involuntarily.

Coffey glanced at her, small eyes narrowing to pinpricks of white. "Captain, ah, Hayward, isn't it?"

She nodded.

"Go ahead, please."

"You haven't mentioned the role of the NYPD in the search."

Coffey's eyebrows shot up. "Role?"

"That's right. I've heard a lot about what the FBI's going to do, but nothing about the cooperation with the NYPD you mentioned earlier."

"Lieutenant Hayward, our latest information, if you've been listening, has Pendergast in Suffolk County. There's not a great deal you can do for us out there."

"True. But we've got dozens of detectives here in Manhattan who are familiar with the case, we've developed virtually all the evidence—"

"*Lieutenant,*" Coffey interrupted, "no one is more grateful for the NYPD's assistance in furthering this investigation than I am." But he didn't look grateful—if anything, he looked more pissed-off than before. "At the moment, however, the matter is outside your jurisdiction."

"Our immediate jurisdiction, yes. But he could always return to the city. And given that Agent Pendergast is wanted in two murders I'm in charge of investigating, I want to make sure that, once he's apprehended, we've got access for interrogation—"

"Let's not get ahead of ourselves," Coffey snapped. "The man's still at large. Any other questions?"

The room was silent.

"Good. There's just one last thing." Coffey's voice went down a few notches. "I don't want anybody taking any chances. Pendergast is armed, desperate, and extremely dangerous. In the event of a confrontation, a maximal armed response will be appropriate. In other words, shoot the son of a bitch. Shoot to kill."

Sixty-two

EORGE KAPLAN EXITED his Gramercy Park brownstone, paused for a moment at the top of the steps to check his cashmere coat, flicked off a speck of dust, pinched his perfectly knotted cravat, patted his pockets, inhaled the crisp January air, and descended. His was a quiet, tree-lined neighborhood, his brownstone facing the park itself, and even in the cold winter weather there were mothers with their children walking the winding lanes, their cheerful voices rising among the bare branches.

Kaplan fairly tingled with anticipation. The call he had received was as unexpected as it was welcome. Most gemologists lived their entire lives without ever having the opportunity to gaze into the depths of a gemstone one-millionth as rare or famous as Lucifer's Heart. He had, of course, seen it at the museum behind a thick piece of glass, under execrable lighting, but until now he hadn't known just why the lighting was so bad: had it been lit properly, at least a few gemologists—himself included—would have recognized it as a fake. A very good fake, to be sure: a real diamond, irradiated to give it that incredible cinnamon color, no doubt enhanced by colored fiber-optic light skillfully delivered from beneath the gem. Kaplan had seen it all in his forty years as a gemologist, every rip-off, cheat, and con game in the business. He chided himself for not realizing that a diamond like Lucifer's Heart *couldn't* be put on display. No company would insure a stone which was always in full public view, its location known to the world.

Lucifer's Heart. And what was it worth? The last red diamond of any quality that had come up for sale was the Red Dragon, a five-carat stone that had gone for sixteen million dollars. And this one was nine times as large, a better grade and color, without a doubt the finest fancy color diamond in existence.

Value? Name your price.

After receiving the call, Kaplan had spent a few moments in his library, refreshing himself on the history of the diamond. With diamonds, it was usually the case that the less color the better, but that was true only up to a point. When a diamond had a deep, intense color, it suddenly leaped in value; it became the rarest of the rare—and of all the colors a diamond could possess, red was by far the rarest. He knew that, in all the crude production from all the De Beers mines, a red diamond of quality surfaced only about once every two years. Lucifer's Heart made the word *unique* sound hackneyed. At forty-five carats, it was huge, a heart-cut stone with a GIA grade of VVS1 Fancy Vivid. No other stone in the world even came close. And then there was the color: it wasn't ruby red or garnet-colored, either of which was exceedingly rare in its own right. Rather, it was an intensely rich reddish orange, a color so unusual that it defied naming. Some called it cinnamon, and while Kaplan thought it more reddish than true cinnamon, he himself could not find a better word to describe it. The closest analogy he could think of was blood in bright sunlight, but if anything, it was even richer than blood. No other object in the wide world possessed its color—nothing. Its color was a scientific mystery. To find out what gave Lucifer's Heart its unique color, scientists would have to destroy a piece of the diamond—and that, of course, would never happen.

The diamond had a short, bloody history. The raw stone, a monster of some 104 carats, had been found by an alluvial digger in the Congo in the early 1930s. Not realizing, because of its color, that it was even a diamond, he used it to pay a long-running bar tab. When the man later learned what it was, he tried to get it back from the barman, only to be rebuffed. So one night he broke into the barman's home, killed the man, his wife, and their three children, and then spent the rest of the night trying to hide his crime by cutting up the corpses and throwing them off the back porch to the crocodiles in the Buyimai River. He was caught, and during the gathering of evidence for the murder trial, part of which involved killing and examining the stomach contents of a dozen river crocodiles, a police inspector was killed by an enraged reptile and a second drowned trying to save him.

The gemstone, still uncut, made its way through the black market (and several other rumored killings) before it resurfaced in Belgium as the property of a notorious black market dealer. The man badly botched the cleaving of the stone, leaving a nasty crack in it, and subsequently committed suicide. The now damaged rough stone bounced around the diamond demimonde for a while, ultimately ending up in the hands of an Israeli diamond cutter named Arens, one of the best in the world. In what was later called the most brilliant cutting ever done, Arens was able to produce a heart-shaped gem from the cracked rock in just such a way as to remove the flaw without fracturing the stone or losing too much material. It took Arens eight years to complete the cut. The process had since passed into legend. He spent three years looking at the stone; then another three practicing the cutting and polishing on no fewer than two hundred plastic models of the original, experimenting in ways to optimize the size, cut, and design while removing the exceedingly dangerous flaw. He succeeded, in much the same way Michelangelo was able to sculpt the *David* out of a badly cracked block of marble other sculptors had rejected as unworkable.

When Arens was done, he had produced an extraordinary, heart-cut stone along with another dozen or so smaller stones, all from the same rough. He named the biggest stone Lucifer's Heart after its grim history, commenting to the press that it was "the very devil to cut."

And then, in an act of extraordinary generosity, Arens willed the stone to the New York Museum of Natural History, which he had visited as a child and whose Hall of Diamonds had determined what his life's work would be. He sold the dozen or so much smaller stones cut from the same rough for what was rumored to be an astonishing sum, but, strangely enough, none of the stones had ever resurfaced on the market. Kaplan assumed they had been made into a single, spectacular piece of jewelry, which remained with the original owner, who wished to keep her identity secret.

Kaplan swung around the corner of Gramercy Park and walked west, toward Park Avenue, where he had the best shot of catching a cab headed uptown. He had half an hour, but you could never predict midtown traffic at lunchtime, and this was one appointment he did not want to be late to.

As he stopped at the corner of Lex to wait for the light to change, he was startled to see a black car roll up beside him, window down. Inside sat a man in a green sports jacket.

"Mr. George Kaplan?"

"Yes?"

The man leaned over, presented the badge of a New York City police lieutenant, and opened the door. "Get in, please."

"I have an important appointment, Officer. What's this all about?"

"I know. Affiliated Transglobal Insurance. I'm your escort."

Kaplan peered closely at the badge: Lieutenant Vincent D'Agosta. It was a genuine shield—Kaplan was well versed in such things—and the man behind the wheel really couldn't be anything other than a cop, despite the unusual choice of apparel. Who else would know about his appointment?

"That's kind of you." Kaplan climbed in, the door shut, the locks shot down, and the car eased away from the curb.

"Security's going to be high," said the policeman. Then he nodded at a gray plastic box on the seat between them. "I'll have to ask you to surrender your cell phone, your wallet with all your identification, any weapons you might have, and all your tools. Put them in that box next to you. I'll pass them to my colleague, and they'll all be returned to you at the vault after they've been thoroughly vetted."

"Is this really necessary?"

"Absolutely. And I'm sure you can understand why."

Kaplan, not very surprised under the circumstances, removed the requested items and placed them in the box. At the next light, at Park Avenue, a vintage Jaguar that had been following them pulled up alongside; the windows of both vehicles went down; and the policeman handed the box through the window. Glancing into the other car, Kaplan saw that the driver had carefully groomed pale blond hair and was wearing a nicely tailored black suit.

"Your colleague drives a most unusual car for a policeman."

"He's a most unusual man."

When the light changed to green, the Jaguar turned right and headed for Midtown, while the policeman driving Kaplan turned south.

"I beg your pardon, Officer, but we should be heading north," Kaplan said. "Affiliated Transglobal Insurance is headquartered at 1271 Avenue of the Americas."

The car accelerated southward and the policeman looked over unsmilingly. "Sorry to inform you, Mr. Kaplan, but this is one appointment you won't be keeping."

Sixty-three

THEY GATHERED in the sitting room of Harrison Grainger, CEO of Affiliated Transglobal Insurance. The executive suite was perched high in the Affiliated Transglobal Tower, looking north up the great canyon of Avenue of the Americas to its terminus, a half dozen blocks north, at the dark rectangle of Central Park. At one o'clock precisely, Grainger himself emerged from his office, a florid man with cauliflower ears and a narrow head, expansive, balding, and cheerful.

"Well, are we all here?" He looked around.

Smithback glanced about. His mouth felt like paste and he was sweating. He wondered why in the world he had agreed to this insane scheme. What had sounded like a fabulous escapade earlier that day, a chance at a one-of-a-kind scoop, now appeared mad in the harsh light of reality: Smithback was about to participate in a very serious crime—not to mention compromising all his ethics as a journalist.

Grainger looked around, smiling. "Sam, you make the introductions."

Samuel Beck, the security chief, stepped forward with

a nod. Despite his nervousness, Smithback couldn't help noticing the man had feet as small as a ballerina's.

"Mr. George Kaplan," the security chief began. "Senior associate of the American Council of Gemologists."

Kaplan, a neat man dressed in black, sporting a trimmed goatee and rimless glasses, had the elegant look of a man of the last century. He gave a short, sharp bow.

"Frederick Watson Collopy, director of the New York Museum of Natural History."

Collopy shook hands all around. He didn't look especially pleased to be here.

"William Smithback of the *New York Times.*"

Smithback managed a round of handshakes, his hand as damp as a dishrag.

"Harrison Grainger, chief executive officer, Affiliated Transglobal Insurance Group Holding."

This set off another series of murmured greetings.

"Rand Marconi, CFO, Affiliated Transglobal Group."

Oh, God, thought Smithback. Were all these people coming?

"Foster Lord, secretary, Affiliated Transglobal Group."

More handshakes, nods.

"Skip McGuigan, treasurer, Affiliated Transglobal Group."

Yet again, Smithback plucked weakly at his collar.

"Jason McTeague, security officer, Affiliated Transglobal Group."

It was like announcing the nobility arriving at a formal ball. A heavily armed security guard shifted on his feet, nodded, didn't offer his hand.

"And I am Samuel Beck, director of security, Affiliated Transglobal Group. Suffice to say, we've all been checked, vetted, and cleared." He gave a quick smile at his own witticism, which was reinforced by a hearty laugh from Grainger.

"All right, then, let's proceed," said the CEO, holding out his hand toward the elevators.

They headed deep into the bowels of the building, descending first one elevator, then a second, then a third, at last winding through long and unnamed cinder-block corridors before arriving at the largest, most polished, most gleaming vault door Smithback had ever seen. Staring at the door, his heart sank still further.

Beck busied himself with a keypad, a series of locks, and a retinal scanner while they all waited.

At last, Beck turned. "Gentlemen, we now have to wait five minutes for the timed locks to disengage. This vault," he continued proudly, "contains all our original, executed policies: every single one. An insurance policy is a contract, and the only valid copies of our contracts are here—representing almost half a trillion dollars of coverage. It's protected by the latest security systems devised by man. This vault is designed to withstand an earthquake of 9 on the Richter scale, an F-5 tornado, and the detonation of a hundred-kiloton nuclear bomb."

Smithback tried to take notes, but he was still sweating heavily, the pen slippery in his hands. *Think of the story. Think of the story.*

There was a soft chiming sound.

"And that, gentlemen, is the signal that the vault's locks have disengaged." Beck pulled a lever and the faint humming of a motor sounded, the door slowly swinging outward. It was staggeringly massive, six feet of solid stainless steel.

They moved forward, the well-armed security guard bringing up the rear, and passed through two other massive doors before entering what was evidently the main vault, a huge steel space with metal cages enclosing drawer upon metal drawer, rising from floor to ceiling.

Now the CEO stepped forward, clearly relishing his role. "The inner vault, gentlemen. But even here the diamond is not kept unprotected, where it might tempt one of our trusted employees. It is kept in a special vault-within-a-vault, and no fewer than four Affiliated Transglobal executives are needed to open this vault: myself, Rand Marconi, Skip McGuigan, and Foster Lord."

The three men, dressed in identical gray suits, bald, and looking enough alike as to be mistaken for brothers, all smiled at this. Clearly, they didn't get many chances to strut their stuff.

The interior vault stood at the far end of the chamber, another steel door in the wall. Four keyholes were arrayed in a line across its face. Above them, a small light glowed red.

"And now we wait for the outer vault doors to be locked before we open the inner vault."

Smithback waited, listening to the series of motorized hummings, clickings, and deep rumbles.

"Now we are locked in. And as long as the inner safe is *unlocked,* the outer vault doors will remain *locked.* Even if one of us wanted to steal the diamond, we couldn't leave with it!" Grainger chuckled. "Gentlemen, take out your keys."

The men all removed small keys from their pockets.

"We've set up a small table for Mr. Kaplan," said the CEO, indicating an elegant table nearby.

Kaplan eyed it narrowly, pursing his lips with tight disapproval.

"Is everything in order?" the CEO asked.

"Bring out the diamond," Kaplan said tersely.

Grainger nodded. "Gentlemen?"

Each of the men inserted his key into one of the four keyholes. Glances were exchanged; then the keys were turned simultaneously. The small red light turned green and the safe clicked open. Inside was a simple metal cabinet with eight drawers. Each one was labeled with a number.

"Drawer number 2," said the CEO.

The drawer was opened; Grainger leaned in and removed a small gray metal box, which he carried over to the table and placed before Kaplan with reverence. The gemologist sat down and began fussily laying out a small collection of tools and lenses, adjusting them with precision on the tabletop. He took out a rolled pad of plush black velvet and laid it out, forming a neat square in the middle of the table. Everyone watched him work, the people forming a semicircle around the table—with the exception of the security guard, who stood slightly back, arms crossed.

As a last step, Kaplan pulled on a pair of surgical gloves. "I am ready. Hand me the key."

"I'm sorry, Mr. Kaplan, but rules require me to open the box," said the security director.

Kaplan waved a hand irritably. "So be it. Don't drop it, sir. Diamonds may be hard but they shatter as easily as glass."

Beck leaned over the box, inserted the key, and raised the lid. All eyes were riveted on the box.

"Don't touch it with your naked, sweaty hands," said Kaplan sharply.

The security director withdrew. Kaplan reached into the box and plucked out the gem as nonchalantly as if it were a golf ball, laying it on the velvet in front of him. He opened a loupe and leaned over the stone.

Suddenly, he straightened up and spoke in a sharp, high, querulous voice. "I beg your pardon, but really, I can't work being crowded around like this, especially from behind. I beg you, please!"

"Of course, of course," said Grainger. "Let's all step back and give Mr. Kaplan some room."

They shuffled back. Once again, Kaplan bent to examine the gem. He picked it up with a four-pronged holder, turned it over. He laid down the loupe.

"Hand me my Chealsea filter," he said sharply, to no one in particular.

"Ah, which is that?" Beck asked.

"The white oblong object, over there."

The security director picked it up and handed it over. Kaplan took it, opened it, and examined the gem again, muttering something unintelligible.

"Is everything to your satisfaction, Mr. Kaplan?" asked Grainger solicitously

"No," he said simply.

The tension in the vault went up a notch.

"Do you have enough light?" the CEO asked.

A freezing silence.

"Hand me the DiamondNite. No, not that. *That.*"

Beck handed him a strange device with a pointed end. Ever so gently, Kaplan touched the stone with it. There was a small beep and a green light.

"Hmph. At least we know it's not moissanite," the gemologist said crisply, handing the device back to Beck, who did not look pleased to be cast in the role of assistant.

More mutterings. "The polariscope, if you please."

After a few false starts, Beck handed it to him.

A long look, a snort.

Kaplan stood up and looked around, eyeing everyone in the room. "As far as I can tell, which isn't much, given the horrendous lighting in here, it's probably a fake. A superb fake, but a fake nonetheless."

A shocked silence. Smithback stole a glance at Collopy. The museum director's face had gone deathly white.

"You're not sure?" the CEO asked.

"How can I possibly be sure? How can you expect an expert like me to examine a fancy color diamond under *fluorescent* lighting?"

A silence. "But shouldn't you have brought your own light?" ventured Grainger.

"My *own light*?" Kaplan cried. "Sir, forgive me, but your ignorance is shocking. This is a *fancy color* diamond, graded *Vivid,* and you cannot simply bring in any old light to look at it with. I need real light to be sure. *Natural* light. Nothing else will do. No one said anything about having to examine the finest diamond in the world under fluorescent lighting. This is an insult to my profession."

"You should have mentioned this when we made the arrangements," said Beck.

"I *assumed* I was dealing with a sophisticated insurance company, knowledgeable on the subject of gemstones! I had no idea I would be forced to examine a diamond in a stuffy basement vault. Not to mention with half a dozen people breathing down my neck as if I'm some kind of zoo monkey. My report will be that it is a possible fake, but that final determination will await re-examination under natural light." Kaplan crossed his arms and stared fiercely at the CEO.

Smithback swallowed painfully. "Well," he said, taking what he hoped were intelligible notes, "I guess that's it. There's my story."

"What's your story?" Collopy said, turning on him. "There's no story. This is inconclusive."

"I should certainly say so," said Grainger, his voice shaky. "Let's not jump to conclusions."

Smithback shrugged. "My original source tells me that diamond's a fake. Now Mr. Kaplan says it may be a fake."

"The operative word here is *may*," Grainger said.

"Just a moment!" Collopy turned to Kaplan. "You need natural light to tell for sure?"

"Isn't that what I just said?"

Collopy turned to the CEO. "Isn't there someplace he can view the stone under natural light?"

There was a moment of silence.

Collopy drew himself up. "Grainger," he said in a sharp voice, "the safekeeping of this stone was *your* responsibility."

"We can bring the stone up to the executive board-room," Grainger said. "On the eighth floor. There's plenty of light up there."

"Excuse me, Mr. Grainger," said Beck, "but the policy is quite firm: the diamond can't leave the vault."

"You heard what the man said. He needs better light."

"With all due respect, sir, I have my instructions, and not even you can alter them."

The CEO waved his hand. "Nonsense! This is a matter of critical importance. Surely we can get a waiver."

"Only with the written, notarized permission of the insured."

"Well, then! We've got the museum's director right here. And Lord's a notary public, aren't you, Foster?"

Lord nodded.

"Dr. Collopy, you'll give the necessary written permission?"

"Absolutely. This has got to be resolved now." His face was gray, almost cadaverous.

"Foster, draw up the document."

"As director of security, I strongly recommend against this," said Beck quietly.

"Mr. Beck," said Grainger, "I appreciate your concern. But I don't think you fully comprehend the situation. We have a hundred-million-dollar limit on our policy at the museum, but Lucifer's Heart is covered in a special rider, and one of the conditions of the stone being kept here for safekeeping is that there's no limitation of liability. Whatever the GIA independently determines the stone's value to be, we must pay. We've *got* to have an answer to the question of whether this stone is real, and we've got to have it now."

"Nevertheless," said Beck, "for the record, I still oppose taking the gem out of the vault."

"Duly noted. Foster? Draw up the document and Dr. Collopy will sign it."

The secretary took a piece of blank paper from his suit jacket, wrote some lines. Collopy, Grainger, and McGuigan signed it, then Lord notarized it with his signature.

"Let's go," said the CEO.

"I'm calling a security escort," said Beck darkly. At the same time, Smithback watched as the security chief slid a gun out of his waistband, checked it, flicked off the safety, and slid it back.

Kaplan picked up the stone with the four-prong.

"I'll do that, Mr. Kaplan," said Beck quietly. He took the handle of the four-prong and gently laid the stone in its velvet box. Then he shut the lid and locked it, pocketing the key and placing the box under his arm.

They waited while Kaplan packed up his supplies; then they shut the inner door and waited for the outer one to open. They proceeded back through the succession of massive doors, where they were met by a brace of security guards. The guards escorted them to a waiting elevator bank, and within five minutes Smithback found himself being ushered into a small but extremely elegant boardroom, done up in exotic wood. Light flooded in through a dozen broad windows.

Beck stationed the two extra security guards outside the doors, then shut and locked them.

"Everyone please stand back," he said. "Mr. Kaplan, will this do?"

"Splendid," said Kaplan with a broad smile, his whole mood seeming to change.

"Where do you want to sit?"

Kaplan pointed to a seat in a corner, between two windows. "That would be perfect."

"Set yourself up."

The jeweler busied himself laying out all his tools again, spreading the velvet. Then he looked up. "The stone, please?"

Beck laid the box next to him, unlocked it with the

key, and raised the lid. The gemstone lay inside, nestled in its velvet.

Kaplan reached in, plucked it out with the four-prong, and called for a Grobet double lens. Using this device, he peered at the diamond, first looking at it through one lens, then the other, then both at once. As he held it, light struck the gemstone, and the walls of the room were suddenly freckled with dots of intense cinnamon color.

Several minutes passed in absolute silence. Smithback realized he was holding his breath. At length, Kaplan slowly laid the diamond down on the velvet, swiveled the Grobet lenses from his eyes, and bestowed a beaming smile on the waiting audience.

"Ah, yes," he said, "how wonderful it is. Natural light makes all the difference in the world. This is it, gentlemen. Without the slightest doubt, this is Lucifer's Heart." He placed it back down on the velvet pad.

There was a relieved exhalation, as if everybody else in the room had been holding their breaths along with Smithback.

Kaplan waved his hand. "Mr. Beck? You may put it away. With the four-prong, if you please."

"Thank the Lord," said the CEO, turning to Collopy and grasping his hand.

"Thank the Lord is right," Collopy replied, shaking the hand while dabbing at his forehead with a handkerchief. "I had a bad moment back there."

Meanwhile, Beck, his face unreadable but still dark, had reached over with the four-prong to pick up the gem. At the same time, Kaplan rose from his chair and bumped into him. "I beg your pardon!"

It happened so fast that Smithback realized what he'd seen only after the fact. Suddenly, Kaplan had the gem in one hand and Beck's gun in the other, pointed at Beck. He fired it almost in Beck's face, just turning the barrel enough so the bullets went past and buried themselves in the wall. He fired three times in rapid succession, the incredibly loud reports plunging the room into terror and confusion as everyone dropped to the floor, Beck included.

And then he was gone, out the supposedly locked door.

Beck was up in a flash. "Get him! *Stop him!*"

As he picked himself up from the floor, ears ringing, Smithback could see through the double doors the two security guards sprawled on the floor scrambling back to their feet and taking off down the hall, fumbling with their guns.

"He's got the gem!" Collopy cried, struggling to his feet. "He's got Lucifer's Heart! My God, get him! *Do* something!"

Beck had his radio out. "Security Command? This is Samuel Beck. Lock down the building! Lock it down! I don't want anyone going out—any*thing* going out—no garbage, no mail, no people, *nothing!* You hear me? Shut off the elevators, lock the stairwells. I want a full security alert and all security personnel to search for a George Kaplan. Get an image of his face from the security checkpoint video cam. Nobody leaves the building until we've got a security cordon in place. No, to hell with fire regulations! That's a direct order! And I want an X-ray machine suitable for detecting a swallowed or concealed gemstone, along with a fully staffed technical team to man it, at the Sixth Avenue entrance, on the double."

He turned to the rest of them. "And none of you, *none* of you, are to leave this room without my permission."

Two exhausting and trying hours later, Smithback found himself in a line with what seemed like a thousand employees of Affiliated Transglobal Insurance. The line snaked interminably around the interior lobby of the building, coiling three times about the elevator banks. On the far side of the lobby, he could see employees trundling carts piled with mail and packages, running them all through X-ray machines of the kind found in airports. Kaplan had not been found—and, privately, Smithback knew he wouldn't be.

As Smithback approached the head of the line, he could hear a hubbub of voices raised in argument, from a large group of people shunted to one side who had refused to allow themselves to be X-rayed. Outside were fire trucks, their lights flashing; police cars; and the inevitable gaggle of press. As each person in line was thoroughly searched and then put through the X-ray machine, finally emerging into the gray January afternoon, there would be scattered applause and a burst of camera flashes.

Smithback tried to control his sweating. As the minutes crawled by, his nervousness had only grown worse. For the thousandth time, he cursed himself for agreeing to this. He had already been searched twice, including a revolting body-cavity search. At least the others in the executive boardroom had been subjected to the same kind of search, Collopy insisting on it for himself and the rest, including the officers of Affiliated Transglobal Insurance and even Beck. Meanwhile, Collopy—almost beside himself with agitation—had been doing all he could to convince Smithback to keep mum, not to publish anything. Oh, God, if they only knew . . .

Why, oh why, had he ever agreed to this?

Only ten more people in line ahead of him now. They were putting the people, one at a time, into what looked like a narrow telephone booth, with no fewer than four technicians examining various CRT screens affixed to it. Someone in front of him was listening to a transistor radio with everyone else crowding around—amazing how news got out—and it appeared the real Kaplan had been released unharmed in front of his brownstone a half hour ago and was now being questioned by the police. Nobody yet knew who the fake Kaplan was.

Just two more people to go. Smithback tried to swallow but found that he couldn't. His stomach churned with fear. This was the worst part. The very worst of all.

And now it was his turn. Two technicians stood him on a mat with the usual yellow footprints and searched him yet again, just a little too thoroughly for comfort. They examined his temporary building pass and his press credentials. They had him open his mouth and searched it with a tongue depressor. Then they opened the door of the booth and put him inside.

"Don't move. Keep your arms at your side. Look at the target on the wall . . ." The directions rolled out with rapid efficiency.

There was a short hum. Through the safety glass, Smithback could see the technicians poring over the results. Finally, one nodded.

A technician on the other side opened the door, placed a firm hand on Smithback's arm, and drew him out. "You're free to go," he said, pointing to the building exit.

As he gestured, the technician brushed briefly against Smithback's side.

Smithback turned and walked the ten feet to the revolving door—the longest ten feet of his life.

Outside, he zipped up his coat, ran the gauntlet of flashbulbs, ignored the shouted questions, pushed through the crowd, and walked stiffly up Avenue of the Americas. At 56th Street, he hailed a cab, slid into the back. He gave the driver the address of his apartment, waited until the cab had moved out into traffic, turned and glanced searchingly out the rear window for a full five minutes.

Only then did he dare settle into his seat, reach into his coat pocket. There, nestled safely in the bottom, he could feel the hard, cold outline of Lucifer's Heart.

Sixty-four

D'AGOSTA AND PENDERGAST sat, without speaking, inside the Mark VII on a bleak stretch of Vermilyea Avenue in the Inwood section of Upper Manhattan. The sun was dropping slowly through layers of gray, setting with a final slash of blood-red light, which cast a momentary glow over the dusky tenements and bleak warehouses before it was extinguished in bitter night.

They were listening to 1010 WINS, New York's all-news radio station. The station repeated its top stories on a twenty-two-minute cycle, and it had been continuously broadcasting news of the museum diamond heist, the announcer's excited voice in contrast to the somber mood inside the vehicle. Just ten minutes earlier, a new story had broken, a related but even more spectacular item: the theft of the real Lucifer's Heart from Affiliated Transglobal Insurance headquarters. D'Agosta had no doubt the police had tried desperately to keep a lid on that one, but there was no way something that explosive could be kept under wraps.

"*. . . the most brazen diamond theft in history, taking place right under the noses of museum and insurance*

*company executives, and following hard on the heels of
the diamond heist at the museum. Sources close to the investigation say the same thief is suspected of both
crimes . . ."*

Pendergast was listening intently, his face as hard and
pale as marble, his body motionless. His cell phone sat on
the seat between them.

*"Police are questioning George Kaplan, a well-known
gemologist, who was on his way to identify Lucifer's Heart
for Affiliated Transglobal Insurance when he was abducted
near his Manhattan town house. Sources close to the investigation say that the thief then assumed his identity in order
to gain access to the diamond. Police believe he may still
be hiding in the Affiliated Transglobal building, where a
massive manhunt is still under way . . ."*

Pendergast leaned over and shut off the radio.

"How do you know Diogenes will hear the news?"
D'Agosta asked.

"He'll hear it. For once, he's at a loss. He didn't get the
diamond. He'll be in agony, on edge—listening, waiting,
thinking. And once he learns what's happened, there will
be only one course of action available to him."

"You mean, he'll know it was you who stole it."

"Absolutely. What other conclusion could he come
to?" Pendergast smiled mirthlessly. "He'll know. And
with no other way to send me a message, he'll call."

Sodium lights had come up, burning pale yellow along
the length of the empty avenue. The temperature had
dropped into single digits and a brutal wind swept up
from the Hudson, blowing before it a few glittering flakes
of snow.

The cell phone rang.

Pendergast hesitated just a second. Then he turned it

over, punching the tiny speaker on the back into life. He said nothing.

"*Ave, frater,*" came the voice from the speaker.

A silence. D'Agosta glanced at Pendergast. In the reflected glow of the streetlights, his face was the color of alabaster. His lips moved, but no sound came.

"Is that any way to greet a long-lost brother? With disapproving silence?"

"I am here," Pendergast said in a strained voice.

"You're *there*! And how honored I am to be graced with your presence. It almost makes up for the vile experience of being forced to call you. But leave us not bandy civilities. I have but one question: did you steal Lucifer's Heart?"

"Yes."

"Why?"

"You know why."

There was a silence at the other end of the phone, then a slow exhalation of breath. "Brother, brother, brother . . ."

"I am no brother of yours."

"Ah, but that's where you're wrong. We *are* brothers, whether we like it or not. And that relationship defines who we are. You know that, don't you, Aloysius?"

"I know that you're a sick man desperately in need of help."

"True: I am sick. No one recovers from the disease of being born. There is no cure to *that* sickness, short of death. But when you get down to it, we're all sick, *you* more than most. Yes, we *are* brothers—in sickness as well as in evil."

Again, Pendergast had no response.

"But here we are, bandying civilities again! Shall we get down to business?"

No answer.

"Then I will lead the discussion. First, a big, fat bravo for pulling off in one afternoon what I took years to plan—and, ultimately, failed to accomplish." D'Agosta could hear a slow patting of hands over the phone. "I assume this is all about making a little trade. A certain personage in exchange for the gemstone. Why else would you have gone to what was undoubtedly a bit of trouble?"

"You assume correctly. But first . . ." Pendergast's voice faltered.

"You want to know if she's still alive!"

This time it was Diogenes who let the silence draw out. D'Agosta stole a glance at Pendergast. He was motionless, save for the twitch of a small muscle below the right eye.

"Yes, she's still alive—at present."

"You hurt her in any way and I'll hunt you to the ends of the earth."

"Tut-tut. But while we're on the subject of women, let's talk a little bit about this young thing you've kept cloistered in the mansion of our late lamented ancestor. If indeed she is 'young,' which I'm beginning to doubt. I find myself most curious about her. Her *in particular,* in fact. I sense that what one sees on the surface is what one sees of an iceberg: the merest fraction. There are hidden facets to her, mirrors within mirrors. And at a fundamental level, I sense that something in her is *broken.*"

During this speech, Pendergast had stiffened visibly. "Listen to me, Diogenes. Keep away from her. You come close to her again, approach her in any way, and I'll—"

"Do what? Kill me? Then my blood would be on your

hands—more than it already is—as well as that of your four dear friends. Because *you, frater,* are responsible for all this. You know it. You made me what I am."

"I made you nothing."

"Well said! *Well said!*" A dry, almost desiccated laugh came over the tiny speaker. Listening, D'Agosta felt a chill of repulsion.

"Let's get to it," Pendergast managed to say.

"Get to it? Just when the conversation was becoming interesting? Don't you want to talk about how *utterly* and *completely* responsible you are for all this? Ask any family shrink: they'll tell you how important it is that we talk it out. *Frater.*"

Suddenly, D'Agosta could take it no longer. "Diogenes! Listen to me, you sick fuck: you want the diamond? Then you cut with the bullshit."

"No diamond, no Viola."

"If you hurt Viola, I'll take a sledgehammer to the diamond and mail you the dust. If you think I'm kidding, keep talking."

"Empty threats."

D'Agosta brought his fist down on the dashboard, making a resounding crash.

"Careful! Easy!" The voice was suddenly high and panicked.

"So shut the hell up."

"Stupidity is an elemental force, and I respect it."

"You're still talking."

"We'll do this on my terms," said Diogenes briskly. "Do you hear me? My terms!"

"With two conditions," Pendergast said quietly. "One: the exchange must take place on the island of Manhattan, and within six hours. Two: it must be set up in such a way that you can't renege. You tell me your plan and I'll be the judge. You have one chance to get it right."

"That sounds like five conditions, not two. But of course, brother—of course! I have to say, though, this is a knotty little problem. I'll call you back in ten minutes."

"Make it five."

"More conditions?" And the phone went dead.

There was a long silence. A sheen of moisture had appeared on Pendergast's brow. He plucked a silk handkerchief from his suit jacket, dabbed his forehead, replaced it.

"Can we trust him?" D'Agosta asked.

"No. Never. But I don't think he'll have enough time to arrange an effective double cross within six hours. And he wants Lucifer's Heart—wants it with a passion you and I cannot comprehend. I think we can trust that passion, if we can trust nothing else."

The phone rang again, and Pendergast pressed the speaker button.

"Yes?"

"Okay, *frater*. Time for a pop quiz in urban geography. You know of a place called the Iron Clock?"

"The railroad turntable?"

"Excellent! And you know its location?"

"Yes."

"Good. We'll do it there. You'll no doubt want to bring your trusty sidekick, Vinnie."

"I intend to."

"Listen to me carefully. I'll meet you there at . . . six minutes to midnight. Enter through tunnel VI and step slowly out into the light. Vinnie can hang back in the dark and cover you, if you wish. Have him bring his weapon of choice. That will keep me honest. Feel free to bring your own Les Baer or whatever fashion accessory you're carrying these days. There'll be no gunplay unless something goes wrong. And nothing's going to go wrong. I want my diamond, and you want your Viola da Gamba. If you know the layout of the Iron Clock, you'll realize it is the perfect venue for our, shall we say, *transaction*."

"I understand."

"So. Do I have your approval, brother? Satisfied that I can't cheat you?"

Pendergast was silent for a moment. "Yes."

"Then *a presto*."

And the phone went dead.

"That bastard gives me the creeps," said D'Agosta.

Pendergast sat in silence for a long time. Then he removed the handkerchief again, wiped his forehead, refolded the handkerchief.

D'Agosta noticed Pendergast's hands were trembling slightly.

"You all right?" he asked.

Pendergast shook his head. "Let's get this over with." But rather than move, he remained still, as if in deep thought. Abruptly, he seemed to come to some decision. And then he turned and—to D'Agosta's surprise—took his hand.

"There's something I'm going to ask you to do," Pendergast said. "I warn you in advance: it will go against all your instincts as a partner and as a friend. But you must believe me when I say it is the *only* way. There is no other solution. Will you do it?"

"Depends on what it is."

"Unacceptable. I want your promise first."

D'Agosta hesitated.

A look of concern settled over Pendergast's face.

"Vincent, please. It's absolutely critical that I can rely on you in this moment of extremity."

D'Agosta sighed. "Okay. I promise."

Pendergast's tired frame relaxed in obvious relief. "Good. Now, please listen carefully."

Sixty-five

IOGENES PENDERGAST STARED at the cell phone, lying on the pine table, for a long time. The only indication of the strong emotion running through him was a faint twitching of his left little finger. A mottled patch of gray had appeared on his left cheek, and—were he to look in a mirror, which he did only when applying a disguise—he knew he'd find his *ojo sarco* looking deader than usual.

Finally, his gaze strayed from the telephone to a small bottle topped by a rubber membrane and, lying next to it, a glass-and-steel hypodermic needle. He picked up the bottle, held it upside down while inserting the needle, drew out a small quantity, thought a moment, drew out more, then capped the needle with a plastic protector and placed it in his suit pocket.

His gaze then went to a deck of tarot cards, sitting on the edge of the table. It was the Albano-Waite deck—the one he preferred. Picking it up, he gave the deck an overhand shuffle, then laid three cards facedown before him in the spread known as the gypsy draw.

Putting the rest of the deck to one side, he turned over the first card: the High Priestess. *Interesting.*

He moved his hand to the second card, turned it over. It showed a tall, thin man in a black cloak, turned away, head bowed. At his feet were overturned golden goblets, spilling red liquid. In the background was a river, and beyond that, a forbidding-looking castle. The Five of Cups.

At this, Diogenes drew in his breath sharply.

More slowly now, his hand moved to the third and final card. He hesitated a moment, then turned it over.

This card was upside down. It portrayed a hand above a barren landscape, thrusting out of a dark cloud of smoke. It held a massive sword with a jeweled hilt. A golden crown was impaled on the end of its blade.

The Ace of Swords. Reversed.

Diogenes stared at the card for a moment, then slowly exhaled. He raised it in a shaking hand, then with one violent motion tore it in half, then in half again, and scattered the pieces.

Now his restless gaze moved to the black velvet cloth, laid out and rolled up at the edges, on which lay 488 diamonds, almost all of them deeply colored, scintillating underneath the bright gem light clamped to the table's edge.

As he stared at the diamonds, his agitation began to ease.

Restraining an exquisite eagerness, his hand roved over the ocean of glittering trapped light before plucking one of the largest diamonds, a vivid blue stone of thirty-three carats, called the Queen of Narnia. He held it in his palm, observing the light catch and refract within its saturated deeps, and then with infinite care raised it to his good eye.

He stared at the world through the fractured depths of the stone. It was like kicking open a door just a crack and catching a glimpse of a magic world beyond, a world of color and life, a *real* world—so different from this false, flat world of gray mundanity.

His breathing became deeper and more even, and the trembling in his hand subsided as his mind loosened in its prison and began to ramble down long-forgotten alleys of memory.

Diamonds. It always started with diamonds. He was in his mother's arms, diamonds glittering at her throat, dangling from her ears, winking from her fingers. Her voice was like a diamond, pure and cool, and she was singing a song to him in French. He was no more than two years old but nevertheless was crying, not from sorrow, but from the aching beauty of his mother's voice. *In spite of myself, the insidious mastery of song / betrays me back, till the heart of me weeps to belong . . .*

The scene faded.

Now he was wandering through the great house on Dauphine Street, down long corridors and past mysterious rooms, many of them, even then, having been shut up for ages. But when you opened a door, you would always find something exciting, something wondrous and strange: a huge draped bed, dark paintings of women in white and men with dead eyes; you would see exotic objects brought from faraway places—panpipes made of bone, a monkey's paw edged in silver, a brass Spanish stirrup, a snarling jaguar head, the wrapped foot of an Egyptian mummy.

There was always his mother to flee to, with her warmth and her soft voice and her diamonds that glittered as she moved, catching the light in sudden bursts of rainbow. The diamonds were here, they were alive, they never changed, never faded, never died. They would remain, beautiful and immutable, for all time.

How different from the fickle vicissitudes of the flesh.

Diogenes understood the image of Nero watching Rome burn while gazing at the conflagration through a gemstone. Nero understood the transformative power of gems. He understood that to gaze at the world through such a stone was to transform both the world and oneself. Light was vibration; and there were special vibrations from a diamond that reached the deepest levels of his spirit. Most people couldn't hear them; perhaps nobody else on earth could hear them. But *he* could. The gemstones spoke to him, they whispered to him, they gave him strength and wisdom.

Today the diamonds, not the cards, would provide divination.

Diogenes continued to gaze deeply into the blue diamond. Each gemstone had a different voice, and he had picked this stone for its particular wisdom. He waited, murmuring to the gemstone, beseeching it to speak.

And after a moment, it did. In response to his murmured question, a whispery answer came back like an echo of an echo, half heard in a waking dream.

It was a good answer.

Viola Maskelene listened to the strange murmuring, almost like a prayer or a chant, that came from below. The sound was so low she could make out nothing. This was followed by an unnerving half-hour silence. Then, at last, came the sound she'd been dreading: the scrape of a chair, the slow, careful footfall of the man climbing the staircase. All her senses went on high alert, her muscles trembling, ready to act.

A polite rap on the door.

She waited.

"Viola? I should like to come in. Please step round the bed to the far side of the room."

She hesitated, then did as he requested.

He had said he was going to kill her at dawn. But he hadn't. The sun had set already, night was coming on. Something had happened. His plans had changed. Or, more likely, had *been* changed, against his will.

The door opened and she saw Diogenes standing in it. He looked different—slightly disheveled. His face was mottled, his cravat askew, his ginger hair a little ruffled.

"What do you want?" she asked huskily.

Still, he gazed at her. "I'm beginning to see what my brother found so fascinating in you. You are, of course, beautiful and intelligent, as well as spirited. But there is one quality you possess that truly astonishes me. You have no fear."

She did not dignify this with an answer.

"You *should* be afraid."

"You're mad."

"Then I am like God, because if there is a God, He is Himself mad. I wonder why it is that you have no fear. Are you brave or stupid—or do you merely lack the imagination to picture your own death? You see, *I* can imagine it, *have* imagined it, so very clearly. When I look at you, I see a bag filled with blood, bones, viscera, and meat, held in by the most fragile and vulnerable covering, so easily punctured, so facilely ripped or torn. I have to admit, I was looking forward to it."

He peered at her closely. "Ah! Do I finally detect a note of fear?"

"What do you want?" she repeated.

He raised his hand, opening it with a twist and displaying a dazzling gemstone between thumb and forefinger. The ceiling light struck it, casting glittering shards about the room.

"Ultima Thule."

"Excuse me?"

"This is a diamond known as the Ultima Thule, named after a line in one of Virgil's *Georgics*. That's Latin for the 'Uttermost Thule,' the land of perpetual ice."

"I read Latin in school, too," said Viola sarcastically.

"Then you'll understand why this diamond reminded me of you."

With another flick of the wrist, he tossed it to her. Instinctively, she caught it.

"A little *going-away* gift."

Something about the way he said "going away" gave her an ugly feeling. "I don't want any gift from you."

"Oh, but it's *so* apt. Twenty-two carats, princess-cut, rated IF Flawless, with a color grading of D. Are you familiar with the grading of diamonds?"

"What rot you talk!"

"D is given to a diamond utterly without color. It is also called white. It is considered by those with no imagination to be a desirable trait. I look at you, Viola, and what do I see? A wealthy, titled, beautiful, brilliant, and successful woman. You have a splendid career as an Egyptologist, you have a charming house on the island of Capraia, you have a grand old family estate in England. No doubt you consider you are living life to the fullest. Not only that, but you've had relationships with a variety of interesting men, from an Oxford professor to a Holly-wood actor to a famous pianist—even an Italian soccer player. How others must envy you!"

Shock burned through Viola at this invasion of her privacy. "You bloody—"

"And yet, not all is what it seems. None of your rela-tionships have worked out. No doubt you're telling your-self the fault lies with the men. When will it occur to you, Viola, that the fault lies in yourself? You are just like that diamond—flawless, brilliant, perfect, and utterly without color. All your sad attempts to appear exciting, uncon-ventional, are just that—sad attempts." He laughed harshly. "As if digging up mummies, rooting in your lit-tle plot of dirt by the Mediterranean, could confer char-acter! That diamond, which all the world considers so perfect, is in reality dead common. Like you. You're thirty-five years old and you're unloved and unloving. Why, you're so desperate for love that you fly halfway around the world in response to a letter from a man you met only once! Ultima Thule is yours, Viola. You've earned it."

Viola staggered. His words felt like one physical blow after another, each one finding its mark. This time she had no answer.

"That's right. No matter where you go, you'll live in Ultima Thule, the land of perpetual ice. As someone once said: Wherever you go, there you are. There's no love within you, and there'll be no love for you. Barrenness is your fate."

"You and your bit of glass can get knotted!" she cried, violently throwing the stone back at him.

He deftly caught it. "Glass, you say? Do you know what I did yesterday while you were here all alone?"

"My interest in your life would be undetectable even to the most powerful microscope."

Diogenes removed a square of newsprint from his pocket and unfolded it, revealing the front page of that day's *New York Times*.

She stared at it from across the room, squinting to make out the headlines.

"I robbed the Astor Hall of Diamonds at the Museum of Natural History. It is a crime I've been planning for many years. I created a new identity to pull it off. And you helped me do it. That's why I wanted to give you that stone. But if you don't want it . . ." He shrugged, slipped it into his pocket.

"My God." Viola stared at him. And now, for the first time, she was truly afraid.

"You played an important role. The pivotal role. You see, your disappearance kept my brother racing all over Long Island, searching frantically for you, desperately worried about your safety, while I robbed the museum and transported the gems out here."

Viola swallowed, feeling a lump in her throat. The fact she was still alive was nothing but a temporary reprieve. He wouldn't tell her all this if he meant to let her live.

He really *was* going to kill her.

"I was giving you that as a little keepsake, a memento, since we shall part, never to see each other in this world again."

"I'm going somewhere?" she said, voice quavering now despite her best efforts.

"Oh, yes."

"Where?"

"You shall find out."

She could see he had his hand in his jacket pocket, fingering something. He took a step into the room. The door remained open behind him.

"Come here, Ice Princess."

She didn't move.

He took a second step forward, and a third. At that moment, she broke for the door. But somehow he had anticipated it, whirling and leaping toward her with the speed of a cat. She felt a shockingly powerful arm, tight as a steel cable, whip around her neck; the other hand slipped out of his pocket now, and in it was the sudden flash of a needle, and then she felt a burning sting in her upper thigh; there was the sensation of heat and an overpowering roar; and then the world abruptly shut down.

Sixty-six

ANY IDEA WHAT this is about?" Singleton said as they rode an express elevator to the rarefied upper floors of One Police Plaza.

Laura Hayward shook her head. If Commissioner Rocker had asked to see her alone, she might have expected it was more fallout over her fingering Pendergast for the murders. But she and Singleton had been asked to meet with the commissioner together. Besides, Rocker had always been a straight shooter. He wasn't political.

They emerged on the forty-sixth floor and walked down the plushly carpeted corridor to the commissioner's corner suite. A uniformed secretary in the large outer office took their names, dialed her phone, had a brief, hushed conversation, and waved them through.

Rocker's office was expansive but not ostentatious. Instead of the shooting awards and grinning photo ops that covered the office walls of most police brass, these walls sported watercolor landscapes and a couple of diplomas. Rocker was seated behind a large but utilitarian desk. Three couches were arrayed in a rough semicircle around it. Special Agent in Charge Coffey sat in the middle couch, flanked by Agents Brooks and Rabiner.

"Ah, Captain Hayward," Rocker said, rising. "Captain Singleton. Thanks for coming." There was an unusual, strained quality to his voice she hadn't heard before, and his jaw was set in a tight line.

Agent Brooks and Agent Rabiner rose as well, leaping to their feet as if tickled by live wires. Only Coffey remained seated. He nodded coolly at them, small pale eyes in the big sunburned face moving from Hayward to Singleton and back to Hayward again.

Rocker waved vaguely at the sofas. "Please have a seat."

Hayward seated herself beside the window. So at last Coffey was deigning to bring them into his investigation. They hadn't heard a word from him or anybody else in the FBI since the meeting that morning. Instead, she'd kept herself and her detectives busy questioning additional museum employees and further developing the evidence. At least it had helped keep her mind off the manhunt going on sixty miles to the east, at what D'Agosta was doing—*committing*—on Long Island. Thinking about him, about the whole situation, gave her nothing but pain. She could never understand why he'd done it, why he'd made the decision he did. She'd given him an ultimatum, and under the circumstances an incredibly fair one. Do the right thing, come in out of the cold. And not just the right thing as a cop, but as a human being and a friend. She hadn't actually said it, but it had been clear enough: *It's either me or Pendergast.*

D'Agosta had made his choice.

Rocker cleared his throat. "Special Agent in Charge Coffey has asked me to convene this meeting to discuss the Duchamp and Green murders. I've asked Captain Singleton to be here as well, since both homicides took place in his precinct."

Hayward nodded. "I'm glad to hear that, sir. We've had precious little information from the Bureau about the progress of the manhunt, and—"

"I'm sorry, Captain," Rocker interrupted quietly. "Special Agent Coffey wishes to discuss transfer of evidence on the Duchamp and Green murders."

This stopped Hayward dead in her tracks. "Transfer of evidence? We've made all our evidence freely available."

Coffey crossed one trunklike leg over the other. "We're assuming control of the investigation, Captain."

There was a moment of stunned silence.

"You don't have the power to do that," Hayward said.

"This is Captain Hayward's case," Singleton said, turning to Rocker, his voice quiet but strong. "She's been living it night and day. She's the one who found the connection between the D.C. and New Orleans homicides. She developed the evidence, she ID'd Pendergast. Besides, murder isn't a federal crime."

Rocker sighed. "I'm aware of all that. But—"

"Let me explain," Coffey said with a wave of the hand at Rocker. "The perp is FBI, one of the victims is FBI, the case crosses state boundaries, and the suspect's fled your jurisdiction. End of discussion."

"Agent Coffey is right," said Rocker. "It's their case. We'll naturally be on hand to assist—"

"We don't have a lot of time to jawbone," said Rabiner. "Let's get on with the particulars of evidence transfer."

Hayward glanced at Singleton. His face was flushed.

"If it wasn't for Captain Hayward," he said, "there wouldn't be any manhunt."

"We're all just as pleased as punch at Captain Hayward's police work," said Coffey. "But the bottom line is, this is no longer an NYPD matter."

"Just give them what they need, please, Captain," Commissioner Rocker said, a note of exasperation in his voice.

Hayward glanced at him and realized he was pissed as hell at this development, but could do nothing about it.

She should have seen it coming. The federal boys were going for the gold, and on top of that, this Coffey seemed to have a personal animosity toward Pendergast. God help him and D'Agosta when the feds finally caught up with them.

Hayward knew she ought to feel outraged at all this. But through the numbness, all she could bring herself to feel was an upwelling of weariness. That, and a feeling of revulsion so strong that she simply could not bear to spend another moment in the same room with Coffey. And so, abruptly, she stood up.

"Fine," she said briskly. "I'll initiate the paperwork. You'll get your evidence as soon as the chain-of-evidence transfers are signed. Anything else?"

"Captain?" said Rocker. "I'm very grateful to you for your fine work."

She nodded, turned, and left the room.

She walked quickly toward the elevator, head lowered, breathing fast. As she did so, her cell phone rang.

She waited, getting her breathing under control. After a minute or two, the cell phone rang again.

This time she answered. "Hayward."

"Laura?" came the voice. "It's me. Vinnie."

Despite herself, she felt her heart rise into her throat. "Vincent, for God's sake. What the hell are you—?"

"Just listen, please. I have something very important to tell you."

Hayward took a deep breath. "I'm listening."

Sixty-seven

D'AGOSTA FOLLOWED PENDERGAST into Penn Station, which—disgracefully—consisted of little more than an escalator entrance in the shadow of Madison Square Garden. It was a quiet evening, a Tuesday of no consequence, and at such a late hour, the area was almost deserted, save for a few homeless people and a man passing out sheets of his poetry. The two rode the escalator down to the waiting area, then took another that descended still farther, to the track level.

They were headed, D'Agosta noted with a certain grimness, for track 13.

Pendergast had barely spoken a word in the last half hour. As the appointed time drew nearer—as they came closer to seeing Viola and, inevitably, Diogenes—the agent had grown more and more tight-lipped and withdrawn.

The tracks were almost deserted, just a few maintenance men sweeping up trash and two uniformed cops at a security station, chatting and blowing on cups of coffee. Pendergast led the way to the far end of the platform, where the tracks disappeared into a dark tunnel.

"Be ready," Pendergast murmured as his pale eyes roved the tracks.

They waited for a moment. The two cops turned and walked into the security station.

"*Now!*" Pendergast said under his breath.

They jumped lightly off the platform onto the tracks and jogged away into the dimness. D'Agosta glanced back at the receding platform, ensuring nobody had noticed.

It was warmer belowground, hovering just around freezing, but it was a much damper cold, and it seemed to cut effortlessly through D'Agosta's purloined sports jacket. After another minute of jogging, Pendergast stopped, fished in his pocket, and pulled out a flashlight.

"We have some way to go," he said, shining the light down the long, dark tunnel. Several pairs of eyes—rat's eyes—gleamed out of the darkness ahead.

The agent set off again at a fast walk, his long legs striding down the middle of the tracks. D'Agosta followed, listening a little nervously for any sound of an approaching train. But all he could hear were their hollow footsteps, his own breathing, and the sound of water dripping from icicles in the ancient brick roof.

"So the Iron Clock is a railroad turntable?" he asked after a moment. He spoke more to break the strained silence than anything else.

"Yes. A very old one."

"I didn't know there were any turntables under Manhattan."

"It was built to manage the flow of train traffic in and out of the old Pennsylvania Station. In fact, it's the only remaining artifact from the original architecture."

"And you know how to find it?"

"Remember the subway murders we worked on some years back? I spent quite a bit of time then, studying the underground landscape of New York City. I still recall much of the layout beneath Manhattan, at least the more common routes."

"How do you think Diogenes knows about it?"

"That is an interesting fact, Vincent, and it has not escaped my attention."

They came to a metal door, set into an alcove in the tunnel wall, fastened with a rust-covered padlock. Pendergast stooped to examine the lock, tracing the heavy lines of rust with his finger. Then he stepped back, nodding to D'Agosta to do the same. Pulling his Wilson Combat 1911 from its holster, Pendergast fired it into the lock. A deafening roar cracked down the tunnel, and the broken lock fell to the ground in a cloud of rust. He leaned to the side and kicked open the door.

A stone staircase led down, exhaling a smell of mold and rot.

"How far down is it?"

"Actually, we're already at the grade of the Iron Clock. This is merely a shortcut."

The staircase was slippery, and as they descended, the air grew warmer still. After a long descent, the steps leveled out, broadening into an old brick tunnel with Gothic arches. Locked work sheds lined the tunnel.

D'Agosta paused. "Lights ahead. And voices."

"Homeless," Pendergast replied.

As they continued, D'Agosta began to smell woodsmoke. Shortly, they came across a group of ragged men and women sitting around a rudely built fire, passing around a bottle of wine.

"What's this?" one of them called out. "You fellows miss your train?"

The laughter subsided as they passed. From the darkness behind the group came the sudden crying of a baby.

"Jeez," D'Agosta muttered. "You hear that?"

Pendergast merely nodded.

They came to another metal door, from which someone had already cut away the lock. Opening the door, they climbed back up a long, wet staircase, dodging streams of water, and emerged onto a new set of tracks.

Pendergast paused, checking his watch. "Eleven-thirty."

More rats scurried away as they walked wordlessly down the tunnel for what seemed miles. No amount of walking seemed to warm D'Agosta against the damp chill. At one point, they passed a siding holding several wrecked train cars. Later, passing a series of stone alcoves, D'Agosta saw an ancient metal gear more than eight feet in diameter. Once in a while, he heard the distant rumble of trains, but nothing seemed to be running on the tracks they were walking on.

At last, Pendergast halted, switched off his flashlight, and nodded ahead. Peering into the darkness, D'Agosta saw that the tunnel ended in an archway of dim yellow light.

"That's the Iron Clock up ahead," Pendergast said in a low voice.

D'Agosta removed his Glock 29, slid open the magazine, checked it, and slipped it back into place.

"You know what to do?"

D'Agosta nodded.

They moved forward slowly and silently, Pendergast in front, D'Agosta close behind. He checked his watch, holding it mere inches from his nose: twelve minutes to midnight.

"Remember," Pendergast whispered. "Cover me from here."

D'Agosta flattened himself against the wall. From this vantage point, he had a good view into the enormous space ahead. What he saw almost took his breath away. It was a huge circular vault built of granite blocks streaked with limestone and grime, an incredible Romanesque underground massing. The floor of the vault was spanned by a railroad turntable: a single length of track stretching from one wall to another, set into a vast iron circle. Twelve arched tunnels, spaced equally apart, entered the vault. Each bore a small, grime-covered light above its mouth, along with a carved Roman numeral, I through XII.

So that's the Iron Clock, he thought.

His dad had been a railroad buff, and D'Agosta knew something about railroad turntables. The revolving carousels were usually found at a railroad's terminus: a single track led into the turntable, and lying beyond would be a semicircular roundhouse with bays for locomotive storage. Here, however, hard by Penn Station and within one of the world's busiest networks of railroad tracks, the turntable clearly had a different purpose: it was simply a nexus, a way to allow trains to go from one series of tracks and tunnels to another.

The sound of dripping water echoed in the vast space, and he could see, far above, icicles on the upper vaulting. The drops came spinning down through a dirty circle of lights to land in black puddles below.

He wondered if—out there somewhere, in the darkness of one of the other eleven railroad tunnels—Diogenes was waiting.

Just then he heard a faint rumble, followed by a growing rush of air. Pendergast retreated back into the tunnel, motioning D'Agosta to do the same. A moment later, a commuter train burst out of one of the tunnel mouths and went thundering over the turntable, windows flashing by as it shot through the space, then rocketed back into darkness. The roar died to a rumble, then a murmur. And then, with a loud clanking noise, the single section of track in the center of the Iron Clock began to rotate, halting with a clang as it connected two other tunnels, preparing for the next train.

The tunnels it now connected were tunnel XII and the tunnel they themselves were in: tunnel VI.

All fell silent again. D'Agosta saw the dark shapes of rats—some the size of small dogs—scurrying along the shadows at the far edge of the roundhouse. Water dripped steadily. The place smelled of rot and decay.

Pendergast stirred, gestured toward his watch. Six minutes to midnight. Time to act. He grasped D'Agosta's hand.

"You know what to do?" he repeated.

D'Agosta nodded.

"Thank you, Vincent," he said. "Thank you for everything."

Then Pendergast turned and stepped out of the tunnel, into the dim light. Two steps. Three.

D'Agosta remained in the shadows, Glock in hand. The great vault of the roundhouse remained empty and silent, the dark tunnels like so many open mouths, icicles gleaming like teeth.

Pendergast took another step, then stopped.

"*Ave, frater!*"

The voice boomed out into the dank, dark space, echoing from all quarters, so that it was impossible to tell its source. D'Agosta stiffened, straining to see into the black openings of the other tunnels visible from his own, but he could see no sign of Diogenes.

"Don't be shy, brother. Let's have a look at that pretty face of yours. Step a little farther into the light."

Pendergast took a few more steps into the open area. D'Agosta waited, gun in hand, covering him.

"Did you bring it?" came the echoing voice. The tone was leering, almost a snarl; yet there was a curious hunger in it.

In reply, Pendergast raised one hand, twisting his wrist as he did so. The diamond suddenly appeared, dull in the dim light.

D'Agosta heard a sharp intake of breath, like the crack of a whip, come out of the darkness.

"Bring me Viola," Pendergast said.

"Easy, now, brother. All in good time. Step onto the turntable."

Pendergast stepped over the iron circle and onto the track bed.

"Now walk forward, to the center of the track. You'll find an old hole cut in the iron plate. Inside that is a small velvet box. Put the stone in there. And do hurry— we wouldn't want another passing train to end all this prematurely."

Again, D'Agosta strained to locate the voice, but it was impossible to know in which tunnel Diogenes might be hiding. Given the peculiar acoustics of the vaulted space, he could be anywhere.

Pendergast walked forward guardedly. Reaching the

center of the roundhouse, he knelt, picked up the velvet box, placed the diamond inside it, replaced it by the track.

Then, abruptly, he rose, pulling out his Wilson Combat and aiming it at the diamond. "Bring me Viola," he repeated.

"Whoa! Brother! This rashness is unlike you. We go by the book. Now step back while my man takes a look to make sure it's real."

"It is real."

"I trusted you once, long ago. Remember? Look where it got me." A strange sigh, almost like a moan, came out of the darkness. "Forgive me if I don't trust you again. Mr. Kaplan? Do your stuff, if you please."

A terrified, disheveled man stumbled out of tunnel XI into the faint light. He blinked, looking around in bewilderment. He was wearing a dark suit and black cashmere coat, muddied and torn. On his bald head was a headband loupe, and he held a light in one hand. D'Agosta immediately recognized him as the man they'd abducted earlier.

He looked like he'd had an unusually bad day.

Kaplan took a tottering step forward, then stopped again. He stared about, uncomprehending. "Who . . . ? What . . . ?"

"The diamond is in a box at the center. Go examine it. Tell me if it's Lucifer's Heart."

The man looked around. "Who's speaking? Where am I?"

"*Frater,* show Kaplan the diamond."

Kaplan stumbled forward. Pendergast waved his gun in the direction of the box.

The sight of the gun seemed to wake Kaplan from his

stupor. "I'll do what you say, but please don't kill me!" he cried. "I have children."

"And you shall see your dimpled lunatics again— *if* you do as I say," came the disembodied voice of Diogenes.

The man stumbled again, recovered, knelt over the diamond, and picked it up. He lowered the loupe over his eye, switched on the small light, and examined the stone.

"Well?" came Diogenes's voice, high and strained.

"A moment!" the man almost sobbed. "Give me a moment, please."

He peered at it, the light blossoming inside the diamond, turning it into a glowing orb of cinnamon. "It looks like Lucifer's Heart, all right," he said, his voice hushed.

" 'Looks like' won't do, Mr. Kaplan."

The man continued to peer into the diamond, his hands shaking. Then he straightened. "I'm sure it is," he said.

"Be sure, now. Your life, and the lives of your family, depend on your accurate appraisal."

"I'm sure. There's no other diamond like it."

"The diamond has one microscopic flaw. Tell me where it is."

Kaplan returned to his examination. A minute passed, then two.

"There's a faint inclusion about two millimeters from the center of the stone, in the one o'clock direction."

A hiss—perhaps of triumph, perhaps something else—came from the darkness. "Kaplan, you may go. Tunnel VI is your exit. *Frater,* remain where you are."

With a grateful sob, the man hurried toward tunnel VI and the waiting D'Agosta, stumbling, half sprawling in his zeal to get away. A moment later, he arrived in the darkness of the tunnel mouth, panting heavily.

"Thank God," he sobbed. "Thank God."

"Get behind me," said D'Agosta.

Kaplan peered at D'Agosta, fear replacing relief as he recognized the face. "Wait a minute. You're the cop who—"

"Let's worry about that later," D'Agosta said, pushing him farther into the protective darkness. "We'll have you out of here soon."

"And now, the moment you've been waiting for." Diogenes's voice echoed around the vaulted space. "I present you—Lady Viola Maskelene!"

As D'Agosta peered out, Viola Maskelene suddenly stepped out of the darkness of tunnel IX. She paused in the light, blinking uncertainly.

Pendergast took an involuntary step forward.

"*Don't move,* brother! Let her come to you."

She turned and looked at Pendergast, took a step forward, not quite steadily.

"Viola!" Pendergast took another step forward.

There was a sudden gunshot, deafening in the enclosed space. A puff of dirt sprang up near Pendergast's outstretched shoe. Instantly, the agent dropped into a crouch, gun in hand, moving its barrel from tunnel mouth to tunnel mouth.

"Go ahead, brother. Return fire. Pity if a stray round takes down your Lady Eve."

Pendergast turned. Viola had frozen at the sound of the gunshot.

"Come to me, Viola," he said.

She stared at him. "Aloysius?" she asked weakly.

"I'm right here. Just come to me, slow and steady."

"But you . . . *you* . . ."

"It's all right now. You're safe. Come to me." He held out his arms.

"What a touching scene!" said Diogenes. This was followed by mocking, cynical laughter.

She took a shaky step, another, another—and collapsed in Pendergast's arms.

Pendergast cradled her protectively, lifting her chin with a gentle hand and looking at her face. "You drugged her!" he said.

"Pooh. Nothing more than a few milligrams of Versed to keep her quiet. Don't be concerned—she's *intact.*"

D'Agosta could now hear Pendergast murmuring into Viola's ear, but he couldn't catch the words. She shook her head, pulled away, swayed. He grasped her again, steadying her. Then he helped her toward the tunnel opening.

"Bravo, gentlemen, I do believe we're done!" came Diogenes's triumphant voice. "Now you may all leave by tunnel VI. In fact, you *must* leave by tunnel VI. I would insist upon it. And you had better hurry—the midnight Acela will be coming down track VI in five minutes, bound for Washington. It accelerates quickly out of the station and will already be going close to eighty. If you don't reach the first alcove, three hundred yards down the tracks, you'll be so much paste on the tunnel walls. I'll shoot any stragglers. So get moving!"

Pendergast helped Viola back into the darkness, passed her to D'Agosta.

"Get her and Kaplan out of here," he murmured, placing his flashlight in D'Agosta's hand.

"And you?"

"I have unfinished business."

This was the answer D'Agosta had feared. He put out a restraining hand. "He'll kill you."

Pendergast gently shook himself free.

"You *can't*!" D'Agosta whispered urgently. "They'll be—"

"Did you hear me?" Diogenes's voice rang out. "You've now got four minutes!"

"*Go!*" said Pendergast fiercely.

D'Agosta shot him a final glance. Then he wrapped his arm around Viola, turned toward Kaplan, gave him a gentle nudge. "Come on, Mr. Kaplan. Let's go."

He switched on the flashlight and, turning away from the Iron Clock, led the way quickly down the tracks.

Sixty-eight

PENDERGAST REMAINED in the darkness of the tunnel, gun drawn, waiting. All was silent. A minute went by, then two, then three, then four. Five minutes passed. No train came.

Six minutes. Seven.

Still Pendergast waited in the dark. He realized his brother, always cautious, would not show himself until the train had passed. Slowly, he stepped back out into the light.

"*Aloysius!* What are you still doing here?" The voice was suddenly panicked. "I said I'd kill anyone who showed themselves again!"

"Then do it."

Once again, a gun fired, kicking up gravel inches from his toe.

"Your aim is off."

A second round ricocheted off the stone arch above Pendergast's head, spraying him with chips.

"You missed again."

"The train's coming through at any moment," came the urgent voice. "I won't have to kill you—the train will do it for me."

Pendergast shook his head. Then he began strolling leisurely along the railroad turntable, heading toward the center of the vault.

"*Get back!*" Another shot.

"Your aim is poor today, Diogenes."

He stopped at the center of the turntable.

"No!" came the voice. "Get away!"

Pendergast reached down and picked up the box, took out the diamond, weighed it in his palm.

"The train, you fool! Put the diamond down! It's safe in that hole!"

"There is no train."

"Yes, there is. It's late, that's all."

"It's not coming."

"What are you talking about?"

"The midnight Acela was canceled. I called in a bomb threat at the Back Bay station."

"You're bluffing! How could you have called in such a threat? You couldn't have known my plan."

"No? Why meet us at six minutes to midnight, rather than midnight? And why here? There could be only one reason: it had to do with the railroad timetable. From there it was elementary." He slipped the diamond into his pocket.

"Put that back—it's mine! You liar! You *lied* to me!"

"I never lied to you. I merely followed your instructions. You, on the other hand, lied to me. Many times. You said you would kill Smithback. Instead, you targeted Margo Green."

"I killed your friends. You know I won't hesitate to kill you."

"And that's precisely what you're going to have to do. You want to stop me? Then kill me."

"Bastard! *Mon semblable, mon frère*—now, *you die!*"

Pendergast waited, motionless. A minute passed, then another.

"You see, you can't kill me," Pendergast said. "That's why you did not properly aim your shots. You need me alive. You proved that when you rescued me from Castel Fosco. You need me, because without me—without your *hatred* of me—you would have nothing left."

Diogenes did not respond. And yet a new sound had been introduced to the vault: the sound of running feet, barked commands, crackling radios.

The sounds were coming closer.

"What is it?" came Diogenes's urgent voice.

"The police," said Pendergast calmly.

"You called the *police*? You fool, they'll get you, not me!"

"That's the whole point. And your gunshots will bring them here all the faster."

"What are you talking about? Idiot, you're what— using yourself as bait? Sacrificing *yourself?*"

"Precisely. I'm exchanging my freedom for the safety of Viola, and for the recovery of Lucifer's Heart. Self-sacrifice, Diogenes: the one end result you could not have predicted. Because it's the one thing you would never, ever think to do yourself."

"You—! Give me my diamond!"

"Come and get it. You might even have a minute to enjoy it before we're both captured. Or you can run now, and maybe—*just maybe*—escape."

"You can't do this, you're utterly mad!" The disem-bodied voice fell in another choking moan, so penetrating and inhuman that it sounded feral. And then it cut off abruptly, leaving only an echo.

A moment later, Hayward burst out of tunnel IV, a phalanx of cops behind her. Singleton followed, speaking excitedly into his radio. The officers quickly surrounded Pendergast, dropping to their knees in the three-point stance, weapons aimed at him.

"Police! Freeze! Raise your hands!"

Slowly, Pendergast raised his hands.

Hayward came forward, stepping through the ring of blue. "Are you armed, Agent Pendergast?"

Pendergast nodded. "And you will find Lucifer's Heart in the left pocket of my jacket. Please treat it with great care. Hold it yourself, don't entrust it to anyone."

Hayward glanced back, motioned for one of the officers to frisk him. Another agent came up behind, grabbing Pendergast's hands, pulling them behind his back and cuffing them.

"I suggest we move away from the railroad track," Pendergast said. "For the sake of safety."

"All in good time," Hayward said. She reached cautiously into his jacket pocket, withdrew the diamond, glanced at it, tucked it into her own breast pocket. "Aloysius Pendergast, you have the right to remain silent. Anything you say can and will be used against you in a court of law . . ."

But Pendergast was not listening. He was looking over Hayward's shoulder, into the darkness of tunnel III. Two small points of light were barely visible there, seemingly mere reflections of the faint light of the vault. As he watched, the lights faded out a moment, then returned— as eyes would do when blinked. Then they dimmed, turned away, and vanished, leaving only blackness in their wake.

Sixty-nine

THE AMBULANCE CREW had already taken away Kaplan and Viola. D'Agosta remained behind, cuffed to a chair in the holding area of the NYPD's Madison Square Garden substation, guarded by six cops. His head was down, eyes on the floor, trying to avoid eye contact with his former peers and subordinates as they stood around, making forced small talk. It turned out to be easy: everybody was assiduously avoiding looking at him. It was as if he no longer existed, as if he'd turned into some kind of vermin that didn't even merit a glance.

He heard a burst of radio talk and saw, through the substation's glassed-in partition, a large group of cops moving through the ticketing area of Penn Station. In the middle, still walking tall, was the slender, black-suited figure of Pendergast, hands cuffed behind his back, two burly cops on either side. Pendergast glanced neither to the left nor to the right, and his back was straight, his face untroubled. For the first time in many days, he looked— if it was possible, under the circumstances—almost like his old self. No doubt they were leading him to a waiting paddy wagon at the station's Eighth Avenue entrance. As

Pendergast passed, he glanced in D'Agosta's direction. Even though the partition was made of mirrored glass, it seemed that Pendergast nevertheless looked directly at him, with what seemed to be a quick, grateful nod.

D'Agosta turned away. His whole world, everything he cared about, had been destroyed. Because of Pender-gast's insistence that he inform Hayward of their where-abouts, his friend was on his way to prison, probably for life. There was only one thing that could make him feel worse, and that would be if Hayward herself made an appearance.

As if on cue, there she was: walking with Singleton, approaching from the far side of the substation.

He dropped his head and waited. He heard footsteps approach. His face burned.

"Lieutenant?"

He looked up. It wasn't Hayward, just Singleton. Laura had simply passed him by.

Singleton glanced around, exchanged greetings with the cops guarding D'Agosta. "Uncuff him, please."

One of the cops uncuffed him from the chair.

"I'd like to have a private word with the lieutenant, if you fellows don't mind."

The cops evacuated the holding area with visible re-lief. When they were gone, Singleton put a hand on his shoulder. "You're in deep shit, Vinnie," he said, not unkindly.

D'Agosta nodded.

"Needless to say, they'll be convening a board of in-quiry, and a preliminary internal affairs hearing will be held as soon as possible, probably the day after tomor-row. Your future in law enforcement is a big question mark at this point, but, frankly, that's the least of your worries. It looks like we're dealing with four felony charges: kidnapping two, grand auto, reckless endangerment, accessory after."

D'Agosta put his head in his hands.

Singleton squeezed his shoulder. "The thing is, Vinnie, despite all this, in the end you came through. You dropped a dime on Pendergast, and we nailed him. A few cars were wrecked, but nobody got hurt. We might even be able to argue that this was the plan all along—you know, you were working undercover, setting Pendergast up."

D'Agosta didn't respond. The sight of Pendergast being led off in cuffs was still working its way into his head. Pendergast, the untouchable.

"The point is, I'm going to see what I can do about these charges, maybe knock some of them down to misdemeanors before they get written up and filed, if you know what I mean. No promises."

D'Agosta swallowed and managed to say, "Thanks."

"There's a bit of a twist here. The kidnap victim's preliminary statement seems to indicate that this Diogenes Pendergast is alive—and maybe even responsible for the diamond heist at the museum. Seems we just missed him down there in the railroad tunnels. The fact that Pendergast had Lucifer's Heart in his pocket is also damned puzzling. This sort of . . . well, opens up the case. We're going to have to take a second look at some of our assumptions."

D'Agosta looked up sharply. "I can explain everything."

"Save it for the interrogation. Hayward already told me about your theory that Diogenes framed his brother for those killings. The fact is, we now know that Pendergast impersonated Kaplan and stole the diamond. Whatever the precise details are, he's going to do hard time, no question about it. If I were you—and I'm speaking to you now as a friend, not as a supervisor—I'd worry about your own skin and quit interesting yourself in his. That FBI bastard's caused you enough trouble."

"Captain, I would appreciate it if you wouldn't speak of Agent Pendergast in that way."

"Loyal to the end, eh?" Singleton shook his head.

The sound of a loud, angry voice came echoing down the substation. A solid mass of federal agents, led by a tall, glowering, sunburned man, came into view outside the holding area. D'Agosta stared hard: the man at the front looked familiar, very familiar. He tried to clear his mind, cut through the fog. *Coffey.* Special Agent Coffey.

Spying Singleton, Coffey veered in the direction of the holding area.

"Captain Singleton?" His fleshy face was red even through the tan.

Captain Singleton looked up, his expression mild. "Yes, Agent Coffey?"

"What the hell's gone down here? You made the collar without us?"

"That's right."

"You know this is our case."

Singleton waited a minute before responding. When he did, his voice was calm and low, almost as if he were talking to a child. "The information came in fast and we had to act on it immediately. The perp slipped your Suffolk County dragnet and made his way back into the city. We couldn't wait. I'm sure you'll understand, given the circumstances, why we had to move without you."

"You didn't contact the Southern District of Manhattan Field Office at all. There were agents standing by in the city, ready to move at a moment's notice."

Another pause. "That was certainly an oversight, for which I take full responsibility. You know how easy it is, in the heat of action, to neglect to dot an *i* somewhere along the way. My apologies."

Coffey stood in front of Singleton, breathing hard. A few NYPD officers snickered in the background.

"There was an unexpected bonus in collaring Pendergast," Singleton added.

"And what the hell was that?"

"He had the diamond, Lucifer's Heart, in his pocket."

Singleton took advantage of Coffey's momentary speechlessness to glance at his men. "We're done here. Let's head downtown."

And, propelling D'Agosta gently to his feet, he turned on his heel and walked away.

Seventy

WEDNESDAY DAWNED brilliant and clear, the morning sun blazing in through the single window of the dining nook of the small apartment on West End Avenue. Nora Kelly heard the door to the bathroom slam. A few minutes later, Bill Smithback emerged in the hallway, dressed for work, his tie unknotted and his jacket slung over one shoulder. The expression on his face was dark.

"Come and have some breakfast," she said.

His face brightened slightly as he saw her, and he came over and sat down at the table.

"What time did you get in last night?"

"Four." He leaned over and gave her a kiss.

"You look like hell."

"It isn't for lack of sleep."

Nora pushed the paper over to him. "Page one. Congratulations."

Smithback glanced at it. His story of the theft of Lucifer's Heart by an unknown assailant was front page, above the fold: the dream of every journalist. It was a stupendous scoop, and along with the arrest of Pendergast, it had pushed Harriman's story of the Dangler capture to B3 of the Metro Section—an old woman had seen the Dangler exposing himself in front of an ATM and, righteously indignant, had whacked him into semiconsciousness with her cane. For the first time, Nora thought, Bill didn't seem interested in Harriman's misfortune.

He pushed the paper away. "Not going to work?"

"The museum's told us all to stay home for the rest of this week—a kind of forced vacation. The place is in lockdown mode until they find out how the security system was breached." She shook her head. "On top of that, Hugo Menzies seems to have disappeared. It seems they caught him on a security camera not far from the Astor Hall at the time of the heist. They're worried he might have stumbled on the robbery and gotten himself killed."

"Maybe he's the thief."

"Diogenes Pendergast is the thief. You of all people should know that."

"Maybe Menzies *is* Diogenes." Bill forced a brittle laugh.

"That's not even funny."

Smithback shrugged. "Sorry. Poor taste on my part."

Nora filled his coffee cup, refilled her own. "There's one thing I still don't get from reading your story. How did Pendergast get Lucifer's Heart out of the Affiliated Transglobal building? I mean, they immediately sealed the building, they X-rayed everyone leaving, they did a count of every single person who had come in and left. And they never found Pendergast. What'd he do, climb down the outside of the building? How'd he get the gem out?"

Smithback smoothed down an unruly cowlick, which popped back up as soon as his hand was gone. "That's the best part of the story—if only I could write it."

"Why can't you?"

Smithback turned toward her and smiled a little grimly. "Because I was the one who walked the diamond out of the building."

"You?" Nora stared at him, incredulous.

Smithback nodded.

"Oh, Bill!"

"Nora, I *had* to. It was the only way. And don't worry— it'll never be traced back to me. The diamond is back where it belongs. It was truly a brilliant plan."

"Tell me about it."

"You sure you want to know? That makes you an accessory after the fact."

"I'm your *wife,* silly. Of course I want to know."

Smithback sighed. "Pendergast worked it all out. He knew they'd seal the building and search everyone on their way out. So he posed as a technician manning the X-ray machine."

"But if security was as tight as you say, wouldn't they X-ray the security technicians, too? I mean, when they left the building?"

"Pendergast figured that out, too. After sending me through the X-ray machine, he pointed me toward the building exit. That's when he slipped the diamond into my pocket. I walked it right out of the building."

Nora could hardly believe it. "If you'd been caught, they would have put you away for twenty years."

"Don't think that wasn't on my mind." Smithback shrugged. "But a life depended on it. And I have faith in Pendergast—sometimes I feel like I'm the only one left in the world who does."

At this, he rose, walked to the window, and stared out restlessly, hands on his hips.

"It's not over, Nora," he muttered. "Not by a long shot."

He turned swiftly, eyes flashing with anger. "It's a travesty of justice. An innocent man's been framed as a horrendous serial killer. The real killer's still loose. I'm a journalist. It's my job to report the truth. There's a hell of a lot of truth still missing in this story. I'm going to find out what it is."

"Bill—for God's sake, don't go after Diogenes."

"What about Margo? Are we going to let her killer go free? With Pendergast in jail and D'Agosta on modified duty or worse, there's no one left who can do it but me."

"Don't. *Please* don't. This is just another one of your impulsive—and stupid—decisions."

He turned back to the window. "I concede that it's impulsive. Maybe even stupid. So be it."

Nora rose from her chair, feeling a surge of anger herself. "What about us? Our future? If you go after Diogenes, he'll kill you. You're no match for him!"

Smithback looked out the window, not answering immediately. Then he stirred. "Pendergast saved my life," he said quietly. He turned again and looked at Nora. "Yours, too."

She wheeled away, exasperated.

He came over and took her in his arms. "I won't do it . . . if you tell me not to."

"And that's the one thing I'm *not* going to tell you. It's your decision."

Smithback stepped back, knotted his tie, drew on his jacket. "I'd better get to work."

He kissed her. "I love you, Nora."

She shook her head. "Be very, very careful."

"I will, I promise. Have faith in me."

And he vanished out the door.

Seventy-one

ONE DAY LATER, and fifty miles to the north, the sun shone dimly through the shuttered window of a small room in the intensive-care unit of a private clinic. A single patient lay under a sheet, hooked up to several large machines that beeped softly, almost comfortingly. Her eyes were closed.

A nurse came in, checked the machines, jotted down some of the vitals, and then paused to look at the patient.

"Good morning, Theresa," she said brightly.

The patient's eyes remained closed, and she did not answer. They'd removed the feeding tube, and she was out of immediate danger, but she was still one very sick woman.

"It's a beautiful morning," the nurse went on, opening the shutters and allowing a ray of sun to fall across the covers. Outside the window of the rambling Queen Anne mansion, the Hudson River sparkled amidst the winter landscape of Putnam County.

The woman's pale face lay against the pillow, her short brown hair spreading slightly across the cotton fabric.

The nurse continued to work, changing the IV bag,

smoothing the covers. Finally, she leaned over the girl and brushed a strand of hair out of her face.

The girl's eyes slowly opened.

The nurse paused, then took her hand. "Good morning," she said again, holding the hand lightly.

The eyes flicked to the left and right. The lips moved, but no sound came.

"Don't you try to talk just yet," the nurse said, moving to the intercom. "Everything will be all right. You've had a tough time of it, but now everything's fine."

She pressed the intercom lever and leaned toward it, speaking in a low voice.

"The patient in ICU-6 is waking up," she murmured. "Get word to Dr. Winokur."

She went and sat by the bed, taking the woman's hand again.

"Where . . . ?"

"You're at the Feversham Clinic, Theresa dear. A few miles north of Cold Spring. It's January 31, and you've been unconscious for six days, but we've got you on the mend. Everything's just fine. You're a strong, healthy woman and you're going to get better."

The eyes widened slightly. "What . . . ?" the weak voice managed to say.

"What happened? Never you mind about that now. You had a very close call, but it's all over and done with. You're safe here."

The figure in the bed struggled to speak, her lips moving.

"Don't try to talk just yet. Save your strength for the doctor."

". . . tried to kill . . ." The phrase came out disconnected.

"Like I said, never you mind. You concentrate on getting better."

". . . awful . . ."

The nurse stroked her hand kindly. "I'm sure it was, but let's not dwell on that now. Dr. Winokur will be here at any moment and he might have some questions for you. You should rest, dear."

"Tired . . . Tired . . ."

"Certainly, you are. You're very tired. But you can't go back to sleep quite yet, Theresa. Stay awake for me and the doctor. Just for now. Okay? That's a good girl."

"I'm not . . . Theresa."

The nurse smiled indulgently, patting her hand. "Don't worry about a thing. A little confusion on awakening is perfectly normal. While waiting for the doctor, let's look out the window. Isn't it a lovely day?"

Seventy-two

AYWARD HAD NEVER BEFORE visited the legendary high-security lockup within Bellevue Hospital, and she walked toward the unit with a rising sense of curiosity. The long, brightly lit hallways stank of rubbing alcohol and bleach, and along the way they passed through almost half a dozen locked doors: Adult Emergency Services, Psychiatric Emergency, Psychiatric Inpatient, finally ending up at the most intimidating door of all: a windowless double set of dented stainless steel, flanked by two orderlies in white suits and an NYPD police sergeant sitting at a desk. The door sported a small, scratched label: *Secure Area.*

Hayward flashed her badge. "Captain Laura Hayward and guest. We're expected in D-11."

"Morning, Captain," said the sergeant in a leisurely tone, who took her shield, jotted down some information on the sign-in sheet, and handed it to her to sign.

"My guest will wait here while I visit the inmate first."

"Sure, sure," said the sergeant. "Joe will escort you."

The beefier of the two orderlies nodded, unsmiling.

The sergeant turned to a nearby phone and made a call. A moment later, there came the sound of heavy automatic locks being released. The orderly named Joe pulled the door open. "D-11, you said?"

"That's correct."

"This way, Captain."

Beyond lay a narrow corridor, the floors and walls of linoleum. Long rows of doors lined both walls. These were metal, with tiny observation ports set at eye level. A strange, muted chorus of voices met Hayward's ears: frenzied cursing, crying, a dreadful half-human gibbering, all filtering out from behind the doors. The smell was different here; underlying the stench of alcohol and cleaning fluids was a faint waft of vomit, excrement, and something else which Hayward recognized from her visits to maximum security prisons: the smell of fear.

The door clanged shut behind her. A moment later, the automatic locks reengaged with a crack like a pistol shot.

She followed the orderly down the long corridor, around a corner, and down a similar corridor. There, toward the end, she could easily identify the room they were headed for: it could only be the one with four men in suits standing guard outside. Coffey had missed out on the actual collar, but he sure as hell wasn't going to miss anything else.

The agents turned as she approached. Hayward recognized one of them as Coffey's personal flunky, Agent Rabiner. He didn't seem happy to see her.

"Put your weapons in the lockbox, Captain," he said by way of greeting.

Captain Hayward removed her service piece and pepper spray and placed them in the lockbox.

"Looks like we're keeping him," Rabiner said with an unctuous smile. "We've got him nailed on Decker, and it fits the federal death penalty statute to a T. Right now it's just a question of getting the psych evaluation over with. By the end of the week, he'll be in the isolation unit at Herkmoor. We're taking this sucker to trial, like, tomorrow."

"You're rather garrulous this morning, Agent Rabiner," Hayward said.

That shut him up.

"I'd like to see him now. First myself, then I will bring back a guest."

"You going in alone or want protection?"

Hayward didn't bother answering. She simply stood back and waited while one of the agents peered through the glass, then unbolted the door, weapon at the ready.

"Sing out if he gets physical," Rabiner said.

Captain Hayward stepped into the garishly lit cell.

Pendergast, in an orange prison jumpsuit, sat quietly on the narrow cot. The walls of the cell were thickly padded and there were no other furnishings.

For a moment, Hayward said nothing. She had grown so used to seeing him in a well-tailored black suit that the outfit looked incomprehensibly out of place. His face was pale and drawn, but still composed.

"Captain Hayward." He stood and motioned her toward the cot. "Please have a seat."

"That's all right. I prefer to stand."

"Very well." Pendergast, too, remained standing, as a courtesy.

A silence settled over the small cell. Hayward was not one to find herself at a loss for words, but the fact was, she still didn't quite know what impulse had prompted her to make this visit. After a moment, she cleared her throat.

"What did you do to piss off Special Agent Coffey?" she asked.

Pendergast smiled a little wanly. "Agent Coffey has an inordinately high opinion of himself. It's a viewpoint I've never quite been able to bring myself to share. We worked on a case together some years ago, which did not end well for him."

"I ask because we tried to get jurisdiction over the case, but I've never seen the FBI stomp down so hard on the NYPD. And it wasn't done in the usual semi-cordial way."

"I am not surprised."

"Thing is, there've been a couple of bizarre developments in the case, not yet official, which I wanted to ask you about."

"Please do."

"Turns out Margo Green is alive. Someone pulled a fast one at the hospital, arranging for her to be medevaced upstate under a phony name, while substituting the corpse of a homeless drug addict about to be sent to potter's field in her place. The M.E. says it was an honest mistake, the medical director claims it was a 'regrettable bureaucratic mix-up.' Funny that both of them happen to be old acquaintances of yours. Green's mother just about had a heart attack when she learned the daughter she had just buried was alive."

She paused, her eyes narrowed, then burst out: "Damn it, Pendergast! Can't you do *anything* by the book? And how could you put a mother through that?"

Pendergast was silent a moment before answering. "Because her grief had to be real. Diogenes would have seen through any dissembling. As cruel as it was, it was necessary in order to save Margo Green's life—and her life is, ultimately, more important than a mother's temporary grief. It was this same need for *utmost* secrecy that kept me from telling even Lieutenant D'Agosta."

Hayward sighed. "Anyway, I just spoke to Green on the phone. She's incredibly weak, had the closest of calls, but she was very lucid. And what she had to say surprised the hell out of me. She's absolutely insistent that you weren't her attacker, and her description fits the other description we have of your brother quite well. Problem is, it was *your* blood at the crime scene and on the weapon Green defended herself with, along with fiber, hair, and other physical evidence. So we've got a major evidence conundrum on our hands."

"You certainly do."

"Our interviews with Viola Maskelene corroborate your story about Diogenes, at least what I understand of it. She's insistent it was he who did the kidnapping, not you. She says he basically confessed to the killings and showed her one of the stolen diamonds from the Astor Hall. No proof, of course, just her word, but she helped lead us to the safe house where she was held. We found quite a setup there, including some pretty conclusive evidence linking Diogenes to the Astor Hall theft—evidence he clearly didn't intend to give up."

"Interesting."

"We almost caught someone in the tunnels who Lieutenant D'Agosta swears was Diogenes. The gemologist, Kaplan, backs this up, as does Maskelene. Their preliminary stories are all consistent, and we know it couldn't have been you. We've asked our British counterparts to open an investigation into Diogenes's death in England, but that'll take time. Anyway, the evidence does seem to indicate your brother may be alive, after all. We have three people who certainly believe it."

Pendergast nodded. "And what do you believe, Captain?"

Hayward hesitated. "That the case merits further investigation. Trouble is, the FBI are moving full speed ahead bringing capital charges on the murder of a federal agent, and it seems they could care less at present about any inconsistencies in the other three. Or rather, two, since the Green killing wasn't a killing, after all. Which makes my continued investigation of those other homicides somewhat moot."

Pendergast nodded. "I see your problem."

Hayward peered at him curiously. "I was just wondering—do you have anything to say about the matter to me?"

"That I have faith in your abilities as a police officer to find the truth."

"Nothing more?"

"That's a great deal, Captain."

She paused. "*Help* me, Pendergast."

"The person to help you is Lieutenant D'Agosta. He knows all there is to know about the case, and you could do no better than use his expertise."

"You know that's impossible. Lieutenant D'Agosta's on modified duty. He can't help anyone at the moment."

"Nothing is impossible. You just need to learn how to bend the rules."

Hayward sighed irritatedly.

"I have a question for you," Pendergast said. "Does Agent Coffey know about the reappearance of Margo Green?"

"No, but I doubt he'd care much. As I said, they're one hundred percent focused on Decker."

"Good. I would ask you to keep that information quiet as long as possible. I believe Margo Green is safe from Diogenes, at least in the short term. My brother has gone to ground and will be licking his wounds for a while, but when he emerges, he will be more dangerous than ever. I ask that you keep a protective eye over Dr. Green during the rest of her convalescence. The same goes for William Smithback and his wife, Nora. And yourself. You're all potential targets, I'm afraid."

Hayward gave a shudder. What had seemed like an insane fantasy just two days ago now was beginning to look chillingly real.

"I'll do that," she said.

"Thank you."

Another silence settled over the cell. After a moment, Hayward roused herself.

"Well, I'd better be going. I really just came as an escort for someone else who wants to see you."

"Captain?" Pendergast said. "A final word."

She turned to face him again. He stood there, pale in the artificial light, his cool gaze resting upon her.

"Please don't be too hard on Vincent."

Despite herself, Hayward looked away quickly.

"What he did, he did at my request. The reason he told you so little, the reason he moved out—those actions were to keep you safe from my brother. In order to help me, to protect lives, he made a grave professional sacrifice—I hope and pray the sacrifice won't be a personal one, as well."

Hayward did not reply.

"That's all. Good-bye, Captain."

Hayward found her voice. "Good-bye, Agent Pendergast."

Then, still without making eye contact, she turned away once more and rapped on the safety glass of the observation port.

Pendergast watched the door close behind Hayward. He stood motionless, in the ill-fitting orange jumpsuit, listening. He heard a few muffled voices outside the padded door, and then focused on the light but determined stride of Hayward as she made for the ward's exit. He heard the security locks disengage, heard the heavy door boom open. It remained so for almost thirty seconds before closing and locking again.

Still, Pendergast listened, even more intently. Because now another, different set of footsteps was sounding in the corridor outside: slower, tentative. They were growing closer. As he listened, his frame tensed. A moment later, there was a rude banging on his door again.

"Visitor!"

Then Viola Maskelene appeared in the doorway.

She had a scratch over one eye, and beneath her Mediterranean tan she seemed pale, but otherwise she appeared unhurt.

Pendergast found he could not move. He simply stood and looked at her.

She stepped forward, stopped awkwardly in the middle of the room. The door closed behind her.

Still, Pendergast did not move.

Viola's eyes fell from his face to his prison garb.

"I wish, for your sake, that you'd never met me," he said almost coldly.

"What about for *your* sake?"

He looked at her a long time, and then said, more quietly: "I'll never regret meeting you. But as long as you have feelings for me—if that is indeed the case—then you'll be in grave danger. You must go away and never see or think of me again."

He paused, then cast his eyes to the floor. "I'm deeply, deeply sorry for everything."

There was a long silence.

"Is that it?" Viola finally asked in a low voice. "We'll never know, never have the chance to find out?"

"Never. Diogenes is still out there. If he thinks there's any connection remaining between us, *anything at all*, he'll kill you. You must leave immediately, go back to Capraia, get on with your life, tell everyone—including your own heart—how utterly indifferent you are to me."

"And what about you?"

"I'll know you're alive. That's enough."

She took a fierce step forward. "I don't want to 'get on' with my life. Not anymore." She hesitated, then raised her arms and rested her hands on his shoulders. "Not after meeting you."

Pendergast remained as still as a statue.

"You must leave me behind," he said quietly. "Diogenes will be back. And I won't be able to protect you."

"He . . . said terrible things to me," she said, her voice faltering. "It's been thirty-six hours since I walked out of that railroad tunnel, and in all those hours I haven't been able to think of anything else. I've led a stupid, wasted, loveless life. And now you're telling me to walk away from the only thing that means anything to me."

Pendergast put his arms gently around her waist, looked searchingly into her eyes.

"Diogenes makes it a game to find out a person's deepest fears. Then he strikes a deadly, well-aimed blow. He's driven people to suicide that way. But his words are hollow. Don't let those words stalk you. To know Diogenes is to walk in darkness. You must walk out of that darkness, Viola. Back into the light. And that also means away from me."

"No," she murmured.

"Go back to your island and forget about me. If not for your own sake, Viola, then for mine."

They looked into each other's eyes for a moment. Then, in the harsh light of the squalid cell, they kissed.

After a moment, Pendergast disengaged himself and stepped back. His face was uncharacteristically flushed; his pale eyes glittered.

"Good-bye, Viola," he said.

Viola stood as if rooted to the ground. A minute passed. Then, with infinite reluctance, she turned and walked slowly to the door.

At the door, she hesitated and, without turning, began to speak in a low voice.

"I'll do as you say. I'll go back to my island. I'll tell everyone I could not care less about you. I'll live my life. And when you're finally free, you'll know where to find me."

She gave a quick rap on the observation port, the door opened—and she was gone.

Epilogue

T
HE FIRE DIED on the grate, leaving a crumbling stack of coals. The light in the library was dim, and the usual cloak of silence lay over all: the baize-covered reading tables neatly stacked with books, the walls of slumbering volumes, the shaded lamps and leather chairs. Outside, it was a bright winter day, the last day of January, but within 891 Riverside it seemed to be perpetual night.

Constance sat in one chair, wearing a black petticoat with white lace trimming, legs tucked up beneath her, reading an eighteenth-century treatise on the benefits of bloodletting. D'Agosta sat in a wing chair nearby. A can of Budweiser sat on a silver tray on a table beside him, unconsumed, in a puddle of its own condensation.

D'Agosta glanced over at Constance, at her perfect profile, her straight brown hair. That she was a beautiful young woman, there was no doubt; that she was unusually, even uncannily, intelligent and well read for someone her age went without saying. But there was something strange about her—very, very strange. She'd had no emotional reaction at all to the news of Pendergast's arrest and incarceration. None.

In D'Agosta's experience, that kind of nonreaction was often the strongest reaction of all. It worried him. Pendergast had warned him of Constance's current fragility and had hinted of dark things in her past. D'Agosta had long had his own doubts about Constance's stability, and this inexplicable lack of reaction only made him wonder the more. It was partly to watch over her, now that Pendergast was gone, that had brought him and his few belongings back to 891 the day before— that and the fact he had no place else to go.

And then there was the problem of Diogenes. It was true he had been crossed, his plans for Viola and Lucifer's Heart had been thwarted, he himself forced back into hiding. The NYPD now believed in his existence and were pursuing him with a vengeance. The recent developments seemed to have dented, but not completely shaken, their certainty that Pendergast was a serial killer—the problem was still the overwhelming physical evidence. The NYPD was at least now certain, however, that Diogenes was behind the Astor Hall theft and had kidnapped Viola. They'd found the safe house and were in the process of taking it apart. The case was by no means closed.

In a way, Diogenes's failure and flight only made him more dangerous. He recalled Diogenes's curiosity about Constance, during the phone conversation in the vintage Jaguar, and he shivered. The one thing he could count on was that Diogenes was a meticulous planner. His response—and there would be one, of that D'Agosta was sure—would not come for a while. He would have a little time to prepare for it.

Constance looked up from her book. "Did you know, Lieutenant, that even into the early 1800s, leeches were often a preferred alternative to the scarificator when performing bloodletting?"

D'Agosta glanced at her. "Can't say that I did."

"The colonial doctors frequently imported the European leech, *Hirudinea annelida*, because it was able to take in much more blood than *Macrobetta decora*."

"*Macrobetta decora?*"

"The American leech, Lieutenant." And Constance returned to her book.

Call me Vincent, D'Agosta thought as he looked reflectively at her. He wasn't all that sure how much longer he was going to be a lieutenant, anyway.

His mind wandered to the previous afternoon, and the humiliating internal affairs hearing. On the one hand, it had been a huge relief: Singleton had been good to his word and the whole misadventure had been chalked up to an undercover operation gone awry, in which D'Agosta had displayed poor judgment, made errors—one of the board had termed him "maybe the stupidest cop on the force"—but in the end they found he had not willfully committed any felonies. The list of misdemeanors was ugly enough.

Stupidity was better than felony, Singleton had told him afterward. There would be more hearings, but his future as an NYPD cop—as *any* kind of cop—was very much in question.

Hayward, of course, had testified. Her testimony had been delivered in a resolutely neutral voice, employing the usual police jargon, and not once—*not once*—had she glanced in his direction. But in its own way, the testimony had been effective in helping him escape some of the heavier charges.

Once again, he dragged the Diogenes file into his lap,

feeling a sudden stab of futility. Ten days before, he had been in this same room, looking at this same file, again without Pendergast there to guide him. Only now, four people had been murdered, and Pendergast, instead of being "dead," was in Bellevue, undergoing some kind of psych evaluation. D'Agosta had learned nothing helpful then—what could he possibly learn now?

But he had to keep plugging. They'd taken everything away from him: his career, his relationship with Hayward, his closest friend—everything. There was only one thing left for him to do: prove Pendergast's innocence. And to do that, he needed to find Diogenes.

A faint buzzer sounded in the depths of the house. Someone was at the door.

Constance looked up. For the briefest of moments, naked fear—and something else, something ineffable—showed in her face before a veil of blankness came down.

D'Agosta stood up. "It's okay. Probably just neighborhood kids, playing around. I'll check it out."

He put the file aside, stood up, surreptitiously checked his weapon, then began walking toward the library door. But even as he did, he saw Proctor approaching from across the reception hall.

"A gentleman here to see you, sir," Proctor said.

"You took the necessary precautions?" D'Agosta asked.

"Yes, sir, I—"

But just then, a man in a wheelchair came into view in the gallery behind Proctor. D'Agosta stared in astonishment as he recognized Eli Glinn, the head of Effective Engineering Solutions.

The man brushed past both Proctor and D'Agosta and wheeled himself toward one of the library tables. With a brusque motion of his arm, he shoved aside several stacks of books, clearing off a space. Then he deposited a load of papers on the table: blueprints, plats, building plans, mechanical and electrical diagrams.

Constance had risen and was standing, book in hand, looking on.

"What are you doing here?" D'Agosta asked. "How did you find this place?"

"Never mind that," said the man, turning to D'Agosta with a gleam in his good eye. "Last Sunday, I made a promise."

He raised his black-gloved hand, and in it was a slender manila folder. He laid it on the table.

"And there you have it: a preliminary psychological profile of Diogenes Dagrepont Bernoulli Pendergast. Updated, I might add, to reflect these most recent events— at least what I could glean of them from the news reports and my sources. I'm counting on you to tell me more."

"There's a lot more."

Glinn glanced over. "And you must be Constance."

She nodded in a way that was almost a curtsy.

"I'll need your help, too."

"I shall be glad."

"Why this sudden interest?" D'Agosta asked. "I had the impression—"

"The impression that I wasn't giving it a high priority? I wasn't. At the time, it seemed a relatively unimportant problem, a way to earn an easy fee. But then, *this* happened." And he tapped the manila folder. "There may not be a more dangerous man in the world."

"I don't get it."

A grim smile gathered on Glinn's lips. "You will when you read the profile."

D'Agosta nodded toward the table. "And what are all these other papers?"

"Blueprints and mechanical plans for the maximum security wing of the Herkmoor Correctional Facility in upstate New York."

"Why?"

"I should think the 'why' would be obvious. My client, Agent Pendergast."

"But Pendergast is in Bellevue, not Herkmoor."

"He'll be in Herkmoor soon enough."

D'Agosta glanced at Glinn in astonishment. "You don't mean we're going to . . . to bust him out?"

"I do."

Constance drew in a sharp breath.

"That's one of the worst pens in the country. No one's ever escaped from Herkmoor."

Glinn continued to stare at D'Agosta. "I'm aware of that."

"You think it's even possible?"

"Anything's possible. But I must have your help."

D'Agosta looked down at the papers and blueprints thrown across the table. Everything conceivable was there—diagrams and drawings of every technical, structural, electrical, and mechanical system in the building. Then he glanced at Constance. She nodded almost imperceptibly.

Finally, he looked back at Glinn's one glittering eye. For the first time in a long while, he felt a fierce, sudden rush of hope.

"I'm in," he said. "So help me God, *I'm in.*"

Another smile spread across Glinn's scarred face. He gave the pile of papers a light slap with his gloved hand. "Come on, my friends—we've got work to do."

About the Authors

DOUGLAS PRESTON and LINCOLN CHILD are coauthors of the bestselling novels *Relic*, *Mount Dragon*, *Reliquary*, *Riptide*, *Thunderhead*, *The Ice Limit*, *The Cabinet of Curiosities*, *Still Life with Crows*, and *Brimstone*. Douglas Preston, a regular contributor to *The New Yorker*, worked for the American Museum of Natural History. He is an expert horseman who has ridden thousands of miles across the West. Lincoln Child is a former book editor and systems analyst who has published numerous anthologies of ghost stories and supernatural tales. The authors are working on their next Pendergast novel. They encourage readers to visit their Web site, www.prestonchild.com.

More chilling suspense in
the new thriller
featuring Agent Pendergast!

Please turn this page
for a preview of

The Book of the Dead

available in June 2006.

DR. FREDERICK WATSON Collopy stood behind the great nineteenth-century leather-topped desk of his corner office in the museum's southeast tower. It was morning. The huge desk was bare, save for a copy of the *New York Times*. The newspaper had not been opened. It did not need to be opened: already, Collopy could see everything he needed to see, on the front page, above the fold, in the largest type that the staid *Times* dared use.

The cat was out of the bag, and it could not be put back in.

Collopy considered himself heir to the greatest position in American science: director of the New York Museum of Natural History. His mind had drifted from the subject of the article to the names of his distinguished forebears: Bickmore, Scott, Throckmorton, Gilcrease. His goal, his one ambition, was to add his name to that august registry—and not fall into ignominy like his two immediate predecessors, the late and not-much-lamented Winston Wright or the inept Olivia Merriam.

And yet there, on the front page of the *Times*, was a headline that might just be his epitaph. He had weathered several bad patches recently, eruptions of scandal that would have felled a lesser man. But he had handled them coolly and decisively—and he would do the same here.

A soft knock came at the door.

"Come in."

The bearded figure of Hugo Menzies, dressed elegantly and with slightly less than the usual degree of academic rumpledness, entered the room. He silently took a chair as Josephine Rocco, the head of public relations, entered behind him, along with the museum's lawyer, the ironically named Beryl Darling of Wilfred, Spragg, and Darling.

Collopy remained standing, watching the three as he stroked his chin thoughtfully. Finally he spoke.

"I've called you here in emergency session, for obvious reasons." He glanced down at the paper. "I assume you've seen the *Times*?"

His audience nodded in silent assent.

"We made a mistake in trying to cover this up, even briefly. When I took this position as director of the museum, I told myself I would run this place differently, that I wouldn't operate in the secretive and sometimes paranoid manner of the last few administrations. I believed the museum to be a great institution, one strong enough to survive the vicissitudes of scandal and controversy that plague most public institutions."

He paused.

"In trying to play down the destruction of our diamond collection, in seeking to cover it up, I made a mistake. I violated my own principles."

"An apology to us is all well and good," said Darling, in her usual crisp voice, "but why didn't you consult me before you made that hasty and ill-considered decision? You must have realized you couldn't get away with it. This has done serious damage to the museum and made my job that much more difficult."

Collopy reminded himself this was precisely the reason the museum hired Darling and paid her $400 an hour: she always spoke the unvarnished truth.

He raised a hand. "Point taken. The truth is, this is a development I never, ever in my worst nightmares could have anticipated—finding that the museum's diamond collection had been reduced to . . ." His voice cracked; he couldn't finish.

There was an uneasy shifting in the room.

Collopy swallowed, then began again. "We must take action. We've got to respond, and respond now. That is why I've asked you to this meeting."

As he paused for their responses, Collopy could hear, coming faintly from Museum Drive below, the shouts and calls of a growing crowd of protestors, along with police sirens and bullhorns.

Rocco spoke up. "The phones in my office are ringing off the hook. It's nine now, and I think we've probably got until ten, maybe eleven at the latest, to make some kind of official statement. In all my years in public relations I've never encountered anything quite like this, and I'm really at a loss as to how to spin it."

Menzies shifted in his chair and smoothed his white hair. "May I?"

Collopy nodded. "Hugo."

Menzies cleared his throat, his intense blue eyes darting to the window and back to Collopy. "The first thing we have to realize, Frederick, is that this catastrophe is beyond, ah, 'spinning.' Listen to the crowd out there—

the fact that we even *considered* covering up such a huge loss has the people up in arms. No; we've got to take the hit, honestly and squarely. Admit our wrong. No more dissembling." He glanced at Rocco. "That's my first point and I hope we're all in agreement on it."

Rocco nodded. "And your second?"

He leaned forward slightly. "It's not enough to respond. We need to go on the offensive."

"What do you mean?"

"We need to do something glorious. We need to make a fabulous announcement, something that will remind New York City and the world that despite all this we're still a great museum. Mount a scientific expedition, launch a grand new exhibition, embark on some extraordinary research project."

"Won't that look like a rather transparent diversion?" asked Rocco.

"Perhaps to some. But the criticism will last only a day or two, and then we'll be free to build interest and good publicity."

"What kind of project?" Collopy asked.

"I haven't gotten that far."

Rocco nodded slowly. "Perhaps it would work. This opening or event could be combined with a gala party, strictly A-list, the social 'must' of the season. That will mute museum bashing among the press and politicians, who will naturally want to be invited."

"This sounds promising," Collopy said.

After a moment, Darling spoke. "It's a fine theory. All we lack is the expedition, exhibition, or event." She glanced around cynically. "It takes a year or more to install a major exhibition—far too long to have the desired effect."

At that moment, Collopy's intercom buzzed. He

stabbed it with irritation. "Mrs. Surd, we're not to be disturbed."

"I know, Dr. Collopy, but . . . well, this is highly unusual."

"Not now."

"It requires an immediate response."

Collopy sighed. "Can't it wait ten minutes, for heaven's sake?"

"It's a bank wire transfer donation of ten million euros for—"

"A gift of ten million euros? Bring it in."

Mrs. Surd, efficient and plump, entered carrying a paper.

"Excuse me for a moment." Collopy snatched the paper. "Who's it from and where do I sign?"

"It's from a Comte Thierry de Cahors. He's giving the museum ten million euros to renovate and reopen the Tomb of Senef."

"The Tomb of Senef? What the devil is that?" He tossed the paper on the desk. "I'll deal with this later."

"But it says here, sir, that the funds are waiting in transAtlantic escrow and must either be refused or accepted within the hour."

Collopy resisted an impulse to wring his hands. "We're awash in bloody restricted funds like this! What we need are *general* funds to pay the bills. Fax this Count Whoever and see if you can't persuade him to make this an unrestricted donation. Use my name with the usual courtesies. We don't need the money for whatever particular windmill he's tilting at."

"Yes, Dr. Collopy."

She turned away and Collopy glanced over the group. "Now, I believe Beryl had the floor."

The lawyer opened her mouth to speak, but Menzies

held out a suppressing hand. "Mrs. Surd? Please wait a few minutes before contacting the Count of Cahors."

Mrs. Surd hesitated, glancing at Collopy for confirmation. The director was a bit taken aback, but nodded a confirmation to her. She left, closing the door behind her.

"All right, Hugo, what's this about?" Collopy asked.

"I'm trying to remember the details. The Tomb of Senef—it rings a bell. And, now that I recall, so does the Count of Cahors."

"Can we move on here?" Collopy asked.

Menzies sat forward suddenly. "Frederick, this *is* moving on! Think back over your museum history. The Tomb of Senef was an Egyptian tomb on display in the museum from its original opening until, I believe, the Depression, when it was closed."

"And?"

"If memory serves, it was a tomb stolen and disassembled by the French during the Napoleonic invasion of Egypt and later seized by the British. It ended up in some Scottish lord's castle. It was purchased by one of the museum's benefactors and reassembled in the basement as one of the original exhibits. It must still be there."

"So who is this Cahors?" Darling asked.

"Napoleon brought an army of naturalists and archaeologists with his army when he invaded Egypt. A Cahors led the archaeological contingent. I imagine this fellow is a descendant."

Collopy frowned. "What does this have to do with anything?"

"Don't you see? This is precisely the exhibition we need!"

"A dusty old tomb?"

"Exactly! We make a big announcement of the gift, set

an opening date with a gala party and all the trappings, and make a media event out of it." Menzies looked inquiringly at Rocco.

"Yes," Rocco said. "Yes. That could work. Egypt is always popular with the general public."

"Could work? It *will* work. The beauty of it is that the tomb's already installed. We could do this in two months."

"A lot depends on the condition of the tomb."

"It would have been bricked up. Of course, it might be in poor condition, but nevertheless it's in place and ready to go. It might only need to be swept out. Our storage rooms are full of Egyptian odds and ends, mummies, canopic jars, ushabtis, that sort of thing, that we could put in the tomb to round out the exhibition. And of course there's always the chance its original exhibits still remain in place, undisturbed. I doubt if there's anyone still alive who really knows what condition the tomb is in, or what it looks like. But the Count is offering plenty of money for its restoration."

"I don't understand," Darling said. "How could an entire exhibition just sit behind a brick wall, moldering and forgotten, for seventy years?"

"That's the way it is." Menzies smiled a little sadly. "This museum simply has too many artifacts and not enough money or curators to tend them. That's why I've lobbied for many years now that we create a position for a museum historian. Who knows what other secrets sleep in the long-forgotten corners?"

A brief silence settled over the room, broken abruptly when Collopy brought his hand down on his desk. "Let's do it." He reached for the phone. "Mrs. Surd? Tell the Count to release the money. We're accepting his terms."

N THE MORNING appointed for the opening of the Tomb of Senef, Nora arrived in Menzies' capacious office to find him sitting in his usual wing chair, in conversation with a young man. They both rose as she came in.

"Nora," he said. "This is Dr. Hugh Wicherly, the Egyptologist I mentioned to you. This is Dr. Nora Kelly."

Wicherly turned to her with a smile, a thatch of untidy brown hair the only eccentricity of his otherwise perfectly dressed and groomed person. In a glance Nora took in the understated Savile Row suit, the fine wingtips, the club tie. Her sweep came to rest on an extraordinarily handsome face: dimpled cheeks, flashing blue eyes, and perfect white teeth. He was, she thought, no more than thirty.

"Delighted to meet you, Dr. Kelly," he said in an elegant, understated Oxbridge accent. He clasped her hand gently, blessing her with a dazzling smile.

"A pleasure. And please call me Nora."

"Of course. Nora. Forgive my formality—my stuffy

upbringing has left me rather hamstrung this side of the pond. I just want to say how smashing it is to be here, working on this project."

Smashing. Nora suppressed a smile. Hugh Wicherly was almost a caricature of the dashing young Brit, of a type she didn't think even existed outside P. G. Wodehouse novels.

"Hugh comes to us with some impressive credentials," Menzies said. "D. Phil. from Oxford, directed the excavation of the tomb KV 44 in the Valley of the Kings, University Professor of Egyptology at Cambridge, author of the monograph *Pharaohs of the XX Dynasty.*"

Nora looked at Wicherly with fresh respect. For an archaeologist of such stature, he was amazingly young. "Very impressive."

Wicherly put on a self-deprecating face. "A lot of academic rubbish, really."

"It's hardly that." Menzies glanced at his watch. "We're meeting someone from the maintenance department at ten. As I understand it, nobody knows, quite precisely, where the Tomb of Senef is anymore. The one certainty is that it was bricked up and has been sealed ever since. We're going to have to break our way in."

"How intriguing," said Wicherly. "I feel rather like Howard Carter."

They descended in an old brass elevator, which creaked and groaned its way to the basement. They emerged in the maintenance section and threaded a complex path through the machine shop and carpentry, at last arriving at the open door of a small office. Inside, a small man sat at a desk, poring over a thick press of blueprints. He rose when Menzies rapped on the doorframe.

"I'd like to introduce you both to Mr. Seamus Mc-

Corkle," said Menzies. "He probably knows more about the layout of the museum than anyone alive."

"Which still isn't saying much," said McCorkle. He was an elvish man in his early fifties with a fine Celtic face and a high, whistling voice. He pronounced the final word 'mitch.'

Introductions complete, Menzies turned back to McCorkle. "Have you found our tomb?"

"I believe so." He nodded at the slab of old blueprints. "It's not easy, finding things in this old pile."

"Why ever not?" Wicherly asked.

McCorkle began rolling up the top blueprint. "The museum consists of thirty-four interconnected buildings, with a footprint of more than six acres, over two million square feet of space and eighteen miles of corridors–and that's not even counting the sub-basement tunnels, which no one's ever surveyed or diagrammed. I once tried to figure out how many rooms there were in this joint, but gave up when I hit a thousand. The place has been under constant construction and renovation for every single one of its hundred and forty years. That's the nature of a museum—exhibits come and go, halls get built and closed, collections get moved around. Rooms get joined together, others get split apart and renamed. Advances in technology mean new labs, new storage areas, new ducts for computer cables and fiber optics. A lot of these changes are made on the fly, without blueprints."

"None of the museum's original Gothic Revival building is even visible from the street," added Menzies. "It's now completely encased by later construction."

"But surely they couldn't lose an entire Egyptian tomb," said Wicherly.

McCorkle laughed. "That would be difficult, even for

the museum. It's finding the entrance that might be tricky. It was bricked up in 1935 when they built the connecting tunnel between the 81st subway station and the museum." He tucked the blueprints under his arm and picked up an old leather bag that lay on his desk. "Shall we?"

"Lead the way," said Menzies.

They set off along a puce green corridor, past maintenance rooms and storage areas, through a heavily-trafficked section of the basement. As they went along, McCorkle gave a running account. "This is the metal shop. This is the old physical plant, once home to the nineteenth-century boilers, now used to store the collection of whale skeletons. Jurassic dinosaur storage . . . Cretaceous . . . Oligocene mammals . . . Pleistocene mammals. . . ."

The storage areas gave way to laboratories, their shiny, stainless-steel doors in contrast to the dingy corridors, lit with caged lightbulbs and lined with rumbling steam pipes.

They passed through so many locked doors, Nora lost count. Some were old and required keys, which Mc-Corkle selected dexterously from a large ring. Other doors, part of the museum's new security system, could be opened by swiping a magnetic card. As they moved deeper into the museum, the corridors became progressively empty and silent.

"I daresay this place is as vast as the British Museum," said Wicherly.

McCorkle snorted in contempt. "Bigger. *Much* bigger."

They came to a set of ancient riveted metal doors, which McCorkle opened with a large iron key. Darkness yawned beyond. He hit a switch and illuminated a long, once-elegant corridor lined with dingy frescoes. Nora squinted. They were paintings of a New Mexico landscape, with mountains, deserts, and a multistoried Indian ruin she recognized as Taos Pueblo.

"Fremont Ellis," said Menzies. "This was once the Hall of the Southwest. Shut down since the forties."

"These are extraordinary," said Nora.

"Indeed. And very valuable."

"They're rather in need of curation," said Wicherly.

"It's a question of money," Menzies said. "If a French count hadn't stepped forward with the necessary grant, the Tomb of Senef would probably sleep undisturbed for another seventy years."

McCorkle opened another door, revealing a dim storage room full of shelves filled with beautifully painted pots. Old oaken cabinets stood against the walls, fronted with rippled glass, revealing a profusion of dim artifacts.

"The Southwest collections," McCorkle said.

"I had no idea," said Nora, amazed. "These should be available for study."

"As Hugh pointed out, they need to be curated first," Menzies said. "Once again, a question of money."

"It's not only money," McCorkle added, with a strange, pinched expression on his face.

There was a pause in which Nora exchanged glances with Wicherly. "I'm sorry?" she asked.

Menzies cleared his throat. "I think what Seamus means is that the, ah, first Museum Beast killings happened in the vicinity of the Hall of the Southwest."

In the fresh silence that followed, Nora made a mental note to have a look at these collections later—preferably, as a member of a large group. Maybe she could write a grant to see them moved to up-to-date storage.

They continued on. Another door gave way to a smaller room, lined floor-to-ceiling with black metal drawers. Half hidden behind the drawers were ancient posters and announcements from the twenties and thirties, with art deco lettering and images of Gibson Girls. In an earlier era, it must have been an antechamber of sorts. The room smelled of paradichlorobenzene and something bad—like old beef jerky, Nora decided.

At the far end, a great dim hall opened up. In the reflected light, she could see that its walls were covered with frescoes of the Pyramids of Giza and the Sphinx as they had appeared when first built.

"Now we're approaching the old Egyptian galleries," McCorkle said.

They stepped into the vast hall. It had been turned into storage space: jumbles of sculptures covered in transparent plastic sheets, which were in turn overlaid with dust, giving the appearance of ghosts. Lining the walls and obscuring the lower parts of the frescoes were large metal shelves crowded with pottery vessels, gilded chairs and beds, headrests, canopic jars, and hundreds of smaller figurines in alabaster, faience, and ceramic.

"Lovely," Wicherly breathed.

McCorkle unrolled the blueprints and squinted at them in the dim light. "If my estimations are correct, the entrance to the tomb is supposed to be in what is now the Annex, at the far end."

Wicherly went to one shelf and lifted the plastic. "Good lord, this is one of the finest collection of ushabtis I've ever seen." He turned excitedly to Nora. "Why, there's enough material here alone to fill up the tomb twice over." He picked up an ushabti and turned it over with reverence. "Old Kingdom, II Dynasty, reign of the pharaoh Hetepsekhemwy."

"Dr. Wicherly, the rules about handling objects . . ." said McCorkle, a warning note in his voice.

"It's quite all right," said Menzies. "Dr. Wicherly is an Egyptologist. I'll take responsibility."

"Of course," said McCorkle, a little put out. Nora had the feeling that McCorkle took a kind of proprietary interest in these old collections. They were his, in a way, as he was one of the few people to ever see them.

Wicherly went from one shelf to the next, lifting the plastic again and again, his mouth practically watering. "Why, they even have a Neolithic collection from the Upper Nile! Good lord, take a look at this ceremonial *thatof*!" He held up a footlong stone knife flaked from gray flint.

McCorkle cast an annoyed glance at Wicherly. The archaeologist laid the knife back in its place with the utmost care, then reshrouded it in plastic.

They came to another iron-bound door, which McCorkle had some difficulty opening, trying several keys before finding the correct one. The door groaned open at last, the hinges shedding clouds of rust.

They entered a small room filled with sarcophagi made of painted wood and cartonnage. Some were without lids and inside Nora could make out the individual mummies, some wrapped, some unwrapped.

"The mummy room," said McCorkle.

Wicherly rushed in ahead of the rest. "Good heavens, there must be a hundred in here!" He swept a plastic sheet aside, exposing a large wooden sarcophagus. "Look at this!"

Nora went over and peered at the mummy. The linen

bandages had been ripped from its face and chest, the mouth was open, the black lips shrivelled and drawn back as if crying out in protest at the violation. Its chest was a gaping hole, the sternum and ribs torn out.

Wicherly turned toward Nora, eyes bright. "Do you see?" he said in an almost reverential whisper, resting a light hand on her shoulder. "This mummy was robbed. They tore off the linen to get at the precious amulets hidden in the wrappings. And there—where that hole is—was where the mummy's heart had been replaced by a jade and gold scarab beetle. The symbol of rebirth. Gold was considered the flesh of the gods, because it never tarnished. They ripped the corpse open to take it."

"This can be the mummy we put in the tomb," Menzies said. "The idea—Nora's idea—was that we show the tomb as it appeared while being robbed."

"How perfect," said Wicherly, turning a brilliant smile to Nora.

"I *believe*," McCorkle interrupted, "that the tomb entrance was against that far wall." Dropping his bag on the floor, he pulled the plastic sheeting away from the shelves covering the wall, exposing pots, bowls, and baskets, all filled with black shrivelled objects.

"What's that inside?" Nora asked.

Wicherly went over to examine the objects. After a silence he straightened up. "Preserved food. For the afterlife. Bread, antelope joints, fruits and vegetables, dates, all preserved for the pharaoh's journey to the afterworld."

They heard a growing rumble coming through the walls, followed by a muffled squeal of metal, then silence.

"The A Line," McCorkle explained. "The 81st Street station is very close."

"We'll have to find some way to dampen that," Menzies said. "It destroys the mood."

McCorkle grunted. He removed an electronic device from the bag and aimed it at the newly exposed wall, turned, aimed again, then examined the readings. He pulled out a piece of chalk, made a mark on the wall, then another. Taking a second device from his shirt pocket, he laid it against the wall and slid it across slowly, taking readings as he went.

Then he stepped back. "Bingo. Help me move these shelves."

They began shifting the objects to shelves on the other walls. When the wall was bare, McCorkle pulled the shelf supports from the crumbling plaster with a set of pliers and put them to one side.

"Ready for the moment of truth?" McCorkle asked with a gleam in his eye, his good humor returning.

"Absolutely," said Wicherly.

McCorkle removed a long spike and hammer from his bag, positioned the spike on the wall, gave it a sharp blow, then another. The sounds echoed in the confined space and plaster began falling in sheets from the old wall, exposing courses of brick. He continued to drive the spike in, bricks splitting, dust rising, and then suddenly the spike buried itself to the hilt. McCorkle rotated it, giving it a few side blows with the hammer to loosen the brick. A few more deft blows knocked a chunk of brickwork away, leaving a black rectangle. He stepped back.

As he did so, Wicherly darted forward. "Forgive me if I claim explorer's privilege." He turned back with his most charming smile. "Any objections?"

"Be our guest," said Menzies. McCorkle frowned but said nothing.

Wicherly took his flashlight and shined it into the hole, pressing his face to the gap. A long silence ensued, interrupted by the rumble of a subway train.

"What do you see?" asked Menzies at last.

"Strange animals, statues and gold—everywhere the glint of gold."

"What?" said McCorkle. "The tomb should be empty."

Wicherly glanced back at him. "I was being facetious—quoting what Howard Carter said when he first peered into King Tut's tomb."

McCorkle's lips tightened. "If you'll step aside, please, I'll have this open in a moment."

He stepped back up to the gap, and with a series of expertly aimed blows with the spike and hammer loosened several rows of bricks, taking them out and handing them to Nora and Wicherly, who stacked them neatly against the wall. In less than ten minutes he had opened a hole big enough to step through. He disappeared inside then returned a moment later.

"The electricity isn't working, as I suspected. We'll have to use our flashlights. I'm required to lead the way," he said, with a glance at Wicherly. "Museum regulations. Might be hazards in there."

"The mummy from the Black Lagoon, perhaps," said Wicherly, with a laugh and a glance at Nora.

They stepped inside, then paused to reconnoiter. In the glow of their flashlight beams a great stone threshold was visible, and beyond, a sloping staircase carved out of rough limestone blocks.

McCorkle moved toward the top step, hesitated, then gave a slightly nervous chuckle. "Ready, ladies and gents?" he asked.